The Ash Spear

OTHER TITLES BY G R GROVE:

The Storyteller Series:

Storyteller

Flight of the Hawk

Guernen Sang It: medieval-themed poetry

Guernen Sang It: King Arthur's Raid On Hell And Other Poems

Guernen Sang Again: Pryderi's Pigs And Other Poems

The Ash Spear

The Third Book
in the Storyteller Series

G R Grove

Lulu.com

Copyright ©2009 by G R Grove. All rights reserved.
Cover image copyright ©2009 by G R Grove.

First Edition: June 2009

Published by Lulu.com
Lulu Press, Inc.
Morrisville, NC, USA

ISBN: 978-0-557-06070-2

Set in 12 pt Garamond and Arial by Aldertree Books,
Denver, CO, USA.

To all those gone before.

CONTENTS

The Storyteller 1
The Third Man 10
The Druids' Island 21
The Dark Path 30
No Way Back 41
The Irish Wind 50
The Black Lake 61
The News-Bringer 70
First Blood 80
Beltane Fires 89
Taliesin's Need 100
The Man From The Sea 110
Riding to War 120
Arfon in Flames 129
Fire in the Night 140
The Hostage 152
The Land of Eagles 163
The Harper's Tale 174
The Black Spears 186
A Long Summer's Day 196
Choices 204
Ghosts 214
Memory 224
Gratitude 233
An Iron Chain 242
The Singer of Tales 251
The Kitchen Girl 262
The Gray Hounds 272
The Halls of Annwn 281
The Ash Spear 293
Samhain 305
Author's Postscript 311
Appendices 314

Settlements

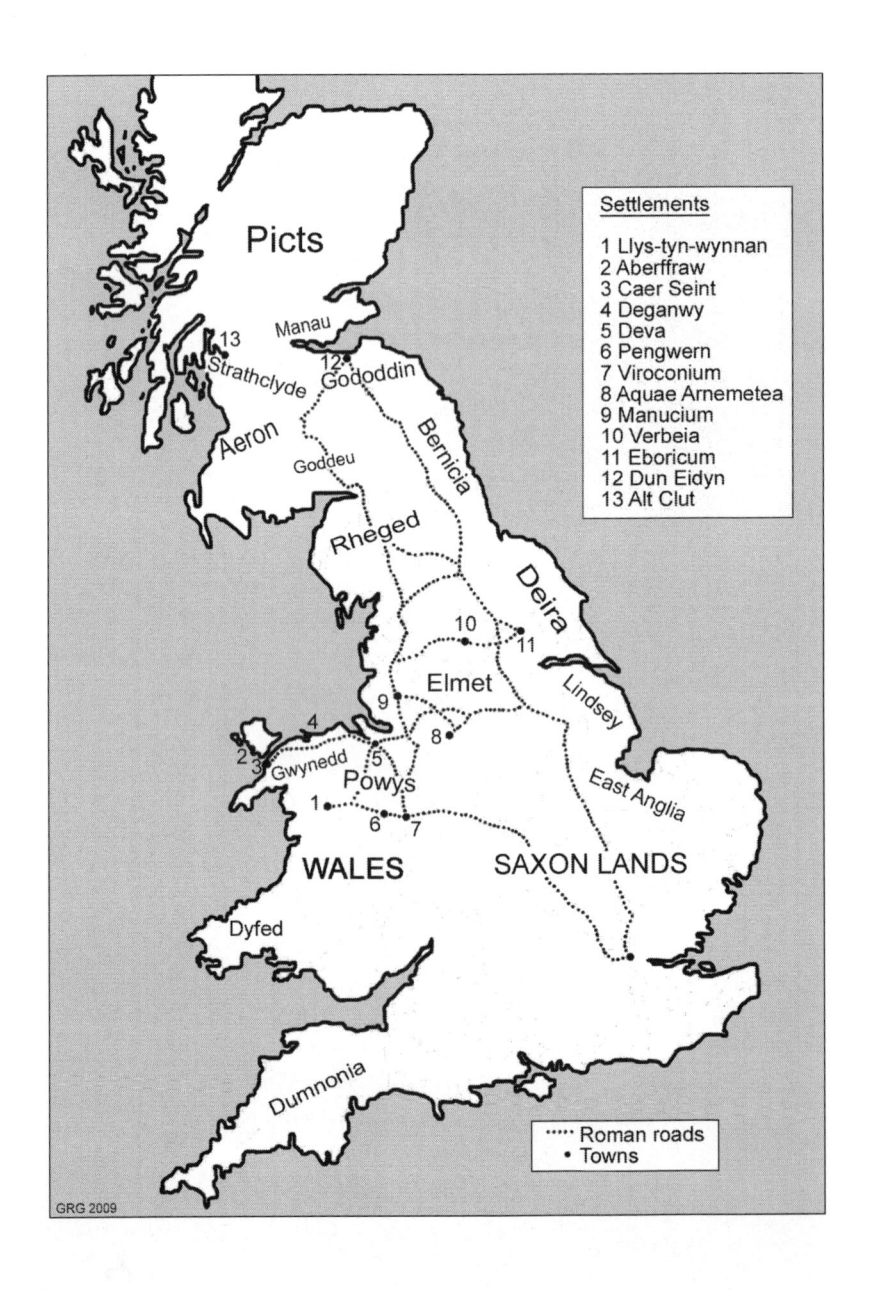

1 Llys-tyn-wynnan
2 Aberffraw
3 Caer Seint
4 Deganwy
5 Deva
6 Pengwern
7 Viroconium
8 Aquae Arnemetea
9 Manucium
10 Verbeia
11 Eboricum
12 Dun Eidyn
13 Alt Clut

····· Roman roads
• Towns

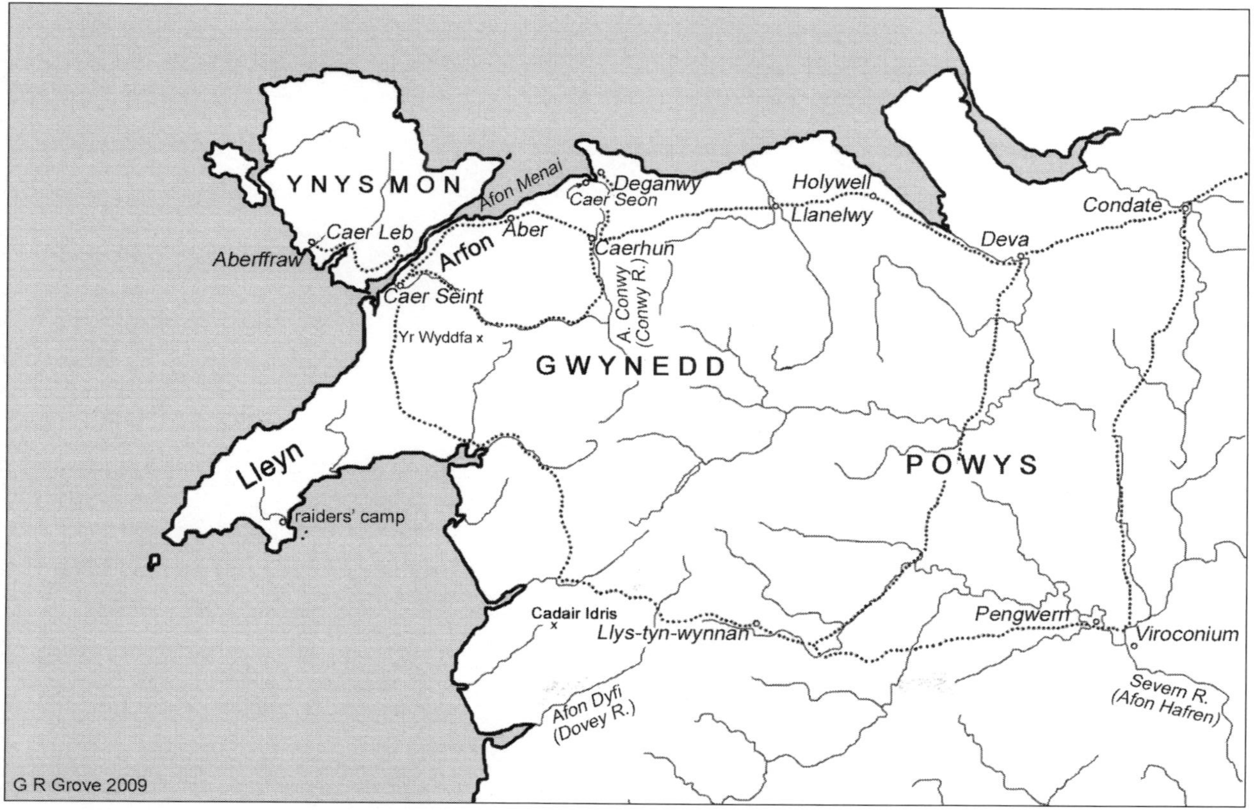
YNYS MON
Afon Menai
Deganwy
Caer Seon
Holywell
Llanelwy
Condate
Caer Leb
Aber
Aberffraw
Arfon
Caerhun
Deva
Caer Seint
A. Conwy
(Conwy R.)
Yr Wyddfa x
GWYNEDD
Lleyn
POWYS
raiders' camp
Cadair Idris
Llys-tyn-wynnan
Pengwern
Viroconium
Afon Dyfi
(Dovey R.)
Severn R.
(Afon Hafren)
G R Grove 2009

Pren onn ydyw fy awen gwen.

My ash spear is my holy awen.

-Taliesin

The Storyteller

Elidyr Mwynfawr, King of Aeron, was a weak, greedy fool, and like many another such fool, he died of his folly. But because he was a king, in his dying he cost many better men their lives as well, and this was the way of it: for I, Gwernin Kyuarwyd, was there, and saw much of it myself, and the tale that I tell you is true.

I was in my seventeenth year when it happened, and in the second year of my apprenticeship to Talhaearn Tad Awen, who was *pencerdd* and harper-bard to Cyndrwyn, Prince of western Powys in mid-Wales. All that winter my master had been working me hard, teaching me my trade as bard and harper and storyteller: *kyuarwyd*, we call that last, a reciter of lore and legends and the descent of Kings. Dry work I found some of it, but it was all a needful part of my craft. Triads and lists had to be memorized, patterns of poetry got off by heart, tales for the dark and the light halves of the year practiced and performed—for the libraries of the bards, like those of our predecessors the Druids, are in our heads, not written on monkish parchment. Even now, as an old man, I remember most of those lessons still, and glad I am to keep them; but in those days I was sometimes gladder to snatch a free hour when I could, and spend it on other pursuits. And chiefest of these was my girl Rhiannedd, the dark-haired delight of my heart.

I had come back the previous Samhain from a summer away in the North, on adventures of which I have spoken elsewhere, to find her patiently waiting for me still. All through that winter we had spent stolen hours together, as and where we could—in the hayloft of the byre wrapped together in my cloak, with the steamy breath of the beasts rising from below to warm us; pillowed in the thick-drifted leaves of the oak woods above the *llys* on a mild afternoon, the bare branches of the trees cutting dark-edged patterns from the sky; now and again in the stables, lying in the straw by my black pony's feet, and giggling like children when he lowered his head to snuffle at us, his mane tickling our faces; and once or twice, with ears a-prick, on my pallet in Talhaearn's quarters when I knew he would be busy elsewhere—for the Prince's wife Angharad had a new boy-child, and summoned the old bard sometimes to play the babe to sleep. And on days when I was free and Rhiannedd was not, I would sit on the bench in her mother's hut and watch as she ground herbs or mixed a draught: for her mother Gwawr was herbalist and sometimes leech to the court, and Rhiannedd also had her own trade to learn.

So it happened, late one rainy afternoon in the spring, that I sat lazily watching Rhiannedd's movements by the flickering firelight of the brazier, as she fetched first one herb and then another from the drying-racks on the wall and added them to the pungent concoction growing in her mortar. The sweet shape of her as she moved warmed my imagination, and after a while I stood up and came behind her, putting my arms around her slender waist, and bending to kiss the back of her neck below the soft dark hair which she had pinned up out of her way while she worked. She suffered my embrace for a moment, then twisted away from me impatiently. "Not now, Gwernin," she said. "Mother will be back soon, and I should have this ointment ready for her when she comes."

"Is it so urgent," I asked, "that we cannot steal a few moments for ourselves first? Talhaearn will have me telling tales tonight until bedtime, and who knows when we will have another such chance? It has been too long already!" And reaching out, I took her by her slender shoulders and turned her toward me, pulling her close to kiss her; but she held me off with her two small hands flat against my chest.

"Na, na," she said, frowning up at me. "This is not the time. I need—I want—we must talk, Gwernin."

"Why, so we shall," I said, puzzled and frowning in my turn. "But cannot it wait?" And I tried again to kiss her, but she pushed me away more strongly, and after a moment I let her go. "What is wrong, *cariad*?" I asked then. "What troubles you?"

"I think—I am not sure..." She paused, biting her lip and not meeting my eyes, her hands busy straightening the front of her blue woolen kirtle. Without thinking I reached out again to hold her, and this time she let me, but turned her head away when I tried to kiss her mouth. "Will you be gone again traveling this summer?" she asked, her voice muffled against the shoulder of my brown tunic.

"Why—I do not know," I said. "It is early days yet to tell. Talhaearn may go with the Prince when he makes a circuit, and of course I would go along. Or perhaps…" I paused in my turn. I had spent the previous summer at the bidding of Taliesin Ben Beirdd, the most famous bard in Britain, traveling most of the time in company with his student Neirin, and before I left them Taliesin had promised that we would all meet again in the spring. But for some reason—I am not sure why—I had not mentioned this to Rhiannedd when I recounted the tale of my adventures to her. Instinct told me now that this was not the time to remedy my omission. Instead I held her closer, and tried again to kiss her. It was not a success, but still I persisted. Her dark hair against my cheek smelled faintly of violets, the sweet early violets that would soon be blooming on the hill above us, and the feel of her, warm and soft in my arms, was driving me to distraction. Closing my eyes, I kissed her again more urgently, and felt her begin to respond, her arms coming up to clasp me in her turn.

Then there was the sound of a voice outside the door and a hand on the latch; and as we fell apart, Rhiannedd's mother Gwawr came into the room, bringing with her a gust of cold air and the scent of rain. "Oh, Gwernin," she said, throwing back the wet shawl which covered her still-dark hair, "I thought I might find you here. Talhaearn wants you in the courtyard: we have guests."

"I will go, then," I said, and with a glance and a smile at Rhiannedd I headed for the door. She did not smile back. Her expression was strange, and somehow made me uneasy; but I had no time to ponder it just then, and in the ensuing excitement I forgot it.

In the early twilight the muddy courtyard was bright with the ragged golden flames of the torches, blown sideways by the wind, and full of people and horses. Talhaearn's lean height and mane of white hair were easy to spot in the crowd, and I made my way toward him. He was speaking with two shorter men, both cloaked and hooded against the rain: presumably the visitors. As I came up the taller of the two pushed back his wet leather hood, showing a familiar head of hair as red as autumn bracken. "Neirin!" I called, and he looked around grinning, his eyes shining amber as a hawk's in the torchlight. "I did not think to see you here so soon!"

"Did you not, Gwernin?" said the second man, turning with a smile. "But I told you that you would see us in the spring. Surely you cannot have forgotten?" With delight I recognized the dark-bearded face of Taliesin Ben Beirdd, whose coming always meant excitement.

Before I could answer him, however, Talhaearn interrupted. "So, Gwernin, here you are at last. Is the Prince on his way?"

"He is in the doorway of the hall behind you, Master," I said: for Talhaearn was blind, or nearly so, and used me often as his eyes.

"Then let us go in, out of this wind and rain," said Talhaearn, taking the arm I offered him. "These two will be glad of a fire and a cup of wine: it is a long ride from Pengwern."

"I will see to the baggage first," said Neirin, "and bring our harps in out of the weather." And with that he turned briskly away, leaving the three of us to climb the steps to the hall.

Cyndrwyn mab Ermid, Prince of western Powys, was a tall, well-built young man not long in his lordship, easy-going and good to look upon, but well able to control his domain. His wedding at Deganwy two years before had been the occasion of my first meeting with Taliesin, who had sent me here to study under his own old master Talhaearn. The Prince was waiting for us now by the central fire-pit in his feast-hall, warming his hands at the flames which set bright highlights in his chestnut hair and beard and glittered on the enameled silver brooch that fastened his red woolen cloak. Beside him, his golden-haired young wife Angharad stood ready to offer the great carved guest cup full of mead to Taliesin, who took it with a word of thanks and a smile.

"Welcome you are always in my hall, Taliesin," said the Prince, when Taliesin had drunk and handed back the cup, "welcome whenever you may come. Well do I remember the songs you made for us at Deganwy, and the speech we had here together last spring. What can I do for you or give you this time? Do your travels take you far?"

"As far as the Island of Môn, Lord," said Taliesin, still smiling. "I go to lose an apprentice and find a Master Bard. My student Neirin won his crown in competition last summer at Dun Eidyn: it is time to let him fly free."

"Ah, I remember him: an excellent young lad," said Cyndrwyn, not many years Neirin's senior. "Is he with you?"

"Indeed he is: he is seeing to our baggage now," said Taliesin, throwing back the heavy damp folds of his leather rain cape and holding out his hands to the fire in his turn. Beneath it he wore the usual short woolen tunic and trews of a horseman, and his boots were liberally splattered with the mud of the spring roads. "But since you offer, Lord," he continued, "I have a thing I would ask of you—though maybe I should have begged his permission first."

"Speak, and you shall have it," said Cyndrwyn, smiling.

"I ask, then, the company of your *pencerdd* Talhaearn on my journey," said Taliesin, his blue eyes twinkling. "Sorry I am to leave you without bard or harper, but it will only be for a month: if all goes well, you shall have them back by Beltane."

"*Them?*" said Cyndrwyn, raising his eyebrows. "You mentioned only one."

"My apologies," said Taliesin lightly. "I had assumed Talhaearn would bring his apprentice Gwernin, to carry wood and water and see to the horses, if for nothing else."

Talhaearn gave a snort of amusement. "He will be good for that at least," he said with a grudging smile, and stroked his gray beard.

"I take it, then, they will go, whatever I say," said Cyndrwyn a little ruefully. "Be welcome to them, Chief of Bards—only bring them back soon, and whole, when you are done!" And he laughed, and the talk became general. For myself, I felt a bubbling excitement not unmixed with apprehension: Rhiannedd, I suspected, would not be pleased to see me leaving again so soon.

"Why Ynys Môn?" I asked Neirin later that evening, as we sat at meat in the smoky babble of the feast-hall. "Cannot Taliesin set you free without traveling the length and breadth of Wales to do it?"

"He can, but there is more to it than that, more than my merely getting my loosing from him," said Neirin, stuffing his mouth with roast boar-meat and grinning. "Much more. He will let me walk the Dark Path there, if—if I can do it. And I want to try."

"The Dark Path," I said slowly, tasting the words. "I have heard of that, a little, but I was thinking it was a Druid thing, from the very-long-ago. And Taliesin knows how to do it, does he?"

"He has done it," said Neirin, and he was not grinning now. "There are not five men now alive who have."

"And you want to—wah!" I said, and shivered. "What happens if you fail?"

"I will not fail," said Neirin, and for a moment a little, dangerous smile that I knew well played about his mouth and narrowed his amber hawk's eyes. "But I may not—succeed." And suddenly he laughed and clapped me on the shoulder, so that I almost spilled my ale. "But that is enough of such talk, for now. How are you and your girl—Rhiannedd, was it not?—getting on nowadays? Will we be seeing a hand-fasting soon?"

"Umm," I said, reminded of my own problems. "I do not know. She has been—strange—of late. And then there is the matter of a bride-price. I should maybe not have spent so much of last summer's silver at the Lughnasadh Fair."

"But she liked the beads, did she not?" asked Neirin, taking a bite of barley bread and brushing crumbs from his checkered woolen tunic and out of his young red beard. "I remember you showing them to me—jewel-bright colors they were, blue and red and amber, fit for the daughter of a king."

"Yes," I said, and sighed. "She likes them very much, or so she says. But she does not wear them often, only on feast days. And even if I *had* the silver for the bride-price, I have no land, no home to take her to. I am no better a match than I was last spring, for all the goods and gear I won on our travels."

"That," said Neirin, frowning, "is why bards should never marry. For us there is always the road in summer, and a snug hall somewhere to winter in—perhaps a lord to serve all year round in old age, if the fates be kind, as they have been to Talhaearn. But it is no life for the women, or the little ones. Better to take love lightly where you can, and move on."

"As you do," I said, and sighed again.

"*Sa*, as I do," said Neirin, still frowning. He drained his ale-cup, and looked around for a woman to refill it. "*Hai mai!* And yet I do not know. It was a long ride from Pengwern today, and the rain cold in my face. How will that be, I wonder, when I am old? Maybe you have the right of it after all, brother."

"Maybe," I said, emptying my own cup, "but I can see Talhaearn looking for me now, to tell a tale for the company. I will speak more with you later."

"Will he give you the back of his hand, if you are slow?" asked Neirin, once more grinning.

"If I am lucky, he will," I said with a laugh, and went to do my master's bidding.

I did not speak with Rhiannedd again that night. I saw her once or twice across the hall, pouring ale for the men of the war-band, and it struck me that she was looking paler than usual. I hoped she was not ill. But the tale I was telling required some concentration, and I lost sight of her; and when I looked for her again, she was gone. Then it was time for me to see Talhaearn back to his quarters, and to seek my own blankets. Tomorrow, I thought, would be soon enough to talk; and in some ways I was right.

In fact, it was two more days before we left Llys-tyn-wynnan, and they were not happy days for me. There was the packing, of course, which took some little time—clothes and gear for traveling and for courts, for fine weather and for foul, with Talhaearn changing his mind three times in an hour as to how I should pack them, and including some fairly biting comments on my ability to pack anything at all. There was the rounding up of the pack-ponies from the upper hill-pasture where they had been let out to graze with the horse-herd, and their bringing in and checking over and grooming before they were let loose temporarily in the home paddock. There were my daily chores and lessons with Talhaearn, from which I was not let off. And then there was my parting with Rhiannedd.

She had heard the gossip already, of course, before I had a chance to speak with her: Talhaearn and Gwernin were leaving with Taliesin, for who knew how long. They were going to the King of Gwynedd's court in Deganwy—in Caer Seint—in Aberffraw. They were going to Ireland—to Alt Clut—to the Western Isles that lay beyond the sunset, in search of King Arthur. They would be gone for a month—for the whole summer—for a year and a day. Such is rumor when it has two days to work.

"Na," I said, "it is not true—the most of it is not!" We were sitting on a mossy rock in the woods above the court, the only place I could think of where we would not be interrupted. It was an afternoon of mixed sun and rain, changing quickly without warning—a fox of a day, the old men call it—and Rhiannedd's moods seemed at one with the weather. "We are only going with Taliesin and Neirin to Ynys Môn," I said, "and we will be back before Beltane. That is all."

"But why Ynys Môn, and why now?" Rhiannedd asked. "It is early in the year to be traveling, and so far."

"There is something there which Taliesin wants to show Neirin, I think," I said slowly. "As to the timing, I am thinking it is something to do with the moon and her waning—or so Neirin said." It sounded unconvincing, even to me, and Rhiannedd was not impressed. When I had tried to put my arm around her earlier, she had twisted away; now she was sitting huddled in her brown cloak with her arms crossed, looking cold and unhappy.

"That does not sound like much of a reason," she said after a moment. "And why should Talhaearn go, too? He is an old man; he should stay here safe by the fire until summer, not go riding about in the mud and the rain!"

I shrugged. "They have not told me, and I have not heard all their talk, to know their minds. But for my part, I should like to see Ynys Môn again. I spent a few days there once, with my friend Ieuan—did I not tell you of it?"

"Na, I am not sure," said Rhiannedd, frowning. "But I have heard tales of that place—and not good ones!" She shivered. "What is it like?"

"It is—just a place," I said, edging closer to her on our rock. "A low, flat land it is, compared with most of Wales, but good for growing grain. It lies across a narrow strait from Arfon, in the northwest part of Gwynedd. Ieuan and I went there for a while when we had to leave Caer Seint in a hurry, after—after some trouble he got into." This, I thought, was an understatement, but I did not elaborate.

"You will not be getting into trouble in this time, will you?" asked Rhiannedd, still frowning. "You almost got your killing last summer, remember—I have seen the scars!"

"Na, nothing like that will happen," I said easily. "Are you not cold? You look it."

"A little—it is no matter. And will you really be back by Beltane? Promise?" Her dark blue eyes were wide and solemn in her winter-pale face, but she was no longer frowning.

"Of course I will," I said, getting my arm around her again. She sighed, and rested her head on my shoulder, and after a while I kissed her. This time she did not push me away. And when at last we went back down the hill, hand in hand, she seemed much as always, and I thought nothing was wrong between us, after all: and this was a mistake.

But that, O my children, is a story for another day.

The Third Man

The Conwy is a big river, and broad near its mouth, though not so wide as the Severn by which I grew up. The east bank is low and marshy at first, though it rises soon to hills as you go south; but the west bank is steep from the beginning, and climbs toward Eryri, the Land of Eagles. The river is tidal as far inland as Caerhun, where the old Roman road crosses on its ford, and it was there that we crossed it, avoiding the tides and the quicksands nearer the sea. Avoiding, too, a side-trip to Caer Deganwy, one of King Rhun's chief strongholds: for Taliesin had got word that the King was currently on Ynys Môn, at his court of Aberffraw, and it was there we would be visiting him by and by. First, though, there was the question of the third man.

Among the native peoples of Britain, as among our cousins the Irish, things of significance tend to come in triads—in groups of three. In the lore and language of the bards, in the case-books of the lawyers, in the prayers and invocations of the priests—Druids and Christians alike—three is the magic number. Our ancient oaths bind us by earth and air and water, by land and sky and sea: nothing else is as perfect, nothing else is as strong. And so it was that for Neirin's walking of the Dark Path, he needed three sponsors, three bards who had walked that path before him and could guide him on his way. Taliesin and Talhaearn were two such men; now we went to find the third man, and that was Ugnach of Caer Sëon.

"Na, I was not knowing he was an initiate," said Neirin, as our ponies plodded up the climbing track toward Sychnant in the thin spring sunshine. "Not when we met him last summer, at any rate. But many things we saw then have become clearer to me since." He had dropped back to ride beside me where I led the pack string in the rear of our little group, leaving Taliesin and Talhaearn to converse more privately ahead of us.

"Such as?" I asked, looking sideways at him. The sea breeze was getting up and bringing us the sour smells of the saltings to mix with the earth scents of last year's bracken and heather; the gulls were crying over the river and the larks singing on the hill; and with my black pony moving easily beneath me, and the sun warm on my shoulders, I was feeling uncommonly peaceful. After the stress of preparations and farewells, it was good to be on the road again.

"Oh, some of the—magical things, I suppose you would call them," said Neirin, grinning. Fine in his dress as always, he was wearing that day a short checkered tunic as variably green as the spring hills around us, and against it his hair and beard shone a dark foxy-red. "I had many questions for Taliesin this winter, after you left us."

"And did he answer them all?" I asked, grinning back at him.

"Some of them." Neirin grimaced comically. "Sometimes his answers do not make things clearer. You will be finding that out for yourself soon enough, I am thinking."

"How do you mean?" I asked, puzzled.

"Na, he had better tell you that himself," said Neirin, and grinned again. "*Hai mai!* I wonder how much farther we have to go? It is been long and long since breakfast, and my belly is empty."

Even as he spoke we reached Pen-Sychnant, the level valley at the top of the Sychnant pass where three ways join—our track coming up from the south; the eastern road which leads past the crumbling fortress of Caer Sëon on its rocky hilltop, before descending to Aber Conwy; and the western road which drops steeply through the Sychnant valley itself toward the sea. To the east we had a wide view over the gray-brown waters of the Conwy and the low green country beyond, although Deganwy on its north-reaching peninsula was hidden from us by the Caer Sëon hill. To the north and northwest, between two lower hills, we got glimpses of the far-off sea, silver-shining as a salmon in the sunlight; but Pen-Sychnant itself was protected from the worst of the western gales by its encircling hills, which rose up green and brown with heather and bracken, crowned with outcrops of rough gray stone, and dotted here and there with grazing sheep.

Ugnach's homestead—a cluster of wooden and dry-stone

buildings encircled by pastures and new-ploughed fields—lay not in the old fortress of Caer Sëon itself, but in the small sheltered valley at its foot. This place, as I learned later, was his family inheritance, not a gift from the King, and the people of Pen-Sychnant were all of his kinship: cousins in one degree or another; aunts and uncles; brothers and sisters; his five children and his old wife as well. However far he traveled, here he had his roots, his belonging-place, his home. Thinking of it, I felt a twinge of envy.

He met us at the door of his reed-thatched wooden hall, a tall grey-haired man with a fine bushy beard, plainly dressed in russet woolen like my own. His smile widened when he saw Neirin, whom he had helped to crown at the Lughnasadh competition last summer. "Why, what a fine company have we here," he said in his strong Gwynedd accent. "Rhys! Llew!"—this to two boys who stood in the courtyard staring at us—"take their horses to the stables—and do you all come in, my friends! It is too long since you have been under my roof!"

"Too long indeed," said Taliesin, following Ugnach into the smoky dimness of the hall, with a hand on Talhaearn's elbow to guide him. "I had no leisure to visit you last summer, old friend."

"And I," said Talhaearn, "have been fixed in Cyndrwyn's Powys these last two years, as you will have heard."

"Well do I know it," said Ugnach, still smiling. "Come you to the fire, do—it is a chill wind we have blowing today, for all that the sunlight is warm. Ah, Mairi, here you are with the guest cup! Drink, friends, and be welcome."

"Ah!" said Talhaearn, drinking and passing the carved wooden cup to Taliesin. "Always a fine hand with the mead, your wife has, son of Mydno."

"Indeed and she has—you will find few better," said Ugnach proudly. "But this batch is my daughter's—is it not, Mairi Fach? Run, now, fetch your mother—in the dairy she is, I am thinking, with your sister Nefydd."

"Fine mead and fine daughters," said Taliesin, smiling as the pretty black-haired girl went out. "Three of them, as I remember—

or has the eldest married?"

"Last summer," said Ugnach, "before I took the road north, to her cousin Gwyn mab Padarn over the hill—and a son in her room already, blessings be on him!"

"Fast work," said Talhaearn, raising his thorny white eyebrows. "These impatient children!"

Ugnach winked at Neirin, who was drinking now from the guest-cup. "Ah, I like to see a lad with juice in him, like your boy here. I told you, Taliesin, how he took the prize from me at Dun Eidyn—and me thinking I had it safe in hand, certain sure."

"An honor it was to contend with you, Master," said Neirin, grinning and passing the almost-empty cup to me. The mead—such of it as was left—was indeed excellent.

"Well, and you deserved your crown, *gwas*," said Ugnach generously. "But what fortune brings you all here together? Not only a desire for the pleasure of my company, I feel."

"Ah," said Taliesin, his blue eyes twinkling, "but the pleasure of your company, Ugnach, is exactly what we desire."

"Is it now, indeed?" said Ugnach, opening his brown eyes wider. "Well, well, you shall tell me the way of it soon enough; but for now, follow me to the guesthouse, and make yourselves at home."

The guesthouse was a small, new-looking wooden hut which backed against the dry-stone wall surrounding the compound, conveniently close to the feast hall. There were only two beds—allotted naturally enough to Talhaearn and Taliesin—but plenty of floor space for pallets, and Neirin and I had slept in many worse places. The two of us set off to the stables to get our gear, only to meet Ugnach's two lads carrying the most of it on their shoulders. In a little while it was all stowed safely in the guesthouse, and we joined our masters in Ugnach's hall for the midday meal.

We found the two of them seated with Ugnach at a trestle table near the fire, with a good spread of cold meat, bread, and relishes set before them, and a generous pitcher of ale to wash it all down. "Of course I will come," Ugnach was saying to Taliesin as we approached. "How not? And I know your judgment on this is better than my own. But he seems full young to me…" He broke off abruptly as he saw us, and smiled. "Ah, and here they are now. Sit, friends, and eat. Is all well?"

"Thank you, Master, it is," said Neirin, as we took the places laid for us. "Do you know my friend Gwernin?"

"Na, I am not sure," said Ugnach, frowning a little. "Was he not with you last summer in the North?"

"He was, and supported me mightily. He is Talhaearn's pupil," said Neirin, "as no doubt you have already heard, and a good storyteller."

Talhaearn gave a sort of snort, and Ugnach smiled. "He is well enough," said Talhaearn grudgingly, "when he stays with me and applies himself. But Gwion here"—he meant Taliesin, who was grinning at him—"will keep borrowing him, and then I have all to do over."

"Na, na, Father of Awen," said Taliesin, laughing, "acquit me of that—this time it is yourself I have borrowed, from your own kind patron, and Gwernin comes along only to serve you. How then am I at fault?"

"Have it your own way," said Talhaearn, smiling despite himself. "You always do. And Ugnach, do you pass me more of that good bread and butter, if it please you."

"Gladly," said Ugnach, buttering a thick chunk of bread lavishly and handing it to Talhaearn. "Neirin, Gwernin, help yourselves: I know the appetite of a growing lad. Two sons do I have, and a need for food on each of them as bottomless as Manawydan's crane-bag! They may yet see me beggared and walking the roads for my keep!" And he laughed, knowing there was no such likelihood: a very good living he got from his farmstead, did Ugnach, not to mention what he won with his *awen* at the courts of Kings. Neirin and I fell on our food with a will, and gladly filled our bellies while our elders talked idly of this and that.

"Have you heard any more news from the North, Taliesin?" asked Ugnach after a while. "I had a sniff of something there last summer which I did not like, but trying to learn more about it was like trying to grasp mist: nothing solid at all, strive as you might. Rheged, Aeron, Strathclyde, Eidyn: all of those Kings are restless, and yet none dares attack his neighbor for fear another will fall on his own back while it is turned. You saw it, did you not, Neirin?"

"*Sa*, I did," said Neirin, hastily swallowing his mouthful of cold pig-meat. "Clydno Eidyn, as you know, is my half-brother, and I will not speak against him; but yes, all the North is working like a loaf with too much yeast, for all that they seem to get along on the surface."

"Rhydderch of Alt Clut got himself a good ally when he married Urien Rheged's daughter last summer," said Taliesin thoughtfully, stroking his short, clipped black beard. "If I were Gwenddolau of Goddeu, or Aliffr Gosgorddfawr, or even Elidyr Mwynfawr, I think I would be looking to my defenses, not planning trouble of my own: they are all of them living in the nutcracker's jaws now, and Urien is the man to squeeze."

"True that is, from all that I hear," said Ugnach, and sighed. "And how is Cynan Garwyn these days?"

Taliesin grimaced. "As ever he was: a generous patron to his friends, and a deadly threat to his neighbors. I do what I can with my songs to sweeten him, but he will be out for plunder every summer, for all my efforts. Cynewald of Mercia is growing stronger to the southeast, and may eat him up one day, but he will not see it: he had rather go raiding among his cousins in Gwent."

"Is that why you are out so early in the year on this quest, then?" asked Ugnach.

"One reason, yes," said Taliesin, and draining his cup, set it down firmly on the table. "For the rest..." He shrugged. "I go where the *awen* sends me."

"And carry us along," muttered Talhaearn.

"To where?" asked Ugnach, smiling. "You have not yet said, Taliesin."

"To Ynys Môn," said Taliesin, "and Bryn Celli Ddu."

"Mmm," said Ugnach frowning. "Is that wise?"

Taliesin shrugged again. "It is the place I found in my dreaming."

"I will need a day or two to be ready," said Ugnach, and sighed. "You can endure my hospitality for that long, I hope?"

"Gladly," said Taliesin, and even Talhaearn smiled.

For two days and three nights, then, we stayed at Ugnach's farmstead while he made ready for our journey. All of this time was good—Ugnach's table was bountiful and his two pretty daughters friendly, and I had light work—Taliesin and Ugnach keeping Talhaearn occupied—and Neirin's company; but for me the evenings were best, because a company of bards can no more keep from friendly competition with each other than they can keep from breathing. Each of us had his turn with song or story, while Ugnach's wife and children, women and farmhands sat around us and listened; and neighbors and cousins gathered from over or under the hill as well, when the news of our presence went round. I had heard all the others perform at one time or another, but not to this extent, and I was proud—and a little nervous—to spin my tales before such an audience, though I had spoken without fear before kings and princes. Neirin's repertoire I knew well from traveling with him, but he had of course been composing new material and polishing old during the winter. Talhaearn surprised me with several pieces I had not heard before; Ugnach displayed an unexpected gift for humorous verse; and Taliesin... Taliesin told a story.

He told it, at Talhaearn's request, toward the end of our last evening at Caer Sëon. Most of the guests had left by then, and the rest of us were thinking of our beds. Neirin had been playing his harp for us, a dark, slow, dreamy piece, intricate as the interlacing designs of the Pictish lands where he learned it. Ugnach was talking softly with his wife in the background, I was trying not to yawn, and Taliesin was staring into the fire as if all our futures were written in its flames, when Talhaearn, who had seemed asleep, looked up and said, "Gwion, tell us your tale of Camlann. I have not heard it in a long time; and these children have never heard it at all, and should. You tell it better than I do, for you were still young then, and saw it with a young man's eyes, while my heart was already old in disappointment."

Taliesin looked up from the fire, and blinked as if to clear his vision. "Do you mean the tale of the battle only, Iron Brow? If I were to tell the whole long story which led up to it, we should be here until Samhain."

"The battle will do," said Talhaearn. "Start with the night before, and go on."

Taliesin took a deep breath, and for a moment looked uncertain—the first time I had ever seen him do so. Without a word spoken, Ugnach's gray-haired wife came with a fresh cup of mead and put it into his hands, and he drank and thanked her with a smile. Then, looking again into the fire, he began.

"Arthur son of Uthur Pendragon, High King of the Britons, was a strong man, and a good general, and for much of his life he was lucky. I did not see his early battles; I was still a child; but I served him as his bard for seven years, from my coming of age until his death. They were years bright and shining and terrible as this fire, and they ended at Camlann in ashes.

"A High King is made by the consent of other Kings, and can be so unmade. Subjugation, even by their own consent, is not a natural state for the Cymry. Arthur united them for a while, partly by his own great strength of will, and partly by their desperate need to stand together against a common foe—to stand against the Saxons. But once that need became less urgent, their underlying nature came again to the surface, and they began to raid and war against each other, even as we see them do today. A little raiding, a little warring at first, put down by Arthur with what means he had to hand: harsher and harsher means as time passed, which brought temporary success, but left a growing resentment.

"As Talhaearn says, I was still young in those days, and saw things with a young man's eyes, still new and full of hope. But to be young is not always to be foolish; and I had walked the Dark Path with Talhaearn and with Emrys, and won my ash spear in the Undying Land, and hope did not blind me to the shadows that move in the darkness. So I saw more clearly than most the perils that surrounded Arthur, and did what I could to aid and to advise him. But it was not enough.

"Medraut was a young king from the southwest, from the lands that lie beyond Dumnonia: a little king from a little kingdom, but not thereby a small man. The whispers had it that he was of Arthur's bloodline, and it may well have been so, for they were much alike in face and build and coloring; much alike, also, in their strength of will, and in their desire for power. This is a desire which grows in some men like a thirst for strong wine, and it is not always base. Arthur wanted power as a general, to best order Britain's forces against her enemies, but Medraut—or so I believe—wanted it for glory, and to be free of all restraints. And he gathered about him allies of a like mind for that end. What sort of High King he might have made, if he could have displaced Arthur, I do not know, for both their paths led them to Camlann fight, and ended there."

Taliesin paused, and drank from his mead cup, and Ugnach's wife came quietly as before to refill it. He gave her a sweet, abstracted smile, like a young boy's, then turned his eyes again to the flames. Their leaping light shone red on his face as blood, and sparkled in his eyes. And he spoke on.

"The river Cam runs through the Summer Country, between Caer Camel and the High Tor. Arthur and his men lay at Caer Camel to the south, and Medraut and his war-bands across the river to the north. There were parleys and discussions, offers and counter-offers. Neither of the Kings had compromise in his nature, yet something held them both back from this last mad expedient, this clash of Cymry against Cymry, of cousins against each other in arms. Maybe they somehow knew that it would be the breaking of Britain; maybe they both remembered the story of Branwen. I know that Arthur did: I had made sure of that. I sang it for him again, that last night in his chamber, and at the end I saw him weep... He had a great heart, had Arthur, and I loved him." Taliesin paused again, and for a moment I saw his mouth set hard as if in pain; in the silence, the crackling of the fire on the hearth sounded loud. Then he went on.

"At last a fragile agreement—how frail, how temporary!—was hammered out, and the two Kings met on a mound between their two armies to conclude it. The day was hot and sultry, there were storm-clouds gathering in the west, and everyone was on edge. The Kings were clasping hands; we were almost into safe harbor; and yet I knew that we were not safe. The feeling was like fire in my head, and in my belly; I looked around, seeking danger, and I saw it. But I was just too late.

"One of the men in Arthur's retinue, restless with waiting, had stepped back into some bushes, and trod unknowingly on an adder which was sheltering there. When the annoyed snake struck him in the leg, the man drew his sword to kill it, and the uplifted blade flashed in the midday sun. Someone in the assembled war-bands saw it; someone shouted 'Treachery!' The spider-thread of restraint which had held them all in check broke in an instant; one and then another group shouted and charged their enemies. Bravely the warriors battled that day, and fell in their scores and in their hundreds, until the River Cam itself ran red with their blood. Then the storm came down upon us with thunder and with rain, and brought an early night with it, but too late: too late for Britain, too late for Medraut and Arthur, too late for all too many of their men. And the little Kings took back their little kingdoms, and rule them still—such of them as are left. But our tide is running out, and the Saxons' is running in. It is for the bards now to keep our language and the memories of our people alive, and to be an ash spear in the hand against our enemies."

Taliesin sighed, and drank off his mead, and stood up. "I am for bed now, friends, and so should we all be—we have a long ride tomorrow over the hills to Aber."

"Master," said Neirin, more subdued than I had ever seen him, "you were on that battlefield—were you with Arthur at the end?"

"I was," said Taliesin quietly, and for a moment I saw a deep sadness on him; then his mouth moved in an almost-smile, and he looked himself again. "But that, O my children," he said, echoing the storyteller's phrase, "is a story for another day." And with that we had for the moment to be content.

The Druids' Island

Ynys Môn is known for many things: for its broad fertile fields, rich in wheat and barley, which have made it in times of need the granary of all Gwynedd; for its herds of wide-horned red and black cattle, with their abundant milk and butter and cheese; for the blue-gray, fish-swarming seas that lap around it; and for the King's high wood-hewed hall at Aberffraw. But I remember it most for the tall gray standing stones, quartz-streaked and gold-lichened, which crown its low hills, and for the green slumbering mounds which lie in its ghost-thronged valleys. For Môn was the Island of the Druids, and their last great stronghold and sanctuary; and there the Romans came with sword and fire, in the year when Boudicca rebelled, and left behind them blood and ashes only, and silence.

I was saying as much to Neirin, while we waited on the shore for slack water and the ferry which would take us across to the island. Afon Menai, the strait between the mainland and Môn, is not wide, but its tides are fast-flowing and treacherous, and it takes a good pilot to know them well. I was watching the choppy gray-green waves with distrust—I am a river man, no salt-water sailor—and a little unease. It was raining again, a little cold mizzle rain that tasted salt on my lips, and our elders were sheltering from it in the boatman's hut behind us, but we had come out to give them more room and to look after the ponies. With us we had Ugnach's elder son Rhys, a skinny boy of thirteen and his father's proud pupil, who had come along to act as horse-holder and helper. In the two days he had been with us he had hardly spoken a word from awe of our masters, and he eyed even me with respect.

"*Sa*, I have heard something of that myself," said Neirin thoughtfully. "It was here at the south end of Menai that they crossed, or so Taliesin told me. The Romans were not brave at first, for the chanting of the Druids, and the wailing of the women, and the shouts and shield-clashing of the assembled warriors gave them pause. But finally they crossed, the foot-soldiers on their flat-bottomed boats and the riders swimming beside their horses. The first-comers gathered on the beach and linked their shields—they had big square-cornered shields, man-covering—and when they moved like that, like one great many-legged, many-headed monster, there was no stopping them. And more and more of them came ashore behind the first, endless as a river; and everywhere they went, they killed, to erase their shame and the memory of their fear, until all the streams of Môn ran red as Camlann ford, and the ravens gorged for a month on man-flesh. And the ghosts of the Druids and their people haunt the island still."

"Hmm," I said. "I did not see any ghosts when I was here before, but that was in high summer, and we kept well clear of the barrows. I would not be for walking abroad there on a winter evening—who knows what you might see!" As I spoke I looked sideway at Rhys, whose eyes were wide and dark in the shadow of his over-sized rain cape. I grinned.

"Na, nor I either, I am thinking," said Neirin, his gaze on the misty shoreline across the water. "But we will not be keeping clear of the barrows this time, not all of them. They are the gateways to Annwn, and there the Dark Path leads. And where it leads, I must go."

This was the most he had yet said about the thing that lay before him, and I would have liked to ask questions, but the boy's presence held me back—that, and something in Neirin's face. "Well," I said after a moment, "I suppose Taliesin knows what he is doing in bringing you here."

Neirin chuckled. "That I am sure of. It is only as to whether I myself know what I am doing, that my heart sometimes misgives me... *Hai mai!* In a few more days it will be over, and—and we will ride on to Aberffraw. It—it is only three days in the dark, after all... Rhys, I think the ferry-man is coming. Can you manage all those ponies by yourself, or is it help you will be needing?" And when the boy shook his head, Neirin took the lead-ropes of his own ponies and started down the path. I followed the two of them with a sort of sinking in my belly. Only three days in the dark, was it? On the road to the Otherworld, alone?

The farmstead at Caer Lêb had not changed much in the two years since I last saw it: a huddle of thatched buildings sitting within a fortified compound, surrounded by two walls with a ditch between, and a gate on the eastern side. The walls themselves were five-sided and ancient, and built perhaps as much for show as for defense, being overlooked by higher ground to the east; the buildings within were newer, though old enough in their own right, having mostly the right-angled shapes beloved of the Romans. The whole looked strong and prosperous as we came riding up the muddy track toward it, through the dark fields already plowed and planted and showing the first faint green shoots of the corn. In the misty twilight the lime-washed walls of the buildings seemed to glow with their own light, and the blue hearth-smoke that hung around the place smelled of warmth and roasting meat, and set my belly growling with hunger.

The old yellow dog chained in the gateway saw us first, and set up a barking which brought out a mixed pack of other hounds and children to greet us, followed by a few curious adults. Among them was a dark, wiry man who seemed familiar to me. It was only when he stood up from quieting the watchdog that I recognized my old friend Ieuan, whom I had last seen two summers ago at Deganwy. He had there been adjudged a thief in the King's court, and would have spent the rest of his life as a slave in Ireland, had it not been for the generosity of the Lord Cadwaladr of Caer Lêb, who bought him free of the Irish and took him home. Now here he was still, clearly a member of the household. It seemed he had found his belonging-place at last.

Our recognition was not mutual; Ieuan's eyes slid over me unseeingly and fixed on the Masters at the front of our party. I was not much surprised; I had changed greatly from the wandering lad I had been two years ago, earning my living with my tongue and carrying all I owned upon my back. I had grown and filled out; I was the proud owner now of a respectable moustache, even though my beard still grew in clumps and patches; and if I led the pack-string at the back of our company, I did so as a free man on my own black pony, and not as a muddy-footed servant. Moreover, I was now a bardic apprentice, and likely to be a master bard myself one day; in all ways my status had improved.

So I was thinking as we rode into the courtyard and dismounted. We were a big party now, five men and a boy and eleven ponies. The Lord and Lady of the place came out to greet our masters and hand round the guest cup, while Neirin and I and Rhys did our best to sort out the ponies and baggage, helped by the men and boys of the place. That was how I came to find myself presently face to face with Ieuan, who was trying to direct the stabling and the bestowal of our gear.

"There is space enough for all your mounts in the covered block," he was saying. "The pack-ponies will have to go into the pasture outside the walls, once we have unloaded them, but they will be safe enough there. There is room in the guesthouse for most of you, though one or two may have to sleep in the hall—you, and you, perhaps"—indicating Rhys and myself. "Let us get your gear under cover, and then we will see."

"Ieuan," I said, and paused. He looked back at me, his black brows drawn together in a frown.

"Yes, that is my name. Do I know you, lad? Something about you…seems familiar."

"It should be," I said, grinning. "We walked enough miles together from Pengwern, and I got you out of trouble more than once."

Ieuan's eyes widened. "Gwernin? It cannot be! Why, boy, you have grown—and come up in the world! I wondered often what had happened to you after we parted. We must share a cup and a gossip presently—but first, the gear and the ponies!" And to the curious eyes around us, "He came here first with me two years ago, as my helper and packman on the road. A good lad he was, if a bit of a dreamer—I got him his start, and look at him now!"

I frowned a little at that, which did not match my memories, but it was no time for arguing. "Where do you want our gear?" I asked. "Better to get it out of the rain."

"Of course, of course," said Ieuan. "Take it over there"—he pointed at a building across the courtyard—"as we unload it."

"The harps first, then," I said. "And carefully, man, carefully!"

Ieuan raised his eyebrows, then stood back, grinning. "You had better unload them yourself, then, Lord!" he said. And looking around, "What a boy, eh?"

At this point Neirin stepped between us. "Na, friend, I shall do the unloading, and Gwernin and Rhys the carrying—if you will direct your lads where to take the ponies? The sooner then will you and Gwernin"—he winked at me—"come to that cup and that gossip of which you spoke, and the rest of us to our dinner!"

"At your will, then, Lord," said Ieuan, knowing his match when he met it. "At your will."

After that things went smoothly, and it was not long before we joined the others in the hall for the evening meal. As we walked across the courtyard I tried to say a few words to Neirin in explanation, but he cut me short. "Na, na," he said, laying his arm across my shoulders for a moment and smiling, "you need not explain, brother: I know his type well. A plausible rogue; well for you that you got shot of him when you did."

"Na, it is not that," I said. "He was good to me often enough on the road, and before; it is only…"

"*Sa, sa,* I know," said Neirin, squeezing my shoulder. "Let it be: there are too many ears here, and I want my dinner." And with that we entered the hall.

In some ways it was like stepping back in time; I had spent several days here on my previous visit, and the people and place were familiar to me. I saw the Lord Cadwaladr, tall and lean and red-headed, seated at his high table with our three Masters; his lady Braint, calm and dark-haired and graceful beside him; girls and boys grown older but still recognizable; and other men and women whose faces I remembered from the long evenings when I had entertained them with my tales. The warmth and comfort of the hall and the good food and drink in plenty lulled me into a sense of contentment, so that I almost forgot our reason for being here. Presently, at our masters' bidding, Neirin and I took it in turns to entertain the company, and got our due in applause: and this too was good.

As the feasting was breaking up one young woman sitting in the shadows at the far side of the room caught my eye, a dark-haired lass much my own age with a dark-haired infant at her breast. I had seen Ieuan seated beside her earlier, but he was now busy with the other men who were taking down and stacking the trestle tables, and banking the central hearth-fire in preparation for the night. As I stood there uncertain, the woman looked up and met my gaze and smiled, and I went over to join her. "Gwernin!" she said. "I am so glad to see you again—it has been a long time!"

"Indeed, and it has," I said, sitting down on the bench beside her. "Anwen, is it not?"

"It is," she said, still smiling, and shifted her grasp on the child. "There, *baban*, have you had enough?"

"Is he Ieuan's?" I asked, remembering her previous interest in my misguided friend.

"He is. A year and more we have been wed." The baby released her breast and she put him against her shoulder to burp him. Young as he was, he had her black curly hair, though I cannot say he looked much like either of his parents otherwise; I am no hand at judging likenesses in babies' faces. "Thanks to you it is," she went on, "that I have him, and his dear father. If you had not brought Ieuan here, we would never have met."

"Na, it was not all my doing," I said, a little embarrassed. "As well thank Ieuan's gambling, which made us flee Caer Seint! Is he good to you?"

"He is," said Anwen, smiling down at her child, who was falling asleep. "He is kind, and grateful to the Lord Cadwaladr, who bought him free and gave him a home."

"That is good," I said, standing up again. "I must attend my master now, but I am glad to see all is well with you."

"It is," said Anwen, "very well. And that is why..."

"Why what?" I asked, pausing and looking back.

"That is why we named the baby after you," said Anwen, still smiling. "This little one is Gwernin, too—Gwernin mab Ieuan!"

A strange feeling it was in me, as I went to join Talhaearn and the others. To have a child—even if not *my* child—named after me, and to know that my name would live on, gave me thoughts I had not had before—for at seventeen one does not think much of one's own mortality. But Talhaearn had tasks for me which soon took my mind from the future and put it back firmly in the present. And that present involved the preparations for Neirin's ordeal.

The round green mound called Bryn Celli Ddu—the Hill of the Dark Grove—lay some two or three miles north of Caer Lêb in the valley of the little river Braint. There were other farmsteads closer to it where we might have stayed, but Cadwaladr was the chief man of the district, and known moreover to our Masters from past meetings. He put workmen at Taliesin's disposal, and with them we rode there the next morning—all of us except Neirin, who stayed behind in the guesthouse; he was not to see the place until it was ready.

Once we had reached the mound and unsaddled our ponies, Rhys and I set to work with two of the men to build a thatched shelter, walled with wicker-work and floored with straw and dry bracken, where some of us could stay overnight. Under Taliesin's direction, three others removed the earth and timber which had closed the entrance to the hill for many years. He himself and Ugnach then went inside with shovels and twig brooms to make what preparations they deemed fit, and returned to supervise the hanging of a bull's-hide curtain over the newly cleared entrance. All this took the better part of the day, and when we rode back again to Caer Lêb the gray twilight was drawing in upon us.

That night Neirin played his harp for us in the feast-hall, and I told my tales, and one after another our Masters sang. All of their singing was unworldly and strange, unlike their usual straightforward praise songs, and all of it touched in one way or another on Annwn, the Otherworld. But the piece I remember best was

Taliesin's, perhaps because he sang last. In the ordinary way of things he was a slight, dark man of less than average height, a finger's-breadth or two shorter than I was in those days, and I am not tall. He wore his dark beard—which had then scarcely a trace of gray in it—clipped short, and his hair, held back on ceremonial occasions with the silver circlet of his rank, fell straight and dark to his shoulders. In plain, well-worn traveling clothes, or when he wished to be unnoticed, he could pass as any small farmer or poor soldier, and draw hardly a second glance. You would have said that tall, white-haired Talhaearn, still lean and straight despite his age, or gray-haired, bushy-bearded Ugnach, a man of no middling height, were either of them more imposing figures. And yet when Taliesin stood up to sing, he somehow dwarfed every other man in the place, and drew and held all eyes, and no voice spoke in the hall but his until he was done. So it was that evening when he stood beside the high table, clothed only in a long woolen robe as brilliantly blue as his eyes, and touched with red firelight; and he sang:

> "I have been in many forms;
> Many lands have felt my tread;
> Many skies my eyes have seen;
> Living, I have long been dead.
>
> In the dark behind the stars,
> In the womb of mother earth,
> In the green depths of the sea
> All alone I got my birth.
>
> Gods have I seen rise and fall,
> Altars built but to decay;
> Names forgot that all men knew—
> Each in turn has had his day.
>
> Through the swirling waterfalls,
> Through the surging currents cold,
> Through the sounding salt-sea waves
> I have swum with skin of gold.
>
> Kings have ridden on the earth,
> Warring, winning famous names;

All in turn have come to dust—
Under oaks all sleep the same.

I have soared on wings of fire
Eagle-pinioned through bright air;
Lightening-crowned and thunder-borne,
Where the ravens never dare.

Peoples speak their thousand tongues,
Poets sing their songs of praise—
Light as leaves upon the wind
Their words vanish in the maze.

I have seen the deathless land;
I have walked cold halls of stone;
In the dark beneath the dark
Silent have I sung alone.

Poet, praise the warrior bold,
Shedding blood to buy his mead—
Only by your *awen* bright
Shall his fame outlive his deed.

I have been in many shapes,
Many births and deaths are mine;
Here within this fire-bright hall
All shall in my *awen* shine."

Well I remember that spring evening in the smoky, flame-lit hall of Cadwaladr Coch, with the rain hushing softly on the thatch and dripping from the eves, the bards all drinking at their ease beside the Lord and his dark-haired Lady, the men of the place lounging on their benches with the women pouring their ale, and the dogs and children rolling together in the rushes beside the central fire. In the midst of it all Neirin sat playing his many-stringed harp, the firelight gilding his face and his thin, clever hands and turning his dark red hair to flame, and the bright notes hanging in the air like sparks thrown up from blazing pine-wood. A peaceful night it was, and a good one, there on the edge of a fate which none of us saw coming, and none who survived it could afterwards forget.

But that, O my children, is a story for another day.

The Dark Path

The day we took Neirin to meet his fate began in fog and drifting sea-mist, bitter and salt on the lips, dewing hair and clothes alike with a million tiny droplets and turning all the formerly solid world to shadows. He and I were up before the dawn, and indeed I think that neither of us had slept much during the night. We went first to the well for a bucket of cold water to wash the grit of sleep from our eyes and slake our thirst, then wandered out past the friendly watchdog, who came wagging and sniffing to greet us, to check on our pack-ponies in the pasture. It was too early for breakfast, and anyway Neirin would be getting none that day.

Instead the two of us stood leaning silently against the dry-stone wall which bounded the pasture and watched the growing light, hearing as we did so the voices of the waking land: the contention of early birdsong in the coppiced thicket north of the farmstead; the crowing of a cock on his dunghill behind the stable; the lowing of cattle and bleating of sheep where they mixed in a nearby field; and sweet and distant, the morning bell of the Christian *clas* at Llangaffo, a mile or so to the west. At last the fog-blurred disk of the sun appeared through the eastern trees, turning the iron-gray mist to gold. Watching it, Neirin drew a deep breath and smiled, and I smiled back at him. Then, still unspeaking, we returned to the compound, he to his seclusion in the guesthouse and I to join the others in the feast-hall for breakfast. The day had begun.

Presently, with the help of the stable-boys, Rhys and I saddled up our ponies, and the six of us rode out through the now-bright morning. Neirin rode with a slight smile on his face, but his eyes were busy on all that lay around him, storing up sights to sustain him in darkness, or maybe taking a last look as a condemned man would at the world he might be leaving soon—for as I learned later, not all of those who walked the Dark Path came back safe and whole. Between the worlds is a perilous place for human-kind, and the greatest of perils there are sometimes those we bring with us in ourselves.

All too soon Bryn Celli Ddu loomed up before us, innocent in sunlight and backed by the dark oak trees of its name, their buds now swelling bronze-golden toward spring. Some of the trees looked old enough to have survived the Romans' fire, but most were young, and all of them were twisted sideways by the wind. Our ponies' hooves splashed through the shallows of the little river Braint, and we came to the shelter which we had built the day before. While Rhys and I unsaddled the ponies and hobbled them to graze, and Neirin joined Talhaearn in the shelter with our saddlebags, Taliesin and Ugnach pulled the bull's-hide curtain to one side, and went into the mound to complete their preparations. White fleecy clouds floated by overhead; it could have been the mildest of summer days. But within the hollow hill it would not be warm.

The morning passed slowly, accompanied by birdsong. Taliesin and Ugnach came back out and joined us, and Talhaearn produced a stoneware jug from his gear and sent me down to the stream for water. Neirin sat cross-legged on a sheepskin, staring at nothing with that same faint smile. Around midday a boy came jogging across the fields from Caer Lêb with a basket which proved to contain bread and cheese and wine, and everyone but Neirin ate. Slowly the sun wheeled over to the west; slowly the shadows lengthened. Sometime in late afternoon Neirin stood up and stretched, and picking up his saddlebags, turned to me with a smile. "Will you come down to the river with me, brother?" he asked. "The need is on me to bathe."

"Of course," I said, wondering at his choice of time, but Taliesin nodded. "Go with him, Gwernin, and help him make ready. Rhys, you may go as well." Then I understood: the ceremony had begun. Behind me as I followed Neirin, I heard the Masters start to talk quietly among themselves.

At the stream-bank Neirin stripped and waded into the cold water. It was not deep: even when he knelt in the deepest pool he could find, the water barely reached his chest, but he ducked his head under all the same and came up spluttering and blowing. His body was very white where his tunic covered it, and the long scar from his last-summer's wounding showed faintly pink on his left shoulder. When he had finished washing he climbed out, shivering a little in the light breeze and slapping his arms to warm them, and dried himself with the thin linen towel he had brought with him. I handed him the sheep-colored woolen tunic I had found in his saddlebags, and gratefully he pulled it on, then sat on a rock for me to comb and braid his wet hair. After I had gathered up his discarded clothes, he rose and we went back to the shelter, young Rhys following silently in our wake.

While we had been gone, someone had kindled a fire, and we found Taliesin on his knees beside it, heating water in a three-legged pot. As we arrived he pulled it back from the flames and carefully poured its contents into a black pottery beaker, from which a pungent steam arose. Then he looked up at the two of us and smiled. "Are you ready, Little Hawk?" he asked Neirin.

"I am, Master," said Neirin seriously, but his amber eyes were bright with anticipation.

"Good," said Taliesin, standing up carefully so as not to spill his brew. "As soon as this cools, we can start. Ugnach, Talhaearn, let us go now."

"What about the boys?" asked Ugnach, brushing straw and bracken leaves from his russet brown robe.

"Let them come," said Talhaearn, arising more stiffly, and Taliesin nodded. "This much they can see."

We went, then, in straggling procession to the waiting portal and the dark leather curtain that closed it. The sun was sinking low now, and soon would drop behind the hill to our west. The entrance to the mound faced away from it, toward the midsummer sunrise. Three evenings hence, if the day was clear, we would see in the west at this hour the slender sickle of the new moon, and Neirin would emerge from his seclusion.

The Masters arranged themselves in a half-circle facing Neirin, who stood with his back to the green mound and the last of the sunlight shining in his dark red hair, while Rhys and I watched them all from behind. There was a moment's pause, as if the world was drawing breath; then the descending sun touched the dark bulk of the hill. Faint and distant from the west I heard the sound of the Christian bell.

"Seeker, are you ready now," said Ugnach in his mellow voice, overriding the bright chime of the bell, "to walk the dark path which lies between the stars?"

"I am ready," said Neirin.

"Then take this token," said Ugnach, "to aid you on your way, and go wherever it may lead you." And stepping forward, he handed Neirin a long feather, the bright barred pinion of a hawk. Neirin took it and worked it through the thongs that bound his right braid, and Ugnach nodded and stepped back. The bell had ceased to sound.

"Seeker, are you ready now," said Talhaearn in his deep voice, "to walk the dark path which lies within the earth?" As he spoke I heard from the north the echoing croak of a raven, and saw its black wings beat heavily across the sky.

"I am ready," said Neirin.

"Then take this tool," said Talhaearn, "to aid you on your way, and go wherever it may lead you." And stepping forward, he handed Neirin a stone knife. Neirin took the knife and pushed it through the leather strap which was all he wore for a belt, and Talhaearn nodded and stepped back. The raven called once more, then was silent.

"Seeker, are you ready now," said Taliesin in his rich voice, "to walk the dark path that lies within the sea?" For a moment I thought I could hear the hushing of the waves on the shores of Aber Menai, a mile and more away to the east.

"I am ready," said Neirin.

"Then take this cup," said Taliesin, "to aid you on your way, and drain it to the bitter dregs." And stepping forward, he handed Neirin the black pottery beaker. Neirin took it in both hands, and stood for a moment looking down at it with a faint smile; then he lifted it to his lips and drank it all down at one draught. Slowly he lowered it, his mouth closed hard as if fighting against pain or sickness, and I saw him swallow once convulsively; slowly he held it out to Taliesin, who took it, and nodded, and stepped back. "The Path awaits you, Little Hawk," he said. "Go you now and walk it, and walk it well."

"I will," said Neirin, a little hoarsely. His eyes were wide and dark, the pupils already dilating as he felt the effects of the drug. Then with that same faint smile he turned and put aside the leather curtain, and bending a little under the gray lintel stone, stepped quickly into the darkness which lay within. The curtain closed behind him, and he was gone.

The three bards nodded to each other. "Come along, Gwernin, Rhys," said Taliesin. "That is all for now; let us go back to the shelter." And he led the way, with the rest of us following slowly behind him. During the brief ceremony, the shadow of the western hill had reached out and swallowed us, leaving only the lingering brightness in the sky to light our way; soon it would be dark.

"Build up the fire a little, Gwernin," said Taliesin. "And the rest of you may as well go back to the hall for your dinner. There will be nothing happening here for a while. Ugnach will be back later, but you, Talhaearn, need not come until tomorrow."

"And do you think, Gwion," rumbled Talhaearn, his grey beard jutting aggressively, "that I am so old and feeble as to fear a little night air?"

"I know you fear nothing, Father of Awen," said Taliesin, smiling, "but I also know you are too wise a man to spend the night needlessly in an open field, when you might be sleeping safe and warm in a good bed."

"Hmm," said Talhaearn. "Glib as usual, boy. Oh, well, you have a point; I will see you tomorrow then. Ugnach, Rhys, let us saddle the ponies. We will send you back some food later, Gwion. Do you mean to keep Gwernin here?"

"If you can spare him," said Taliesin.

"For the one night at least, I can," said Talhaearn dryly. And with that he turned and followed the others into the twilight. I went on adding wood to the fire, and wondered what was coming next.

For a long while nothing happened. Taliesin sat cross-legged on a sheepskin idly watching the flames, and sometimes tilting his head a little as if listening to something that only he could hear. Once he frowned; twice he smiled to himself. The fire burned down and I added more wood, and the night grew darker and colder. My empty belly rumbled its discontent, but I did my best to ignore it and to maintain a dignified silence. Finally Taliesin sighed and stretched, and looked across the fire at me, and I felt emboldened then to speak.

"Master," I asked, "what is happening to Neirin? Is there anything you can tell me?" For the thought was on me that I might wish to walk the Dark Path myself one day, and this seemed my best chance to learn.

Taliesin sighed again and held out his hands absently to the fire, his eyes never leaving my face. The flickering light sparkled in them, and painted red highlights in his dark hair and beard, and on the intricately carved brooch that closed his heavy woolen cloak. "I cannot tell you much, Gwernin," he said slowly. "You are not ready to hear it, and you may never be. But some questions I can answer. Neirin's body is lying in the hollow hill, and I think resting peacefully. Ugnach, when he returns, will go in to make sure that it is so, and to…do other things. Neirin's spirit is out of his body and walking the Dark Path. He has gone a long way already."

I sat and thought on this for a while. "What is happening to him there?"

"That," said Taliesin, "I cannot tell you. It is a knowledge that can only be got by doing; when your time comes, if it ever does, you will know." He smiled. "But now I think I hear Ugnach coming back, and I hope bringing our dinner. Later, perhaps, I will answer another question—or perhaps not!"

When we had eaten the bread and meat that Ugnach brought, and he had gone into the mound, Taliesin rolled himself in his cloak and lay down beside the fire to sleep. "You had better rest while you can, Gwernin," he said yawning. "There is nothing you can do now to help Neirin, and our watch will be long." After a moment I took his advice. I fell asleep sooner than I had expected, and I dreamed. I dreamed...

Neirin was floating in darkness. Around him were shining points of light, and a chiming as of silver bells, or of ice-covered branches bending and clashing in the wind. He was gathering the lights like berries and putting them into a pale skin bag, but they were all of them sharp as broken crystal, and each time he touched one, he bled. His hands and his arms ran red with it, his own blood dripping and falling into the darkness, one gout of bright blood for every point of light. And though the pain of it was great, he was laughing, laughing with delight as his life bled away before his eyes...

I opened my own eyes and stared up into darkness, my heart pounding. Dry bracken rustled faintly under me as I moved, reminding me of where I was. The fire beside me had burned down to embers, and the night was cold and still. Across the shelter from me Taliesin lay breathing softly in sleep, but Ugnach was nowhere to be seen. Slowly I got up and added wood to the fire, then sat beside it holding out my hands to warm them. My hands...*Neirin's hands*...had it been only a dream? I had shared thoughts with him in dreams before, when our need had been great. But then, as now, there had been nothing I could do to help him. At last I lay down once more and slept, and when I woke again it was to sunlight and the sound of voices.

Taliesin was kneeling by the fire, toasting bread-and-cheese on a flat rock beside it. Across from him Ugnach sat on a camp stool, looking weary and drinking something from a wooden cup. The morning was bright and breezy, and the sun had been up for some time. The good smells of food and ale assailed my senses, and I sat up hurriedly; it had been a long time since supper. Taliesin saw me and smiled, and tossed me a piece of his bread-and-cheese.

"Just like my lads," said Ugnach, grinning. "They will sleep through fire and tempest, but wave a piece of warm bread at them, and up they come. Rhys, now, I would wager is still abed, unless Talhaearn has been at him."

"You would lose your wager," said Taliesin. "Here they come now. Talhaearn has a way with slug-a-beds—has he not, Gwernin?"

I grinned and swallowed my mouthful. "I am thinking you would know that as well as I, Master?"

Taliesin laughed. "You are right," he said. "How that takes me back! Though I swear I was never so oblivious as you... Good morning to you, Talhaearn. Have you brought us more breakfast? Your pupil will be starving otherwise, for Ugnach and I have eaten all that was left."

"I have," said Talhaearn, taking the camp stool as Ugnach vacated it. "Bottomless as Llyn Tegid, these boys, and just as easy to fill. Rhys has the basket, unless he has eaten it empty on the way. How are things here?"

"Well enough," said Ugnach. "A quiet night, at any rate. I will be off now to my watching—do you save me some food for later."

"I will if Gwernin leaves us any," said Taliesin, grinning. Just then Rhys arrived with a covered basket, and I fell to with thanks.

This second day passed as slowly as the one before. By and by Taliesin stood up and left us for a while, and Talhaearn, determined to make up for lost time, began testing me on my poetic forms. Rhys sat and watched, at first open-mouthed in surprise at my errors, and then slyly grinning, but he discovered his mistake when my master began shooting questions at him as well. He had been well taught, had Rhys, and was farther along in some things than I was, for all that he was four years younger; but then I had not had a bard for a father, nor been tutored in tongue-craft since I could speak.

Presently Taliesin came back, and after listening for a while, he began to argue with Talhaearn about some of our answers. This was much better entertainment from my point of view, and I listened entranced until their discussion became general. Then I got up and went to check on our ponies. Without my noticing it, my apprehension for Neirin had come creeping back, and I was restless. I wandered down to the river, and found Rhys there throwing stones in the water. "Hello," he said when he saw me. "What are you doing?"

"Nothing," I said. "There is nothing I *can* do." I looked him over thoughtfully, seeing him for the first time as a person rather than simply an annoyance. Brown eyes, curly brown hair, a wide mouth, and a slender, coltish body in a well-worn, too-large tunic, cut down from someone else's use and torn at the shoulder; in the warm afternoon he had been wading, and his big bare feet were covered with mud from the stream. "What are *you* doing?" I asked.

"Nothing," said Rhys, mimicking my tone of voice. "There is nothing here *to* do. Why are you so bad at poetry, at your age? You do not *look* stupid."

I flushed a little, but kept my temper. "I have only been studying it for two years—before that I was a storyteller. A circuit round Wales I have gone, all on my own, and last summer I traveled with Neirin in the North, and won fat prizes."

Rhys nodded. "*He* is good—he does not make stupid errors. Do you think he will succeed in his walking? My father says that some people come back crazy, or feeble—and some never come back at all. After a while their bodies starve to death, and stop breathing—and who knows where their spirits go? Lying like a log until you rot—that would not be a good way to die!"

My heart sank within me, but I tried not to show it. "This is foolish talk. Neirin will succeed—he always does. He won the bardic competition at Dun Eidyn last summer with only two nights to prepare, against bards three times his age, and your father himself, who was one of them, helped to crown him."

Rhys cocked his head, considering. He had a smudge of dirt on one cheek, and bramble-scratches on his legs. "That is true. But poetry is not the same as magic. When I come of age, I will walk the Dark Path, too—I have been preparing. No one has ever done it that young, except Taliesin. I will be as famous as he is."

"Neirin has done magic, too," I said, stung by his boasting. "I have seen him do things that would take your breath away, were you not too young to hear of them."

"Windy words," said Rhys dismissively; I got the feeling he was quoting his father. "They cannot have been too great, if *you* were there. I was a better poet than you are when I was ten years old."

"And have you walked with ghosts, and talked with dead men?" I asked. "Have you sat yarning with Gwydion mab Dôn, and done him a favor afterwards, and had him do you one in return? I do not think so. You are a silly little boy—come and talk to me of magic when your beard has grown. Your father should beat you, to teach you manners." And I turned away.

"You will never be a poet," said Rhys. "You are too old to start now. You will be a storyteller all your life, and never a bard, as I shall be."

"Maybe," I said, turning back slowly. "But I know one thing that you will be soon, and I will not, if you do not shut your mouth."

"And what is that?" asked Rhys, taunting.

"Thrown in the river!" I said, and made a lunge for him; but he twisted out of my grasp and was away, running up the slope like a hare and laughing as he went. I did not follow; I had no taste for vengeance just then. My heart was sick with worry for Neirin, and the rest of the day seemed very long indeed.

At last evening came. This time it was Talhaearn who stayed with Neirin, replacing Ugnach, and all the rest of us who rode back to the hall for our meal. The place seemed very bright and warm and full of people after the chill silence of the fields, and I was glad to get a hot dinner, but part of me was longing every moment to be away. When we had eaten and Ugnach had retired to the guest-house to make up his lost sleep, I followed Taliesin to the stables and found him saddling his red mare. "Master," I said, "let me come with you again. It is only right, when my own master is there, that I should serve him there as well."

Taliesin looked me over with a stern face but a hint of a twinkle in his eye. I stood my ground, waiting. "Very well, Gwernin," he said at last. "You may come back with me for one more night. Go to the kitchen and get Talhaearn's food, then saddle up and follow me." Then he grinned. "I think you would come anyway, so you may as well make yourself useful."

Once more at the shelter I built up the fire, and we settled down to wait. It was not long before Talhaearn came striding through the starlight toward us like a tall ghost—for he was not wholly blind, and best he could see in dim light. "How is he, Iron Brow?" asked Taliesin quietly as he sat down.

"As he should be," said Talhaearn briefly. "His body stirs from time to time, and can still swallow—I got a little watered wine into him just now. I think he will do well enough. Now I am for my dinner." He ate with relish the barley bread and cold meat I had brought him, and I refilled his ale cup twice. Then he stood up and stretched, and left us without a word. Straight toward the hill he went, and vanished into it. In the darkness I did not even see the curtain stir.

"Yes," said Taliesin as if I had spoken. "He sees by more than eyesight when he wishes. Eye-blind is not always head-blind, Gwernin—remember that when the day comes that you need it."

I looked at him, surprised, and saw the weariness heavy on him. "Master," I said tentatively, "is Neirin really well? I had a dream last night…"

"Ah," said Taliesin, sounding amused. "I thought that might be the way of it. *Sa, sa*, I did not send the two of you off together last summer for nothing. Yes, I think all is still well with Neirin—but he has yet a long way to go, on a road which allows no turning back. Now I am going to sleep, and you should do so as well. Trust in the Hawk, as I do, to find his way home safely at last." And with that, he rolled himself up in his cloak again beside the fire, and slept at once. More slowly I followed his example, but it was long before sleep came to me; I think I was afraid of what I might see in my dreams…

But that, O my children, is a story for another day.

No Way Back

A road which allows no turning back, Taliesin had said: that is the nature of the Dark Path, as I have proved in my turn. Only at the beginning, when the perils which have already been passed are few and small, and the Seeker's strength and courage still burn high and bright, could he turn and retreat as he had come: and at that point, for that very reason, he would not do so. Once past the first major challenge, there is no way back: the only road home lies forward, come what may...

This time when I saw him, Neirin was walking through a deep cavern. The floor of it was rough, strewn with rocks and rubble, and treacherous with dark pits and pools, but he could see his way clearly by the glow from the skin bag he carried. His hands were wrapped in stained bandages, but seemed to trouble him not at all. Briskly and lightly he walked, like a man just setting out on a pleasant journey. Ahead of him the walls of the cavern stretched dimly into the gloom, and the only sounds were the crunch of his footsteps and the plop and tinkle of dripping water—the only clear sounds. Somewhere on the edge of hearing there was a formless roaring, more felt through the bones than heard, but growing steadily louder as he walked.

Now and again there were side branches to the cavern, and Neirin paused at each of them, looking carefully back and forth and listening, but always he continued straight ahead, toward the swelling roar. Now it shook the air, and the rock itself trembled. Ahead of him the path ended, where a great cataract leapt roaring from the right-hand wall of the cave and plunged into unfathomable depths. The only way forward was a narrow bridge no wider than a sword-blade, wet and slippery with the breath of the falls, which spanned the torrent and led on into darkness.

Neirin stood and thought for a moment, his eyes measuring the bridge and the maelstrom beneath it. To slip was to fall; to fall was death and destruction; but he had no choice. With one bare foot he tested the silvery span, and felt its icy cold stab through him like a lance. He frowned, then nodded to himself and stepped out upon it, his eyes fixed not on his feet but on the far side of the chasm, where something small and golden was glowing ever brighter in the dark. With each step he took the cold became more bitter, and his body shuddered like a grass-blade plucked by the wind. Step…step…step… Surely he must be halfway there by now. The roar of the falls was deafening him, as its mist was blinding. Then his foot slipped and he wavered, throwing out his arms to save his balance. The glowing bag dropped from his bandaged fingers and disappeared into the void, leaving him in darkness. And in that darkness, he closed his eyes and laughed…

Again I awoke to darkness, my heart pounding in my ears and my breath coming in gasps. I could feel the chill of the ice bridge in my own body, making me shiver. The fire had burned down almost to ashes, and the night was still and cold. I got up and added wood—small sticks of kindling at first, and then larger branches—until it blazed up like a beacon, and my trembling hands at last grew warm. Even then I sat for a long time staring into the flames, willing their warmth to Neirin, wherever he was. It was almost dawn before I rolled myself in my cloak again and slept.

Sunlight on my face woke me, sunlight and voices and the scent of warm bread. Groaning, I rolled over and opened bleary eyes, feeling a thousand years old. Gradually the faces around the fire came into focus: Taliesin, looking amused; Ugnach, looking angry; and Rhys, managing to look both sullen and afraid.

"This lad, or so he tells me," Ugnach was saying, "has been vaunting his abilities and causing bad blood amongst us. I have told him before that it takes more than technical prowess to make a bard, but he will not believe me. Maybe he will pay more attention to you, Taliesin."

"Well, we will see," said Taliesin, and to me, "Good morning, Gwernin. You have slept so late there is breakfast ready and to spare. Now tell me"—switching his attention back to Rhys—"what you have been doing to put your father in this state. What were you boasting of, and to whom?"

"I—it was only..." said Rhys unhappily.

"Yes? What was it only?" asked Taliesin.

"I was telling Gwernin," said Rhys in a rush, "that I am a much better poet than he will ever be—and it is *true*. I listened to him yesterday, he cannot answer even baby questions! He is useless! Why does Talhaearn keep him as a student, wasting his own efforts, when Gwernin will never make a bard? He is only a storyteller, after all."

"That is *Master* Talhaearn to you, *gwas*," said Ugnach, giving his son a cuff on the head that knocked him sideways.

"Wait, Ugnach," said Taliesin. "Only a storyteller... *only* a storyteller! Rhys, where do you think the bards draw their inspirations, if not from storytellers? How many stories can *you* tell?"

"Why..."—Rhys' eyes crossed momentarily as he counted—"two and twenty, at least. That is probably more than *he* knows."

"A master bard in Ireland, a member of the *filid*," said Taliesin softly, and he was not smiling now, "knows a tale and its brother for every night of the year, and three-score more besides. You have some way to go before you meet that standard. You have heard Gwernin's stories, both in your own hall and here: were you not entertained? Did he bore you?"

"Well—no, he did not," said Rhys reluctantly, "and yes, I was. But that was before I knew..."

"Not every bard is equally good at all aspects of his craft," said Taliesin, "especially at the beginning. That does not make him any less a bard. It is true that the poetic measures are the crown of our art, its highest glory. But a poet is only as good as his *awen*, and *awen* breathes where it will. Without it you have only a pretty mouth-music, an amusement for children, and no sense. Any fool can manage that, with enough practice. Do you understand me, Rhys?"

"I—no," said Rhys, confused. "How can you be a bard, and not a poet? I thought..."

"You cannot," said Taliesin. "Not in Wales. But you can be a poet, and not a bard, if you have only craft and no inspiration.

Gwernin is doing very well for the amount of time he has had to study, which is not much: as Talhaearn will tell you, I keep interrupting his schooling. You, on the other hand, have a clever tongue and little sense to go with it. Now run away and think on this, before your father stops holding his hand, and in a day or two you can tell me your conclusions! Gwernin," he added, with a total change of tone, "your breakfast awaits—if you are not too embarrassed now to eat it!"

I sat up, blushing, as Rhys fled: but the scent of toasted bread-and-cheese recalled me to my senses, and I made a hearty meal.

"Well for him," said Ugnach apologetically, "that Talhaearn was not here, too. The little devil is clever, I grant you, but a fool."

"Oh, I expect he will grow out of it," said Taliesin lightly. "Were you not a fool at his age? I know I was."

"Hmm," said Ugnach. "Your folly outdoes most men's wisdom, but never mind. Has Talhaearn been out yet this morning?"

"Yes, before you came," said Taliesin, frowning. "He looked a little worried, but would not say why—you know his way. Only that my boy was still alive and on his path." His mouth set hard for a moment, and then relaxed.

"Well, it is not an easy road," said Ugnach. "Or it was not so for me. I thought more than once I was done for, but somehow I pulled through." Taliesin glanced at me, where I sat all ears, the food forgotten in my hand. "Ah, well," said Ugnach. "I am not saying anything he does not know already. I am away now, in search of my idiot child—do you get some rest before evening, you look worn out."

"I will, in a while," said Taliesin absently, still frowning and looking at me. "Gwernin, is there something you can tell me? Have you been dreaming again?" And then gently, when I nodded, "Is he hurt?"

"Not—badly," I said. "Not when I saw him last. But he has been in pain, and in such danger..." I stopped, remembering the ice bridge. "Master, what happens to him if—if he dies there?"

"Then he will not come back," said Taliesin simply. "But I do not think he is near that point yet. Finish your breakfast, then go down to the river and wash your face—it will make you feel better. I am going to take Ugnach's advice, and get some more sleep while I can. Tonight I may need all my strength."

It was another long day, with little in it to remember. In the afternoon clouds came up from the west, and brought rain with them. The three of us—Rhys had been banished to the farmstead—sat around the fire in the shelter and talked, the sort of slow, rambling talk that fills the time and leaves few memories behind it. Some of it, though, I do remember because of what came later. The Irish, said Taliesin, were expanding their settlements in the North, in the area they call Dál Riata, and causing some trouble to Rhydderch Hael of Strathclyde. This he had got from Cadwaladr, who had heard it at King Rhun's *llys* not long before.

"Well for Rhydderch's neighbors, then," said Ugnach, tugging gently at his bushy beard and frowning. "Not that any on that coast can count themselves safe if the Ulaid are stirring again."

"True enough," said Taliesin thoughtfully. "And yet it may relieve their minds a little, if Urien's chief ally has problems of his own. Now I wonder... Gwernin, you two met Irishmen on Aeron's southern border last summer, did you not?"

"We did," I said, and frowned at the memory. "Slave-takers, they were, with a base in the mountains there. They almost had us; it was a close-run thing. We told King Elidyr about it when we came to his court, but if he acted against them, I never heard of it."

"Maybe," said Taliesin, "he had reason... It would not be the first time that a wolf at the door was tamed, and made a dog. And if one wolf, why not the pack? Well, no doubt we shall see in time..."

The talk drifted on to other subjects, and the day wound at last to its end. Toward sunset two boys rode over from Cadwaladr's hall with baskets, bringing us food and ale, and we made a hearty meal. We were still eating when Talhaearn appeared suddenly out the gloom. "Gwion," he said abruptly, "I think you should go to him now. He is talking but not making sense; I cannot understand him. Maybe you can."

Taliesin put down his food and stood up; then, seeing me about to follow, set a hand on my shoulder and pressed me back to the ground. "No, Gwernin," he said. "Here you cannot go. Stay in the shelter with Talhaearn—and if you dream tonight, be careful what you do!" And on the word he was gone, leaving us staring after him.

No one went back to the hall that night despite the rainy weather. Instead we sat around the fire and dozed, gripped by a feeling of impending crisis. More than once Talhaearn started to snore, and only my shaking his shoulder kept him from falling into the fire. Ugnach sat counting on his fingers and mumbling, and I was torn between a desire for sleep and fear of what I might see. At last, when I could keep my eyes open no longer, I rolled myself up in my cloak and lay down again, and almost at once I dreamed...

Neirin was walking through green darkness, darkness thick enough to touch. In his right hand he carried a golden lamp, which showed him the path he followed. Now and then things moved in the darkness, floating creatures like fish, but like no fish that I had ever seen. Neirin looked pale and tired, but he was still smiling, and as he walked he sang. The words rose from his mouth in bubbles like bright sparks, like harp notes caught in amber. The words were his *awen*, and his life.

Ahead of him something bulked large in the darkness, tall as a fort or a tower. In the gloom the stones of it glowed faintly green, and beyond its high gateway there shone a glimmering golden light, the honey-gold light which sometimes shines beneath the clouds at sunset. The closer Neirin came to it, the taller the tower appeared, until it seemed to touch the sky—if sky there was in this place. The stairs to its gateway were very steep, and their steps beyond counting. Neirin paused for a moment at their base, and then started to climb.

At first he climbed lightly, almost easily, past waving seaweeds and scuttling many-legged things with glowing lights for eyes; but soon the steps grew steeper, so that the effort required to make each lift increased, and the drop behind him grew cliff-like and bottomless. Step after step, effort after effort, stretched out in endless time. He was moving slowly now—step and pause, step and pause. He had lost sight of the light above him, and now there was only the climb.

Gasping, he stood still at last, and looked at the lamp in his right hand. He had nothing else to throw away, only the torn robe he wore, which floated almost weightless on his body. His belt was gone, and with it the stone knife; the feather was gone from his hair. The lamp was his only prize, won with such effort and pain, and even its glow was fading. Soon he would be wholly in the dark…

I opened my eyes to dim firelight, and a hand shaking my shoulder. "Gwernin!" said Talhaearn's deep voice. "Gwernin! Tell me now, what did you see?"

"He is…in the ocean," I said, half-asleep still. "In the darkness, climbing a stair. The higher he climbs, the farther he can fall, but he never reaches the top. I do not know…if he can get out…"

"Hmm," said Talhaearn, peering at me with clouded blue eyes. At least, I thought groggily, he had stopped shaking me. "I know that stairway, and so should he. Why did he ever start?"

"I think," I said, "he was too tired to remember…" Despite myself I yawned. "Is it almost morning?"

"Close enough," said Talhaearn. "Gray and still raining. Get up, boy, get up—or do you want to go back?"

"No," I said, and then, "Yes… I do not know. Taliesin said…"

"Gwion is very good," said Talhaearn firmly, as if I had argued with him, "but I am older at this game than he is. Get up for now—it is a long time until evening. We may need you later for one final throw."

I do not know how I got through that day. I felt half alive, and wholly confused. Talhaearn and Ugnach took it in turns to keep me awake, lest I drift back into Neirin's world unintentionally. I think I ate and drank, I think I even talked, but I have no clear memory of any of it.

Towards evening the rain stopped, and the clouds began to

break up, letting a little watery sunlight leak through. I blinked at it wearily, knowing that for some reason it was important. Sunset…and Neirin. Neirin…and the dark. This time…I would help…

He was very near the top now, crawling on bandaged hands and bloody knees, pulling himself up step by step. The lamp, barely glowing, hung from a cord around his neck, twisted from one more strip of his ragged robe. His eyes were closed; there was nothing to see in the darkness; but still he wore a trace of his faint, mischievous smile, and still, very softly, he was singing.

I saw him from above, looking down. This time I was present, and solid; this time I had hands, and a voice. I tried to call his name; I heard nothing, but he looked up, and his eyes opened, and he saw me. I reached down my hand—my arm was incredibly long—and he took it. He was standing—he was climbing—he was at the top and smiling at me as I let him go. Then he looked over my shoulder, and his eyes widened, and he held up the lamp, which flared in my vision like the rising sun. I turned to look behind me, and the light there, which had been gentle as sunset, now burned fiercely white, brighter than midday, a soundless explosion of blinding fire that struck me like a wave, knocked me off my feet, and sent me tumbling into the void. Sightless, mindless, bodiless, I fell, and fell, and fell, through time without meaning, without measure…

Light, and pain, and hard hands holding me. An echoing voice shouting, calling my name. I had been dead, and was alive. I was reborn. I was Gwernin…

I was lying on my back on the muddy turf beside Bryn Celli Ddu, and Taliesin was shaking me. When he saw my eyes were open, he stopped, and helped me to sit up instead. "Gwernin," he said, "Gwernin…" He was paler than I had ever seen him, haggard and drawn and weary, and at first I thought he was angry; but there was no anger in his eyes, or in his voice.

"Did I…do it right?" I asked. My voice sounded strange in my own ears. My head ached, and I did not feel quite solid.

"Come and see," said Taliesin, and pulled me to my feet. In the west the sun stood balanced on a golden bar of cloud, and above it floated the merest sliver of a new moon. As we came to the entrance of the mound, the bull's-hide curtain was pushed aside, and Neirin stood there, wobbly as a new calf, but with such happiness in his face as I have seldom seen. And just for a moment the sunlight on his hair seemed to shine like a golden lamp—but I must admit my vision was none too clear, for I was weeping, and grinning at the same time.

There was feasting that night at Caer Lêb, and Neirin was in the midst of it, although it was little enough he could eat after his three-day fast. Instead he drank cup after cup of thrice-watered wine, and smiled and smiled at everyone around him. Few of the people there had any idea of what he had done, but they felt that it was something magical and impressive, which perhaps could only have been done in this time and place, and therefore reflected well on everyone in the area. And with enough mead and ale, harp-song and singing, firelight and laughter and friendship, the celebration soon became cause enough in itself to rejoice.

I sat on a bench at the side of the hall that night and watched the others perform. I was too tired and too confused, but also too full of joy, to want to be the center of attention, and after a few cups of mead I was too drunk as well. Instead I sat happily if muzzily smiling while Ieuan told me—in great detail—all the things he had accomplished since we parted at Deganwy two years ago, and all his plans for the future. He had been a quiet man on the road, had Ieuan, but marriage seemed to have loosened his tongue. I am not sure at what point in his monologue I fell asleep, or who eventually put me to bed in the guesthouse; I only know I slept without dreaming, and woke up very late the next day: and in this I was not alone.

We stayed two more days at Caer Lêb, until everyone was recovered, and then we rode on to the King's court at Aberffraw. And if I never got a clear explanation from Taliesin for my part in the story I have just told you—well, some kinds of knowledge have to be experienced, and not explained.

But that, O my children, is a story for another day.

The Irish Wind

The Kings of North Wales—of Gwynedd—have many fortresses and strong places, and many high timber-built halls. Deganwy is the chiefest of these, and there they built with Roman stone on Roman foundations, and in the Roman style. Caer Seint, which faces the Menai and the Irish Sea, is another such, with Roman roots beneath its wood-framed buildings and Roman walls around them. But the great wooden hall at Aberffraw within its wooden palisade is wholly British, and there have been Kings of Gwynedd there ever since Rhun's great-grandfather drove the invading Irish out of Ynys Môn and took it back for the Cymry.

Aberffraw lies only a few miles west of Caer Lêb, so near that Cadwaladr sent one of his men along to relieve me—and of course Neirin—from our duties with the pack string, leaving only Rhys to bring up the rear with his father's pack-pony. He had been keeping his distance from me—and from Taliesin!—since his chewing-out, and I was glad to continue that arrangement. I was less happy with Cadwaladr's choice of packman, though it was well intended; I had already seen—and heard—enough of my old friend Ieuan.

It was afternoon before we set out, the day before having been spent in seeing the mound put to rights and closed again. Much of this work had fallen to Neirin, as the youngest initiate, and I wondered what he had thought of the task. We had had no time for private talk since his emergence from the hill, and I felt a reluctance now to mention my dreaming, and my interference—if that was what it had been—in his private quest. Besides, with the passing of time, it had all begun to fade and seem a little unreal to me.

Real enough, however, was the afternoon sun warm on my face, and the cool north-west wind, smelling of fresh-turned earth and new grass and all the other delights of spring. My black pony moved faster of his own accord to walk beside Neirin's dapple gray, with whom he was good friends, and Neirin, seeing the two of us out of the corner of his eye, reined back to join me, leaving the older bards to their talk. "A fine day it is," he said grinning, "and good to be on the road again, even with the Irish wind blowing."

"The Irish wind?" I asked, puzzled.

"Taliesin says they call it that here," said Neirin, "when it blows from the north and west. Ireland is not so far away in that direction, and often enough they come raiding, though it is early yet in the year for them now. Had you not heard?"

"I remember something of that," I said slowly, "from two years ago: the Lord Cadwaladr does not love the Irish."

"And he has reason," said Neirin, nodding. "The walls around his *llys* are not only for show."

"No," I said, "I suppose they are not." And thinking back to that place and its people, I added, "Did you hear my old friend Ieuan has a son now, and they have named him after me?"

Neirin laughed. "*Sa, sa,* what a thing for you! Which girl is she—the pretty redhead?"

"Na, the little dark one with the curly hair—she was sitting by the wall the first night we were there."

"Let me think—oh, yes, the one with the small baby. I do not notice them so much," said Neirin simply, "once they are mothers. *Hai mai!* I am hoping there are some decent single ones at Aberffraw! It has been far too long for me!"

I laughed. "I thought you had a girl at Pengwern last winter! Did she take against you, then, while we were gone?"

"Who? Oh, her—na, na, it was not that," said Neirin, grinning. "Though I doubt me not that she was spoken for before I was out of sight! Na, there were other reasons. And just as well, for I will not be going back to Pengwern with Taliesin when this trip is over."

"Why not?" I asked. "Is it because you are *pencerdd* now? But that was so last autumn."

"Well, that is part of it," said Neirin. "Taliesin gives me my freedom now, so it is right that I should journey and find myself a patron. I had thought of going first to my mother's-brother in Elmet—you remember him, of course."

"How could I forget?" I said and smiled, thinking of that burly good-natured King. "I wish I might come with you."

"Why, as to that—perhaps Talhaearn would spare you," Neirin suggested.

"Na, I think not," I said, and sighed. "Unless I mistake him, he has a deal of work stored up for me—my poetics are not what they should be, not at all. You did not hear him testing me the other day, while you were—elsewhere. It was not pretty—Rhys can run rings around me!"

"Well, as to that," said Neirin again, and paused, frowning slightly. "I am thinking—but never mind. I will give my uncle your regards—have you kept up your practice with the sword he gave you?"

"As well as I could," I said, smiling. "Cyndrwyn's *penteulu* gave me some lessons this winter, he and one or two others in the warband, but they are most of them spearmen, as I was used to be. It is in my baggage now... Do you remember the bouts we had last summer in Aeron, while you were teaching me to use it?"

"Do I not!" said Neirin, and laughed. "You almost had me once or twice, through my own incompetence... That must be Aberffraw ahead, and glad I am of it: I am ready for my dinner!"

Indeed I saw that he was right. Ahead of us was the *llys* on its slight mound, the wooden perimeter walls standing up dark and strong against the late afternoon sky, with lighter stripes showing here and there where palings had been renewed. On our left as we approached was the harbor where the little river Ffraw met the sea, with a few small boats pulled up on the pale sandy beach and a larger ship lying at anchor. Peat smoke from the fishermen's bothies mingled with the scents of fish and seaweed, and white-winged seagulls crying raucously circled overhead. Our ponies splashed through the gravelly ford of the stream, half exposed now by the ebbing tide, and turned onto the muddy track which led to the *llys*.

At the iron-bound gates, the soldiers leaning on their spears waved us through smiling, knowing us for what we were, and when we reined up in the courtyard stable-boys came running to take our ponies, and girls to lead us to the King's guesthouse. One of the latter was a fine slender young maid with rich golden hair, and I saw Neirin's eyes rest upon her consideringly; nor did she appear displeased by his regard. For myself, I have always preferred dark girls; besides, once they had seen Neirin, they seldom glanced at me twice. Sighing, I sleeked down my pale mustache with a damp thumb and forefinger, wishing my beard would grow faster, and prepared to do my best.

The girls led us to two large rooms, brought us wine and water and fresh wheaten bread, and left us to refresh ourselves until it was time to go to the feast hall. I joked with Neirin, who was lodged with Rhys and myself, that he had come down in the world again, but he only laughed. Rhys said nothing, and looked wary at this arrangement: on the one hand, he did not want to be alone with me, but on the other, he did not know how much I had told Neirin of what had passed between us.

That evening Neirin dressed himself with all his usual care, and even something over. He was always fine—finer than I have ever been—but this was his first coming before a King as full *pencerdd*, and he wanted to make the most of it. His knee-length tunic was of fine-combed wool woven in a rich checker of green and blue and gold, with narrow bands of red silk gleaming at neck and shoulders, and under it he wore a soft linen shirt, and woolen trews of a deep double-dyed black. The dark leather of his new belt and boots gleamed softly with polishing, and the bronze fittings on his belt and knife sheath glittered like red gold. His dark red hair he had pulled back and tied at the nape of his neck, and his young beard and mustache made a brave display. All he lacked was the silver circlet he had won last summer at Dun Eidyn: but that had been destroyed by an envious thief, and only the hacked remains had come home with him.

"Na, I do not have it with me," he said when he caught my questioning glance. "I have not seen it since the autumn. I looked for it when I was packing, but could not find it. It does not matter; no doubt I will win another, one of these days. I am not less *pencerdd* for losing it."

"Of course not," I said hastily. Neirin smiled.

"If my *awen* does not show in my singing," he said, "it does not matter if I am crowned with gold. And if it does—why, I think no one will notice."

"You are right," I said; and indeed there was a shining on him that night which needed no crown to prove it. I remembered the golden lamp he had carried in the underworld, and understood.

At that moment there came a tapping at the door, and it opened to show Ugnach, also dressed very richly. He was smiling, but it changed to a frown when he saw his son. "Rhys," he said, "that tunic is all very well, but wash your face, do! And have you lost your comb again?" And as the blushing Rhys made haste to follow his commands, he added, "Neirin, Gwernin, Taliesin wants you in the other room. I will be along in a moment, as soon as I have put this lad to rights."

In the other room we found Talhaearn sitting on a stool while Taliesin combed out his long white hair. I flushed with shame when I saw this, saying, "Master! I am sorry, I am neglecting you! Taliesin, let me do it!"

"Na, na," said Talhaearn complacently, "there is no need—Gwion has done this task for me before, and it will not harm him to do it again. But next time, boy, come sooner."

"Master," I said to Taliesin, "will you let me finish?"

"No need, Gwernin," said Taliesin, laying aside the comb and starting to braid Talhaearn's hair. "It is as he says. Where is Ugnach?"

"Seeing to his son," said Neirin with a grin. "*Hai mai!* What is that?"—at a sound of raised voices without.

"New arrivals, I think," said Taliesin, pausing in his task to listen. And to Ugnach, who entered almost dragging a refurbished Rhys, "Who is making the noise outside?"

"A new party, come up from the harbor," said Ugnach. "Irish, from the sound of them, and demanding the loan of horses for their lord. Well, well, I am thinking we outrank them, and there is plenty of room here besides. Are we ready?"

"Almost," said Taliesin, finishing the plait he held and binding a thong around the end to hold it. "Neirin, look in the nearer saddlebag on my bed-place and bring me what you find. You will know it when you see it."

Neirin's brows shot up, but he said no word in response, merely doing as he was bidden. When he looked into the saddlebag, I heard him suck in air through his teeth in surprise, and for a moment he stood quite still. Then he turned to Taliesin with something in his hands, something which caught the lamp-light and gleamed. "Master..." he said in a queer voice.

Taliesin smiled and held out his hands, and Neirin put the shining thing into them. Reaching up—for Neirin was the taller by a hand's-breadth now—Taliesin placed the re-forged silver on his former pupil's dark red hair. "Not your Master any longer—*Pencerdd*," he said softly. "Fly free, Little Hawk, fly free!"

It was a brave company we made in Rhun's hall that night, the four *Pencerddiaid* silver-crowned and in their best clothes, myself in the red woolen tunic I had got in Pictland the summer before, and even Rhys looking almost respectable in good brown wool. Taliesin wore his customary dark blue, Ugnach a long robe of amber-gold and green, and Talhaearn outshone us all in the gown he had worn when I first met him, a deep red-purple in hue like almost-ripe blackberries, enriched at neck and cuffs and hem with wide bands of many-colored embroidery. On top of this he had piled three massive necklaces of red amber, which glittered in the torchlight as he moved. Even King Rhun, who had made room for the four Masters at his high table that evening, was hardly dressed finer than Talhaearn.

A tall man was Rhun mab Maelgwn Gwynedd, tall and broad and strong, and his thick curly hair and beard still showed more red than gray. It did not need the purple and red of his fine-combed, gold-embroidered robe, or the narrow golden band, set with polished rubies, that crowned his head, to proclaim him royal. Heavy gold bracelets glittered on his sinewy arms, and his blue eyes were bright and keen as he welcomed his guests—all of them familiar from past encounters—to his well-laden table. Rhys and I meanwhile found seats lower in the hall and prepared to enjoy the feasting, for the savory scent of roast meat hung heavy in the air, and my belly, at least, was growling with hunger. Servants brought us cups and bowls, and pretty young girls—Neirin's golden-haired fancy among them—poured out clear mead and foaming ale from red-glazed pitchers. Near the top of the hall Rhun's harper was playing, but he had hard work to make himself heard over the clamor of the feasters. Then the door to the hall crashed open, and with a gust of wind that shook the torches, a body of armed men tramped in.

In the sudden silence every man's hand felt for his weapon. But it was not the custom to come armed into the King's hall, and these men carried swords, bright blades blue-bare and shining. Of Rhun's men there, only the *penteulu*—the captain of his war-band—and a few of his men were armed. These came now hurriedly to their feet and moved to put themselves between the armed intruders and their Lord, but Rhun stayed them with a word. Still seated at his ease, he ran his eyes over the leader of the in-comers, now close before him, and said coolly, "Greetings, Brother-in-Law of Aeron! I heard your sails were sighted off the northern headland this morning. You come somewhat tardily to our feast—will you stack your arms and join us now, or have you some message which first demands our attention?"

Elidyr Mwynfawr, King of Aeron—for such he was—paused at this, and his men behind him stopped. "You know my errand, son of Maelgwn," he said loudly, his broad brown face flushing darker with anger. "I have come this time to take what is my due."

"Why, I think you have it, and have held it now for long," said Rhun, smiling like a wolf. "As for your visit, you are welcome, but there is no need for this war-like mien—or do you feel threatened? I assure you, you are in no danger here."

Elidyr's dark eyes narrowed and he met Rhun's hard blue stare for a long moment. Then, abruptly, he sheathed his sword. "Na," he said deliberately, "I know that I am not." His tone was menacing, but at his gesture his men sheathed their weapons as well, and the rest of us in the hall began to breathe again.

"Join me, then, Brother, at my table," said Rhun, and at his gesture a space was cleared beside him. After a moment Elidyr took the offered seat, while his men found places among Rhun's *teulu*. The harper began to play again, and the hall-folk slowly returned to their interrupted meal.

Rhun had seated Elidyr at his right hand, between himself and Taliesin, and as the King of Aeron settled himself in his place, I saw the bard speak to him and receive some answer. After a moment he introduced Neirin as well, and the conversation became more general among the three of them, although I could see Elidyr occasionally stealing distracted looks over his left shoulder toward Rhun, who sat placidly eating his dinner, as if such incursions were an common matter. Maybe for him they were.

In looks the two Kings were not unalike, both being tall, strongly built men past their first youth, but Elidyr was the younger and darker of complexion, and his hair and beard were browner than Rhun's grizzled red curls. I remembered him well from the time Neirin and I had spent at his court the previous summer: a man of sudden tempers, quick to kindle and slow burning, sensitive to slights and prone to resentments. His wife, as I had heard, was Rhun's half-sister, a younger daughter of Maelgwn's by a different mother. Elidyr had maybe married her expecting more from the match than he got, for Rhun was as stark a man as his great father, and unlikely to diminish his inheritance for the sake of a distant brother-in-law. In the five years or so since Maelgwn died, hostilities had rumbled on between the two of them, flaring up from time to time with threats of violence. Now Elidyr, as it seemed, was minded to go beyond threats. If so, this show of force might be the first move in a new and more dangerous game.

When I had satisfied my first hunger, I got up, leaving Rhys still gorging himself on roast cow meat, and made my way toward the high table to see what commands Talhaearn might have for me.

I did not want to be guilty of neglecting my duties twice in one evening. As I passed the table where Elidyr's soldiers were seated, I overheard some of their conversation—overhead, but did not understand, for the language was strange to me. Frowning, I stopped to listen. Irish? It might well be—the Irishmen, perhaps, that Ugnach had mentioned hearing outside the guesthouse earlier that evening. But why was Elidyr, British King of Aeron, traveling with an Irish escort?

At the high table, Talhaearn had no orders for me, but bade me keep alert. "I do not know what plans Gwion has, but one of us should entertain: Neirin, perhaps. Or Rhun may summon one of his own bards first—I know he has several."

"Yes, lad," said Ugnach beside him, overhearing us, "keep your eyes and ears open—and help me keep a watch on my young cub. There is no telling what he may be up to here, no telling at all."

Before I could answer, one of Rhun's court officials began to call for silence. As the crowd quieted, Taliesin stood up with Neirin beside him and made a half-bow toward the King. "My Lord King, and all lords here assembled," he began, and quietly though he spoke, his voice carried to the very back of the hall, and even the Irishmen fell silent to listen. "I bring to you now Neirin mab Dwywei ferch Lleenawg Elmet, youngest son of Cynfelyn Eidyn, who was King of Gododdin in his day. For six years he has been my student, and learned all I could teach him. Last summer he won his Crown at the Contention of the Bards in Dun Eidyn, as Ugnach of Caer Sëon can testify. He has traveled his circuit, and carried the Green Branch into the land of the Picts at peril of his life; he has walked the Dark Path of the Druids, and won his ash spear in the land of Annwn. Now he is wholly *pencerdd*, and I set him free. Here he is: ask of him what you will." And with that Taliesin sat down, leaving Neirin standing alone. I could not see his expression, for he faced toward the King, but I knew he was smiling.

"Welcome to my court, Neirin mab Dwywei," said Rhun. "Glad am I to welcome the student of such a Master, though he be student no longer. What would you bring me this night? For on such an occasion, I ask only what you would give."

"Gladly would I give you whatever entertainment you desire, Lord King," said Neirin, and I heard the smile in his voice. "But if the choice is mine, I would offer you—a song."

"Gladly would I hear it," said Rhun. "Pray, when you are ready, begin."

"Then let me stand before you in the hall," said Neirin, and at Rhun's nod, he circled the high table to stand in the open space between it and the central hearth, that all might see him clearly. Just for a moment he paused to summon his *awen*, and then, in the half-singing, half-chanting measures of the bards, he began.

> "Long years ago, four men's full lifetimes,
> north-country cattle-lord, Cunedda came
> forth from fair Manau, riding to Menai,
> mighty men with him, the Irish to tame.
>
> Blue steel their blades, blood-bordered in battle;
> high-crested horses between their strong thighs;
> ready to redden the dark earth with corpses,
> down the long hills from their homeland they ride.
>
> First in green Gwynedd they settled their homesteads;
> stone-built their fortresses, faultless gainst foes;
> hill-top and river-mouth, held in their mastery–
> where once ruled Roman men, Cunedda rode.
>
> Sowed he his many sons wide through the wastelands,
> each in his country a king stark as stone;
> forced out the Irish wherever he found them,
> building his palaces on their white bones.
>
> Right line of Cunedda, long may they conquer:
> Cadwallon Lawhir, the Long-Armed High King,
> Maelgwn the Mighty, red War-Hound of Gwynedd,
> and Rhun the Great ruler whose praise all bards sing.
>
> Long years ago, four men's full lifetimes,
> north-country cattle-lord, Cunedda came
> forth from fair Manau, riding to Menai,
> mighty men with him to make him their king."

"Finely done," said Rhun when the applause had died down.

"Taliesin, I expected no less of your—former!—pupil: I make you my compliments. And as for you, my newest suppliant"—this to Neirin with a smile—"a small fraction of the worth of your praise." And he held out to Neirin a leather bag, small but heavy, which one of his officers had just placed on the table beside him. Neirin took it with a grin and a word of thanks, and returned to his earlier place. "Now," said Rhun, still smiling, "let us see what my bards can do in response. Cyan, what do you have for us tonight?"

The feast went on in its accustomed way, with one after another of the local bards rising in turn to praise their patron. I stood in the background and watched through the drifting wood-smoke, keeping my eyes and ears open as I had been told, but I saw and heard nothing worth noting: only that Elidyr Mwynfawr, seated beside his host but getting only crumbs of praise from his table, looked blacker and blacker as the evening wore on, and his eyes went now and again to the war-band which had followed him down the Irish wind from the North. I had the uneasy feeling that trouble might be coming sooner rather than later from that discontented man: and I was right.

But that, O my children, is a story for another day.

The Black Lake

We spent three more days at the court of Aberffraw, and except for the brooding presence of Elidyr Mwynfawr, they were good days. All of our party but Rhys took it in turns to perform, and even he earned his place at table more than once by accompanying his father on Ugnach's small harp. A clever lad, Rhys, so long as he kept his mouth shut—but of course that state of affairs could not last.

It was the second afternoon of our visit, and Talhaearn had been drilling me again on my poetic forms. The day being warm and pleasant, he had chosen a bench at the side of one of the main courtyards for this exercise—a more exposed spot than would have been my preference. None of the passers-by, however—and there were many—showed much interest in us, and after an hour or so I began to relax, insofar as that was possible while being the focus of Talhaearn's attention. His temper had not grown milder with the years, nor had his tongue lost its edge, and he had a quick way with what he considered foolish errors, so that I needed all my wit and memory to keep out of trouble. After a couple of hours, his throat being dry from correcting me, he sent me into the guesthouse to fetch him a cup of watered wine. I decided to take my time about this errand.

In the guesthouse I found Ugnach, engaged in composition. He waved away my apologies for intruding, and pointed out the cups and flagons I had come to seek. Sighing to myself—for I had meant to have my own drink before preparing Talhaearn's—I mixed wine and water in one cup, and went out again, carrying it carefully. Indeed, the cup was so full that I stopped to have a sip. That was when I heard giggles and low whispers from the adjacent room which I shared with Rhys and Neirin. Curious, I pushed aside the door-curtain and looked in, but there was no luck for me there either. Neirin had come to terms with his golden-haired lass, and was busy making the most of it. Neither of the two intertwined figures on the bed had heard me come, and neither saw me go.

As I stood irresolute outside, not eager to return to my lesson and yet with no excuse to prolong my absence, I saw Rhys approaching from the direction of the stables. From the looks of him he had been grooming the ponies, for there was dirt on much of his exposed skin, and wisps of hay on his tunic. In the last day or so he had recovered his self-confidence, and now came up to me, fearless-proud, with a sort of a smirk. "Do you not be going in," I said to halt him. "Your father is busy in one room, and Neirin in the other. Better you find a horse-trough and wash yourself before anyone else sees you, or they will take you for our groom—and they will be right."

"You are not my master," said Rhys, but paused none the less. "Should you not be at your lessons? I saw Talhaearn in the courtyard waiting for you. You had better run away before he comes seeking you."

"That is none of your business," I said, looking him over with disfavor. "Snotty little boys should mind their elders. Have you lost your comb again?"

"You may be older than I," said Rhys, flushing, "but you have learned less. Be careful I do not make a satire on you—you could never match it!"

"Well, go in," I said, grinning, "if you want the back of your father's hand, or Neirin's. I will stand and laugh, O great poet. Only do not bleed on my blankets when they are through with you."

"I would not waste my clean blood," said Rhys, "on your smelly blankets. I am *bonheddig*, a land-owner's son, and what are you? What peasant hovel did you escape from, *taeog*? I have not heard your lineage."

"I need not recite it for you, bearer of burdens," I said disdainfully. "But I am as well born as you are, bed-wetter, and very much cleaner. How does your father, a man of renown, endure being served by a little mouse's-turd like you? Be careful, or Taliesin will catch up with you again, and ask you questions." For looking beyond him, I had seen a familiar figure crossing the courtyard toward us.

"Do not tempt me, storyteller," said Rhys, now red in the face and almost dancing with fury, "or I will make good my threat! I can curse the beard from your chin—what little there is of it!—and the sight from your eyes, the harp-strings from your fingers and the words from your lips, the tongue from your mouth and the breath from your body, the iron from your tool and the stones from your bag! I can call the wind to flog you naked, the seas to rise and drown you, the earth to gape and swallow you! I have learned the four-and-twenty measures, and the twelve variations; I have forgotten more lore than you have yet learned; I have—"

"—not learned to keep your temper, or lower your voice in public," said Taliesin, coming quietly behind Rhys and seizing him by the neck-band of his dirty tunic, half-choking him. "Gwernin, you may go on your way; Rhys and I are going to have a talk with his father." And pushing the now white-faced Rhys ahead of him, he closed the door behind them. I went back to Talhaearn, carrying his wine-and-water carefully; and if I was smiling like a cream-fed cat, he did not see it to question me.

Rhys did not come to the hall that night at all, and when I went to bed, he and his blankets were missing from the room he had shared with us. I cannot say I thought much of it; my mind was running too much on the performances I had just heard, and the poem I was trying to compose at Talhaearn's direction. If it was good enough, he might even let me sing it in the feast-hall before we left, instead of my usual storytelling. But when Rhys did not reappear the next morning, I was surprised, and commented on it to Neirin upon our return to the guesthouse.

"Na, na," Neirin said grinning, "no cause for worry, brother. He is confined to the stables until we leave, at his father's orders—and lucky if he gets off with that, I am thinking." He was polishing his belt and boots and whistling as he worked. I had seen him exchange glances with his golden-haired lass at breakfast, and deduced that another meeting was planned for later in the day. So I thought no more of Rhys, being preoccupied with the song I was still shaping.

I was busy with Talhaearn in the courtyard when the next thing happened. It started with a trampling of men and a neighing of horses somewhere nearby. Next we heard shouts, but of two voices only: and one I recognized as King Rhun's. "Go and see what is passing, Gwernin," said Talhaearn, and I needed no urging.

The main courtyard of the *llys* was swarming with men, some mounted and some not. In the midst of the crowd was a clear space, and in it stood the two Kings, garbed as if for riding in green and red woolens, and in much the position of two big dogs about to fight. As I came closer I heard Elidyr say loudly, "Is that your final word?"

"It is," said Rhun, in a voice of hard-held patience. "Not one more foot of land, not one piece of silver, will you get from me above what you have already, though you stay here until Doomsday. Is that clear enough for you?"

"By God, it is!" said Elidyr, his russet beard quivering with affront. "But long may you rue this day's work, Gwynedd!"

"Do you threaten me here in my own *llys*, Aeron?" asked Rhun, his right hand going as if unconsciously to his sword hilt. "Take care!"

"It is not I who need take care," said Elidyr, and to his men, "Pack my gear and bring it to the ship. I am leaving now!"

"Go with a following wind!" said Rhun, and turning abruptly on his heel, mounted the steps to his hall. Elidyr stood for a moment as if he would say more, then swung himself back up onto the sweating bay horse from which he had just dismounted, and rode clattering out of the gateway with some of his Irishmen following him, their red and saffron cloaks streaming behind them in the afternoon sunlight. The remaining men sorted themselves out, Rhun's to lead their horses to the stables, and the visitors to collect their gear from the hall and depart. With nothing more to see, I went back to Talhaearn.

"Hmm," he said, when he had heard my account. "Not a good ending, but inevitable. With luck he will go back north and stay there—but when were the Cymry lucky?" He sighed. "Now let me hear the verse you have prepared."

I did my best, but the interlude had shaken my concentration, and I stumbled on more than one line. "No," said Talhaearn simply when I was done. "Work on it more, and I will hear it again tomorrow or the next day. You can tell a tale tonight—and I may tell one myself as well. Now take me back to the guesthouse; I need to speak with Gwion."

With Elidyr's departure, the hall seemed a happier place. If Rhun had concerns about his brother-in-law's future plans, he did not show them that evening. He received my tale well—it was the story of how Gwydion the Magician stole Pryderi's pigs by magic, and brought them home to Gwynedd with Pryderi's army hot-foot in pursuit—and he rewarded me with silver, which I was glad of. Neirin gave him another praise song, Taliesin one of Arthur, and Ugnach an amusing tale of five and a half men riding a sea-going horse (the half was the man who swam along behind, holding the horse's tail). Rhun's local bards did their best to match us, but were a little over-stretched. Then, when the hour was growing late, and all were thinking of their beds, Talhaearn stood up. "Lord King," he said, "I would tell you a tale before we end this feast."

"Gladly would I hear it," said Rhun, his blue eyes bright with interest. "Let you begin."

"Not all of this tale is good hearing," said Talhaearn. "Yet it should be heard and remembered. I learned it from Emrys, my own great master, who dwelt once upon this island."

"Indeed, I remember him well," said Rhun, smiling. "I saw him once, when he was as old as you, and I a young lad still at my foster-father's table. I treasure that memory. Speak on."

"This is the tale of the Black Lake," said Talhaearn, and he directed his voice now to the hall, where all who heard him grew quiet to listen. "Many men's lifetimes ago it happened, not long after the men of Rome first came to Britain. The Romans were greedy for tribute, and their armies were mighty. They conquered first the rich farmlands of the southeast, the lands which the Saxons hold today in their turn, and there they built their towns—the towns which now lie in ruins. They conquered the hills and plains of middle Britain, as far north as her narrow waist where their Wall still runs; the Brigantes fell under their sway, and the southern lands of the Votadini, those people whom we now call Gododdin. Their armies marched into the south and west, into Dumnonia and the isles beyond; and they crossed the Severn and subdued the Silures, the forefathers of the men of Deheubarth, and set them in chains to dig for gold at Dolaucothi. And at last they came to Gwynedd.

"The tribes of the Venedoti fought them fiercely, and retired at need into the mountains, into the great fortress of Eryri which had always been their refuge when they were hard-pressed. But the people who lived here on Môn had no such retreat: they had never needed one. They were the Druids, and in their power they had always been secure—until the Romans came.

"The Romans crossed the Menai strait, and wrought here much destruction, burning and slaying until the streams ran red, and corpses covered the fields. Many a good man and woman they slew—yes, and children too—from end to end of this island, and where there had been songs, they left silence. But they did not come everywhere. Some of the Druids had withdrawn to Môn's Colt— the little island at the big one's flank—and raised there a magic mist to hide them from their enemies. And before their power could weaken, and the mist blow away, the Romans received a message of recall which took them from these shores in haste. For in the Iceni lands of the east, which the Saxons hold now, Boudicca had raised her revolt, and fallen on Roman London with fire and sword, even as the Romans fell on Môn. So the legions marched away to fight her, and made there a great slaughter, and afterwards they sowed fire and death throughout the land in revenge. But for a brief time Môn was safe—what remained of it.

"Among those who had taken refuge on the little island, some were Druids, and some were Seers, and some were Bards, while others were young men still studying these disciplines, as well as their women and children. Not knowing when the Romans would return, but only that they *would* return—for long ago they had driven out the Druids from Gaul—the chief men of the Orders made provision for the future. The women and children and the younger men they sent away into Ireland for safety, to one of the Druidic sanctuaries there, and these carried with them some of the island's treasures—such of them as had escaped the Roman pillagers. The rest of the treasure, and all goodly things which could be salvaged from the ruins, was offered to the Gods at a reed-bordered lake which had long received such sacrifices, and there it rests to this day. There was no need of victims to accompany it, for by then all the island was one huge reeking pyre, and all its earth drunk with blood. Then the men who remained turned their backs on Môn, and went to join their cousins in Eryri, to take up the tasks which lay before them; and the chiefest of these would fall upon the bards.

"Among the Druids was one who would have been a prince to his people, had the Gods not summoned him to a greater calling. Not a young man, he was then, and yet not old: for his beard was still dark, and his back was still straight, and his eyes saw clearly. His birth-name he had given up when he become a priest, and took instead the name Lovernos, which in today's common tongue means Fox. Like his namesake he was clever, and more than clever, for he had the gifts of prophecy and of *awen*, and beyond his years he was wise. And it was he who took command of the survivors of Môn, and set them about their tasks.

"The Druids and Seers put aside their white robes, and dispersed into all the corners of Britain, wherever the Romans were not, that their wisdom and learning should not be wholly lost to their people: for they were become the Knowledge of the Land. The Bards set out on their travels as well, but more openly, wherever they went learning and preserving all the songs and tales of the tribes, and teaching them in turn to all who would learn: for they were become the Memory of the Land. And Lovernos the Fox looked into the smoke, and into the fire, and he watched the flight of birds, and the turning of the stars in the night sky, and listened to the silence of the mountains. And in time he knew what his role was to be, and his alone. And his eyes wept, but his spirit rejoiced.

"The Druid priests were not celibate like the Christians; they did not preach distain for the good things of this world. There was in the place where Lovernos was then staying a most beautiful maiden, young but not yet wed, the daughter of a Chieftain, and he of a line which had produced many bards. When Lovernos knew his fate, he went to her, and asked her to lie with him until she be with child. And she looked at him, and saw that he was comely, and of great renown; and also she knew that he was kind. So she agreed, and her father gave his consent as well. For a moon, and another moon, they lay together; and before the third moon was full she knew that she had conceived. Then Lovernos kissed her, and told her she must go again to her father's house, and told her why; and he held her while she wept. And the next day he went away with his last few companions, and she never saw him again; but in nine months she bore him a son.

"Lovernos came down out of the mountains and traveled east, to a place of ancient magic. Often he and his friends moved by night to avoid the Romans, who were everywhere in the land. The marks of their burning and oppression were plain to see, and the earth groaned beneath them. And when Lovernos saw this he wept afresh, for he knew there would be worse to come, and all that he could do would not prevent it. But something, at least, he could save.

"They came to the place they sought, and lay up there in secret, waiting until the season was right. They talked by day and by night, and made sacrifice in the sacred grove, and bathed in the holy springs. And at last, they went back down the long hills to the Black Lake which lies hidden at their feet, cupped in the hand of the Goddess. And there Lovernos gave away his second name, and submitted himself to the Triple Death, to become the spirit of the land, the King in the Ground: for always," said Talhaearn, turning his pale eyes upon Rhun, "kingship requires sacrifice. Whether he be Druid or Christian, the wise king knows that he who would lead must be a bridge: a bridge between his people and their Gods, and a bridge between his people and their land; and always he must be willing to lay down his life for them at need. When we forget this, the seas will truly rush in and drown us, the earth gape and swallow us, and the sky of stars fall upon us and crush us out of life forever."

There was a long silence. Then Rhun smiled, and raised his cup to toast Talhaearn. "I thank you for you wisdom, Father of Awen," he said. "Not many would offer that story before a king. Twice today I have been—let us say advised, for threatened is too strong a word for your warning!—here in my own court. He who warned me first I sent empty away, but for your words I will pay their worth in gold." And standing, he went to the old bard, and pulled off one of his own gold bracelets, and put it on Talhaearn's arm; then he embraced and kissed him. And the silence of the hall broke up in applause.

"Master," I said later as we were making our way back to the guesthouse, "I have a question for you."

"Only the one?" said Talhaearn dryly. "That is not usual. Well, ask it then, boy."

"In the story you told," I said, "what became of the child—the son of the Druid? Did he become a Druid in his turn?"

"I have wondered about that myself," said Talhaearn, "but the tale does not say. Maybe, Gwernin, you will have to look for your own answer someday." And in this he spoke truer than he knew.

But that, O my children, is a story for another day.

The News-Bringer

Just as one pebble falling on a mountain slope can start a landslide which wipes out a entire village, so can one man's anger lead to war. In both cases it needs the right circumstances, the right weight and placement of pebble or man, but once the thing has begun, it acquires an unstoppable momentum of its own. Then may the Gods take pity on anyone who stands in its way, for he will need it.

I was in the courtyard outside the guesthouse the next morning, loading gear on our pack-ponies, when the sound of hoof-beats made me look up. Into the courtyard on a sleek brown mare rode my old friend Ieuan. "Gwernin!" he said as soon as he saw me. "Is Taliesin still here? I have a message for him from my Lord."

"He is here somewhere," I said. "I saw him last in the feast-hall, talking with the King. Is it urgent?" For I saw that he had a bruised face and a fresh gash on his forehead, as if he had been fighting.

"Urgent enough," said Ieuan, dismounting and giving his mare to a stable-boy who came forward to take her. "Can you bring me to them?"

"Surely," I said, and leaving the ponies standing I led him though the maze of the *llys*. The feast-hall was empty of King and bard, but a little enquiry brought us to the door of Rhun's private quarters. The young soldier who stood there leaning on his spear was happy to carry news of a messenger within, and returned in a moment to hold the door wide for us. Inside we found the two we sought, seated by an open casement and nursing morning cups of ale. Strong spring sunshine streamed through the window, bringing to brilliant life the colors of an embroidered hanging on the wall behind the King and shining on the thick furs which covered his bed. Taliesin was dressed today for travel in serviceable dark wool and leather, but Rhun's loose woolen gown was blue as the bright morning sky, and trimmed at throat and cuffs with strips of red brocaded silk. Both men looked up inquiringly at our entrance.

"Good day to you, Lord King," said Ieuan, making a half-reverence to the King. "I bring news to you from my master, the Lord Cadwaladr. I was sent to Taliesin, but the news is for both of you."

"Speak, then," said Rhun, looking shrewdly from one of us to the other. "Or is your message secret?"

"No, Lord," said Ieuan. "Indeed, it may soon be known to all too many; I am only the news-bringer. My master sends to tell you that King Elidyr of Aeron is seeking support for his cause among your *uchelwyr*. He came to us last night at Caer Lêb for this purpose, and has now gone on to Arfon. He has Irish soldiers with him, thirty at least. My master thought it better to let him think we might aid him, for we were outnumbered, and feared lest he fire the thatch above our heads if he was displeased."

"Were any of your people harmed?" asked Rhun, frowning.

"No, Lord—or at least, none seriously," said Ieuan. "There were one or two scuffles, when the Irishmen presumed too much on our hospitality to make free with our women, but Elidyr still has them in hand—for now."

"Then the sooner he is dealt with, the better," said Rhun, and raising his voice, he summoned the guard from outside his door and gave rapid orders. "We will go by sea to Caer Seint," he said then, when the young man had left at a run. "Taliesin, you and your party are welcome to join me, but I cannot take your horses."

"My thanks, Lord, but we will follow by the ferry," said Taliesin, standing up. "I want to speak with the Lord Cadwaladr on my way. Ieuan, Gwernin, come with me now." And we followed him out of the King's room, leaving Rhun calling loudly behind us for his personal attendants and his armor.

As we crossed the courtyard toward the guesthouse, Taliesin said to Ieuan, "Tell me now what else you did not tell the King."

"There is little more to tell, Lord," said Ieuan. "Only that King Elidyr was like a barely-banked fire, cool enough on the surface, but burning with anger within. It came out once or twice, when something vexed him, and then he fell to cursing like a hag-wife. I was serving him and my Lord at table and heard more than most, maybe. That is a bitter man!"

"Yes, we saw that clearly enough while he was here," said Taliesin. "What else? Did you hear what aid he wanted of your Lord?"

"Men and horses, chiefly," said Ieuan, "to join him on the mainland in pillaging. My Lord put him off, but pledged to see him at Caer Seint in three days. And what he has pledged, he will perform—but I swear he means nothing against the King! He would not else have sent me here to warn him!"

"I believe you," said Taliesin. "Gwernin, are we nearly packed?"

"Nearly so, Master," I said, and it was true. All the pack-ponies but mine and Talhaearn's were ready-laden, and boys came leading our mounts from the stables as I spoke. "I have only a few things more to bring out."

"Good," said Taliesin. "Bring them out now. We should be away as soon as we well may be. Ieuan, sit and rest yourself while we finish our preparations. I think we still have wine in our rooms, if you would like some."

"That would be welcome, Master," said Ieuan, smiling for the first time that morning. "Riding in the sun is thirsty work. I had to skirt well upstream of the ford, for the tide was full in. Will you cross to the mainland today, or spend the night with us first? You would be welcome."

"I think," said Taliesin, frowning, "we may accept that offer. But it will depend on what your lord has to tell me, and on the tide. For now, come in and have that cup. Then we will see."

In our room I found Neirin digging through the contents of his saddlebags like a dog in search of a bone. "What are you about?" I asked him. "Taliesin is eager to be gone."

"*Sa, sa*, I will be ready soon enough," said Neirin, upending the saddlebag on his bed so vigorously that rings, bracelets, and other small objects bounced off onto the floor. "*Hai mai!* Let him be patient only a little while longer!" And dropping to his knees, he began to gather up the escapees.

"You are kneeling on your comb," I said helpfully. "Take care or you will break it, and then you will be no better than Rhys."

"Na, that is not likely," said Neirin, grinning and retrieving the object in question from under his right leg. "Never in my life was I that untidy! I think that is all." And rising, he plucked a string of river pearls out of the middle of his belongings and put it in his belt-pouch, then began to cram the rest rapidly back into the saddlebag. Before I had finished collecting my remaining gear, he was done and going out the door whistling with the saddlebags over one shoulder. I cast a hasty glance around the room for any forgotten items, and finding none, followed him out into the sunshine.

In the few minutes I had been indoors, the scene had changed again. All of our party were gathered around their ponies, even Rhys—though he was also trying to keep as far from Taliesin as possible. Not only our group, however, was on the point of departure; the *llys* echoed with the sounds of men and horses in orderly movement. Neirin put his saddlebags on his grey pony, and with a word to Taliesin, set off purposefully across the courtyard to where a couple of giggling girls stood watching us. A flash of yellow-gold hair told me all I needed to know about his destination, and grinning, I turned my attention to my own packing. By the time I had finished and was in the saddle, Neirin was back. "Are we ready?" asked Taliesin, looking around at us. "Then let us be off, before the King's party clogs the road."

In the main courtyard soldiers were mustering, but we wound our way through them without much trouble. The ship which had been moored in the harbor when we arrived was now tied up at the dock, and men were going aboard carrying gear and weapons. "They will have a fair wind for Caer Seint," I said to Neirin, who was riding beside me.

"Is that where we are going in such haste?" he asked, grinning.

"Yes," I said. "It seems King Elidyr has gone to Arfon to cause trouble."

Neirin laughed. "They will have the Irish wind," he said. "And that is only right—it brought them down upon us, and now it brings us down on their backs. Tell me the rest of what your friend Ieuan had to say." And when I had done so, "*Hai mai!* I do not like the sound of that. I am thinking there will be bloodshed before Beltane this year."

"I think you may be right," I said soberly. "But what do you suppose Elidyr hopes to win by this? He cannot believe Rhun will give him a free hand to raid and spoil for long."

"Na, I am not sure even he knows," said Neirin. "A balm for his wounded self-esteem, maybe—and enough gold to pay off his Irishmen! They cannot have come here only for the sport of it."

"Hard luck for the people of the country," I said, "who get their roofs burned over their heads through no fault of their own."

"That is always the way with war," said Neirin. Then he grinned. "But it will give us bards much to sing of afterwards."

"If we survive it," I said, but I was grinning back at him. If I had known what lay ahead I might not have been so confident.

Caer Lêb, when we came to it, showed the effects of its unwelcome guests. The green paddock outside the walls where our ponies had grazed was trampled into mud by the feet of many men, and now held only the black burn marks of several fires, and the bloody bones of a butchered cow. The friendly watchdog who had lain in the gateway now cowered back in his kennel, growling and barking savagely, and those who came to his summons were armed men, not women and children. Some of these, like Ieuan, showed fresh cuts and bruises. Their strained expressions vanished, however, when they saw who came, and almost before we had dismounted the tall Lady of the house was waiting beside her red-bearded Lord at the entrance to the hall with the mead-filled guest-cup in her hands. "May you be welcome, Taliesin, and all who come with you," she said, offering him the dark wooden cup bound with silver. "You will have heard from Ieuan what befell us."

"A blessing on the house, and on all who dwell within it," said Taliesin, drinking and looking around the courtyard. "Yes, I heard, and am relieved to see things no worse than they are."

"Yes, I have had Irishmen here before who did me more damage," said Cadwaladr dryly. "But I offered them a hotter welcome, and they went away empty-handed, as these, alas, did not. Do you come within now, all of you, and take food and drink. Will you stay the night with us? You come late for the ferry over Menai."

"The one night, we will, if it is no hardship to you," said Taliesin smiling.

"I am not yet so poor that I cannot feed and house my friends," said Cadwaladr. "Be at home, then, all of you: you know the ways of the place. We will talk more presently—your advice would be welcome to me, Masters."

"Of that," said Talhaearn, taking the cup from Taliesin, "we have a good store. Sometimes some of us may even agree with each other."

When our gear was in the guesthouse and our ponies let into the paddock for what grazing remained, I found myself at unexpected liberty. The older bards were in the hall, conferring with the Lord Cadwaladr; Neirin was amusing himself by flirting with the red-haired girl he had noticed on our previous visit; and Rhys had taken himself off somewhere out of sight. I decided to make myself scarce as well. I had the song I had been composing at Aberffraw to polish, and some ideas for another one. I got bread and cheese from one of the women in the kitchen and headed out the gate. The day was fine and fair, and it seemed a long time since I had wandered on my own. The world beckoned me, and I was ready to go. For no good reason I turned south, toward the path which had brought me to Caer Lêb two summers ago.

That had been a summer of marvels for me, the summer when I first left my home and my foster parents and set off around Wales to earn my living as a storyteller. I had traveled first with Ieuan, then an itinerant peddler who wintered always in my home town of Pengwern, helping to carry a part of his stock-in-trade—small lightweight goods, things that he had carved himself or traded for—until he lost it all to his unfortunate passion for gambling. Long before summer's end it was I and my tales which had mostly earned us food and lodging at the poor homes where we usually stopped. I it was also, though my strange encounters with Gwydion mab Dôn, the supernatural magician and half-god of North Wales, who had brought us indirectly to Ynys Môn. Since then I had only met Gwydion once, though I had often felt his presence, and that last meeting had been a frightening one, beset with ghosts and magic. Now, walking in bright sunlight on the green fields of Môn, I found myself thinking of him again. So when the next thing happened, I was not as surprised as I might have been.

About a mile south of Caer Lêb, on the low ridge which lies between the Afon Braint and Menai, there is a cluster of oak trees. It had caught my eye as I walked, and spoke to me of peace and solitude, both of which I wanted, so I turned my steps toward it. As at Bryn Celli Du, the trees here were mostly young and wind-stunted, with one or two older ones which might have been saplings when the Romans came to Môn. Even in the handful of days since Neirin's walking of the Dark Path, spring had progressed visibly, and the swollen bronze-green buds on the oak branches had opened into tiny bronze-green leaves which glowed in the afternoon sunlight like jewels. There was nothing so substantial as a burial mound here, or even a standing stone; nothing but the hard grey bones of the island, thrusting themselves here and there from the soil around the roots of the trees. Finding a softer spot padded with last summer's dried grass and bracken, I sat down with my back against a tree trunk and gave myself over to poetic composition.

I am not sure how long I sat there, chasing an elusive word or rhyme for the pattern which was growing in my mind, before I noticed that the light around me was changing. Fog is not rare on Môn, though it is not usual on a bright afternoon. But sometime during the day the Irish wind must have dropped, for here the fog came, drifting in from the coast. Already the landscape around me was disappearing in a gray haze.

It is no use at such times to curse or complain, still less to blunder about in haste. The weather was mild; even if I found myself lying out overnight, I would hardly take my death of it. And

I had just come across a very satisfying sequence of rhymes, which showed great promise. So I went on sitting where I was and thinking—until I heard the sound of wings. Then I looked up and saw it.

Not a hawk, not an owl, but an eagle—the great sea eagle whose wings span more than the reach of a tall man's arms. He was coming straight toward me, as if I were a salmon, or a hare, or some other hapless creature destined to be dinner. His wings went up in the braking movement that comes at the end of the dive, dark feathers splayed by the wind of his passage; the fierce talons stretched forward to seize and rend; and the sharp yellow beak parted a little in anticipation. Then, as I scrambled to my feet in sudden panic fear, my back still braced against the oak tree, the whole shape of the bird wavered and changed, and became a man standing in front of me, arms outstretched in a dark cloak, knees a little flexed as if he had just dropped from the heavens. His hair was as black as the raven's wing, his eyes as green as springtime, and his smile was the eagle's smile on a human face, cruel and pitiless and full of hunger. "Good evening to you, Lord," I said, trying to keep my voice steady and almost succeeding. "It is a while and a while since I saw you last, Gwydion mab Dôn."

"Well met, Gwernin," said Gwydion, dropping his arms to his sides and standing erect, the heavy folds of his cloak swinging closed around him. "It is good to see you back in my country again. You have been a long time away."

"True enough," I said. "It is a long way to the land of the Picts, and a longer one around the wheel of the year. But as you say, I am back. Where have you been wandering?"

"Ah," said Gwydion, his eyes narrowing in amusement. "A question, is it? There are those who would charge you dearly for an answer. But because it is springtime, and I am feeling generous, I will give it to you for free—almost for free." He came a step closer, and I would have liked to back away, but there was oak bark behind my shoulder blades, and nowhere to run. Besides, I felt instinctively then what I later proved with experience: never run from the Gods. Like the flight of a mouse from a cat, it only attracts their attention, and their reflexes are much faster than yours.

"What—what price would that be, Lord?" I asked. Gwydion's smile was wide and white as a wolf's.

"That," he said softly, "would be a second answer." Then he laughed. "Na, do not look so frightened, Gwernin *bach*. By my own name, I mean you no harm. You did me a good turn once, and though I paid you back, I have not forgotten it. Will you have your first answer, then, free and for nothing?"

"If it please you, Lord," I said, a little reassured, for his wolf-look had faded with the laughter. "I have not forgotten the help you gave me, either, which brought me to these very shores."

"I was a good boatman, was I not?" said Gwydion, grinning. "Almost as good as my sister's-son... Sit down, then—you know you are not going to run away." And he sank down himself, cross-legged in the young green grass and bracken, and I joined him. "That is better," he said approvingly, pushing back the dark hair from his lean brown face with sinewy, long-fingered hands. "I have been going about the world a bit since you met me last, and I do not like what I see. There have been too many changes in the Island of the Mighty, while I kept my pigs in Meirionydd. And not even I can turn back the years!" And for a moment there was a sadness on him such as I saw there the day we first met. Then it passed. "And you, Gwernin?" he asked, grinning. "Where are you bound? Away north again this summer?"

"I do not know, Lord," I said, and sighed. "Like enough, back to Llys-tyn-wynnan with my master, and no farther. But there is trouble in this land, and maybe bloodshed before Beltane. Elidyr King of Aeron has come down from the North to threaten Gwynedd, and brought the Irish with him."

"As to that, he will get what he came for: the land-hold due to him here," said Gwydion, and the wolf-smile was back. "Whether it will content him is another matter. But you, Gwernin..." He paused, looking at me intently, with his head a little tilted to one side like a curious raven.

"What about me, Lord?" I asked, smiling back at him. "Not

that I am asking," I added hastily. Gwydion gave a low chuckle and stood up suddenly.

"Do not lose hope," he said. "You will find yourself where you should be, when the time is right. That is all that I can tell you now—do not forget it!" And turning, he spread his cloak, and was an eagle again, leaping with powerful wing-beats into the foggy air, and then gone.

I stood up more slowly, and taking my direction from the faint glow of the westering sun, started back down the hill toward Caer Lêb. I had forgotten the new song I had been making: Gwydion had taken it with him in payment for his second answer. But as I was to find in time, it would prove more than a fair exchange.

But that, O my children, is a story for another day.

First Blood

The old fortress of Caer Seint which was built by the Romans—Segontium, they called it—stands on a low hill above its harbor. The last time I saw it, not so many years ago, it lay in smoking ruins, but on the day when I first followed Taliesin there, it seemed a fine strong place, with its corn-lands and lush pastures spread like a green mantle around it, and a straggle of prosperous fisher-huts stretching along the shore at its feet. In the clear waters of the Afon Seint, King Rhun's ship rode at anchor, and at his castle gates his soldiers stood guard with braced spears. Behind the fortress hill Arfon heaved herself up, higher and higher, mass upon mass, to the heights of Eryri and Yr Wyddfa, the great snow-hill which stands at the heart of Gwynedd. The day was warm and bright, the blue depths of the sky flecked with lambs-wool clouds, and the Irish wind was blowing—but gently—from off-shore. All the land seemed wrapped in a dream of peace.

Dreams were not on display in Rhun's court, however. Within the stone-built walls of the old fortress a small army was gathered, quartering its men in the patched-up barracks blocks near the gate and grazing its horses on the parade ground nearby. The smoke of their cooking fires hung over the place, and the air was thick with the smells of horse-dung and roasting meat and latrines, all of it mingling with the sea-smells from the shore below. Men came and went on brisk business, or sat around the fires talking and polishing their gear, and the sound of a smith's hammer somewhere nearby hinted at repairs in progress. It seemed that Rhun was taking Elidyr's threats seriously, and gathering his forces for war.

We made our way through the orderly confusion of the camp toward the inner *llys* where the King and his nobles were housed. Here the Roman commander's headquarters had been reinforced with new walls of stone and timber, a defensible strong place within the great tumble-down sprawl of the fortress itself, meant as it had been to house many hundreds or thousands of men. Within this inner compound lay mead-hall and cookhouse, stables and stores, courtyards and dwelling-places, all in good repair. Here we were welcomed as at any of the King's courts, our gear safely bestowed in a guesthouse and our ponies led away for tending, and we ourselves brought respectfully to the King's presence.

Rhun was in his torch-lit mead-hall, lounging in his high seat with three great rough-coated hounds a-sprawl at his feet. Some sort of conference seemed to be taking place; men sat around him on benches or stools, well-dressed and well-armed men, the *uchel-wyr*—the high men—of this land. Headmen of fishing villages with a few sons or cousins, one-valley chieftains with their small proud war-bands, under-kings of a *cantref* leading their hundred spears: a score and more of these lords of Arfon had come together at their King's call. Gray-beards wise in war and hot-blooded youngsters sat together and argued, or listened to the reports coming in from Rhun's scouts. Elidyr, it seemed, was also gathering supporters, but not so many as yet, for such of Rhun's subjects as did not love him still respected his prowess at war, and knew the formidable weight of his anger when aroused.

Taliesin made his way forward to the King's side, leaving the rest of us to sit in the back of the hall and listen. Talhaearn found himself a comfortable seat with his back against the wall and dozed, and I was tempted to do likewise; Rhys had disappeared yet again; but Neirin and Ugnach were following the discussions with interest. At last the conference broke up with a string of orders from Rhun to his chief war-leaders.

"I do not want him vanishing into the mountains," said the King, "nor yet taking ship only to land again somewhere else in my domains. I will have this settled now, once and for all. Those of you I have named, prepare your men and ride north with the twilight. You know your ground—get behind him and block his bolt-holes; cut him off from the passes. The rest of us will follow in the morning, and close the trap. Then we will make an end to this Northern fox. Go you all now, and prepare!" There were shouts of agreement, and most of the men left the hall. But I saw that Taliesin, still seated beside the King, was frowning; and Rhun, turning toward him with some remark, saw this too. "You look concerned, my friend," he said more quietly. "Have you yet more advice for me?"

"My Lord, I do not know," said Taliesin, but the frown was heavy on his brow. "I only see..." He stopped and closed his eyes for a moment as if in pain.

"See what?" asked the King, frowning in his turn. "What do you foresee, Chief of Bards?"

Taliesin opened his eyes, and for a moment the torchlight shone red in them. "War," he said, and his voice was harsh—

> "Fire in the thatch, and the corn-fields burning.
> Wine-red the ford, as at Camlann field.
> Dark ruin and death, and the meat-crows gorging
> On torn man-flesh after morning fight.
> And many a woman wantonly weeping..."

"That," said Rhun dryly, "is the lot of all warriors in this world, and nothing new. But I hope this time to cut short the slaughter. Do you see a better way, Font of Poetry?"

"No," said Taliesin, and he sighed. "I am sorry, my Lord King: I have no better counsel for you now."

"Then perhaps," said Rhun, standing and including us all with his glance, "you will have a song—each of you—for me tonight. Now I have many things I must see to." And turning, he left the room, with his remaining officers following him.

In the feast-hall that night none of us drank deep, and the King did not sit late over his wine. All of the Masters offered some brief song, praise to the King and his valor, and to that of his soldiers, but none of it sticks in my memory. With all the visiting lords, the *llys* was very full, and we were lucky to be given even one room in the guesthouse. Taliesin and Ugnach drew straws for the second bed, Talhaearn of right having the first, and Ugnach lost, and joined the rest of us on the rush-strewn floor. "It could be worse," he said, yawning and rolling himself in his cloak beside his already-snoring son. "At least it is dry here, and warm enough...

Taliesin, what are your plans for tomorrow?"

"I ride with the King," said Taliesin, blowing out the candle, and I heard the ropes beneath his straw mattress creak a little as he settled himself more comfortably in his bed. "I must see...what is coming." He yawned in his turn. "The rest of you would be wiser to stay here."

"I think I will do so, then," said Ugnach, yawning again. "Talhaearn and I both have students to teach—have we not, my old friend?"

"True, true," said Talhaearn sleepily, and sighed.

"I will ride with you, I think," said Neirin, from where he lay close beside me, his shoulder warm against mine. "Gwernin? You would like to come with us, would you not?"

"Indeed and I would," I said wistfully. "But my master may require me."

"Na, he can surely spare you for the one day," said Neirin, and I heard the smile in his voice. "Talhaearn? May not Gwernin come, too?"

There was silence, and then a snore. I heard Taliesin chuckle. "I think," he said, "we will have to ask him in the morning. But yes, Gwernin, I think you may come with us as well."

The next morning the *llys* was astir long before dawn, for Rhun planned to set out early. Talhaearn having given grudging assent, I found myself on my black pony and riding beside Neirin and Taliesin in the wake of the King while the day star still shone bright in the eastern sky. I had brought my sword, and felt its unaccustomed weight slapping against my thigh, but I did not expect to use it. Neirin wore his as well, but Taliesin rode his red mare unarmed, his cloak floating loose about him in the wind of his going and his dark head uncovered in the dawn chill. For myself, I was shivering as much with excitement as with cold; there is nothing like riding into battle—or at least in the direction of one!—to make you feel the life strong within you, beating like wings with the beat of your blood.

We had not gone far when we saw a horseman breasting the

hill ahead of us and heading at a gallop for the King's banner. At the sight of him Rhun signaled his forces to halt, and drew rein, waiting. Even before he reached the King, the man was calling out his news. "They are not far ahead, Lord," I heard him shout. "Fifty of them at least, and riding at their ease, with no scouts that I could see."

"Good," said Rhun, and with a few commands he changed the disposition of his force, so that when we moved on it was in the shape of a bent bow, the riders on either wing moving ahead of the center. This was not an easy maneuver for scratch troops unused to working together, and the need for constant corrections slowed our advance, so that by the time we came over the hill ourselves and saw the enemy before us we were riding in full sunlight. Before the surprised Irishmen could react, Rhun drew his sword and charged, and with a shout his army followed him, pounding down the hill like a roaring wave that breaks upon the beach and sweeps all before it.

I was not in that charge. Even as I started to kick my black pony to a gallop, Neirin beside me, Taliesin's voice stopped us. "Na, na!" he said, holding up his hands. "Both of you, remember, we are here to watch! You cannot do that from the midst of the battle—it is not as warriors that we are here today!"

"*Sa, sa,* you are right as usual, best of bards," said Neirin, reining his gray pony to a halt and sheathing his sword, but I could see the disappointment on his face. "*Hai mai!*" and he laughed suddenly, throwing back his head, his dark red hair bright as flame in the early sunlight. "I must admit I was looking forward to the fight, though it was none of mine... Well, we will watch, then—and this is a fine place for watching."

Indeed it was. As I sat my fretting pony, I saw the whole of the battle spread out before me. The Irishmen fought fiercely, but they were outnumbered and taken by surprise. Soon there were dark bodies—theirs and ours—lying in the green spring grass, and riderless horses. The knot of the fighting drew tighter and tighter around the tall red-cloaked man at its center, whom I recognized even at that distance as Elidyr Mwynfawr. There were bright blades flashing in the sunlight and the clash of steel on steel, shouts and grunts and the screams of wounded men and horses. Shields were hacked to splinters, and blood was flowing freely. As the fight went against them, one or two of the Irishmen tried to turn and run, but they were cut down with sharp steel, or tumbled headlong with a spear between their shoulder-blades to bleed out their lives on the ground.

Then it was I saw Rhun charging the small clot of his remaining enemies. His big roan horse crashed through their feeble line, and his bloody sword shone red in the sunlight as he swung it. Elidyr saw him coming, and turned in the saddle to catch that first blow on his lime-washed shield. His own blade struck splinters from Rhun's war-board in return, and he shouted something which I could not understand. The Kings circled each other at a little distance then, their snorting, trampling horses throwing up clods of the good black earth and their bright cloaks swirling like banners about them, while all around them their men fell back to give them room.

Rhun shouted in his turn, a word which sounded to me on my hill-crest like "Surrender!" and on the instant Elidyr struck spurs to his mount and charged. Maybe he hoped to catch his opponent off-guard, but if so, he failed. Instead Rhun pulled his well-trained stallion up into a rearing, lashing turn, and as Elidyr's horse swerved aside from those deadly hooves, Rhun's sword flicked out like an adder's tongue and caught his rebellious brother-in-law from behind. It took Elidyr between neck and shoulder, almost beheading him, and bore him down to darkness. His blood-gushing body toppled from its saddle, the few surviving Irishmen threw down their weapons, and the fight was over. But the war, as we found later, had only begun.

As the clash of steel ended, Taliesin sighed. "We can go down now," he said to me. "But think first of what you just saw, Gwernin, and how you would sing it in hall tonight when Rhun feasts his war-band." And with those words he set his mare in motion, and started down the hill.

King Rhun was sitting his horse and listening to a report from his *penteulu* as we rode up. "Ah, there you are," he said to Taliesin when he saw us. "I have a problem, and could use your advice, and perhaps your aid. We will be putting this"—he flicked his fingers at Elidyr's body where it lay unmoving in the blood-soaked grass—"underground soon, with what honor is due him. But it seems to me that it might be politic, considering who he was, to send—let us say, an ambassador—to the North, to bear the news of his death to his widow, and to those of his kindred who are the most concerned. And who better to send on such a mission than a bard, and one who stood outside the fighting and can give a true report?" And here he glanced at Neirin, who smiled.

"I will gladly be your messenger in this, Lord King," he said, his amber eyes sparkling. "For as you well know, I am of the Line of the North myself, and kin within the fourth degree to this man you have just killed. And I say that his killing was lawful, for he attacked your domains, and was taken in arms against you, and neither *sarhaed* nor *galanas* is due to his kin. Yet to pay some reparation might be better, to sweeten his death."

"Na," said Rhun, "that I will not do: I will give for him, dead, no more than I gave to him alive. But his sword, and his armor, and such other things of value as he had with him, you may take to his widow."

"As you wish it, Lord King," said Neirin, but he was not smiling now. "How would you have me travel, and when?"

"My messengers have told me," said Rhun, "that his ship lies at anchor farther up the coast, near Aber of the White Shells. I will send one of the Irishmen, under guard, to take them the news of his death, and tell them that if they come to Caer Seint, I will pay your passage to Aeron. Thus they may get some profit out of their loss. Will it content you?"

"It will, Lord King," said Neirin. Then turning to Taliesin, he added, "I had meant to go north at some time this summer, though not so soon."

"It will be well for you," said Taliesin, nodding, and to the King, "It seems that your problem is solved."

"My thanks for it, then," said Rhun, and to Neirin, "We will speak more of this tonight, O my messenger, and you may set forth as soon as the ship comes and you are ready." And with that he turned back to his *penteulu*, and continued hearing his report. We sat our ponies for a few minutes in silence, surveying the battlefield, and then we rode back to Caer Seint. Already the black-winged ravens were circling in the sky behind us.

There was food and drink in plenty in the hall that night, and praise songs as well, both from our Masters and from some of Rhun's own bards; but I chose instead to tell a story. It was the tale of how Gwydion mab Dôn, pursued by Pryderi Prince of Dyfed for the theft of his magical pigs, chose to meet his opponent face to face on the Great Sands of Aber Dwyryd, and slew him there. Blow by blow I told it—the shouting of insults; the casting of spears and the splintering of shields; the hacking of sword against ringing sword, against shield boss, against war-cap and armor and naked flesh; the blood that trickled and dripped and gushed, making sword-hilts twist in the hand, blinding eyes, and reddening the sea-foam where waves washed around ankles with the rising tide…

There was magic, too, in that fight, magic that darkened the sunlight and brought the winds of death-cold winter howling around them both, so that sweat froze on brow and salt-spume in hair and beard, and eyes darkened and breath rasped in the throat, as if the very air they breathed was congealing with cold. Ghosts were in that wind, dead enemies and lost lovers, moaning, begging, and pleading, grasping at arms, licking the hot blood that flowed from wounds to give themselves voice, calling, shouting like the storm winds that roar around a house at midnight when the gales try to tear it from its foundations and fling it into the sea…

All these things I spoke of, and the hall quieted to hear me. Then I told of the final blow, of Gwydion's sword crashing down like a lightning-bolt through Pryderi's last defense, cutting through steel and leather, flesh and bone, to come to the heart; and how

Pryderi toppled down like a great tree when it feels the final blow of the axe-man, and makes all the earth around it shake when it falls; of the gush of bright blood bubbling out of the broken body; of the wallowing in the waves as they flung him higher and higher up the beach, to leave him there at last like a stranded whale, or a ship driven ashore by storm. And I told of Gwydion's shout of triumph, and of the exaltation in his heart which almost overcame the pain in his wounded body; of his utter weariness, so that every step he took through the surging water and up the sucking sands required the last desperate dregs of his strength; and of his sadness at striking down so brave a warrior, and his joy at being the one left still standing, still alive.

And that night, I said, there was feasting and music for Gwydion in the hall of his uncle in Caer Dathyl, which stood on this very hill before ever the Romans came to build their fort; but Pryderi lay cold and alone in his grave at Maen Twrog, and there he lies still, and shall until the end of the world. So should we all, I said, give thanks to our Gods that we live and feast and drink tonight, and enjoy our lives while we may; for to all men death will come, be it soon or late, and those who meet him bravely in fair fight, and win thereby a great name, may be the luckiest of us all.

The hall was rather silent when I was done, and some there gave me a thoughtful look, but when one calls the *awen*, one must take what comes—or who. So I thought then, and so I think still.

But that, O my children, is a story for another day.

Beltane Fires

Five led ponies are more than enough for one man to manage, up-slope and down through the mountains, even if four of them are pack-ponies well used to being in a string. Three of them I had expected: Taliesin's and Talhaearn's two, and my own shaggy little red mare. But the other two were Neirin's, and this is how it came about.

The Irish ship had come to Caer Seint in response to King Rhun's message on the day after Elidyr Mwynfawr got his well-deserved killing. The sailors had, after all, no particular loyalty to the dead man, beyond that which he had bought and paid for, and they had every reason to wring such profit as they could out of a bad bargain by taking Neirin back to the North with them as a passenger. Meanwhile, to provide a surety for their good faith in this undertaking—for ambassadors and news-bringers can be kidnapped and enslaved as easily as lesser men!—Rhun was keeping such of the Irish soldiers as had survived the battle in chains as his hostages until Neirin should return safely from his mission. How long this would take no one was very sure, least of all Neirin himself.

"Better it might be," he had said to King Rhun that morning in the hall, over a breakfast of cold meat and fresh barley bannock, "if I were to go on from Aeron to Alt Clut and Dun Eidyn, and spread the word firsthand amongst Elidyr's kindred, rather than let rumor run its course. This will take some time, and it is not likely that the Irish ship will be wishing to bide for me at Ayr-port or Clydemouth whilst I do my talking. Nor am I sure, Lord King, where I will find you when I do return. But if I do not come back before midsummer, I will find a way to send you word, so that you may honorably ransom your prisoners to their kinsmen, if they so choose."

"How shall I know that the message comes from you?" asked Rhun, smiling and brushing crumbs from his curly red-gray beard onto his embroidered purple tunic. "Parchment and ink may counterfeit as easily as words."

"Na, it is well thought of," agreed Neirin, reaching for another of the little honey-scented brown cakes which filled the wooden platter set between us. "But I can send instead to Taliesin: he will know if the message comes from me, or not." And he turned to Taliesin, who sat beside them at the table wearing a robe as deeply blue as his eyes. "Would you not know, my once-and-always master?"

"That goes without saying, Little Hawk," said Taliesin, looking up with a smile from the fresh ewe-milk cheese he was spreading on his own bannock. "But do you send your message to the King, for I think that when it comes I shall be close at hand."

So it was arranged, and Neirin went aboard the Irish ship that afternoon, and she sailed with the evening tide. But there being no space on the ship for ponies, he left his two in my keeping. "The pack-pony," he had said earlier that day in the stables, where the two of us had gone to talk, "is neither here nor there, and I can get another if I must; but I would not be for trusting my old friend Brith to the King's grooms for who knows how long. He will be safer with you, brother; and if you take the one, as well for you to take the other, too." And he drew his hand slowly down the dapple-gray's soft nose, and Brith snorted and butted his master in the chest, impatient for the treat which he knew was coming. Neirin smiled and offered it on his open palm, a piece of his last breakfast bannock which he had saved for this purpose, and the pony lipped it up delicately. These two had been together since Neirin's boyhood in the North, and had traveled many a mile in partnership; only last summer Neirin had risked his own life and freedom rather than lose his old friend.

"You will miss him," I said, teasing, "more than any girl you have ever left behind."

"Indeed I will," said Neirin, rubbing Brith's broad forehead and smiling, his amber eyes as bright and dark in the shadowy stable as the pony's own. "And he has never played me false, unlike one or two I could mention. But you will keep him safe for me, brother, until I come again."

"I wish I were going with you," I said as we crossed the courtyard from the stables. "You might need me along to get you out of scrapes again, especially if you are going to Alt Clut." For at Alt Clut dwelt the silver-haired young woman whom Neirin had seen and vainly desired last summer, before her marriage to King Rhydderch Hael.

"Na, na, I will be more careful this time," said Neirin, grinning. "And someone must stay here to help Taliesin when he needs it."

"What do you mean?" I asked in puzzlement. "It is back to Llys-tyn-wynnan with Talhaearn I am going, remember—not off with Taliesin, wherever that might be."

"Of course you are," said Neirin, and laughed. "*Hai mai!* Where are my wits wandering to? And I am not even at sea yet—something that I have not done before, in truth! They are saying it is three day's sailing to Aeron with the wind in this quarter—I wonder, will I be very sick?" And he grimaced comically.

"Na, that I cannot foretell," I said, laughing, "not having been to sea myself! You shall tell me all about it when you come back to reclaim Brith."

"Indeed, and I shall," said Neirin, and laid his arm for a moment across my shoulders. But he did not look worried at all.

I was thinking of that conversation now, as I led my pack string behind Taliesin and Talhaearn. The three of us were not going back the way we had come, north around Eryri, but instead were taking a different route, south through Ardudwy and Meirionnydd, and skirting the eastern flanks of snow-capped Cadair Idris, to come at last into Powys from the west. We had parted with Ugnach and Rhys three mornings ago at Caer Seint, much to the latter's apparent relief, and had covered much ground since then, for Taliesin had promised to have us home again by Beltane, and meant to keep his word. Some of the country was familiar to me from two years before—indeed, we had lain the previous night at Maen-Twrog, near the place where I first met Gwydion mab Dôn—but all that day we had been passing through lands new to me, for between Aber Dyfi and Harddlech, Ieuan and I had followed the coast.

Looking at the thickly-forested slopes towering above me on either side, I could see why Ieuan had chosen that way. We were threading a narrow valley between steep hills, following the swift-running Afon Eden on its way to Aber Mawddach and the sea. This would be dark country in the summer when the branches above us shut out the sun, a land more fit for deer and wild boar—and maybe wild men—than for wandering travelers on foot. Even now it was lonely, as if the old god Idris still cast his brooding spell over the land. That afternoon, however, the oaks and alders all around us were in pale new leaf, and the willow-catkins by the water shone bright gold with pollen. Beside our track the grass and bracken-fern grew lush and green, a temptation to Brith and the pack-ponies, who wanted to stop and graze. Squirrels chittered and chased each other through the oak branches, and somewhere a woodpecker drummed his ownership of his territory. Above us the sky was a ruffled sea of thin broken cloud, through the gaps of which the late afternoon sun poured down from time to time, showing me now and again a partial view of Cadair Idris' snow-crowned head, silver-bright above the darkness of the intervening hills, as our track bent back and forth. It haloed, too, Talhaearn's gray-white mane as he rode straight and tall in the saddle, now behind and now side by side with Taliesin, his hair sometimes shining bright as the mountaintop, sometimes eclipsed by the flickering shadows of the trees.

An old man, I remembered Rhiannedd had said Talhaearn was, one who should be biding safe by the fireside, not braving the cold winds and rain of an uncertain season. How old he was in truth I had no idea; but from tales he had told me, I knew him to have been man grown and a master bard himself before ever Arthur came to be High King—and Arthur died at Camlann fight three years before I was born. Talhaearn seemed ageless to me then, a man of iron; yet all of us come in time to our ends, and even the immortal gods may grow old. Or so Taliesin told me once, and he should know.

Be that as it may, the three of us were glad to find shelter that night in the reed-thatched hall of Rhodri mab Pedr near the water-meet of the rivers Eden and Wnion. Not a rich lord, Rhodri, with wide green acres and herds of cattle; but he had salmon from the river, deer and boar from the forest, a few bee-skeps for their honey, and lived as well in his way as any king. He gave us spit-roasted venison and clear golden mead, and the best straw pallets by the hearth that night. Taliesin, who might deny kings but was generous with lesser folk, made him a shining praise-song, and I told a tale afterwards which held even the noisy children of the place silent for a while and won me good applause at the end. We did not sit late, for we were bone-weary with riding, but bedded down after the feasting was done with all the other folk in the hall. Neither the snores of my neighbors, nor the rustling of the mice in the rushes, and certainly not the occasional pounce of the yellow-eyed cat who hunted them, kept me long awake that night.

There in the breathing darkness, close beside the flanks of Cadair Idris, I slept and dreamed. I dreamed first of an eagle, flying high in the sky, and knew he was not Gwydion, but someone else familiar to me. Higher and higher he soared above the slopes of the mountain until he was a speck against the swirling clouds that wrapped the peak; then he was gone. It was a loss to me, that disappearance; it made me feel alone. Then I looked down, and saw around me a strange world, a gray world, a world from which all the light was draining, like wine from a cup. Ahead of me opened a path through an unknown wood, and half-unwillingly I began to walk along it. The wood grew darker still, and fear came upon me, and I began to run. Faster and faster the trees whipped past me; darker and darker became the wood. And behind me I heard the huntsman's horn, and the baying of hounds...

I awoke, gasping in fear, on my pallet by the hearth. All around me was peace and the dim flickering of the firelight: the small noises of a wooden house at night, the snores and soft breathing of the sleepers, the faint rustle as someone turned in his bed. If I had cried out in my dreaming, it seemed that no one had heard me, no one had awakened. I lay still for a long time, listening to the life of the place, and at last slept again. But I did not quite forget the dream.

The next day we were on our way early—or as early as might be, what with grooming, harnessing, saddling, and loading eight ponies, and snatching a bite of breakfast for myself—though I admit I had some help with the first part. This was our hardest day yet, fording first the swift-running Afon Wnion, and then its tributary the Afon Clywedog, though well upstream from their junction. Crossing a broad valley, we came next to the narrow Oerddrws pass—the *Cold Door*, its name means—where rocky slopes frowned gray above us, just visible through the leafing trees. Beyond the pass we dropped steeply into a deeper valley squeezed between the mountains, and followed its little river while morning changed to midday. At last we forded it, and stopped on its eastern bank for our noontime meal. With Taliesin's help I slacked the saddle-girths and set ponies and pack-ponies alike to grazing, then joined him and Talhaearn on a sunny bank beside the silver stream.

"Which river did we just cross, Gwion?" asked Talhaearn as we settled down to our food—barley bannock and hard-boiled duck's eggs, I mind it was, with a sprinkling of salt from our bag.

"The Afon Dyfi," said Taliesin between mouthfuls. "Not so many miles downstream from here is a place I know well. I spent three summers there as a boy before you and Emrys found me, Talhaearn, and I have still a piece of land there, a farmstead which Arthur gave me once to hold. No one in the long years since"—and here he smiled slightly—"has ventured to take it away again." His blue eyes narrowed against the sunlight, he seemed to be looking into a great distance, and for a moment his face was sad. Then, seeming to feel my regard, he smiled at me. "Time, Gwernin," he said, "is like this river, which moves always toward the sea. Venture onto it in a coracle without a paddle, and it will sweep you away; and however much you may wish to return to a particular bank, to a deed undone or ill-done, you cannot do it. No one can walk back through time to change the past, though he would give his own heart's blood to do so—is that not true, Talhaearn?"

"True, true," said Talhaearn, and shook his head; but whether at Taliesin's words, or some thought of his own, I did not know. After a moment's silence he asked me for another barley bannock, and the conversation, like the river, moved on. Then it was time to gather the grazing ponies, tighten the girths, and be on our way again. Yet long afterwards I was to remember Taliesin's words.

That afternoon we rode east, following the little Afon Dugoed, whose name means *black forest*—and a darkly wooded land it was. Soon enough our track led us to a wide, low pass, and crossing it we reached the headwaters of the Afon Banwy, a stream which flows at length into the Severn and passes Pengwern on its long journey to the sea. But that trip we did not make that day. Instead, in late afternoon we found ourselves at the mouth of the Afon Twrch, and looking up its valley, saw Llys-tyn-wynnan, and knew that Talhaearn and I, at least, were home.

When we rode into the familiar courtyard of the *llys*, Prince Cyndrwyn himself was standing by the door-post of his hall. "Well met again, Taliesin," he called. "I see you have kept your word, and brought them back—though none too soon!"

"I said before Beltane, did I not?" laughed Taliesin, swinging down from his tall red mare. "And behold, we are here, and I have yet a day in reserve!"

"True enough," said Cyndrwyn, smiling. "You will stay on with us for a day or two and share the feast, I hope—you owe me some recompense for the month I have been without song!"

"Then I must repay you a little of that debt, and in the same coin," said Taliesin lightly. "Unless Talhaearn perhaps feels he has had enough of my company for now?"

"I suppose," said Talhaearn dryly, "I can bear a few more days of it, if I must. Only do not trouble with the guesthouse this time, Gwion; you may have Gwernin's bed in my room. I am sure"—and here he smiled—"that he can find another place to sleep for a night or two." At this we all laughed, though I admit I blushed as well; it was true that I had been thinking for many a mile of another bed than my own. As soon as the ponies were unloaded and turned out in the home pasture, I went to look for Rhiannedd.

I did not find her in her mother's room, though Gwawr herself was there, grinding herbs in a mortar. She gave me a long, assessing look when I came in, but answered my enquiry in friendly enough fashion. "I think you will find her down by the stream—I sent her there to look for comfrey roots, a while and a while ago," she said, then added as I turned to leave, "She will be glad to see you back, Gwernin." It seemed an odd comment—I had not been away all that long—but I thought no more of it at the time, for I was in a hurry to find my girl.

I found her on the riverbank below the *llys*. She must have seen or heard me coming—I was not going slowly—and stood waiting for me with a bright, welcoming look on her face which I had not seen in a while. Just so she had looked last autumn, when I came back at last from my summer's journeying with Neirin. I had no rich presents to bring her this time, no jewels nor weight of silver, only myself. But she opened her arms as I came closer, and I walked into them, and wrapped my own around her. Then in sheer high spirits, I lifted her and swung her round like a child; and she laughed, that sweet bubbling laughter that I loved, and I laughed with her. I set her down and kissed her, her red mouth soft against mine, her dark hair brushing my cheek with its faint scent of violets. Her arms tightened around me as if she would never let me go, and beneath her full breasts her heart was beating in time with my own. My need for her rose up in me and filled my mind, and I felt her body trembling in response. There on the riverbank in the afternoon sunshine, we lay down in each other's arms, and took our pleasure as we had done often before; and all around us the birds sang merrily.

At last, when we were lying quietly, and I at least was drifting into sleep, I felt Rhiannedd stir beside me and reach up to stroke my hair. "Gwernin," she said softly in my ear, "are you awake?"

"Mmm," I said, my eyes still closed. The sunlight on my eyelids was warm and red, and I felt very peaceful.

"Gwernin," said Rhiannedd again, "wake up, *cariad*."

"Mmm," I said, and blinked, and focused with an effort on her face. She was looking anxious, her dark brows drawn together in a frown. This pierced my contentment and roused me. "What is it, *calon fach*?" I asked.

"I—I do not know how to tell you this," Rhiannedd said, "but—but I think, no I am sure, it has been two months now…"

"What?" I asked, bewildered. "What has been two months?"

"Gwernin, I am—I have—I am going to have a baby. Your baby." She was frowning fiercely now, and her voice trembled.

"What?" I said again, fully awake now. "How… when? Are you sure?"

"I am sure," said Rhiannedd more firmly. She was, after all, her mother's daughter. "It will be next winter—early next winter, I think. I hope… I hope you are glad?"

"Oh!" I said, and paused. I was not sure at first how I felt—there was a cold sinking in my belly, and at the same time, a sort of warmth. Then I remembered the child named after me in Cadwaladr's court on Ynys Môn, and suddenly the warmth won out. "Yes," I said, "I am. I am glad, Rhiannedd!" And I put my arm around her, and kissed her. Presently I realized she was crying. "*Cariad fach*," I said, "why these tears? Are you not glad yourself? Surely it is a great thing, to be going to have a child?"

"Yes—yes, I am glad," said Rhiannedd and smiled, though her tears still flowed. "I am happy now—now that I know that you are! I did not tell you before you left, because I was not sure, and I have been wondering—I have been afraid—you will not be going away again this summer, will you, Gwernin? Not again?"

"Na, na," I said, smiling back at her, and kissed her wet cheek. "I will be here, *annwyl*, working hard with Talhaearn. Neirin has gone off to the North on his own, and left me behind. Maybe—maybe if I work very hard this summer, and—and next winter as well, Cyndrwyn will make me *bardd teulu*, bard to his war-band, and—and maybe give me land. Then we can marry properly, and I can give you the home you deserve—you and my son!"

"Or daughter," said Rhiannedd, and giggled unexpectedly. "That would be wonderful indeed, *cariad*—but just to have you here, and not leaving again, is enough for me now." And with that she kissed me gently, and I kissed her back, and one thing led to another. Not until the sun dropped behind the western hills, and the evening chill recalled us to the world around us, did we rise and go back to the *llys*, and then we went hand in hand, leaving the herbs Rhiannedd had been seeking when I found her forgotten on the riverbank beside our erstwhile bed. And that night I spread my blankets in Gwawr's room, and knew that I was accepted there, if not yet wholly approved.

The next day was *Nos Calan Haf*, Beltane Eve. The year before, when I was about to leave for the North with Neirin, Rhiannedd and I had jumped the fires hand in hand as an informal marriage, and afterwards spent the night together upon the hill. It had been an act of desperation then, our pledging of a love and a commitment we could not publicly declare. This year it was different. Although my ability to support a wife was not materially improved, we now had hope for the future, and plans, however uncertain. Rhiannedd's child-to-be—our child-to-be—had already by its very existence changed many things.

That evening the two of us stood hand in hand while the Beltane fires were kindled, which were to bless the herds before they were driven up to their summer pastures. We watched as the black and brown cattle ran bawling between the fires, the cows with their new calves at their heels and the sparks flying wild about them; and after the cattle, the sheep, with the sheepdogs barking and nipping behind. Then, as the flames were dying down, the men and women went through: the young ones running and laughing, some of them holding hands; the older ones more deliberately. This time we did not wait until most of the people were gone, but ran through with the rest of them, proud to show our commitment to the world. But as we had done the year before, we did not go back to the court, but spent the night together on the green hillside like many another young couple, with one cloak beneath us, and another above, and the pale stars of summer overhead. And when we went home in the dawn, still hand in hand, our future together looked bright and sure to us as the rising sun, and our love was as warm as its rays.

But that, O my children, is a story for another day.

Taliesin's Need

Taliesin stayed with us for three days and then departed, riding alone and leading his own pack-pony. Rhiannedd and I stood in the gateway to watch him go, long after the others who had gathered to bid him farewell had dispersed about their business. Seen thus from a distance, he looked surprisingly small and ordinary, and oddly lonely. Without Neirin he seemed incomplete.

"He will miss Neirin," said Rhiannedd softly. I looked down at her, surprised to hear the echo of my own thoughts, but she was still watching Taliesin.

"Yes," I said after a moment. "I think he will. They were together six years; that makes a bond."

"What will he do now?" asked Rhiannedd.

"Look for another apprentice, I suppose," I said. "For all I know, he may have one already waiting for him at Pengwern." I sighed, and Rhiannedd looked around.

"Talhaearn missed you last summer while you were gone," she said. "He would not admit it, of course, but I know he did. And I missed you, too. I am glad you will be staying at home with us this year."

"*Sa*, I am glad, too," I said smiling, and put my arm around her. But over her dark head, I was still watching Taliesin, until a bend in the track took him out of sight. And a small disloyal part of me wished that I was riding with him.

I did not have long to indulge such thoughts, for Talhaearn was waiting for me, prepared once again to make up for lost time. Whether because of my last summer's absence, or because of my poor showing against Ugnach's son Rhys, he seemed determined to cram my head with poetic knowledge as quickly as possible, and it was all I could do to keep up. With Taliesin's going I had reluctantly reclaimed my bed in the old bard's quarters, and that night and for many nights to come I fell on it dead tired, and slept to dream of poetic meters, resounding endlessly in my ears. It was a while before I realized that he was pushing himself as hard, or harder, than he was me, and it was Rhiannedd who first put the thought into my mind.

"Talhaearn seems tired tonight," she said, looking across the feast hall at my master where he sat near the Prince. "Is he sleeping badly again?"

"Why—I do not know," I said. "I have not been keeping awake myself at nights, that I should notice. Why do you think so?"

"I expect his back is hurting him again," said Rhiannedd wisely. "You can see it sometimes in the way he sits, or walks, or holds his shoulders. All that riding was not good for him: he is an old man, after all. Mother made him a draught for it over the winter, but I expect he has used it up, and is too proud to ask for more. I will get her to help me make more tomorrow, and you can take it to him, and see that he uses it. You can do that, can you not?"

"Mmm," I said. "I can try. But why did I not notice this, and I with him every day?" For truly Talhaearn had seemed much the same to me, and I had put his recent irritability down to my own incompetence.

"He would not show it to you," said Rhiannedd, getting up from the bench against the wall where we had been sitting together. "I must go refill my pitcher now, and pour more ale. Will you be telling a story soon?"

"Na, something different this time," I said. "A song, unless Talhaearn changes his mind."

"Wait until I come back, then," said Rhiannedd, smiling. "This I must hear."

This was the first time I had stood up in hall to sing, rather than to speak a tale, and truth to tell I was more than a little nervous. Better, however, to do it now, on an ordinary evening, and in a place where folk were used to me, and I to them. The first public step in a new art is always an unnerving one, no matter how accustomed one is to having an audience. I had not drunk much that night of intent, but it was not only lack of drink that dried my mouth when the moment came. And Talhaearn's introduction, of course, did not help.

"My Lord Prince, and others," he had said, in a voice which carried all too well through the hall, "my student Gwernin has something new for you tonight. Not a story, this, but a song of praise: I pray you therefore indulge him, and forgive him if he falls short in his attempt, for we must all of us start somewhere."

"I am sure," said Cyndrwyn smiling, "that any student of yours cannot help but excel. Gwernin, when you are ready I will hear you gladly."

I stood up before the high table, where I had stood often before, and tried to work some moisture into my mouth. "My thanks to you, Prince," I said. My voice had long since broken and stabilized, but I felt a sudden wild fear that it might betray me now. This would not do: I took a deep breath, tried to call my *awen* to me as I had never done before, and began:

> "White trees blossoming, flowering in the spring,
> And a war-band comes riding, riding.
> Who is their leader tall, Lord or Prince or King,
> And whither is he riding, riding?
> Fairest Lord in all this land, Cyndrwyn is that man,
> And to his home comes riding, riding.
>
> White trees blossoming, fragrance on the wind,
> And silver in their branches is chiming, chiming.
> All the goodness of the earth that any God can send
> Now in this fair valley is shining, shining.
> In his hands he holds us all, golden are his lands,
> And harp-song in his hall now is chiming, chiming.
>
> White trees blossoming, fairer than the spring,
> And the Lady by our Prince now is singing, singing.
> Fair one worthy of his love, daughter of a King
> Like silver her sweet voice now is ringing, ringing
> Golden Lord and Lady fair, all praise to them I bring,
> High praises in their hall I am singing, singing.
>
> White trees blossoming, see the petals fall,
> And on the warm wind now they are blowing, blowing.
> Summer follows spring so soon, harvest and leaf-fall,
> And winter's petals cold will soon be growing, growing.

Warm and safe here with our Lord we'll feast within his hall,
Until spring's war-horns loud once more are blowing, blowing."

I reached the end without a stumble, and almost sighed aloud. Truth to tell, I have done worse since, though not often; for a beginning it was not bad. I even got some little applause, partly on novelty value, and a few kind words from Cyndrwyn and his lady. Then I sat down, and Rhiannedd came to pour for me: not ale this time, but clear golden mead. And her smile was as honey-sweet as the mead, but without its bitter aftertaste—as were her kisses later.

The next afternoon I found an excuse to join her and her mother in their workroom. A bright, warm, early-summer day it was, and the door to their wooden hut near the back of the *llys* stood open wide for light and air. The sunlight streaming in lit the scrubbed wooden table, the edge of the brazier, and a strip of the packed earth floor, but the rest of the room, with its shelves of jars and boxes, and its bunches of hanging herbs, was in relative darkness. In that darkness, the brazier's fire glowed sullenly red under a three-legged stoneware pot from which steam was rising. Rhiannedd stood beside it, dropping something dark, piece by small piece, into the liquid within. As my shadow crossed the doorway, she looked up, and her last piece of material missed the pot, and fell onto the coals instead. A thin wisp of aromatic smoke rose from it, grew, and then it burst for a moment into flame, leaving only a small bright spot behind.

"I am sorry," I said, coming into the room. "That was my fault."

"It is no great matter." She smiled and brushed a loose strand of dark hair back from her moist forehead; the heat of the brazier had put warm color into her cheeks. "The brew will be strong enough without it."

"What was it?" I asked, looking with interest at a row of little clay dishes laid out on the table. "And what are these?"

"It is willow twigs in the pot," said Rhiannedd, "picked and dried three months ago when the sap was rising strongly in them. This," and she pointed at one of the dishes, full of small dark things, "is poppy seed, and goes in next." She suited her action to the words, and the stream of little back granules disappeared into the boiling liquid. "Both of those," she said, "take away pain, and the poppy gives sleep as well. They must seethe in the pot for a while now before I add the rest."

"And the rest is——?" I asked.

"Meadowsweet," and she pointed at a dish full of pale dried flowerets and leaves, "picked last summer in the Lughnasadh moon, and hung here to dry. Fresh would be better, but these will serve. It is good for aching joints, and takes away pain and fever. Mullein"—a dish of small yellow flowers and bits of pale fuzz—"also for release from pain, and for sleep. And chamomile"—another dish of pale cone-shaped flower heads, none of them bigger than the end of her little finger—"for sleep, and to give a pleasant scent and taste. When it is done I will strain it and add honey as well, to help cover the bitterness of the willow twigs."

"How long will it need to cook?" I asked, with a glance at the hanging curtain at the back of the room which divided the work-room from the bed-place where the two women slept.

Rhiannedd smiled, following my glance. "Not long enough for that, and Mother will be back soon. Sit you down and watch, if you like: I have more work to do. What excuse did you give Talhaearn for being here this afternoon?"

"I said that your mother had offered to teach me a little herb-craft if I had the time, and that I would like to learn it; I saw enough of wounds and blows last summer to know how useful such knowledge is to a wandering man. And what I said is true, and Talhaearn agreed. Not," I added hastily, "that I am planning on wandering anywhere again soon."

Rhiannedd gave me a long look at that, but made no comment. Instead she brought a stone mortar and pestle from a corner and set it on the table. "If you really want to learn," she said, "you can help me grind some herbs. Bring me that bunch hanging on the wall beside your head—no, that one…"

I was still at it when Gwawr came back. Like her daughter, she was a woman of no more than average height, with thick dark curling hair only a little touched with gray, and laughter lines around her mouth and at the corners of her blue-gray eyes. A widow of some years standing, she earned her place in the Prince's *llys* by her trade, providing draughts and salves to all who needed them. Her husband had been a member of the Prince's *teulu*, killed in some raid or battle, and Gwawr had chosen to stay on at the court after his death, and had done well thereby. Today in the warm summer weather she wore a sleeveless dress of lightweight wool the color of distant hills at twilight, and a good silver bracelet on her right wrist which the Prince's wife would not have distained. When she saw my task she smiled.

"Well, Gwernin, have you come to prepare your master's draught yourself? I spoke with him just now, and he told me I would find you here."

"What did you say to him, Gwawr?" I asked, pausing in my use of the pestle.

"Only that I would gladly teach you what you wished to know. That was after he thanked me for offering to do so. I did not tell him," she added, her eyes narrowing with amusement, "that it was not I who made the offer."

I flushed a little. "Na, that was my idea, to excuse my absence from his teaching. Though as I said just now to Rhiannedd, I would gladly learn some of your craft."

"Well, that is as may be," said Gwawr cryptically, coming to the worktable. "Is the draught ready, daughter dear?"

"It is," said Rhiannedd, holding up the brown pottery flask. Gwawr took it and sniffed the contents, then caught a drop on her forefinger and tasted it. "Yes," she said, "that is strong enough, and not too bitter." She pushed the waiting stopper into the neck of the flask and set it back on the table beside me. "Gwernin, I will leave this delivery to you." She smiled. "And I look forward to hearing of your success."

A little while later, coming into the main courtyard, I found Talhaearn drowsing on a bench in the sun with his back against the wooden wall of his lodging. In repose his lined brown face looked old as the mountains; his hair and tufted brows were white as the winter snows on Yr Wyddfa, and his beard descended like an ice-filled gully on her slopes in the spring. I paused for a moment, wondering how to approach him, and remembering how I had first encountered him so, two summers ago, sunning himself in a courtyard of King Rhun's great fortress at Deganwy. That time I had been sent by Taliesin, who had just caught me out in a public lie, and whether he had sent me out of kindness, or as a punishment, I was still unsure. I only knew that I had come to love this old man, plague me as he might, both for the brilliance and generosity of his teaching, and for something more which I would have been hard pressed to describe.

While I stood thus lost in thought, Talhaearn sighed and stirred. "Are you there, lad?" he asked without opening his eyes. "Do not hover; come up and say what you will."

"Yes, Master," I said, obeying. "Gwawr has had enough of me for the afternoon, and I have come back to see if you needed me, and to bring you—to bring you…"

"To bring me what?" asked Talhaearn, opening his faded blue eyes and peering at me. "I cannot see you in this sun-dazzle. What have you brought?"

"A draught Gwawr sent you," I said, holding up the flask, "of the kind she made for you last winter, to help you sleep at night."

"Ah," said Talhaearn, his craggy brows drawing together as he frowned. "More of the herb-wife's meddling—or was this your own idea? How would you know if I sleep or not, and you snoring in your blankets like a barm-fed sow as you do?"

"How would you know that I snore, Master," I asked carefully, "if you yourself were not awake to hear it? If it is my snores that keep you wakeful, I could sleep elsewhere—you have only to say the word!"

"Would you leave me, then, for the herb-wife's teaching?" asked Talhaearn bitterly. "And for the herb-wife's pretty daughter?"

"And how would you be knowing whether she is pretty or not,

blind as you are?" I asked. To my surprise Talhaearn laughed.

"I may be blind," he said, "but I am not deaf; I know what goes on in this court. Well? Would you leave me?"

"Master," I said, "you know that I would not. I am not half a bard yet, and I know it. This is all my desire, to bide with you and learn all that you can teach me."

Talhaearn chuckled. "All? And forego the herb-wife's daughter?"

"Mmm," I said, and paused. "I do not think I can do that. It is…a little late. She is…"

"A little late," said Talhaearn maliciously, and chuckled again. "Na, na, did I not tell you I know what goes on around me? When did you get her with child?"

"I…am not sure," I said, blushing. "Two months ago, she said, or maybe more. But how did you…?"

"By listening," said Talhaearn, "a habit you should acquire. Remember, boy, that nothing goes on in a place such as this which someone does not see or hear, and if it makes a juicy bit of gossip, tell to someone else—usually to several someones! Sit in the hall long enough and listen, and you will be like Math son of Mathonwy—whatever words the wind hears, you will hear them." He stood up stiffly. "Now come inside with me, where there are fewer listening ears, for I have words to say to you I would not have overheard. But first, run to the kitchens and bring me a measure of good red wine. If I am going to try your nasty draught tonight, I will certainly need a drink afterwards to take the taste away!"

When I had done this errand and joined him in his room, I found Talhaearn sitting silently in the gloom, sunk in thought. "Close the door," he said without looking up, "and light the candle if you wish." And while I was fumbling with the flint and steel, "Gwernin, did you pay much heed to what Gwion and I discussed while he was here?"

"Well…no," I said. "I was busy at first, with the gear and the ponies, and…"

"And the girl," said Talhaearn, and gave a short laugh. "*Sa, sa,* it was ever so. And after?"

"Afterwards," I said, "I did not try to overhear you, and of course I do not know what the two of you said privately in this room at night. Am I at fault?"

"Hmm," said Talhaearn. "No, not really. But I must start at the beginning. Gwion is thinking of leaving Cynan Garwyn and Pengwern. It will not be this summer, or at least not permanently—it may not be for a year or more. But he has a need to journey around Britain, inciting peace where he can, and war where he must, and gauging the intentions of kings. And in this journeying he will need an apprentice, to be his eyes and ears, and guard his back if need be, and do all those tasks which it is not proper for him to do for himself. Neirin did this for him in the past, but Neirin has now flown free, and Gwion has not another, lesser student ready at hand to take his place." He paused, and looked at me.

"That is sad hearing," I said, puzzled. "But surely Taliesin could have his pick of students? Anyone would be glad to serve him and learn from him. I myself, when I first met him…" I stopped. "Do you mean what I think you mean?"

"I am not sure," said Talhaearn dryly, "what you think, lad, or sometimes whether you do think at all. But yes, Gwion is looking about him for a new student, and has asked if I would consider releasing you to him, at least for a while." He paused again. "Or, of course, if you are too firmly rooted here, there is always Rhys mab Ugnach, who shows some talent, and could certainly use the discipline of a different master."

"*Rhys!*" I said in shock. "That little—that little rat, to travel with Taliesin? Master, you cannot be serious!"

"Indeed I am," said Talhaearn. "Gwernin, I am not sending you away. I know you have your hopes here, and your responsibilities. And I have grown—I have grown used to you. Journey if you will with Gwion this summer; and come back to us, if you wish, at summer's end; and in the meantime I will take Rhys and see what can be made of him. Or stay here, and let Rhys go in your place, to fill Gwion's need. The choice is yours to make, but make it soon, for Gwion will be back here with the full moon, on his way to Deganwy."

"That is in two days," I said, still not believing my ears.

"Yes," said Talhaearn, and smiled thinly. "Now blow out the candle, boy, and let us go to the hall, for I think it must be nearly time for meat, and I am hungry even if you are not." I did as he said; and though I told a tale that night to entertain the company, I had hard work to keep my mind on the words. I said to myself that I had two days yet in which to decide, and did not have to do so at once, but I already knew what my decision would be. My only problem would be how to tell Rhiannedd.

But that, O my children, is a story for another day.

The Man From The Sea

I have never been a willing sea-farer, though I have voyaged in boats now and again when need drove me. It is not that I cannot swim; no boy growing up as I did by Severn-side can fail to learn the arts and the enjoyment of the water. In my youth I could paddle and float, dive and sound, and hold my own against any; I could row a coracle, that willow-woven cup of oiled cow-skin, catch my salmon and bring him aboard without overturning. But the sea—the sheer unending wind-tossed, wave-backed, spume-crested, gray-green extent of it—is a foreign country to me; and looking at it, my heart always misgives me. So it was on that day at Deganwy, when I stood on the ramparts of Rhun's fort and watched, far-out, a storm-driven ship struggling toward the land. So has it been for me on many days since.

I had gone up there for a breath of fresh air and a few moments of quiet rehearsal, before the evening meal and the tale that I would telling that night to entertain the court: for Taliesin was as concerned to widen my repertoire and experience as Talhaearn had been, if in somewhat different ways. "Well, Gwernin," he had said to me on the morning we rode away from Llys-tyn-wynnan, "tell me what Talhaearn has been teaching you since I saw you last." And when I had finished my recital, "Good enough. I will set you some lessons presently to use what you have just learned, lest your fine new tools rust and Talhaearn scold us both when you come home. But in the meantime, there are other things than poetry that a bard must know. Have you ever heard the tale of Aranrhod and the Man from the Sea?" And when I said no, he told it to me briefly. Even on that bright summer morning, riding at our leisure with the pack-ponies clip-clopping along behind us, and the birds singing merrily, and all the world at peace, it sent a shiver down my spine. On a stormy evening, such as this would be, in the flame-flickering, torch-lit darkness of the hall, it should be a tale to remember indeed. "Now make it your own," Taliesin had said when he had finished. "That is the thing which sets the bard apart from the reciter: the raiment of the tale. See that you dress this one well!"

The sun was near its setting; it was time for the evening meal. With one more glance at the wind-harried ship, battling to reach the land, I went down from the wall-walk. The courtyard was warm and still by comparison, and heavy with the summer odors of men and horses, laced through with wood-smoke and the rich smell of roasting meat. Already the torches showed golden-bright in the shadows, and the door to the hall was as dark as the mouth of a cave. Inside was the usual babble of voices as the men of King Rhun's household gathered for their meal. I found Taliesin at the top of the hall as usual, waiting for the King's entrance. His eyes met mine for a moment and he smiled, but absently. "Get your food as soon as you may, Gwernin," he said, "and be ready to perform when I call you." Then he turned away as the King came into the hall.

Rhun was dressed as splendidly as ever, in a wine-red robe of fine-spun wool heavily embroidered with gold. In it he shone like the summer sun amidst the flower-bright colors around him at his high table. On his left this evening was a visitor, Cyndeyrn Prince of northern Powys, whose court at Deva I had visited briefly the year before with Taliesin and Neirin. An aging gray-beard, he made Rhun look a mere youth by comparison. On his far side was his young daughter, the Lady Denw, now talking with animation to Taliesin beside her. Somewhere in the hall, I knew, would be their harper-bard Bluchbardd, a lean dark man whose face seemed set in a perpetual scowl.

Food began to arrive on the trestle tables, and I took some and applied myself with a will. As soon as I had satisfied my first hunger, I stood up and went to where I could see and be seen by Taliesin. He still seemed deep in conversion with the Lady Denw, but after a few moments he looked over at me and nodded. Before the relative silence due to full mouths and rapidly champing jaws could die away, I approached the high table and bowed to Rhun. "Lord King," I said, "would it please you to hear a tale?"

"Gladly," said Rhun, to whom I was now a familiar figure. "Speak your tale."

"My thanks, Lord," I said, and taking my stance beside the central hearth, I began.

"Long ago, in an earlier age of this world, there was a king ruling in Gwynedd who was called Math son of Mathonwy. Now Math had no children himself, but he had a niece and three nephews, his sister Dôn's children, and in the manner of the men of those days he planned to chose his successor from among them: for no man knows beyond doubt who fathered a child, but of its mother all the world can be sure.

"The eldest of the children of Dôn was called Gofannon, and he was a smith: the best smith that has ever been in all the Island of Britain. All the power and the knowledge and the magic of fire and of iron was in his hands, for like all his family he was a wizard; and his strength was very great. A huge black-bearded bear of a man he was, with hands as broad as shovels, and the marks of fire like tattooing on his massive chest and arms, for he went bare to the waist from one midwinter to the next. The gold-hilted swords that he made could fight by themselves, and no spell could turn aside his spear-points. But Gofannon cared nothing for kingship: only the tumult of war could move him from his forge, and that only to do battle. So Math was forced to look farther afield for his heir.

"The second of the children of Dôn was called Amaethon, and he was a farmer: the best farmer that has ever been in all the Island of Britain. Seedtime and harvest, all the fruits of the fields, and also the herds and their increase, were his concerns. Every plant that he touched grew three times as tall as any other; all his cows bore twins and his ewes triplets; and the milk from them at one milking could have made a great white lake, with golden islands in it of butter and cheese. His bees were as big as sparrows, and the mead that he made from their honey could have brought the dead back to life, always supposing the living had left as much as a drop of it for them. But Amaethon cared nothing for kingship: only the tumult of war could move him from his fields and herds, and that only to protect them. So Math was forced to look farther afield for his heir.

"The third of the children of Dôn was called Gwydion, and he was a Druid: the most powerful Druid that has ever been in all the Island of Britain. The wisdom of the forests and of the mountains; of the sun and the moon and the stars; of the clouds and the rain and the great green rolling sea, and all that moved within it, was his concern. He sought knowledge in all these elements: in the smoke and in the fire, in the night and in the day, in the turning of the tides and the stars and the seasons. Transformation and subtlety was his art, and the changing of what was into what might be. And he cared nothing for kingship, but like all things in the world it interested him. So Math chose Gwydion his nephew to be his heir.

"Now Gwydion had one sister, and her name was Aranrhod, and she was as fair as he was dark. Her eyes were as green as forest shadows, and her hair as golden as the flowering broom, and her clear skin shone like pale heather honey in the sunlight. She was the youngest of the children of Dôn, and she was as yet unwed; nor did she have any interest in men, or in marriage, or in the bearing of children of her own. Her dwelling place was in Arfon, in a strong fortress by the sea, and there she spent her time in the study of music and poetry, and the hearing of songs and tales and harping; and not a man came into her castle from one midsummer until the next, except that he was a bard.

"Now Gwydion saw this, and it concerned him that his only sister might bear no son to rule after him in Gwynedd. So he determined that Aranrhod must be got with child, and he bent all of his arts and all of his powers of persuasion to accomplish this.

"First he sent the King of Ireland, Conchobhar Mac Nessa, the lustiest man who then walked the earth, to try and seduce her. But Aranrhod said that Conchobhar's singing was like the croaking of an old meat-crow with a rusty throat, and she would not even let him past her gate; and so Conchobhar went away again disappointed. Next Gwydion sent King Simonides of the Greeks, the best singer and poet who then walked the earth, to try and seduce her. But although Aranrhod enjoyed his singing and his poetry, she said that he was the ugliest man that she had ever seen, and she would not even let him into her feast-hall; and so Simonides went away again disappointed. Finally Gwydion sent King Aeneas of the Romans, who was a singer and a poet and a fine warrior as well, to try and seduce her. But although Aranrhod enjoyed his singing and found him fair to look upon, she said that he was no storyteller, and she would not let him into her bedchamber; and so Aeneas went away again disappointed. And at last Gwydion decided to go himself and get his sister with child.

"He took upon himself the semblance of Manannan Mac Leirr, the King of the Island of Man, and no good friend to the children of Dôn. And he went to the shore near Aranrhod's castle, and from the dulse and the seaweed and the driftwood that he found there on the shore, he made by his magic a boat. He put a sail on it of spindrift, and he went aboard it, and he came sailing down the wind from the North, as if he came from the Island of Man. But in his haste to accomplish his purpose, he forgot that Manannan King of Man was also a powerful magician, and also a proud man and a jealous one.

"When Manannan saw by his arts what Gwydion was about in his seeming, he was angry. He sent a great wind from the North, which came roaring over the waves, pushing them into gray-green mountains with hissing white crests of foam, and above them were blue-black storm clouds armed with swords of lighting and arrow-sharp torrents of piercing rain and hail. These fell upon Gwydion and smashed his boat into splinters, and locked him into his false shape, and took from him his memory of who he was and what he was doing, so that only by dint of his magic did he stay man alive. And as a ship-wrecked sailor he was washed ashore at the very gates of Aranrhod's castle. Aranrhod herself saw him lying there at the edge of the surf, and he more than half drowned, with the dulse and seaweed tangled in his long black hair and his beard, and his strong body all bruised and bleeding from the rocks and the battering waves. And although she did not know him for her brother, she felt her heart moved with pity for him; and she had him carried into her castle for tending.

"When he grew better, he told her that he was a bard from Ireland, and he sang and told stories in her feast-hall, both to prove it and to entertain her—and Gwydion was the best teller of tales in the world. And Aranrhod enjoyed his singing, and found him fair to look upon; but most of all she enjoyed the power of his words, and his telling of tales. So at last she took him into her chamber, and into her bed, and he lay with her as a man does with a woman. And after a time it came to pass that she was with child.

"When Gwydion heard this news, his memory came back to him, and he knew who he was and what he had been doing, and that his plan was accomplished. He told Aranrhod then that he was in truth Manannan King of Man, who had been coming to make her his wife, but that he had lost his memory when he was shipwrecked. Now he must go back to his kingdom and make all ready for her, and when the time was right he would return and claim his bride. So he took a little boat and sailed away to the North; but once out of her sight, he changed himself into his own shape again, and turned the boat toward his home at Caer Dathyl, and there he went ashore.

"Aranrhod waited some time for her husband's return, but at last, when she felt the child move strongly within her, she determined to go herself and join him. She took ship to the Island of Man, and sailed into Manannan's harbor, and his people greeted her and brought her to the King. Manannan was astonished to see her there, for he had forgot the spell he had placed on Gwydion; but also he was glad, for Aranrhod was young and exceedingly beautiful. So he took her into his chamber, and into his bed, and that night they lay together as man and wife.

"Thus they lived together for some time, and every evening Manannan's bards entertained them with songs and music and stories. But at last there came an evening when for some reason there was no bard in the hall, and Aranrhod asked her husband to sing for her himself. 'For,' she said, 'I know that you sing better than any bard I have heard since I came here; and I will not sleep tonight, even with you, my husband, unless I first hear singing and harping, and a tale.'

" 'Alas,' said Manannan then, 'you have asked of me the one thing that I cannot do: for I am no bard.' And he told her the truth, that the man who had first got her with child was her brother Gwydion. 'But,' he said, 'by my magic I can promise you this: you shall have your revenge. For you will bear two boys, and one of them you will lose, and one of them Gwydion will keep and cherish, thinking it is his own. But the one you will lose will be his, and the one he will keep will be mine: and so shall your vengeance be served on your brother, for what he has done against you and against me.'

" 'That is a good prophecy,' said Aranrhod, who had never wanted to bear any man's child, much less her brother Gwydion's. 'But now, my dear, I must leave you and return to my home: for I cannot bear to abide with any man who is not a bard, and for all your power and your learning and your magic, you are none. In that respect, if in no other, my wicked brother is your better.' And so she took ship, and went away to her home in Arfon, leaving Manannan desolate.

"In time Manannan's prophecy came to pass, and Aranrhod gave birth to two sons, both of them with hair as golden-yellow as her own. The first-born of them was a big bonny child whom she named Dylan, which in the tongue of those days meant *sea*, in memory of the sea-storm which brought his father to her; and she sent him to be fostered by an old servant of hers who lived on the north coast of Ynys Môn. The second boy, who was tiny and weak and seemed very like to die, she left unnamed until it should be seen whether he would live or no: for a child born untimely does not count as a child until it reaches its first birthday, and as such it requires no name. This one she put out to nurse with a maid-servant in the town, and tried to put him out of her mind, for she knew that he was the son of her dear husband Manannan, the only such a one she was ever likely to bear; but also he was to be the means of her revenge on her brother Gwydion.

"When Gwydion heard the tale of the two births he was puzzled, and he took himself to Aranrhod's castle, to see what was the true story. As he was riding through the town, he saw the maid-servant, sitting on a stool in the doorway of her hut and trying to give her breast to a tiny whimpering something. 'Why, what is this?' he asked her smiling. 'This is a tiny fair one that you have indeed.'

" 'Fair as his mother,' the dark-haired maid-servant agreed. 'But likely soon to be underground, for all the power and the magic that she owns, and she the Lady of the Castle. They do say she rejected him because of the way he was begotten on her, and wants him to die. I am thinking it is soon she will have her wish, the cruel one, for look you, he is too little to nurse, too little to live.'

" 'Give him to me, then,' said Gwydion, 'for I am a Druid, and it may be that my magic will succeed where hers has failed.' And he reached down his hands, and the maid-servant placed the babe in them; and behold, he was so little that he fitted easily in Gwydion's two cupped hands. 'If your mistress asks,' said Gwydion, 'you may tell her that the child died. I will take care of him now.' And he placed the child inside his robe against the bare skin of his chest to keep it warm, and he went away to his own place. And he called the boy Llew, which means 'the fair one,' and raised him tenderly and lovingly. And in time he got for the boy, by magic and enchantment, both a name and arms and a wife, and the lordship of one of the best cantrefs in Gwynedd. And after Gwydion himself passed from the knowledge of men, his sister's-son Llew was King of Gwynedd in his turn.

"But the first-born child, the true son of Aranrhod and Gwydion, grew up on the wild north coast of Môn, and became a sea-mage, and a wind-master, and much more besides, before he came to his death on the iron spear of his twice-uncle Gofannon. But that, O my masters, is truly a tale for another day."

"That was well told," said Rhun smiling when the applause had died down, and he gave me a silver bracelet for my pains. But as I went back to my seat, I saw the black-haired bard Bluchbardd, and he was gazing at the Lady Denw with a sort of naked hunger in his face that made me uneasy to see it. And I remembered last summer, and wondered again what was coming to those two in the future.

While I had been telling my tale, the wind had risen with the coming storm, and the long summer twilight outside had darkened into night and pouring rain. I resumed my former place at one of the tables, and was helping myself to more meat and stewed greens, when one of the maidservants came to fill my cup with ale. She was a pretty brown-haired lass whom I had noticed before, and she smiled as she poured for me. Then she looked beyond me, and gave a cry of surprise, and jerked the pitcher she was holding so that ale went across my arm and into my lap, and soaked the front of my good tunic. I fended her off, and then looked where she was looking, and forgot her waste of good drink. There was a man standing framed in the half-darkness of the doorway who could have been Gwydion himself come up from the sea. Streaming wet as a drowned man he was, with a white face, and dark eyes, and a bloody wound on his forehead. Then the torches flared up, and despite his sorry state I knew him. It was my friend Neirin, come back from his mission to the North.

Only for a moment he stood there, leaning against the doorframe as if gathering his strength; then he walked on up the center of the hall, trailing a wake of sudden silence behind him like a cloak. Even as I leapt up to go to him, he reached the space in front of the high table and stopped, swaying slightly, before Rhun. "Lord King," he said, his voice strangely hoarse and rough, "I have carried your news to the Men of the North as you bade me, and am come back with their answer. Their answer is war, and with war they are on their way. By morning there will be fire and slaughter in Arfon." He paused for a moment, then added in a lower tone, "I am sorry: I have failed you."

"Na, na," said Rhun, shaking his head, "it is only what I expected, and you have come back to bring me the news of it, I think at no small cost to yourself. Rest now and take food and drink; then you shall tell me all." And to the captain of his *teulu*, who had appeared as if by magic at his shoulder, "Send out scouts and messengers now, and have the rest of your men ready to ride with me at dawn. We will pick up more war-bands as we go; if the Men of the North have come down with fire and vengeance on Arfon, we will need them all."

In this he was to be proved right, and more than right. I could see, as I helped Neirin to a bench at the side of the hall and got him meat and ale, that my expectation of a peaceful summer had gone down the Irish wind; and being young, I could not then say that I was sorry.

But that, O my children, is a story for another day.

Riding to War

When I was first serving Talhaearn, there was a young man named Goronwy in the Prince's war-band who used to call me "Horse-boy". This was partly because caring for Talhaearn's mare and leading his pack-pony on foot when we traveled were indeed part of my duties, but mostly because of the competition between us—the very unequal competition—for a certain red-headed girl. There had been times since, however, when I felt that he had in some ways the right of it, and one of those times was the morning after Neirin's return. Somewhere ahead of me—no doubt halfway across Eryri by now—he and Taliesin were riding with Rhun's war-band, while I and our three pack-ponies followed with the baggage train. It was not the way in which I had dreamed of riding to war.

As I jogged along, I thought back to the night before. Warmed, dried, and fed, and with the bloody cut on his forehead tended, Neirin had recovered most of his usual energy. He had answered Rhun's questions readily enough, if sometimes with a certain lack of detail. The main outline of the story he had to tell was clear enough, however.

"I went first, as you asked, to Elidyr's court in Aeron," he had said, sitting on a stool in Rhun's private chamber while the King and Taliesin listened, and I stood leaning against the wall by the door. "I had outrun the news, if not the rumor, of his death, and was welcomed by his Queen and treated well, though the tale I had to tell could not but distress her. I took with me Elidyr's sword and his jewels, and it was the latter, I think, which convinced her that my story was true. She wept when she saw them, poor lady, but as one whose worst fears have been realized, not in surprise. Her fate and that of the kingdom are now uncertain, for Elidyr had no sons. He did, however," said Neirin grimly, "have many cousins."

"That," said Rhun, thinly smiling, "I know all too well. Indeed, I am by marriage one of them. Well, and then?"

"Then," said Neirin, "I traveled on to Alt Clut, where I also got a good welcome. Rhydderch Hael was away from his court, on a small matter of the men of Dál Riata breaking his borders, and I had some days to wait before he returned. Again I was well lodged and well entertained, and spent some little time in conversation with his Queen, who as you will know is Urien Rheged's only daughter. I doubt not but that the news went hot-foot from there to Urien, if he had not heard it already."

"Likely indeed," said Rhun dryly. "Urien is not famed for his lack of spies and messengers. Well, and then?"

"Rhydderch Hael came back victorious, as I would judge, from his border foray," said Neirin, "and with him several of his cousins, in particular Mordaf mab Serfan and Nudd mab Senyllt. Their good spirits, however, were much diminished by my news, and over their drink they fell to threatening vengeance on you and on the men of Arfon, who they felt had betrayed their cousin Elidyr to his death. I did what I could with songs and stories to sweeten their mood, but with little success. So after a few days I left them, and rode on to see my half-brother of Gododdin, Clydno Eidyn."

"Ah, yes," said Rhun. "Elidyr's other royal cousin. Well, and then?"

"My welcome was good," said Neirin, but with a little constraint in his voice. "And he seemed at first unconcerned at my news—though that might have been because it had already reached him. He did, however, ask me many questions, not least about your own dispositions, Lord King. I told him, I hope, only what he knew already."

"Which doubtless is a great deal," said Rhun. "As I myself know of his. I have long been thankful that Rheged lies between us: your brother is not a man with whom I should like to share a border. Not that Urien Rheged is much better... Well, and then?"

"He entertained me for some days," said Neirin, "and that most generously. But whenever I spoke of leaving, or of sending you a message—my mission, as I conceived it, being at an end—he had always some distraction or temptation to prevent me from doing so. At last I decided to ride back to Alt Clut myself the next day, and find my messenger there. That was the morning," said Neirin tersely, "that I woke to find a guard at my door, and myself a prisoner."

"Ah!" said Rhun, frowning. "Now we come to the meat of it! Well, and then?"

"To my questions and curses alike they returned no answer," said Neirin. "My gear had been searched while I slept, and my weapons taken. They brought me food and drink, and—and everything else that I might want, except my freedom. But no one came to speak to me that day, or for many days thereafter. Then at last my half-brother came."

"Yes?" said Rhun. "And he said?"

"That he was going south with the men of Alt Clut to seek vengeance for Elidyr, and that I had a choice," said Neirin. "To take his ring, and be his sworn bard, and ride with him on this adventure, or to bide where I was in my comfortable cage until all was done. He wished me, he said, no harm in the world: only he could not let me go to bring you news of his intentions. For I believe," said Neirin, frowning, "from things I once heard and now remember, that such a plan had long been in his mind."

"Like enough," said Rhun briefly. "Yet I see you here, and I think not forsworn. What happened then?"

"I told him," said Neirin, his eyes sparkling with remembered anger, "that I could not take his ring: my honor and my *awen* alike forbade it. And he nodded, as if he were not surprised; and without a word he went away; and I have not seen or spoken to him since. But once he and his war-band had left Dun Eidyn, a friend of mine in his household guard found means to release me. Not daring to seek a ship at Alt Clut, where it seemed to me the war-bands must assemble, I took a horse and rode south with all speed. On the shore of the Gulf of Rheged, near Luguvalium, I found a fishing boat, and paid the captain to bring me here. Before the storm closed in around us tonight, we saw many sails on the northern horizon; if they have not foundered—as I feared for a while I might do!—they may be in Arfon by now. And that," said Neirin bluntly, "is all my tale, Lord King."

"And for it I owe you much," said Rhun, smiling, "which I will presently repay. Any loss of goods or gear you have suffered in my cause I will amend as well, so far as I am able. Do you ride with me in the morning?"

"I do," said Neirin firmly, and his eyes went briefly to Taliesin, who nodded. "I have made my choice, bitter though it was, and by all the Gods, I will stand by it!"

"I expected no less," said Rhun. "Go then and get you what rest you may, for by the One God, you look in need of it!" He smiled, showing big yellow teeth in his grizzled red beard. "I will see you—both of you!—at dawn, when I ride to Arfon!"

Later, as we lay in our blankets in the guesthouse, with Taliesin already asleep nearby, Neirin said softly to me, "I have been a fool."

"Na, you may have been many things, brother, but not that," I said. "The blame does not lie with you, but with the one who deceived you."

Neirin gave a short laugh. "Well," he said after a moment, "that is as may be, but I will not be for trusting him again, blood kin or no." And with that he turned on his side and sighed, and sleep took him. But I lay awake for a long while pondering the mind and the motivations of Clydno Eidyn.

The war-band had left at dawn, and Taliesin and Neirin rode with them—not as warriors, but as advisors to the King, and ambassadors should the need arise. I had watched their departure disconsolately, then turned back to loading our gear on the pack-ponies. At least I would not be the only one leading a pack-string that day. Soldiers and kings alike might travel light, and food and drink be requisitioned locally, but tents and camp-kettles, extra spears and shields, not to mention gear and clothing for the King and his officers, must all be transported somehow, and wagons fared poorly on the mountain tracks. With our party also would come the King's judge and his priest, his physician and his steward, and all the other officers who made up his court—for where King Rhun was, was the center of Gwynedd.

The day was fine after the storm, the sky a high soft blue with only a few retreating scraps of cloud, and all around us the land was clad in the rich greens of early summer. We first went south along the east bank of the Conwy as far as the old ford at Caerhun. This usually marked the top of the Conwy's tidal range, but the moon being new, the tides were at their highest, and we were glad to cross at half-tide in mid-morning. Splashing through the wide brown river, we set our sights on the mountain wall ahead and began to climb, following the course of the Romans' old road. I tried to imagine what it would have been like to march with those armies, up a stone-paved road, string-straight, which had room for five full-armed men to pass abreast. Even now, many men's lifetimes after its makers had abandoned it to the seasons, it was still a good road, and much used.

As we climbed higher, we began to see flocks of gray and brown sheep with their white lambs frisking about them, and herds of sturdy red cattle with their calves at suck, all grazing here in their summer pastures under the watchful eyes of their herders. Now and again we passed clusters of huts, dark-thatched with heather and bracken above ancient dry-stone walls, where black-haired women with their infants at their breasts watched us from the doorways, and small half-naked boys and girls ran beside us calling out questions. The pack-men called back, throwing joking answers to the children and words of admiration to the women, and garnered a harvest of laughter in return. Then we were past the huts and heading on toward the pass, with only the sheep-cropped slopes rising to the sky on either hand.

At the top of the Ddeufaen Pass we met Rhun's rear-guard, ten or twelve men sent back to give us instructions and escort. The Men of the North, they said, were ravaging here and there as opportunity served, and the King had no mind that his supply train should fall prey to them. As might be expected, this duty was less than pleasing to the soldiers. They had spent the day lounging in the shadows of the two boundary stones which gave the Pass its name, sleeping or playing knucklebones as the whim took them, but they were glad when our train appeared and they could saddle up and go.

The leader of the troop was a lean, ugly young man some few years older than I, whose straw-pale hair and beard suggested Irish blood—or Saxon!—but whose accent was pure Gwynedd, with the nasal intonation of Ynys Môn. Gwyn mab Dafydd, I think his name was, but everyone called him Blaidd—*Wolf*, in the common tongue—for his big yellow dogteeth, which he showed frequently in a wide grin; and also, as I learned later, for his savagery in a fight. He took command of our party with the easy assurance of long practice, ordering us to our best advantage with the most valuable part of the pack train in the center, and most of his fighting men ahead or behind. The King's officers and dependants were allotted their own places depending on their fighting abilities. After a surprisingly short period of milling about in confusion, we moved off again in our new order. I was pleased to find myself near the head of the line now, with a better view of the country and less dust. I loosened my sword in its scabbard and looked around eagerly as I rode, half-hoping for a chance to distinguish myself.

Once through the pass, the road bent left-handed, following the contour of the hill, while on our right the land dropped away steeply toward the sea. As we rode, the north end of Ynys Môn gradually came into sight, her low green fields hazy with distance, and the Laven Sands showing golden through the sparkling turquoise waters of the Menai strait that lay between us. On our side of the channel most of Arfon was still hidden by the hill itself, and by the bulky outliers of Moel Wnion to the south. Rather to my disappointment, it seemed a peaceful enough landscape, with no signs of burning crops or homesteads. I said as much to Blaidd, when he walked his horse past me after one of his periodic checks on the rear-guard, and he laughed.

"Na, na," he said, "it is not on this northern shore they would have landed, not with the storm we had last night doing its best to drive them onto the Sands in the black darkness. They will have set their course toward Ireland instead, and weathered Ynys Môn, and come ashore somewhere near Caer Seint in the green dawn. Trust me, once around Moel Wnion, you will see smoke enough! Thanks be to God, they have come early in the summer when the corn is still too green to burn, or they could have done us greater damage than they have."

"Will we be reaching Caer Seint today?" I asked.

"Na, my orders are to keep you all safe at Aber tonight, unless the King sends to tell me otherwise," said Blaidd, grinning. "He has gone on himself to Caer Seint, where the war-bands will be joining him tomorrow. Then we will crush these God-curst Northerners in short order, and drive them into the sea!" And with a friendly nod he rode on up the line, leaving me to ponder his words. Taliesin and Neirin, I thought, would be expecting their gear and goods tonight, not tomorrow. And I did not care to feel like a child or a woman, being guarded lest I come to harm, I who had ridden once into battle and killed two men with my ash spear alone. The sun was still high in the afternoon sky, and it would be light very late; and this part of the road I knew well, having traveled it only two months ago on our way to Caer Lêb. So I rode, pondering adventures.

It was late in the afternoon, however, before we came to the King's *llys* at Aber of the White Shells. Wood-built like Aberffraw, but none the worse for that, it lay at the mouth of a steep-sided valley where the little Afon Aber reaches the coastal plain. I admit I was glad to arrive, for we had not stopped for food that day, but only made do with bread and cheese as we rode, and my belly was growling with emptiness. Like the other packmen, I unsaddled my ponies and led them to water, then turned them out into the paddock near the *llys*. Our gear I stored in a protected corner of the crowded stables—no guesthouse room for me here!—and made my way to the hall with my blankets, still turning over in my mind my half-formed plans for the evening. But the rich smells of roasting meat and fresh-baked bread brought the warm water into my mouth and gave my thoughts another direction, and maybe saved me much pain.

Einion Goch, the King's man who held Aber for Rhun in his absence, was standing near the central hearth taking reports from

Blaidd and some others of the *teulu* as I came in. A stocky gray-bearded *uchelwr* who looked to have been a fighting man himself in his youth, he was familiar to me from my previous visit; but as one of the least of our prestigious company, I did not expect to be recognized or remembered, and I was surprised when presently a serving-man appeared beside me and said that his lord wished to speak with me. Einion was still in earnest conversation with the soldiers as I approached, so I paused, watching and listening, and glad of an excuse to do so.

"...drove off all the horses and fired the thatch behind them," one of the *teulu* was saying, a wiry black-haired lad with a blood-soaked rag bound around his upper left arm. "Three of the bondsmen cut down in the fields that we saw, and maybe others taken prisoner. The few who were left could not be telling us for sure, so mazed of wit they were."

"Gathering mounts and remounts," said Einion to no one in particular, and then to Blaidd beside him, "Bring all the horses and pack-ponies inside the stockade tonight—picket them wherever there is room—and double the watch on the gate." And to the others again, "Did you see any of them?"

"Na," said the boy with the wounded arm, and the rest shook their heads, agreeing. "Only their tracks, and their handwork. Eight or ten at most, we thought—maybe less. But there will be more."

"How far away was it?" asked Blaidd, frowning.

"Two or three miles at least, in the edge of the forest," said the boy.

"Gruffudd's land," said Einion, and another man nodded. "That will be the smoke we saw this afternoon. Anything else?" And when the boy shook his head, "Go and get your arm dressed then, Gwrgi, and the rest of you can help with the picket lines." Then as the men nodded and walked away, he saw me still waiting and beckoned. "You, lad—were you not here before, two moons ago, with the bards?"

"Yes, Lord," I said, coming up to him. "I was. I told a story for you that night, a tale of King Arthur."

"Hmm—yes," said Einion. "I think I remember something of it. Do you be telling us some tales in the hall tonight, then, if you will—something to amuse us and make us laugh."

"Gladly, Lord," I said, and Einion nodded and turned away to speak to another of his servants. I sighed to myself, and went to see what was happening with the ponies. It seemed that my choice had been made for me, after all. Taliesin and Neirin would have to wait until tomorrow for their gear—and maybe that was just as well.

I told three tales in the hall that night, and none of them had I learned from my masters. Instead, they were light stories, things I had heard or overheard on my travels, and dressed now in better language for the *uchelwyr* and the *teulu*. I cannot even call them to mind after all this time, but I remember the ringing laughter in the hall that night, and how it warmed me like strong mead. I got me, too, rewards beyond my expectation. Einion Goch paid me in silver at the end of my performance, and that was pleasant; but better by far were the smiles of the little dark serving girl who brought me a measure of ale when I sat down again at last, and stayed with me afterwards to help me drink it. And if her sweet shape reminded me somewhat of my girl back home—why, that did not stop me kissing her, and making the most of my chances, then and later. To have got a girl to myself, in that hall full of lusty soldiers, seemed a small miracle to me, and I have never believed in turning away the gifts of the Gods.

It was only afterwards, on the edge of sleep, that I remembered Taliesin and Neirin again, and wondered how they were faring. I found out soon enough, of course.

But that, O my children, is a story for another day.

Arfon in Flames

I had been lucky in my childhood, though I did not know it at the time; our local Prince Brochfael Ysgithrog and his successor Cynan Garwyn were both of them stark men whom their neighbors took good care to leave alone, and until the previous summer I had seen nothing worse than a few cattle raids. But exchanging awkward spear-casts in the summer twilight with the lads of the neighboring *cantref* while running off a few of their young heifers, or even riding down a band of half-awake Saxon raiders in the gray dawn—as Neirin and I had done with his uncle in Elmet the summer before—is no more like full-fledged warfare than a brief summer shower is like the winter tempest which drowns wide valleys and lays whole forests low. Now that I am old and have seen the worst of it, I know that warfare is no game, but every young man has to get that lesson for the first time—supposing that he lives long enough to learn it. So it was with me.

Our party spent the night peacefully enough at Aber, and were up with the dawn. Once the ponies were fed and watered, and everyone had snatched a quick breakfast in the hall, the grooms and packers and I set about preparing our beasts for travel, while Blaidd ranged about the courtyard encouraging us to hurry. He had us all out of the gates of the *llys* and onto the road south before the sun was well up over the mountains. The day was fresh and fine, the larks were singing in the meadows and the gulls crying from the shore, and most of us—I especially!—were in a good mood. I noticed, however, that our escort was larger today, and more alert. It did not take me long to see why.

Before we had ridden a mile, the clean morning air had acquired a taint of burning. It came from the forest edge to the east of us, where tendrils of dark smoke were wafting from the trees, like the last traces of a dying fire. At Blaidd's orders two of the soldiers left our party and went galloping off along a track which led toward the source of the smoke, but they were soon back, shaking their heads. We had not stopped to wait for them, but after hearing their reports, Blaidd sent them on ahead to scout the road while he himself ranged back along our party to make sure there were no stragglers. I was near the front of the group again, and pleased at the time to stay there, for I was still looking forward to a fight. Behind me I could hear the packers, who were less eager for trouble, muttering to each other.

Three more times as the morning wore on we passed burnt-out homesteads, two of them closer to the road—too close for my liking. We saw no people—no living ones, at least—but more than once disturbed the red kites and the meat-crows at their work. Those piles of torn flesh on which they were feeding had yesterday been men or women, cut down in the fields or left sprawling in the dirt beside the ashes of their homes: though it may be fit work for heroes, war is a filthy business, and only the young can truly love it well. Increasingly as we went, we found our road was littered with the dung of many beasts. Not all the cattle had been driven into the mountains for the summer, and most of those remaining must have fallen prey to the Northerners. Horses too they would want, having brought few or none in their ships. Where they had passed, they had stripped Arfon clean of both.

After some time the road swung inland, and we found ourselves in forest. Blaidd and his men redoubled their watchfulness, and even the stolid packmen grew silent: it was a fine place for an ambush. Suddenly around a corner ahead of us came our two scouts, returning at a gallop. They were waving and calling as they came, but even without words their message was clear. Blaidd looked over his shoulder. "Stop and make ready!" he shouted, and his soldiers passed the command back down the pack train, drawing their weapons as they did so. For myself, I had already reined my pack-ponies to a halt and was struggling to draw my sword, made clumsy by haste and excitement and inexperience. The sword was a good one, given to me by Neirin's uncle the summer before, and better by far than befitted my modest station, but I had only used it once in battle. The blade flashed silver-bright in the morning sunlight as I pulled it free, and I grinned despite myself. Then I looked down the road again in the direction from which the scouts had come—to see a flying skein of strange horsemen thundering toward us.

Six—eight—ten, I counted; it was hard to be sure in the shadows and the swirl of dust they were raising. I lifted my sword, trying to remember what I had learned the summer before and wishing I had a shield. Under me my black pony danced in sudden nervousness, feeling my excitement, and I tried to calm him. Blaidd and his men had intercepted the first of the raiders, but some had slipped past on either side. One of them was coming straight toward me. I twisted in the saddle to meet him, but Du was having none of it, and I realized too late that the pack-ponies' lead rope was still looped around my left wrist, pulling me off-balance. The raider, a big burly red-bearded man in dark wool and stained leather, was almost upon me. His sword arm rose and started to descend in the slashing stroke that would take off my head if it landed, his blade shining in the sunlight as it came down. I tried to get my own sword into position to block the blow, but I knew I was moving too slowly. He was going to hit me... I was going to die, here and now.

It was Du who saved me. Whether because I kicked him accidentally as I twisted to keep my balance, or for some other reason of his own, he suddenly jumped forward. The pack-ponies, on the other hand, did not move, and I was pulled sideways out of the saddle by their lead rope. As I started to fall, I jerked up my right hand, still clutching my sword. The red-bearded man's descending blade met it and knocked it spinning, but it had deflected his blow just enough to miss me. Then, as he passed on with a thunder of hooves, Du gave another jump, and I fell off—fortunately not on the sword. By the time I could untangle myself from the snorting pack-ponies and pick up my weapon again, the fight was over, and the surviving raiders were clattering off along the road in the direction from which they had come.

I had fallen very awkwardly, and my left arm and shoulder were wrenched and painful, having been nearly dislocated by my clutch on the lead rope. In truth, I was lucky not to have broken my neck, though I did not think so at the time. But these hurts, not to mention the bruises on other parts of my body, were nothing compared to the wound to my self-esteem. So much, I thought, shakily mopping the blood one-handed from my grazed face and bleeding nose, so much for riding like Cuchulainn to war. Fortunately everyone else had been too busy to notice my antics. As it was, I sheathed my sword clumsily and stood leaning against Du— who fortunately had stopped as soon as he felt me fall off—while Blaidd got his party back in order. Two of our attackers were dead, and one of our escort as well—a man I had shared a joke with in the courtyard only that morning—and there were other men among us more or less badly wounded. Bruised though I was, I was lucky.

"Be you hurt, lad?" one of the packers asked. I looked up and shook my head, hoping that my tears did not show, and he turned back to his string. Painfully, using my left arm as little as I might, I pulled myself back onto my black pony, and catching the lead rope again, waited for the order to start. I could see it was going to be a long day.

By the time we reached Caer Seint that afternoon, we had survived two more attacks, each more determined than the last, and I had seen enough of burning homesteads and dead men to satisfy my thirst for war. Yet that was only the beginning. The Men of the North had ridden through Arfon like the Wild Hunt, killing and plundering at will, until Rhun came down upon them with his *teulu* and what men he had gathered on his way. Then the slaughter was more equal, and many a Northerner left his body to feed the ravens, and his bones to fertilize green Gwynedd fields. But in those first days Rhun had not yet enough men with him to sweep Arfon clean of marauders. The four Northern lords had brought each of them a hundred men and more, and if it had come to a pitched battle Rhun himself might have ended as food for crows. I think Clydno would have kept his allies together if he could, but Rhydderch Hael and his wild cousins had no such discipline, and scattered each in pursuit of his own violent ends. So Rhun and his troop had punched through their ragged cordon, killing as they came, and relieved the hard-pressed garrison at Caer Seint. Neirin told me something of it—he and Taliesin had kept close to the King on that wild ride, and bloodied their own swords; Neirin indeed had done much slaughter.

"Na, I do not know how many I killed," he said to me that evening, shaking his head at the memory. "I was not for stopping to count, not then. I struck until my arm was weary, and glad I was to see the walls of Caer Seint!"

"Did Taliesin fight?" I asked, glancing across the crowded hall to where he sat close beside the King, looking slight and dark as ever among the burly battle-stained warriors. "Somehow, I did not think…"

"Na, he can use steel when he must," said Neirin, following my gaze. "It is only that he prefers not to. He told me once that he saw enough bloodshed at Camlann fight to content him for many lives."

"Mmm," I said. "I am always forgetting he was there. It seems so long ago—before you or I were born or thought of… Well, and then?"

"They had burned the town already," said Neirin, "everything along the harbor, and set fire to the gates here—well, you saw that when you rode in!—and forced the garrison back into the inner *caer*. Some of them had already driven a herd of stolen cattle into the outer fortress, and slaughtered a few, and they were busy building their cook-fires when we came down upon them. We are eating some of that cow-meat now—where they have gone, they will not miss it!" And he grinned, and stuffed another piece of it into his mouth. For sure, it was good cow-meat, probably from a young bullock, tasty and tender, and well-roasted on the big iron spits in the kitchen courtyard. Despite my still-painful shoulder, I laughed and followed Neirin's example, washing the meat down with good brown ale, and we spoke no more of fighting for a while.

I had hoped my sprains and bruises would subside overnight, but when I tried to roll out of my blankets the next morning, I found I could hardly move, and gave such a groan that I attracted Taliesin's attention. He felt me over and told me there was nothing broken, but that it would be some time before I had much use of my left arm again. His hands were strong and gentle, and seemed to take away some of the pain where they touched, and he made me a sling for my arm and told me to keep it there. I would have liked to ride out with Neirin, who was planning to join the King on his forays, but Taliesin said with a smile that I had done enough fighting already, and needed to look to my lessons, lest we both be shamed before Talhaearn at summer's end. It was not to be a warrior, after all, that I had followed him on this trail. I sighed, but knew he was right, and thereafter was kept busy at my poetic measures. As Neirin pointed out to me afterwards, it was never any use arguing with Taliesin: he would always win.

As his reinforcements arrived, Rhun began to scour the country from his base at Caer Seint, but his opponents were elusive. He was one and they were four, and it was not in their interests to come to pitched battle with him. Even when he tried to sweep them into the Lleyn peninsula, where their ships were anchored, they evaded him and struck again in Arfon and Ynys Môn. It was like trying to fight a swarm of stinging wasps; and all the time they went on laying waste to the countryside, until there was hardly a village or a homestead without its burnt-out buildings and fresh graves.

Three days after my arrival, it was Neirin's turn to come to grief. Despite Taliesin's disapproval, he had been riding out each day with Rhun, and I knew he was hoping for a chance to serve as a Green Branch herald between Gwynedd and the Men of the North, feeling himself still somehow to blame because of the failure of his earlier diplomacy. Near the King, however, was a perilous place to be in the fighting, and that day Neirin found how perilous. I was watching from the gate-tower at Caer Seint when they rode in that evening, and saw him, slumped in his saddle and almost last in the line of weary men. The torn woolen rag wrapped around his left thigh was juicy-wet with dark blood, and his face below his iron-bound leather cap was white and sweating with pain. But he was less concerned for his own injuries than for his gray pony, who had suffered a shallow gash along his ribs from the same spear-stroke.

Only after he had seen Brith fed and watered and salved did Neirin consent to have his own wound tended, and let me help him back afterwards to our guesthouse room, joking as we went that the two of us were a fine pair, with three sound legs and three sound arms between us. The wound was deep and ragged and slow to heal, and left him limping painfully and unable to ride for many days. So the three of us sat in Caer Seint and talked, and entertained Rhun whenever he returned from the field, and the war dragged on toward midsummer.

It was about this time that I saw my old friend Ieuan again. I came across him on some errand in the camp—the outer fortress at Caer Seint was now all tents and horse-lines and rough-thatched, broken-down barrack-blocks for Rhun's levies as it had been when we hosted there before Beltane, with only the King and his officers and our fortunate selves housed in the inner fort. I almost did not recognize Ieuan at first, for his face was thinner and set in a permanent frown, and there was more gray in his beard than I remembered. "Ieuan!" I said. "Is the Lord Cadwaladr here?"

"Na, he bides at home," said Ieuan, "keeping our defenses— what is left of them. I am here only as a messenger to the King."

"Did they strike at Caer Lêb, then?" I asked. "I heard there had been raids on Ynys Môn. Is—have you had many losses?" I could not bring myself to mention his girl Anwen and their baby son; I had seen too many burnt-out homesteads and too many dead on my ride south.

"Na, not yet," said Ieuan, "but by the One God, it was a near-run thing!"

"Come back to the hall with me, and tell me over a cup of ale," I said. "Have you the time?"

Ieuan wavered visibly. "I should be going, but…riding in the sun is thirsty work. Yes, I can spare you a little time, and still catch the ferry." And with that he turned and followed me to the court.

In the feast-hall I found a servant who brought us bread and cheese and ale, and we settled down at one of the trestle tables to eat and drink. It was mid-afternoon, and most of the fighting men were out with Rhun, trying yet again to come to grips with the Northerners, so we had the place to ourselves. In the shadowy darkness of the hall the lines on Ieuan's face showed less, and he seemed more like the man I had known in my boyhood in Pengwern, not so many years ago. A quiet man he had been in those days, a refugee from the Saxon inroads to the east, with little to say about his past. A man full-grown even then, he had kept himself to himself, and if he had gone with a women now and again, he had taken none to wife. To a boy, the people he grows up with have always been as they are, and I had thought nothing of it. Now as a man I wondered for the first time what Ieuan's life had been before the Saxons came; but this, I thought, was not the time for asking. "Tell me," I said instead, "what happened at Caer Lêb?"

Ieuan sat staring into his ale-cup for some moments, then looked up and met my eyes, his own shadowed with more than the dimness of the hall. "It was," he said deliberately, "a little piece of Hell—of what the priests tell us Hell is like, at least. They came at night, when we were all asleep, all of us except the watchman—may his soul rest in peace! He gave the alarm, and paid for it with his blood. The gate was closed and barred, but they came with fire— fire for the timbers of the gate, fire for the thatch of the hall, and the byres... They came trailing fire from their torches, and yelling like fiends from Hell." He closed his eyes for a moment, as if in pain.

"Did they break in, over the walls?" I asked, remembering those low grassy mounds of stone.

"Na," said Ieuan, opening his eyes again. "The Lord Cadwaladr has kept us busy this last moon since you were there, strengthening our defenses. Our walls are higher and stronger than they were when you saw them last, and our spears and bows were ready to hand. They did not break through the gate despite their fire, and their torches served as targets for our arrows. But without our defenses we would have been overrun, murdered in our beds or dragged away to slavery..." He shook his head as if shaking off memories. "As it was, they lost more men than we did, and I think will not be back. Most of our horses and some of our best cows were inside the walls, but not all of them. The Lord Cadwaladr led a troop, gathered from all the free farmers in our area, which followed the cattle thieves the next day. We caught them before they could cross the Menai with their plunder, and cut many of them down before they could escape..."

"That is good hearing," I said. "I am glad you came through it safely."

Ieuan's face relaxed in an almost-smile. "So too am I!" he said. "The Lord Cadwaladr sent me with a report to the King, and I was glad to come. My Lord may be leading a war-band from Môn to join Rhun here, and in that case I may see you again soon enough." He drained his cup and stood up. "Now I must go, if I am to catch the tide."

"May your God go with you, then," I said, rising as well. "And give my best wishes to Anwen, and little Gwernin. Tell her—tell her I will be a father soon, too!"

"*Sa, sa,*" said Ieuan, grinning. "That is news indeed. Yes, I will tell her, lad. She will be pleased... I think at last you begin to be a man!" And with that we left the hall, and he went on his way.

Two or three evenings after that, Taliesin provided the spark which was to end the siege of Arfon; and being Taliesin, he did it with a song. All that day he had been quiet and withdrawn, brooding inwardly on some idea, so that Neirin and I took ourselves to another part of the fortress and left him alone. The day before, one of Rhun's war-bands had been badly cut up in an ambush; several of the men came back tied to their saddles, and some came back not at all. The sky to the south and east of Caer Seint was dark with the smoke of burning, and I knew that soon the ripening grain—such of it as had not been trampled by horsemen—would be able to carry fire. There began to be mutterings in the camp and in the court, and men's faces were bitter and weary. Arfon could not stand much more of this destruction.

That night before we went to the hall, Taliesin said to Neirin, "Bring your harp with you this evening, Little Hawk, and play while

I sing, if you will."

"Gladly," said Neirin. "But what shall I play?"

"You will know," said Taliesin, and for once he did not smile. Neirin's eyebrows quirked up in surprise, but he made no comment, merely picking up his leather harp case. I followed them in curiosity, wishing my sprained arm would heal faster so that I might play again. I had prepared a tale instead—one of my Cuchulainn pieces—but in the event I did not have a chance to use it.

After everyone had satisfied his first hunger that night, Taliesin stood up to sing, and such was his manner that all eyes turned immediately toward him, and a growing silence spread through the hall. He glanced once around his audience, then turned to Rhun and began his song. Under his words Neirin's harp-strings beat the time like spears crashing on shields before battle.

> "Fire in the night, so baleful-bright burning,
> weapon or guardian, killer or friend—
> fire in the night, now ripe for returning,
> shall with its fury this ravaging end!
>
> In the long war twixt the Greek and the Trojan lands,
> Troy's brave war-leader, his people to save,
> charged with his hearth-friends one night bearing fire-brands
> to burn the Greek ships where they rode on the waves.
>
> Fire in the night...
>
> 'Burn the black ships!' he cried, 'burn them and sink them!
> Then all the Greeks will die here on our shore,
> or wearing our slave chains, rebuild what they've broken,
> home to their cities returning no more!'
>
> Fire in the night..."

By the second chorus, men had begun to beat on the tables in time to the song, and Rhun began to smile. And Taliesin sang on:

> "Charged then the Trojan men—had they succeeded,
> their city unsacked would still stand fair and free.
> Stronger and braver, fierce Rhun and his war-bands
> can conquer our enemies now by the sea!
>
> Fire in the night...

'Burn the black ships!' I cry, 'burn them and sink them!'
End now the burning of Arfon and Môn!
Right-line of Cunedda, conquer your cousin-kind!
Rich with their red blood our beaches will run!

Fire in the night now, so baleful-bright burning,
a spear in your strong right hand, thrusting and keen!
Fire in the night for their ship-timbers yearning
now with its fury our land can burn clean!
Go, take your torches, and follow King Rhun!"

The thudding accompaniment came to an uneven end when Taliesin stopped, and for a moment there was almost silence; then the hall broke into an applause which seemed to shake the roof beams. I saw hope and understanding in Neirin's face, and a hardening purpose in Rhun's. He nodded once to Taliesin, then stood up. "Men," he said, and the hall fell silent again to hear him, "the Pencerdd has spoken truth, and shown us the way to victory. Now we must plan how to seize it. In the morning we will not ride out as usual, but meet here for a council. Then tomorrow evening we will carry fire to the ships in Lleyn, and end this scourge from the North forever!" And beckoning Taliesin to him, Rhun pulled a gold bracelet from his own arm, and set it on the bard's wrist with a few soft words. And in the King's face was a fierce eagerness, but beneath his usual smile Taliesin's face was sad, with a sadness which I only later came to understand and to share.

But that, O my children, is a story for another day.

Fire in the Night

The one flaw in Rhun's plan was the phase of the moon: she was full. When we walked out of the feast-hall that evening, I saw her high in the eastern sky, a great globe of silver swimming amidst the pale stars and pouring her pure light like balm on the wounded countryside. The great fortress lay quiet around us in the mild summer night, with only muted voices here and there showing where a few weary men were still awake. In the stillness I could clearly hear the distant hushing of waves on the shore, the cries of the nighthawks circling above us, and the high thin squeaks of the bats as they pursued their insect prey. The smoke of the field kitchens still hung lazy and pungent in the air, but the smolder from the burning in the south and east was hidden by darkness.

Outside the door to our quarters Taliesin stopped. "Go in now, if you wish," he said to the two of us. "I think I will walk for a while before I sleep." The moonlight washed all color and detail from his face, making it a white oval framed by the blackness of his hair and beard, in which his eyes gleamed darkly, but I thought from his voice that he was weary. In the hall that night he had been all fire, like the fire of his song; now that fire had sunk to gray ash and embers.

"I am thinking I will go in," said Neirin with a grimace. "*Hai mai!* Will this leg never heal?" I had noticed he was limping worse again that evening, having overtaxed himself during the day. Taliesin chucked.

"Certainly it will not heal the slower for being rested," he said, with a certain gentle emphasis on *slower*. "Gwernin, do you go in with him now and help him salve it. You know which ointment to use?"

I nodded. "The one in the green jar, with comfrey and milfoil in it." I was remembering my herb-lore, such as it was, and knew the scent well. No more than a moon ago, I had watched Rhiannedd making just such a ointment, her slender white hands strong and sure on the mortar and pestle, grinding the herbs… "Master," I said abruptly, "what about the moon?"

Taliesin looked up at the sky consideringly, and half-lifted a hand, as if to grasp and weigh a palm-full of her pale light. "I think…there will be clouds by tomorrow," he said slowly. "Listen to the sea… There is a storm on the way." Suddenly he smiled. "Go in now, lads," he said to us. "I will not be gone long, but I have…things to do, before I sleep." And turning, he walked away from us toward the gate of the inner fortress, and vanished into its shadows without a sound, even the light crunch of his footsteps on the gravel of the yard swallowed up by the darkness. Neirin and I looked at each other and shrugged, and went in reluctantly to our cramped and stuffy room. But though the salving and re-bandaging of the wound took some time, and though afterwards we lay awake for a long while drowsily talking, we were both asleep before Taliesin returned.

He had been right about the cloud. By the time we rose and went to the feast-hall for breakfast, a thin sheet of it covered the sky, half-veiling the midsummer sun. A small, fickle wind was blowing, now from the north, now from the west, and the gulls were crying loudly above the harbor. I saw Taliesin glance up at the sky and nod to himself before we went inside, but he said no word. He did not look, however, as if he had slept well when he finally came to bed: he was pale under his summer tan, and the lines in his face seemed graven deeper than usual.

The feast-hall was full and over-full that morning, what with all of Rhun's under-kings and *uchelwyr* and their captains, and they were all of them talking very loudly. We found ourselves seats near the foot of one of the long trestle tables, and Neirin grabbed a basket of flat wheaten cakes before someone else could snatch them away. I managed to catch a dish of fresh cheese as it was passed, and a serving-maid brought us cups and a pitcher of small ale. Neirin's wide grin and words of thanks drew a quick smile from her, before she scurried away and we settled down to eating.

The King was already in his seat at the high table, and deep in conversation with his *penteulu* and some other members of his retinue. A parchment was spread on the table before them—a map of some kind, perhaps—and they seemed to be pointing at spots on it. A stack of other papers and wax tablets littered the board, and a clerk was taking notes on one of the latter. A tall young man with curly brown hair whom I remembered from Aberffraw and Deganwy was standing behind Rhun, looking over his shoulder: Beli mab Rhun, the King's oldest living son. He had not come with Rhun's war-band or with our baggage train, but had arrived later, bringing reinforcements from Gwynedd-Is-Conwy beyond the mountains. Yesterday he had been out leading a scouting troop to the south. Now he leaned forward and pointed with one square-tipped brown finger at a spot on the map, and said something I could not catch. The other men looked, and then nodded, and the discussion went on.

Presently the lists were finished, the map was rolled up and stacked with the other documents, and the King's Silencer struck the pillar beside him with his iron-shod staff and called for quiet in the hall. It was none too soon; the babble of talk and scraping of benches had been steadily rising as men finished their breakfasts and grew restless. Now as the noise subsided, a boy appeared beside us, saying that the King wanted the bards. Taliesin, who had long since finished his meal, nodded and stood up, and made his way through the thickening crowd toward the King's high seat with Neirin limping after him. I tagged along behind them, trying to look as if I were summoned, too. A little way short of the high table, I stopped and worked my way through the impatient throng to the side of the hall. When I found a spot where I could both see and hear reasonably well, I leaned my shoulders against the smoke-stained wooden wall and waited. I did not have long to wait.

Rhun stood up, a tall burly figure, his grizzled hair and beard shining red in the torchlight. He looked the crowd over for a moment, waiting until he had absolute silence before he began. "Men," he said, "those of you who were in this hall last night will have heard Taliesin's song; those of you who were not will have heard of it by now. He tells us to carry fire to our enemies' ships and burn them, and he is right to do so. If they know that they cannot get home by sea, all the treasure they have ripped from our land will be to no avail to them: we can block the passes and the narrow road along the north coast, and trap them here in Gwynedd. They must come to terms then, or die here: we will have them by the stones, and when we squeeze, they will scream!"

A roar of approval went up from the crowd, but Rhun lifted a hand, and they grew quiet again. "Our only challenge now," he said, "is how to come at those ships. My scouts tell me that most of them are anchored off-shore—not far off-shore, but too far for a land assault to surprise them. This means our attack must be in two parts: first, a land attack by night, not driven home, but serious enough to draw their attention; and secondly, a sea attack by a small force to seize and fire the ships. I want to organize both of these today if I can, so that Arfon will not suffer their attacks one hour longer than needed." There were shouts of agreement again, but Rhun overrode them. "Our only problem was the full moon, which might have betrayed us: and see, God has sent us cloud to veil her light! We have only to settle the details of our plans, and by tomorrow we will have them in our trap. War-leaders, stay here with me now; the rest of you, go to your camps, and make sure no man leaves this fortress unless I send him." He nodded once, then showed his teeth in a grin that was half snarl. "That is all."

In the ensuing tumult, I worked my way back toward Taliesin and Neirin, who were standing not far from the King. "What next?" I asked. "Do we stay, or go?"

"I must stay," said Taliesin. "You may stay or go as you wish, Gwernin. It will be a long day, and much of it tedious, while they work out the details... Rhun will have sent out orders already to gather boats from all along the coast. They will need larger ones to cover the distance around the Lleyn quickly, and smaller ones to approach the ships unseen. His own ship was at Aberffraw, I think, but should be here soon."

"*Hai mai!*" said Neirin, grinning. "You have all the details at your fingertips as usual—I am not knowing why the King needs war-leaders when he has you!"

"To lead their war-bands in battle, and to fight," said Taliesin half-seriously, looking at the huddle near the King. "I can only give them ideas—they must do the work."

"Was it so when you were with Arthur?" I asked, greatly daring. Taliesin looked at me for a long moment, and his eyes were dark with memories.

"Sometimes," he said, and turned away.

It was, as he had prophesied, a long and sometimes tedious day, but it was also in many ways an interesting one, and I learned much before it was over. This was another face of war, this slow and detailed fitting together of men and materials and knowledge—reports on the enemy's dispositions and strengths and movements—while planning how best to deny him the same knowledge of our own plans. From time to time there were breaks, as one man and another got up to stretch or to go outside and relieve himself; food and drink was brought by silent servants, to be consumed by men who had hardly noticed thirst or hunger. Messengers came and went, carrying tidings of the enemy or orders for the scouts. Sometimes Taliesin would be drawn into the discussion, but mostly he sat close beside the King, listening and now and then adding a word. Neirin had fetched his harp and sat nearby, playing softly on it from time to time, but so caught up in following the discussion that his hands seemed to be acting without his will or knowledge.

As Taliesin had said, there were boats to be gathered for the attack on the ships: small boats, coracles for the most part, to carry those who would attack and burn each vessel, larger ones to deliver the men and the coracles within striking range. There were sea-wise men—fishermen or crofters—needed to paddle the coracles and fight any crews that might be on the ships. These were not hard to come by, for the shore-dwellers had suffered much from the invaders, and were eager to strike a blow in return. They would be equipped with firepots or dark lanterns, and torches or grease-soaked rags to be lit at the last minute. All of this body of men and equipment must be moved to the right place and kept there undetected until the land assault began.

The men who would deliver that assault were in the outer fortress now, making ready their gear and horses and snatching what rest they might before evening. Starting at dusk, they would have a long ride to reach the raiders' camp on the south shore of the Lleyn before dawn, but Rhun was adamant that they not start sooner. Traveling by daylight, they might be seen by enemy scouts, which would warn the target that something was amiss, or they might even be intercepted by an equal or stronger force. All of our plan depended on surprise; once the enemy realized our intent, they could move their ships to a safer anchorage, or even embark their men and plunder and set sail, possibly striking again somewhere else along the coast. If we did not succeed tonight, there might be no second chance. This was why Rhun himself would be leading the attack.

"Na, there is no room for argument," he had said when the question arose. "I will not send men where I fear to go myself. It is the King's place to lead…" He looked at Taliesin. "Your old friend Talhaearn said that, or something like it, at Aberffraw back in the spring. '*He who would lead…*' "

" '*…let him be a bridge.*' Yes." Taliesin nodded. "I understand. And this is Midsummer Eve."

Rhun grinned suddenly. "So it is… Well, we will light such a Midsummer fire tonight as will not soon be forgotten, either in Arfon or the North, God willing!" And with that he turned back to his captains, and the planning went on.

At last everything was done that could be done. Rhun sent his captains to deliver their final orders to the war-bands, and to get what rest they could before dark. Then, as we all stood up and stretched, he turned to Taliesin again. "Font of Song," he said quietly, "will you ride with me tonight? Not to fight, but to watch, and to make the song afterwards. I only ask: I would not compel you if I could."

"Gladly," said Taliesin, and then to Neirin who stood beside them, "Little Hawk?"

Neirin grinned. "How not?" he said. And to Rhun, "Yes, I will ride with you as well, Lord King: I have thrown in my lot with Gwynedd in this war, as I told you at Deganwy."

Rhun smiled at that. "Then I am content. Go, both of you, make ready, and take such rest as you can: so will I now do likewise. I will see you at sunset."

As we walked back to our lodgings, Taliesin said, "Gwernin, can you prepare our horses and gear for us while we rest?"

"Gladly, Master," I said, "but may I not come too?"

"I—think not," said Taliesin. "This will be a grueling ride, with a desperate fight at the end."

"I have ridden far, and fought hard before," I said.

"Na, let him come with us," said Neirin. "I think we will none of us be fighting tonight."

"I will do as you bid, Master," I said pleadingly, "but only let me come, that I may see the fight and make a song of it myself one day."

Taliesin made a tutting noise with his tongue. "You will see little enough in the dark... Oh, very well. We will all get our gear ready, and then take what rest remains to us." He looked up at the sky, where the cloud had been growing steadily thicker all day. "And be sure to pack your rain-cloaks—you may have need of them before morning."

Afternoon was turning imperceptibly into evening beneath a heavy deck of dark-gray cloud when I led our three ponies into the courtyard. The rest we had got had not been long, but I at least was too excited to feel weary. The courtyard was very full of men and horses, in an orderly confusion of voices and neighing. I found a less-crowded corner near our lodging, and the three of us loaded our saddlebags and other gear onto our ponies. Neirin took especial care to make sure that his gray pony's wound—which had healed faster than his own—was not rubbed or chafed by any of his gear.

We were finishing our preparations when Rhun rode into the courtyard on his big red stallion. He was dressed for fighting in steel and leather, his helmet slung on one side of his saddle-bow and his round shield on the other like any of his captains; but his height and bulk would have made him stand out among the others even if the quality of his gear had not done so. He was grinning broadly as he came, greeting this man and that one, but he waved to us when he saw us.

Taliesin swung easily up on his red mare and walked her over join the King, while I went to gave Neirin a leg up. His healing wound was well bandaged, and his pony used to being mounted from either side, but it is not so easy to make the steed-leap with a game leg, as I knew well from my own past experience. Then it was my turn to scramble up onto Du. My sprained arm and shoulder were better, and I had discarded my sling some days ago, but mounting still cost me more than a few twinges. By the time I had dragged myself onto my pony, Neirin and Taliesin were speaking with the King. I made haste to join them.

"We will be starting soon," Rhun was saying as I rode up, "as soon as the scouts come back. Keep close behind me; I do not want to lose my bards in the darkness!" With that he set his horse in motion, heading for the gate of the inner fort and the muster outside. The King was taking two hundred men, less than half his available force, but enough to crush any roving band we might meet. That afternoon he had sent a few decoy troops out, not to engage the enemy but to shadow them at a distance, so that a sudden lack of opposition would not alarm them. Caer Seint he was leaving strongly manned—he could not afford to lose it—but a reinforcing troop was due to follow us the next day. The ships carrying the all-important fire boats had already started on their way south; now it was our turn.

The mounted war-bands were waiting for us in the outer fortress as we rode out, the last scouts just returning through the main gate. Rhun reined his stallion to a halt and looked them over, noting their readiness—two hundred blooded warriors, most of them young, sitting their tough mountain-bred ponies, their ash spears bristling like a barbed thicket and their helmets and round shields darkened for surprise. Then he addressed them, his big voice carrying easily to every man there. "Men of Gwynedd," he said, "you all know our mission. The blow we will strike tonight will lay the enemy at our mercy. For your homes and your herds and your kin, strike hard and true, and I will do the rest!" A deep-throated roar came back from the war-bands. Rhun waved his hand at them in acknowledgement, then turned his horse toward the gate, and all his men followed with a will.

What can I say of that long, dream-like ride? Despite the cloud cover, the slow midsummer twilight and the full moon above combined in a ghostly gray light through which we moved as shadows in a shadowy landscape. We had scouts out ahead, and an advance guard; but once we had splashed through the ford above Caer Seint we made little noise: now and then the ring of a bridle as a horse shook his head; a soft word of command passed back along the line; the smother of sound made by many unshod hooves on stony ground. We mostly moved at a walk, for secrecy was more precious to us than speed; when our road took us nearer to the coast, the booming of the surf was louder than any noise we made. The wind was getting up, too, first in little fretful puffs of salt-scented air, then in stronger gusts which now and then carried a spatter of raindrops. After a while, reaching behind me, I untied the thongs that held my leather rain-cape to the saddle and put it on; ahead of me I could see others doing the same.

When we turned away from the ocean, into the hills of the Lleyn, the sea-scent diminished, and the smells of damp horses and men, wet leather and wool, crushed grass and herbs, grew stronger to take its place. My pony's warmth beneath me was real, and the rhythmic shift of his muscles as he walked; my own body moving in time with his; and the sting of wind-blown raindrops on my right cheek. All the rest was ghosts, was shadows; tonight, it was we who were the wild hunt, the company of Annwn, on our way to wreak destruction on sleeping men. The sound of the rising wind covered our hoof-beats, and we moved on the wind, with the wind, as part of the night.

At one point I found myself riding beside Blaidd, he who had led our pack-train from Deganwy, a handful of days and a thousand years ago. He was back now in his usual place as part of the King's bodyguard, Rhun's own personal *teulu*. He turned his head to see who was riding beside him, and I saw the pale gleam of his eyes and his teeth as he grinned. "Well met, Storyteller," he said quietly. "Better hunting, this, than on the road from Aber."

"Well met, Blaidd," I said. "Yes, it is. How have you been faring?"

"None too ill," said Blaidd, still grinning. "I am alive, and five-and-ten Northerners are not. Tonight I hope to better my score." And he laughed, and his pony moved ahead of mine. My right hand went without thought to my sword and caressed her hilt. Maybe, maybe, I too…but probably not tonight.

The light was beginning to strengthen again, although sunrise was still far away, when we came to a halt in a brushy combe among low hills. There had been a few rest breaks during the night for horses to drink and men to get down and relieve themselves, but this pause was different; I could feel it. Around me the warriors were donning their helmets, loosening swords in their sheaths and taking up their shields. I found Taliesin and Neirin again, close by the King, and eased my pony up beside them. "What now?" I asked.

"Waiting to make contact with the scouts who have been watching the camp," said Neirin softly. "Ah, here they come." Two horsemen appeared quietly out of the trees and the thin salt-tinged morning mist, and joined the King. Presently the word was passed to be ready to move again: the camp was quiet, and the scouts had seen the signal from our ships off-shore. Then we rode on, up a gentle slope and along a flat-topped ridge—and there, before us, was the sea, with a dark cluster of ships anchored just beyond the low-tide range, and another darker cluster, barely to be seen, some way out. Below us, but still out of sight, was the enemy camp, on the far side of a little river. We started down the last slope, Rhun leading, and our horses broke into a trot as we went; then, as we hit the flat, into a canter. I heard Taliesin's voice somewhere behind me, calling my name; but my blood was up, and I did not stop. There was a yell ahead of us, suddenly cut off, as a sleepy sentry gave his last alarm. Rhun's full-throated battle cry of "Arfon!" answered him, and then we were all of us shouting. We bust yelling out of the last trees and splashed across a shallow ford, and there ahead of us was the enemy camp, and beyond it the sea. And on that sea, even as I looked, the anchored ships bloomed one by one with red-gold fire.

Then my pony crashed over the low thorn-brush barrier after the others, and I was into the fight, with confusion all around me. I swung the sword I did not remember drawing at an unmounted man; the blade bit home with a shock that jolted my arm, and I felt a warm splatter of blood on my wrist. Du carried me past, and I swung again at another shadowy figure. From the corner of my eye I could see the growing blaze off-shore, but had no time to look at it. My blade swung again and met steel; again my pony's speed carried me on. Then Du swerved and stumbled, and I almost came out of the saddle, saving myself only by a desperate clutch at his mane. Someone cut at me from my unshielded left, and I felt a burning pain in my leg; I swung at another man and hit him, and hot blood spattered my sword-hand. All around me was the deep-voiced shouting and screaming of men, the neighing of horses, the clang and crash of steel on steel. A shower of sparks went up from a campfire; there were thatched huts around me, some of them burning—the remains of a fishing village, taken over by the raiders for their base, their inhabitants slaughtered or fled. Fire and blood—fire on the sea—fire in the mist and around me wherever I looked—fire in my eyes and in my head—the whole world was on fire. I was shouting with exhilaration and anger and pain, and with the sheer drunken joy of battle. I saw a man running, and rode after him, and struck him down from behind so that he screamed and fell and rolled still screaming into a fire, and I rode on laughing. And on the sea every anchored ship burned bright as a torch, wrapped in flames from the deck to the masthead, and then vanished one by one, until the only ships left afloat were our own.

Then the shouting had stopped, and the red mist was gone, and I was sitting my weary pony in the gray dawn light, watching the windswept rain put out the smoldering thatch on a half-burnt fisher-hut and feeling the growing pain of more than one wound on my body. I wiped my bloody sword as well as I could on the sodden skirts of my tunic and sheathed it, and turned my pony back toward the ford, looking for my friends. Around me Rhun's soldiers were putting things to rights with practiced efficiency: picketing their horses, dragging bodies aside for burial, building up the cook-fires, rough-bandaging their own wounds. Here and there the last screams stopped abruptly, leaving an echoing silence in which I could hear the sound of the surf and the first distant croaks of the circling ravens, ready for their meal. Ahead of me I saw the King in the center of a group of horsemen, and recognized Taliesin and Neirin among the others. There was a reckoning waiting for me there, I knew it: I had been meant to watch this battle, not fight in it: but just for the moment I felt at one with Cuchulainn, and content.

But that, O my children, is a story for another day.

The Hostage

I was right about the reckoning, but not about its timing. Neirin, although sorely tempted, had sat out the battle with Taliesin, and had not seen much of it aside from the burning ships. "That," he had said wryly, while binding up the gashes in my hide, "was a sight well worth the seeing, for sure; but I am wishing I might have swung a sword with you as well, brother." Taliesin had said nothing, only looked at me with narrowed eyes and an unsmiling mouth: a thing which made me more uneasy than any threats of punishment. I would rather, on the whole, have been beaten then and there: but that was not his way. No doubt he had learned it as a boy from Talhaearn.

The three of us were sheltering from the rain in a corner of the largest surviving hut, where Rhun had established his headquarters. The first part of his plan for ridding Arfon of her tormentors had succeeded; now it was time for the second part. Only one of the northern leaders had been in their camp when we attacked: Mordaf mab Serfan, Rhydderch Hael's second cousin, now slowly dying of a belly-wound and no use as a hostage. Even if some of our enemies had escaped us in the darkness, it would be a while before they could carry the ill news to the other raiders, and Rhun did not intend to waste that time. Whatever loot had been already loaded on the burned ships was lost, but the fire parties had freed some captives, and more were found hiding in the village: mostly young women and boys, meant for the slave-ports of Ireland. There was also much spoil in the way of arms and armor, silver and jewels and other precious things. Part of this Rhun loaded onto his ships, together with the freed captives, and part he distributed among his war-band in the usual way.

Mordaf mab Serfan and a few other badly wounded prisoners who might yet be worth a ransom also went on the ships, together with our own wounded, while some of the men of the fire-parties came ashore to make more room. These Rhun could mount on captured horses, of which we had more than enough; the rest of the prisoners—there were not many—would be tied bare-back on their led mounts, their ankles roped beneath the horses' bellies and their wrists bound behind them: an uncomfortable position which would keep them too busy staying astride to leave much time for thoughts of escape.

In and around all these arrangements, men and horses had to be fed and rested, and a strong watch kept lest we be surprised in our turn. It was late afternoon before Rhun formed up his troops and we all set off again for Caer Seint: a dirty gray afternoon of wind and driving rain, more like early spring than mid-summer. Men rode huddled miserably in their cloaks; ponies slipped and slid in the trampled mud. Weariness and discomfort led to short tempers. My own wounds were aching, and I was hungry: no one had really had enough to eat that that day, not even the King. But Rhun and his soldiers had seen worse, and knew what they were about: scouts and outriders preceded and followed us, and despite the weather all the men kept alert.

This time we were not worrying about concealment; but there was no fast or easy path through the tangled hills and marshes of the Lleyn, and the light was fading toward evening when we reached Bwlch Derwin, the Oak-tree Gap where the Romans' old road coming up from the south skirts the great mountain mass of Eryri on its way to Caer Seint. As the King's party crested the low pass, I saw three of our scouts spurring up the muddy slope toward us. At a word from Rhun, his captains called a halt, and while the war-bands rested he and a few of his *teulu* trotted forward to meet the scouts. Taliesin and Neirin went with him, and I followed after them as a matter of course.

As the scouts drew nearer, I could see that the middle one of the three was wounded, swaying in the saddle as he came, while the two other men flanked him to catch him if he should fall. This he almost did as they drew rein, but fended off their helpful hands and pulled himself erect in the saddle. For a moment, what with the blood streaming down his face from a scalp wound, and his pale hair sodden-dark from the rain, I did not know him; then he showed his teeth in a grimace, and I recognized Blaidd.

"What news, man?" asked Rhun impatiently.

"Ill news, Lord," said Blaidd, wiping the blood from his eyes. "The Northerners are on the road between us and Caer Seint, and coming this way: a good force of them, maybe as many men as we have."

"Do they know that you saw them?" asked Rhun. Blaidd showed his teeth again, but this time in a grin.

"Not unless they saw me from a distance, and I think they did not," he said. "The two that I met at close quarters will carry no tales."

"Good!" Rhun nodded in understanding. "Then perhaps we can arrange a surprise for them. Llew, Pedr"—this to his two captains—"split the force, half in the trees on either side of the road. Blaidd, how close are they?"

"Within a mile or two by now," said Blaidd, still grinning.

"Good!" said Rhun again, and to the other scouts: "You two, see to him. The rest of you, follow me." And leaving the road, he set off at a trot toward the wood-shore on the western slope of the pass.

We had not long to wait. No sooner, it seemed, had the branches that concealed Rhun's war-bands settled from our passage than we saw the first of the Northerners: two scouts on mired ponies, trotting slowly along the road. We let them go by undisturbed. Next came another mounted party, moving without caution, some of them talking idly among themselves: forty or fifty sturdy dark-haired men in stained leathers, riding stolen horses and carrying seven-foot spears at the rest. Just behind them came a better-armed group, clearly their leaders: even in the gray twilight I could see the wet gleam of steel on their shoulders, and on the helmets slung at their saddle-bows. Behind these came more spearmen, and then at the back a herd of driven cattle, lowing dismally: reavers on the way home with their spoils.

Even as I looked, even as I felt a growing anger at the sight, the calm twilight rang with the notes of a hunting-horn: Rhun's signal to his men to attack. Horsemen erupted from the trees on both sides of the pass and thundered down upon the raiders. I did not thunder with them: even as I drew my sword and started to kick Du forward, Taliesin beside me grabbed my rein. "Not this time, Gwernin!" he said, and such was the force of his words that I desisted. Instead I sat and watched the battle before me: a brief, brutal fight in which two or three of the other side fell for every one of ours. The Northerners fought bravely enough, but they were taken by surprise. A few broke and ran, but most fought steadily and stubbornly around their leaders—fought and died. The payment for mead is always made in blood.

"That is my brother Clydno!" said Neirin beside me suddenly, and I turned, startled, to look at him, then looked back at the fight. In the growing darkness I could hardly tell man from man: certainly I could not recognize Clydno Eidyn, though I had sung in his court and eaten at his table the previous summer. Blood calls to blood: Neirin seemed to be in no doubt; when I looked at him again, I saw a sort of agony in his face. Whatever of betrayal or broken trust lay between those two, there was also a blood tie, too strong to be easily parted.

"Look!" said Taliesin on my other side, and I turned my attention back to the fight. In that fleeting moment things had changed. The Northerners, not entirely surrounded, were making a fighting retreat. Even as I looked I heard Clydno's battle-cry of "Gododdin!" He and a few others had charged where the line around them was thinnest and broken through, followed by most of their surviving force. I heard their yells of triumph; then they were pounding off down the pass in the direction from which they had come. A few of Rhun's *teulu* started to follow, but he whistled them back like a huntsman calling back the wild youngsters of his hound pack; it was no time for pursuit, with the night closing in, and we with a long way yet to ride. Unopposed now, I thought, and I was right: so in blood ended a bloody day. Beside me I heard Neirin heave a sigh before we rode down to join the King.

In the event, with weary men who had fought two battles already that day, and fresh wounded, some of whom could not sit a horse, Rhun decided to camp for the night. Around the hill-shoulder to the west lay Bwlch Derwin homestead, half-burnt and abandoned for now but better than no shelter at all. There we carried the worst injured, and there we improvised a well-guarded camp. Even a musty barn or a half-roofed hall was better than a night spent in the open in the rain, and once we had picketed our ponies in the close-paddock and started some cook-fires, the place began to look more cheerful. Men caught and slaughtered two or three of the cattle the raiders had been driving, and soon the smell of roasting meat filled the muddy courtyard. Rhun sent messengers to Caer Seint, asking for reinforcements, and we settled down to wait for our supper. This time there would be enough for all.

The next morning was brighter in many ways. Sometime in the night the rain had stopped and the clouds crept away, and we woke to a world suffused in sunlight, where every rain- or dew-drop was a sparkling jewel. Our reinforcements arrived early, led by Beli mab Rhun, and bringing bread and ale for our breakfast, and horse-litters for the most sorely wounded. Well before noon we were on the road again, and glad we were to see the walls of Caer Seint, with its well-manned gate-towers and its green fields spread around it— green fields in which the corn was slowly getting ripe. And Arfon was not yet free of raiders.

Rhun had been talking with Taliesin and Neirin as we rode, though I had not heard much of it; my wounds were still painful, and I was feeling a little feverish. They seemed to be discussing what should be done next to bring the Northerners to a parley. This, said Taliesin, was better than more fighting if it could be achieved, and Rhun reluctantly agreed. The question was, how to do it?

"I could maybe ride to my brother with a Green Branch," said Neirin. "I am thinking he might listen now: he lost a-many of his men last night." He was frowning, his usual gaiety absent, and I thought that he had recognized one or two of the dead.

"Na," said Rhun, "how would you find him? I would not myself ride out man alone among them now, not while they are smarting from their losses: they might cut your throat before ever you came near him, Green Branch or no, and that would help neither of us. Na, there must be some other way... What do you think, Font of Song?"

"Let one of your captives go, to carry the news," said Taliesin promptly. "They lost a third of their strength yesterday, and their best way home, not to mention most of their spoils: that must give them pause. Send them all the news, and let them chew on it, and I think they will come of themselves to parley with you before long. Otherwise they will have a weary road home by land, and every man's hand will be against them."

"You are right," said Rhun nodding, and to one of his *teulu*: "Bring me one of the captives." And when a man was brought, dirty and blood-stained but defiant on his bare-backed pony: "Cut his bonds. You"—to the prisoner—"who do you serve?"

"Mordaf mab Serfan, Lord, if he yet lives," said the man, rubbing his wrists where the rope had chafed them. He was a typical Strathclyder, black-bearded and blue-eyed, dressed in stained leather and dark woolens, and with rough bandages wrapping his head and right arm. "Why do you ask?"

"Good!" said Rhun. "That means we took you when we burned the ships. I am letting you go now—ride to your friends and tell them all the news! I will be at Caer Seint for a day or two if they want to parley. I have Mordaf and three of his captains—if no one comes for them soon, they will hang. After that I will come hunting the rest of you. Do you understand?"

"Yes, Lord," said the man grimly. "I will carry your message. And if no one else will parley with you, I will come back to Caer Seint myself in three days' time to take my Lord's place on the gallows."

"Good man!" said Rhun, suddenly smiling. And to the soldier who held the pony's lead rope: "Let him go!"

"That," said Neirin softly as the former prisoner rode away, "is a brave man. I am wishing I knew his name: he deserves a song."

"Maybe you will learn it yet," said Taliesin, and we rode on into Caer Seint.

It was more than two days before the Northerners came to parley, but at last they came. They were in a trap, and they knew it: even though they made a desert of Arfon, Rhun held all the passes through Eryri, and they had no other way home. So on the third morning while we were still at breakfast we heard the sound of a horn, and going to look I saw before our eastern walls a strong force of two or three hundred mounted men: all that was left of the four war-bands which had come south for plunder and revenge. A man rode out from them as I watched carrying the herald's Green Branch: halfway to our gates he rode, and then stopped and waited, and sounded his horn again. The next move was Rhun's.

He had prepared for it, and was ready. Before the notes of the horn had well died away, the gates of Caer Seint opened, and our herald rode out: Huwel mab Rhodri, a young cousin of the King's from Ynys Môn. The two heralds met and conferred for a time, then returned to their respective forces. Next a troop of Rhun's soldiers rode out and took up station outside the fortress walls, ready to counter any treacherous attack. Finally the leaders of both forces and their advisors rode slowly forward to meet between the armies: Clydno, Rhydderch and Nudd mab Senyllt with three of their captains on the one side, and Rhun with his *penteulu* and three of his retinue on the other, as well as Taliesin, Neirin, and myself. I was not, strictly speaking, invited, but I had got my pony ready with the other two, and no one sent me back. So it was I saw all that happened that day, and can report it.

Rhun was mounted as usual on his big bay horse, and splendidly dressed in the purple and gold that suited him. The morning sunlight brought out the red in his thick grizzled curls and beard, and sparkled in his blue eyes. Gold bracelets shone on his sinewy arms, and the heavy jeweled chain he wore on his broad chest was solid gold as well. In contrast the two Northern Kings and their cousin looked the worse for wear, their clothing stained and dirty from much rough living, although their jewels matched Rhun's in splendor. Rhydderch Hael was a tall, broad-shouldered man some ten or fifteen years younger than his opponent, with curly black hair and blue eyes and a tanned, open face which was normally good-tempered, and his cousin Nudd was much like him, though not so tall. Clydno Eidyn, although much the same age, was made in a different mold, a thinner, darker man than his cousins, with brown eyes and dark brown hair that yet showed a hint of Neirin's red. As always his expression was closed and controlled; one never quite knew what he was thinking. His dark gaze went first to Rhun, and then to Neirin, and for a moment something moved in his face which might have been anger; then it was gone. There was a momentary silence, and then Rhun spoke first.

"So here you are at last," he said heavily, "come to ask for terms after your despoiling of my land." There was an undercurrent of anger in his words, but he had himself well in hand. "Listen, then, to what I have to say, if you want to reach your homes alive." He ticked off the points on his blunt fingers as he made them. "First, you will give me hostages to add to those I have already, hostages who will answer for your deeds with their blood if you break my peace again. Secondly, you will dismount half of your force now, and the rest when you leave my lands, for all those horses you are riding were bred here in Gwynedd. Thirdly, you will take no captives with you, not one man, not one woman, not one child. And lastly, you will take the route through my mountains that I give you, and no other, with some of my men going before you, and some following after, to see that you keep the peace. In return I will provide you with enough food to keep you all alive and marching—for I want you gone, all of you, from my lands, as soon as may be! Do you agree?"

"How can we agree to this?" said Rhydderch loudly. "You treat us like slaves, or like fools! Once we dismount our men, what is to stop you attacking and killing us all?"

"You are in no position to make demands," said Rhun. "Remember, it is I who hold the whip hand here. I will leave you your clothing and your weapons and your pitiful lives—that is more than you deserve!"

Rhydderch started to bluster, but Clydno cut in coolly: "You must give us more surety than your word, Gwynedd. If you take hostages, you must expect to give them. They will be safe enough with us as long as we are safe, too."

"That is reasonable," said Rhun, nodding. "Who will you offer me?"

"You already have my uncle's son Mordaf," said Nudd, speaking for the first time. "Is he not enough?"

"He would be," said Rhun, "if he were not so sorely wounded. As it is I cannot guarantee his life, and a dead hostage is of no value. Give me someone else as well."

Nudd's mouth set hard, and he flushed with anger. "Your hospitality, Gwynedd, is a dangerous thing! Perhaps we are safer as we are—you cannot close all the passes through Eryri!"

"You are welcome to try them," said Rhun indifferently. "Your corpses may keep the mountain eagles from this year's lambs."

"Who do you demand, then, Gwynedd?" asked Clydno quietly. "One of us? You will not get it."

"Three captains," said Rhun, "one from each of you, and one of them related to you by blood."

"That is fair," said Clydno, interrupting Rhydderch's protest. "And who will you give us in return?"

"Two men from my retinue, and my cousin Huwel, who rode out to you this morning," said Rhun.

"That is—almost enough," said Clydno, "but I will have one more."

"Who, then?" asked Rhun, frowning. But with a sinking in my belly, I knew.

"That one," said Clydno, and pointed at Neirin. "He cannot fear to join us, for he is our cousin, too—or so his mother told my father. Neirin mab Dwywei, you change sides so readily—will you ride now with me?"

There was a little silence, then: "Yes," said Neirin, and smiled.

"Yes, brother, I will."

Rhun looked at him for a moment, then nodded. "If he consents, so be it. Have your hostages ready in an hour, and I will have mine. This parley is at an end."

Back in the guesthouse, watching Neirin while he packed his gear, I said at last, "Why? Why did you agree? You could have said 'no' so easily!"

"Na, do not press me, brother," said Neirin with a twisted smile. "I cannot lay out my reasons so clearly as you would like. I only did what I must do. It is not easy to live in two worlds."

" 'Two worlds,' " I said slowly. "Is it so different, then, North to South? It did not seem that way to me last summer."

"Na, I am not sure what I mean," said Neirin, frowning. "It is more... All my life I have been half one thing and half another, like...like Dylan ail Ton, who was a man upon the land, and a selkie in the sea... It is only in motion, maybe, that I can find a balance." He looked at Taliesin, who all this time had sat watching in frowning silence. "Do you understand...Gwion?"

Taliesin gave him a sudden, startled smile—I think it was the first time Neirin had ever used his boyhood name to him; then his face sobered again. "Yes, Little Hawk," he said, using Neirin's nickname. "I do...oh, I do!" He looked over at me. "Do not worry, Gwernin. I think...I think he will be safe."

"Of course he will be," I said half-angrily. "It is only—oh, a curse on it all! Neirin, do you take your harp?"

"Na, I think she will be better with you, brother," said Neirin, again with that halfway smile. "You had better keep my sword, too, until I come back for it—I will have no need of it while I am a hostage... *Hai mai!* What a long face! I am not going beyond the sunset, not yet—only as far as Deva!" And putting down the sword-belt he was holding, he came over and embraced me.

"I know it," I said, hugging him back, and feeling the lean strength of him hard against me; then, trying for a lighter note: "Only—only do not make me have to come and rescue you again, as I did last summer!"

"Na, I promise," said Neirin, smiling. "This time it will be my turn to rescue you. But mind, there must be a pretty girl in it for me somewhere!" And he laughed, and I laughed with him. Only Taliesin did not laugh, but frowned instead, like a man who hears a portent, and his blue eyes were looking into shadows.

But that, O my children, is a story for another day.

The Land of Eagles

Eryri, the rugged mountain mass which forms the greater part of north-west Gwynedd, means in the common tongue *land of eagles*, and many are the fierce birds that make their homes there. Fierce, too, are its people: yet they can also be kind, as I have found more than once in my travels. But it is not for nothing that Gwydion, one of the Old Gods of that land, travels often in eagle shape.

It was not of eagles I was thinking, however, on that sunny afternoon, as I rode lazily through the deep valley that borders the north side of Yr Wyddfa. Instead I was thinking of girls: girls in general, and the present lack of them in my life; and also of my particular girl, Rhiannedd, back at home in Llys-tyn-wynnan, and now almost four months gone with child: my child, which I would need to support. Every time my thoughts reached this point, they recoiled, and I returned to where I had begun: the unavailability of girls. Riding as I was in the baggage train of an army, and following another army through a land scantily populated at the best of times, the one was as far out of my reach as the other. But that did not stop me thinking, or quench my desire.

Two days had passed since Neirin had gone as a hostage: two days of hurry and confusion and impatient waiting. Food had to be gathered for both armies from a land already ravaged; arrangements made for the dismounting of half the Northern soldiers, with accompanying disputes and ill-feelings; and Rhun's advance party, which was to lead the way through the mountains, had to set off, and his messengers go out as well to the sub-kings and chieftains along his planned route of march. Through it all Taliesin had been silent and even absent-minded, as if his thoughts were elsewhere, and I had been nervous. I had disobeyed him during the night attack on the ships, and I knew that sooner or later there would be a reckoning between us for that. So far he had held his hand, but I did not think my offense was forgotten—or forgiven.

Ahead of us now, near the north end of Llyn Peris, one of the two lakes which filled much of the floor of this valley, I could see wood-smoke rising from the *llys* of a local lord where we would be stopping for the night. Although I knew that Taliesin would be provided for—perhaps in the King's own chamber!—I myself would do well to find a corner of the stables to sleep in, let alone space in the overcrowded hall. Since it was high summer, and fine dry weather, I might be more comfortable in the fields outside. It would depend on whether I could find a safe place to store all our gear, or whether I would need to sleep near it to guard it; in such a large mixed force as this was, it might be that not all men could be trusted, although theft from comrades is a great offense. Indeed, I have seen men hanged for it, and not felt the punishment too harsh.

Thinking of our gear, however, reminded me of another problem. My wounds from the fight in the Lleyn had been clean, and were healing well; but my trews, unlike my leg, would not mend themselves, and I had only one other pair, which I was wearing now. I had washed out the blood from the damaged ones, but was no hand with a needle; and though I might go bare-legged in the warm weather and take no harm, it would do nothing for my status, or my self-esteem—or, I thought with a sigh, my chances with girls. The one problem seemed as hopeless as the other... And my thoughts began their well-worn circuit again.

Fortunately, before I could become too discouraged, we arrived at the court of Ifor Hen. This was a set of wooden-walled and bracken-thatched buildings inside a palisade, situated on a rocky knob not far from the banks of the lake. I was busy for some time with our five ponies: unloading our gear at the stables; taking them to drink at the lake; picketing them in the horse-lines; and then unsaddling and grooming them. By the time all this was accomplished, I was hot, tired, and dusty from head to heel. I should next have gone to see if Taliesin needed me for anything, but the sparkling blue waters of the lake looked cool and inviting—and I was not the only one to think so: many of the soldiers, with less duties than I had, were already splashing naked in it. I made haste to join them, adding my pile of boots and clothing to many similar piles on the fine brown sand of the lakeshore and wading straight into the water.

Fed by mountain streams, the lake was cold enough to take my breath away at first. I ducked underwater and came up spluttering, then swam a bit to warm up. The exercise felt good, and I swam out farther for the sheer pleasure of it, then turned over and stretched out on my back, floating. The warm sunlight on my face and chest made a pleasant contrast to the cold at my back, and I stayed so for some time, watching the eagles circling high above me on outstretched gold-bronze wings. Against the hazy blue of the summer sky, the white tails and pale heads of the big birds almost disappeared; they seemed to float on the air as I floated on the water, and behind us both lay immense unplumbable depths. The shouts of the men splashing in the shallows seemed faint and far away, like the piping cries of children at play; the warm breeze from the land brought me the rich dry scents of summer, sweet as forgotten perfumes used by ancient queens. I was drifting away on the depths of time, one bright leaf caught on the current of Taliesin's river, which carries us ever onward toward the unknown sea.

If I turned and looked down into the water, I thought languidly, what would I see there? And when I came ashore, would I meet only strangers? Despite the summer sunlight, the chill of winter seemed to be seeping into my bones, stealing my strength. Echoing in my ears was an unearthly music, like harp-song heard far off in the hollow hills; a ringing, chiming sound of silver and crystal which I knew that I had heard before. A little longer and I would know it again, I would know the truth, all the truth...

With an effort I turned over in the water and set out for shore. I had drifted some way down the lake, caught in its slow current, and had farther to swim than I expected. Rather than returning to where I had started, I headed for the nearest land, a rocky point which pushed out through the ragged thickets of alder and willow-herb clothing this part of the lakeshore like a bare elbow through a fraying sleeve—or a knee through a torn pair of trews. Even this seemed a long way, and by the time I came wading ashore, stumbling and slipping on the slimy, water-smoothed rocks of the shallows, I felt as weary as if I had fought a battle. At the foot of the hill which loomed above me was a patch of smooth green sheep-cropped turf, dappled with sunlight, as enticing as a new-made bed waiting for me alone. I lay down on it to rest. After the chill of the lake, the grass was warm. The earth held me up. I sighed, and closed my eyes, and slept.

When I awoke in the cool blue shadows of the mountain the valley was quiet, with only the distant bleating of the lambs and a few late bird calls to disturb the stillness. I knew at once that I had overstayed the leave I did not have. Leaping to my feet, I set off along the lakeshore toward the place where I had left my clothes. Stumbling barefoot through the reeds and the sharp alder-roots, and rousing the shore-birds to noisy flight, I wondered if they would still be there. Taliesin had enough reasons to reproach me without my appearing bare-arsed at the feast, which must already be in progress—if indeed it was not over. My empty belly hoped there would be a few scraps left for me.

The trampled sand of the shore was full of footprints, but empty of boots and clothing. I cursed briefly but wholeheartedly. Whether my clothes had been stolen, or merely removed for a joke, the effect was the same: I would have to find others, and quickly. I could not steal, I would not beg, but perhaps I might borrow. In the soldiers' camp I would be teased, but I would not lose as much face as in the hall, and I thought there were one or two men there who might help me, at least by lending me a spare tunic until I could retrieve my own from our baggage. My good trews, alas, were the ones which had disappeared.

Halfway up the hill I had a better idea, and turned toward the horse-lines. Although I had unloaded our baggage in the court, the saddles and harness were piled near where the horses were picketed, with the oiled pack-cloths spread over them in case of rain. One of those, I thought, would make a cloak of sorts, enough to cover my nakedness for the short time I would need it. Passing through the fringes of the camp, I came in for a few comments from the soldiers, joking or lewd as the fancy struck them. I answered as best I could, trying to turn the joke, but I could feel myself blushing, and not only on my face. Then, when I was approaching the horse-lines, I heard a familiar voice behind me calling my name. Turning, I saw one of the last men I wanted to meet at that moment: my old friend Ieuan.

"Why, what is this, Gwernin?" he was saying, laughing. "What has happened to you, boy? Have the girls here been tearing your clothes off to get at your lovely body? Or did you have to pay them for what you got instead?"

"Ieuan," I said, interrupting, "do you have a spare tunic I can borrow for an hour? Someone took my gear while I was swimming, and I cannot go into the King's hall like this!"

"Na, that is true enough," said Ieuan, still laughing. "And you such a well-provided, well-set-up young man, with a horse, and a harp, and a sword, and all! Well, come along, come along, I think I can find you something—not that I have much to spare, poor man as I am. But if it was a girl, mind that she does not catch up with you—she or her father!" And he laughed again, very pleased with his own feeble wit. From the look and smell of him, there was plenty of beer in camp tonight, if nothing stronger; and Ieuan had never had much of a head for drink.

"Never mind about that now," I said, taking his arm to hurry him along. "Where is your troop camping? I suppose you are here with the Lord Cadwaladr's men?"

"And with the Lord Cadwaladr himself," said Ieuan, still chucking. "Though he dines with the King tonight, not in camp. A pity you are not there to entertain them—you always were a good teller of tales! You might have won at least a pair of breeches, bright lad that you are!"

"Maybe I will yet be in time, if you help me," I said coaxingly. "Come on, Ieuan, show me where you are camped. Is it this way?"

"Na, farther to the right, I think," said Ieuan with a resounding belch. "Somewhere—somewhere over there, I am sure." I got him along a few more yards before he stopped again. "Where are we going?" he asked.

"Back to your camp, so you can lend me a tunic," I said. Men were passing us with broad grins on their faces, and I heard a word or two which did not please me. Soldiers are not known for polite speech. "Come on, Ieuan," I said, losing patience. "Do you not know where your own camp is?"

"*Sa, sa,* of course I do," said Ieuan, and pulling his arm out of my grasp, he draped it across my shoulders. "Come along, then, Gwernin my boy, come and drink with us."

"Gladly," I said, staggering as he leaned on me. "Only show me the way. Is that your fire ahead?"

"Fire?" said Ieuan, and I felt him shiver for a moment. "Fire? No—no, it is only our camp. Yes—only our camp. Come on, Gwernin, have a drink with us, do, and tell us a tale."

"Surely," I said as we stumbled toward the campfire. "Only find me a tunic first, and we will drink. Where is your gear?"

"Over—over here," said Ieuan, blinking. To my relief he let me go, and kneeling beside a pile of equipment, began to dig in a pack, mumbling to himself as he did so. "Na, not this, not this. Maybe—maybe—yes, here it is." And he produced at last a brown tunic, almost clean and only a little too large. I took it from him eagerly and pulled it on over my head. The coarse woolen cloth felt rough on my skin, and smelled of stale sweat and horses, but it was a great improvement over my former state.

"I will bring it back in the morning," I said, preparing to leave. "Thanks, Ieuan."

"Na, na," said Ieuan, getting to his feet unsteadily. "Have to drink with us—drink with us first. And tell us a story. All friends here." And he waved his hands around the circle of grinning men who were watching this comedy. I saw familiar faces there from Caer Lêb, and knew I could not leave yet: to do so would give offense. A black-haired man I remembered from earlier in the summer held out a cup to me, friendly-fashion, and I took it and drank a swallow. It was strong barley wine, fresh-brewed and hardly sour at all. I took another swallow, and felt it start to warm my empty belly. I drank the rest of what was in the cup, and someone else held out another one. "A story," said the first man. "Tell us a tale, Storyteller."

If I went now, I thought, I might still get some scraps at the King's table. I drank another swallow from the second cup, feeling the sweet warmth spread. But then, I thought, I would have to face Taliesin, and explain where I had been. I finished the cup, and a red-headed lad filled it again for me from a jug. Through a sort of haze I saw Ieuan grinning at me; everyone here was smiling, and I was smiling, too. I had got a belly-full for now, I thought, of bardic measures and stable-boy work. Maybe I would just spend the night here among friends, and get drunk... So I did.

The next morning began badly, as might have been expected. A voice I knew was calling my name, and a hard hand shaking my shoulder. When I forced open my gummy eyes, it was to the sight of a pair of brown leather boots, a hand-span in front of my nose. I knew those boots well, though they were not mine; I had brushed mud from them more than once this summer. I groaned and rolled onto my back, then shut my eyes again as the sun's bright arrows pierced my aching brain. I had no need of sight to tell me who was standing over me; I already knew.

"Gwernin," said Taliesin's voice from somewhere above me, "you had better get up now; the King will be riding on soon. Go down to the lake and wash yourself, then meet me at the horse-lines. We have things to discuss."

"Yes—yes, Master," I mumbled, my tongue feeling like a piece of old leather in my dry mouth. I opened my eyes again reluctantly, but Taliesin had gone. I had better do likewise. Besides, I had an uneasy feeling that I had done more than get drunk last night; performance might have come into it. As I sat up and looked around, blinking, the grins on the faces of some of Cadwaladr's soldiers suggested I was right. Lurching to my feet, I set off toward the lakeshore at an unsteady trot. It seemed unlikely I would get any breakfast that morning, but for once I did not care.

The cold lake water restored me somewhat, though it did not

banish my headache. Ieuan's spare tunic was much the worse for wear; after brushing at it ineffectually, I gave up and washed it as well. This made me smell like a wet sheep, but there are worse things, and in the warm morning I would dry soon enough. Combing my damp hair roughly back with my fingers, I headed toward the horse-lines, limping painfully over the stony ground and wondering where I would get a new pair of boots. But this was not the chief of my worries: first I had to face Taliesin.

He was waiting by our pack-ponies, watching as one of Cadwaladr's men finished saddling the last of them. His expression was grim, and I was suddenly reminded of his chastising of Rhys on Ynys Môn earlier that summer. Then I had looked on and smiled, deriving pleasure from the sight; now it was I who was the offender. His first words, however, surprised me. "Much better," he said, looking me up and down. "Take these three to the court and load our gear; I will follow with Du as soon as Dai has finished with him." The red-haired lad in question gave me a sympathetic grin, and I remembered him filling my cup the night before. I did not stay to chat, but took the lead-rope he handed me and headed briskly for the court.

In the courtyard of the *llys* the King's party was already assembling, and I had to wend my way through them to reach the stables. I did not stop to change into my own clothes, but loaded our gear on the pack-ponies as quickly as I could. Taliesin was as good as his word; by the time I was ready he was in the courtyard, mounted on his red mare and leading Du. I joined him and swung up onto my black pony, and he gave me a nod of approval. "Take your usual station with the pack train for now," he said. "I will speak to you later." And he turned away toward the King, leaving me to comply with all haste.

Barefoot, bare-legged, and bleary-eyed as I was, I was glad to hide myself amidst the packers that day and contemplate the extent of my stupidity. Perhaps, I thought, Taliesin had held his hand so long because he did not think me worth correcting. All the approval I had got from him earlier in the summer was forgotten, washed away by the tide of my foolish stubbornness. I wondered if I was to be sent home in disgrace in a day or two when we reached the Conwy Valley. In my sorry state, I could not decide whether I wished for this or not; at least if it happened I would be with Talhaearn again, who valued me, and with Rhiannedd. Then I remembered that Rhys was in Llys-tyn-wynnan now, making himself useful to my master—who might even prefer him!—and my spirits plummeted again. I would have less chance than ever of making a home for my girl, and she would reject me; the Prince would cast me out to wander the roads and starve, or creep home to my aunt and uncle in Pengwern, who might find me a place in the stables... Perhaps, I thought, I should cut my throat at once and be done with it—that would be better. Unfortunately, my knife had gone with my clothes.

But I was seventeen, and at that age even black despair cannot persist forever in the midst of a fine summer's day. As we continued on our way toward the top of the pass, with Yr Wyddfa's crags towering above us on our right, and Glyder Fawr on our left, and the hunting eagles tracing their slow circles against a bright blue sky, I felt my heart lift again despite myself. Birdsong from the oak woods on the lower slopes and from the brushy steeps above mixed with the bleating of the sheep; lambs frisked and played in their rocky pastures, and fat black and brown cattle grazed placidly on the river's lush banks with their small calves sleeping beside them. The sunlight warmed me and dried my borrowed tunic, and even my headache gradually departed, leaving me with a growing desire for food. Held to the slow pace of the Northerners' dismounted troops, the packers talked and laughed among themselves as we ambled along. The odors of men and horses mixed with those of bruised grass and herbs underfoot, and with the sun-warmed scents of flowering gorse and heather on the mountainsides. My body moved easily to the rhythm of my pony's walking, and my mind followed it; without thinking, I began to weave it into a song.

The song was only half-finished when I saw Taliesin up ahead. He was sitting his red mare by the roadside, watching the pack-train pass, and I knew at once that he was waiting for me. Beside him was the red-headed lad from Cadwaladr's war-band, and as we came abreast the two of them set their ponies in motion and matched my pace. "Gwernin," said Taliesin, "give your lead rope to Dai here and ride with me awhile."

I did as he bade me, then followed him as he reined his mare to the roadside again. Looking around at him, I found him watching me with a frown between his black brows. His blue eyes were narrowed in concentration, and his mouth set in a straight line within the frame of his clipped beard. There were gray hairs in that beard now, and a few at his temples as well; a few more lines, too, in his face and at the corners of his eyes. Time was no longer passing him by.

His silent stare, however, was making me nervous. I started to say something—to ask a question—anything to break that silence, but I overcame the impulse, remembering certain experiences with Talhaearn. Instead I forced myself to meet his eyes and waited. It was not easy, that waiting; I felt sweat start on my forehead. My jaw ached with clenching it; my hands were white-knuckled fists on Du's reins; and the sound of my own heart-beat was loud in my ears. I felt like the hare, frozen in her form, waiting for the eagle's stoop; yet still I waited, and still I met Taliesin's questioning eyes. And at last a strange thing happened: his face lost its set expression, and slowly, unbelievably, he began to smile. "Well done, Gwernin," he said. "Something you have learned, at least. Now tell me what else you know."

I sighed, and wiped the sweat from my forehead with the back of my hand. "I know I have been a fool, Master," I said. "I disobeyed you in the Lleyn, following my own wishes, and would have done so a second time had you not stopped me. And yesterday I left my tasks half-done, and went to seek my own pleasure; and when it brought me into trouble, I persisted, and made bad worse. I do not remember last night very clearly, but I know—I think… I think I behaved very foolishly, and brought no credit on myself, or on your teaching." I paused for a moment, but Taliesin said nothing, only watched me with a half-amused expression. I sighed again. "I—I am sorry, and if you send me away, I will have deserved it, but—but I do not want to go. Not yet. I—I am waiting for your judgment."

After a moment Taliesin shook his head. "*Sa, sa, sa...* I think you have delivered it already. What do you think you deserve, lad, for all those misdeeds of yours? A beating?"

"I—if that is what you want." I swallowed. "Now?"

"Na, I think not." Taliesin grinned. "I have a different ordeal in mind for you, Gwernin. You have told stories enough this summer while you have been with me, but you have made no songs. Make one for the King tonight. Show me what you have learned, and I may—I may!—let you continue with me. Is it good enough?"

"It is," I said, nodding. "*Sa*, I will show you—you and the court—tonight!"

"Mind that you do it well, then," said Taliesin seriously. And turning his mare, he set off after the army. I followed, wondering what song I should make for the King. Maybe the one I had been working on earlier that morning…

But that, O my children, is a story for another day.

The Harper's Tale

Again we were camping by a lake, but not in summer sunshine: our golden day had ended in clouds and mizzle rain. The King's *llys*, a substantial fortified steading which guarded the junction of the Nant-y-Gwryd stream with the bigger Afon Llugwy, was stuffed as full with men as a sausage is with meat, and some of the war-bands were setting up canvas and leather tents in the wet fields outside. Across the river below the water-meet, the Northern war-bands were camping wretchedly in the rain, although I could see a few tents and improvised shelters being prepared for the leaders, and hear the sound of axes in the adjacent woodland. There would be leg-weary men with short tempers over there, after the long march they had made today through the mountain passes. I wondered how Neirin was faring, and whether he would be sleeping safe and dry with the Kings tonight, or huddled in his cloak by a smoky fire trying to stay warm: for even in high summer the mountain nights could be cold. The weeping skies hid the tall peaks around us, but I knew they were there: I had been this way before.

Meanwhile, it was time I turned my mind to my business. Our ponies were grazing with many others in the paddocks outside the *llys*; our gear was stored under shelter; and I had come up on the wall-walk in search of a quiet place to finish polishing my song for this evening. But it is hard to concentrate with an empty belly, and mine was empty indeed. I had begged a little bread and cheese earlier from the kitchen, but had got no more; they were all going mad there preparing the King's feast, and had no attention to waste on a horse-boy—for so I still looked in my bare feet and borrowed brown tunic. Soon I would have to go down and change into my other clothes—my only clothes—still packed safely with the rest of our gear, but for now I was searching for a better ending to my song. A word—a rhyme—a closing couplet—yes, it would have to do. One more glance I threw across the river, thinking of Neirin; then I went down.

Taliesin was waiting for me, sheltering in the fore-porch of the hall, his leather rain-cape drawn close about him against the unseasonable chill. He looked me over briefly, his eyes dark in the shadowy light, and nodded. "Go and change your clothes," he said, "and make haste: the feast will start soon." And as I turned away, he added, "Oh, and Gwernin…"

"Yes, Master?" I said, turning back.

"Look in the top of my pack as well as your own." He smiled slightly. "You will find some things there you need."

"Yes, Master," I said again, and went on my way, puzzled. I found our gear where I had stored it in the dim horse-scented stables, crowded now with baggage and men's blanket-rolls, all the beasts turned out to graze. Taliesin's pack was stacked on top of mine, and seemed fuller than usual. Frowning, I unbuckled its straps and pulled back the cover, then stared in astonishment. Neatly folded on top of his gear were my lost tunic and trews, with my belt and boots tucked in above them. After a moment I shrugged and took them out, then looked in my own pack. My better tunic lay where I had had left it, with my torn trews beneath. There was no time to waste on wondering; I began rapidly to change clothes. I put Ieuan's tunic in with my own gear, buckled the straps on both packs, and headed for the hall in haste. Answers could come later: it was time for me to perform, and at least now I was dressed for it.

In the crowded feast hall the air was thick with wood-smoke and the scents of roasting meat, of wet wool and warm bodies and heady heather-ale. Under-kings and captains thronged the trestle tables, and the babble of their voices shook the well-shaped roof-beams above. Fire flickered brightly on the central hearth as I wove my way between the frantic servants, heading for the high table where Taliesin sat close beside the King. The food-smells set my belly growling like a hungry wolf and brought the warm water into my mouth, but I could not think of eating yet: first I must sing. In the curve of my arm I carried my own small harp, protecting her as best I could from the crowd. Sturdy and plain she was compared to

Neirin's carved beauty, but dear to me beyond words. Earlier in the summer—in another life, it seemed—I had played her to accompany Taliesin's songs at Deganwy. Now I must, if I could, accompany myself: not an easy thing to do, or one I had much practiced. But there was no one else to do it for me.

Or perhaps there was. Wedged into a corner close beside the King sat a harper, a thin brown man in faded clothing whom I had never seen before. Perched on a low stool with his harp between his knees, he was working with the tuning key, testing now one string and now another, but so softly that he could not be heard above the clamor of the hall. His face was half-hidden by his loose-hanging hair as he bent over his work, but I thought that he was not young. Perhaps he would help me—but first I must speak to Taliesin, who had turned and was watching my approach with a faint smile. "Master?" I said when I reached him. "When would you have me sing?"

"As soon as the food comes out and the first noise drops," said Taliesin. I had to bend over to hear him and to be heard. His eyes went to my harp and he frowned slightly. "Are you ready to play?"

"I hope so, but—Master, might I ask the harper by the wall to play for me? It would be better, if he will do it." Taliesin's eyebrows rose.

"Kieran?" he said thoughtfully. "Well, you may ask him. But I do not know…" A fresh burst of noise overwhelmed his words, and from behind him the chamberlain touched his shoulder to get his attention. "Do what you will, Gwernin," he mouthed through the uproar and turned away. I threaded my way with difficulty through the press toward the harper, who had finished tuning and now sat softly fingering his strings, his head still bowed on his breast as if he were half-asleep.

"Kieran?" I said, to get his attention, and he looked up—or rather raised his face. I stopped and stared, forgetting what I had been about to say. It was clear that this man was blind, but not, like my Master Talhaearn, by the gradual dimming of the years. Kieran's blindness had been abrupt and total: his eyelids hung half-closed over scarred and empty sockets, where someone years ago had taken out his eyes.

"Who is it?" he asked in a low but carrying voice. "You know my name; now tell me yours, and what you are wanting of me."

I moistened my dry lips, and tried to arrange my thoughts. "I am Gwernin Storyteller, apprenticed to Taliesin Ben Beirdd, and we came here with the King. My master has bidden me sing tonight, and I wondered if you would play for me. I have my own small harp here, but truth to tell, I am not well-practiced at doing both things at once. Would you help me?"

"Give me the measure," said Kieran. "Sing me your first line." And when I had done so, "Yes, I can play for you. What shall be my cue?" We talked for a few moments, arranging details, and I saw that before the loss of his eyes he must have been a handsome man. He was past his first youth now, but had only a little gray in his russet beard, and his voice had an Irish twang, softened as if by many years spent in Gwynedd. I wondered what his story was, but this was not the time to ask. Before I knew it the servants were crowding past us with their platters of smoking meats and fresh-baked bread, and I had to get out of their way as best I could. A final roar of talk dropped abruptly to near-silence as hungry mouths were filled. I caught Taliesin's eye, and he nodded. Leaving my small harp in Kieran's care, I stepped out before the high table and bowed to the King. Then, clapping my hands twice quickly as the blind harper's cue, I began to sing.

> "Twice-nine score of horsemen riding,
> twice-nine score of shining shields,
> twice-nine score of piercing spear-points
> followed Rhun through Lleyn's dark fields—
> moonlight bright upon their shields.
>
> Silent as the gray hunt riding,
> silent in the mist and rain,
> silently to win their vengeance
> Rhun's men rode to deal death's pain—
> strike the raiders down in shame."

Under my words the harp chords, strong and rhythmic, emphasized the beat.

> "Twenty score of reavers sleeping,
> twenty score of red-tusked boars,
> twenty score with blood-lust sated
> snored unknowing by the shore—
> they would see their homes no more!
>
> Swords flashed silver in the moonlight,
> swords rang bright in fight with foe,
> sword-blades blood-red blazed by firelight—
> burning ships gave brighter glow,
> till they sank the waves below!
>
> Fierce our warriors cleaving shields there,
> fierce their spear-thrusts, pangs of pain,
> fierce great Rhun, red wolf of battle
> reaping men like Irish grain—
> sowing bones about the plain!"

Many in the hall now were slapping the tables in time with the harp; most had even stopped eating to listen.

> "Praise King Rhun whose wisdom led us,
> praise all men who did great deeds,
> praise those most who fell in battle
> paying blood-price for their mead—
> let all bards proclaim their deeds!
>
> Gwyn the Strong sits not at table,
> Ifor Goch no more will fight,
> Cynan Hir dines with his fathers,
> Dinfael knows no more the light—
> these and more have left our sight."

My voice rose, anticipating the ending, and the harp-song followed, bearing me up like wings.

> "Twice-nine score rode forth to battle,
> twice-nine score to kill or die,
> twice-nine score did mighty slaughter—
> for the fallen praise I cry—
> not forgotten will they lie!"

When I stopped there was a silence, and then a shout of applause, a drumming of cups and fists on the trestle tables, and a stamping of feet on the hard-packed earthen floor. I stood for a moment without moving, feeling both empty and exalted. It was the best song I had yet made, and I knew I had sung it well. Would it be good enough? I turned toward the high table, where King Rhun was smiling and beckoning me, but it was at Taliesin's face I looked first. After his nod of approval, I did not need the King's words of thanks and present of silver to feel content—though needless to say I did not turn them away. Reclaiming my harp from Kieran, I found myself a seat near the foot of one of the tables and proceeded to fill my poor empty belly with good roast pig-meat and tender wheaten bread, washed down with foaming ale. I refused the cups of mead I was offered; I had learned my lesson, at least for a while.

When my first hunger was satisfied, I rose and went to see if Taliesin had any commands for me. He met me with a quizzical smile, and shook his head. "Na," he said, "they are not in the mood for a story tonight, or at least not yet. But do you wander the hall and listen to what they are saying. There is an undercurrent here I do not like." It was true the noise was still loud, more so than on most evenings. I nodded and walked away, carrying my harp as if I meant to play her. At first I only heard such talk as was usual, but as I went slowly down the hall I began to pick up other snatches of conversation which made me frown.

"We should have fought," a burly black-bearded man was saying to his neighbor. "Our men dead, our woman raped, and they ride out of Gwynedd free as you please, on our horses! We should have fought!"

"A night attack," a gray-haired captain farther down the table suggested. "It worked in the Lleyn, it can work here. Now, while the mountains still hem them in! We could crack them like a nut!"

"What do the hostages matter?" asked a thin, foxy man with a long mustache of his bald friend. "They must take their chances, the same as we would. It was soft of Rhun to allow this, soft..."

There was more of it, mixed in with the normal talk of weather and horses and women, the usual background bragging and complaining of any group of men on the march. Much of it came from the men of Arfon, the black-speared war-bands whose homes and families had suffered the most from the Northern raiders, but the men of the Lleyn and of Môn had their say as well. It was not a reassuring thing to hear. Well, I thought, in another day or two we would be out of the mountains, and then no doubt the mood would change. And in half of this I was right: but in half wrong.

In the meantime, my wanderings had brought me back to the top of the hall, where Kieran was still seated on his stool, harping now for the King and his table companions. I paused nearby, listening and enjoying his music. It was not like Neirin's or Talhaearn's; there were more runs and repeats, and more chords. I wondered if some of the melodies were Irish. The harp was larger than most I had seen, not an instrument for a traveling bard, but Kieran's fingers danced quickly and surely across the strings, and more accurately than I could manage with two good eyes. Watching him, I felt ashamed of my poor prowess, and vowed to practice more.

When he paused for a moment, shaking his hands to ease the tension of playing, a young boy came to him with a cup of ale. The harper took it with a smile and a word of thanks, and the boy squatted down beside him, talking as the man drank. Father and son, I thought: for the likeness was unmistakable. In a little while the boy took back the now-empty cup and went away, disappearing into the crowd. Kieran returned to his playing, and I to my slow circling of the hall, but I got little good of it. Conversations were dying down; the food had all been eaten; and men were thinking of their blankets. Presently the King left the hall, and the servants began to clear away the trestle tables. I could not see Taliesin; perhaps he had gone with the King. But I saw the harper rise from his stool and went to join him, saying a few words of thanks for his playing. He smiled. "Na, it was no great thing. It was a good song you made, I liked it. Have you been long with Taliesin?"

"Na, only a little while," I said. "My own master Talhaearn has loaned me to him for the summer, to replace his prentice Neirin who got his Mastery this Beltane past. But in that little while he has taught me much."

"He is a good teacher," said Kieran. "I should know... Will you drink a cup of ale with me and talk for a while?"

"Gladly," I said. "But first I should go and claim my blanket-space in the stables while I still can."

"Look for me in the bake-house when you return," said Kieran. "My woman works there, and we will be sleeping there tonight, with the hall so full."

I met Taliesin coming out of the stables with his saddlebags over his shoulder, and told him what I had heard in the hall. Even in the rainy twilight I could see his frown. "Rhun will have heard some of this already," he said, "but I will tell him more. It was only to be expected. Gods send the weather is better tomorrow... Are you on your way to bed?"

"Na," I said, "I am only coming to claim a spot for my blankets, if there is still room left. Kieran has offered me a cup of ale and some talk before sleeping."

"Good," said Taliesin. "You should hear his tale." And he nodded and went on his way.

The bake-house was at the back of the *llys*, set apart from the hall like the kitchens for fear of fire. Inside it was warm and sweet-smelling still from the day's baking, and dimly lit by rush-lights in prickets on the walls. At one side of the room three women were working at the dough-tubs with big wooden paddles, mixing the barm and water into the flour for next morning's bread. Two young girls were helping them, while in a nearby corner several smaller children slept tumbled together on a blanket like a litter of puppies. The blind harper sat on a bench against the other wall tuning his harp: wet weather is not good for horse-hair strings, and several had been going out of tune toward the end of his playing. When he heard my step on the threshold, he turned his face toward me. "Is it yourself, Gwernin?"

"It is," I said, coming to join him on his bench. "I am sorry to have been so long; it was hard to find bed-space. I think every foot of floor is taken, in the stables as well as the hall. You have a roomy palace here by comparison."

"Indeed, I know it," said Kieran, smiling. "And I am as well-served as any king in Ireland." As he spoke his young son came up to us, carefully carrying two wooden cups. The ale was fresh and sweet, better than what I had got in the hall earlier, and I said so. "Ah," said Kieran, "and so it should be: the brew-man is my wife's brother, and always sends us the best. To your health!"

"And to yours, and that of all here present," I said, and drank again. We sat in silence for a moment, I watching the women working, and the harper following some thought of his own. "You have been here some years, have you not?" I said at last. "Taliesin said I should hear your story. Would you tell it to me?"

Kieran was silent for so long that I thought I might have offended him, and began to apologize, but he cut me short. "Na, na, friend," he said. "I was only thinking how to begin… Tell me first, how old are you?"

"Seventeen," I said. "Eighteen come harvest month."

"*Sa, sa…* I was much your age when I lost my sight, and that was twenty years ago. Had it not been for Taliesin, I would be a slave now, or dead. But when I was sixteen, I was the younger son of a king and a good warrior, riding to battle on a gold-maned stallion and sleeping in purple, as strong and proud as any man in Ireland…until my father died. In Ireland the kingship comes by election from the close circle of the royal kin, not from father to son only, as among the Britons. I was well-liked by many, and might have been king in my turn, though I was young for it, but as it happened they chose my one of my older half-brothers—I had many, for my father had known many women—because he was a proven war-leader. That was when I first met Taliesin; he had come over to Ireland on some business of Arthur's, he and his former master Talhaearn, and they stopped by our *rath* for the king-making. He was a year or two older than I—much the same age you are now—and we took a liking to each other, and spent some time together while our elders were talking."

Kieran fell silent for a moment, staring into his inner darkness, while I tried and failed to think of Taliesin as a youth. "What did you do together?" I asked at last.

"Hmm? Oh, rode about the countryside, I think—I mind me he wanted to see some of old places, the stones and the fairy hills. And he told me about Arthur's battles—that was what I wanted to hear. He did not sing in hall—he was not a master bard then, as the Irish know it—but he told a tale or two." Kieran smiled briefly to himself. "Then he rode away, and my life went on as before—for a while."

"What happened to change it?" I asked when he had sat some time silent. The women had finished mixing the dough and kneading it; now they were shaping it into loaves. The harper's son sat cross-legged on the floor nearby, listening silently, and outside the rain dripped from the thatch into the shallow ditches under the eaves. At my prodding Kieran shook his head and sighed, and went on with his tale.

"It was a time of unrest, of border-raids and midnight murders. My half-brother led out his war-band to fight, and I went with them. But the neighboring king was quicker; he took us in an ambush, and many of our men were killed, and the rest of us would have been, had not my brother sued for peace. He gave hostages, and I was one of them. This was nothing out of the ordinary, you understand; hostages are given and taken often there, as they are here in Wales. But what happened to me was not ordinary; it was vile..." He stopped and compressed his lips for a moment, an old anger burning in his scarred face. His little son sat wide-eyed and silent, listening. At last Kieran went on.

"I believe my brother himself gave the orders, though I did not hear them. He had failed in battle; his kingship might have been in question; he may have seen me as a threat. But a king must be without blemish, and a blind man cannot be king..." Unconsciously he put his hands to his face, covering the eyes he no longer had, then realized what he was doing and dropped them again to his lap.

"I am sorry," I said awkwardly. "You do not need to tell me

this. I should not have asked." Kieran shook his head.

"Na," he said, "I am telling it for Taliesin. I owe him that... Well, when I was healed enough to travel they took me to the coast, and sold me to the slave-traders. After a time I ended up in Dumnonia—Kernow, as some call it now. A blind slave is not valuable; there are too many things he cannot do; he gets all the roughest jobs, the hardest bed and the least food. It was I who ground the corn, turning the quern all day; I who led the mule hour after hour around his track in the winnowing yard; I who scoured filthy pots in the kitchen by touch, and washed the new-shorn fleeces before they went to the dye-vats. The language was strange to me, and I was slow at first to learn it, and was beaten often for my stupidity; but the smell of the country—the wind from the sea, the new-plowed earth, the corn-fields in summer and leaf-mold in autumn—was much like my own land, and filled me sometimes with longing. Now and then a bard would come, and there would be music in the hall, and sometimes I could linger for a while by the door-post to listen, and imagine that I was still a king's son in Ireland...

"I had been three years a slave in that place when Taliesin came. I think he had not meant to stop there; it was no great lord's court, though it was a big farm; but it was cold autumn and raining, and he came seeking shelter. He sang in the hall that night, and I knew his voice. I did not think he would recognize me, or I would have stayed away from him; I had still some rags of pride. But after his singing one of the kitchen-women gave me a basket of bread to take to the high table, and while doing so I stumbled over the hounds in the rushes and fell, and cursed the bread-loving dogs in my own tongue as they fought for the loaves which I would have fain eaten myself. And the women cursed me in my turn for an Irish fool, and I would have had a beating for my clumsiness, but in the midst of it all I heard Taliesin's voice calling my name—my name which no one had called me by in three years and more! And I answered, and he knew me."

One of the women came with a pitcher and filled our cups, speaking first to the harper and rumpling the child's red hair as she passed. Kieran turned his face up to her, and she bent down and kissed him—a plain, brown woman she was, no longer young, but with a sweet smile. "My beautiful wife," he said proudly to me, putting his arm around her for a moment. "One of the best things in my life."

"What was the end of the tale?" I asked when the woman had gone back to her bread-making.

"Oh, Taliesin took me," said Kieran, "as the least part of the payment for his song that night. He found there was music in me, and taught me the harp. And he got me a place here in Gwynedd, at one of old King Maelgwn's courts, and set me free." He yawned suddenly and stretched, his scarred face relaxing into a smile. Seeing him easier the boy got up and came to him, and Kieran gave him the harp to put away. "Yes," he said, half to himself, "I am as well off here as any king in Ireland. I have my woman and three healthy children; bed and food and fire; and my harp to play in the hall. I am a rich man, Gwernin, richer than many who are of higher rank. And praise be to God, I know it, which is the greatest gift of all!"

We finished our ale, and I went out into the rain to find my bed in the stables. And sometime in the night I dreamed of my girl Rhiannedd, and woke to lie awake and wonder how she was—she and my soon-to-be child.

But that, O my children, is a story for another day.

The Black Spears

I have said it before, and I will say it again: for bloodshed and insult there must always be a payment. For blood the price may be blood, and it may be gold, and it may be something else; but however long in it is coming, it must be paid. Otherwise there is no peace—no peace for the living, or for the dead. Always *galanas* must be paid. But where does the paying stop?

The day after I sang in hall was no good day for riding. It is true the rain had stopped—almost stopped—but the roads were deep in mire, black and thick and sticky, churned up by the passage of many horses and men. Whenever a few rays of sunlight broke through the clouds, the countryside steamed, and we steamed with it. To the summer smells of plowed fields and green forests were added those of crushed vegetation, fresh ordure, and many unwashed bodies. I fancied even the eagles circling high above us moved aside to avoid our stink.

Nevertheless, I was feeling happier with my lot, for that day I rode with Taliesin, and not with the pack train. He had arranged for one of the packers to add our three ponies to his string, saying with a smile, "I think I need to keep you more under my eye, Gwernin. It was not to be a horse-boy I borrowed you from Talhaearn. You sang very well last night, but there were one or two spots where your lines might have been stronger. Let us work on them together, and see what we can achieve." And he proceeded to point out several weak points in my ornament and rhyme scheme, and helped me to improve them. At our midday stop he ate with the King, and I with the King's *teulu*, so by the end of the day I was feeling myself a bard again—or at least a bard in training!—and not a barefoot servant.

We made a long ride that day, for Rhun was impatient to push his enemies out of Gwynedd, and especially out of the narrow mountain valleys where his restless war-bands might think to set a trap for them. "He wants no more fighting," said Taliesin that afternoon when I remarked on our pace. "It will not serve his purpose, either to lose more of his own men, or to breed more hatred among the Men of the North, lest what has happened once should happen again. The Cymry have no need of other enemies, when we can find so many among those who should be our friends. So it was with Arthur; so it will ever be, unless we unite under some new leader." His face was sad for a moment; then he began to question me on my poetic forms, and I was kept too busy to think of the past. But I remembered his words later.

Despite Rhun's best efforts, it was early evening before we came to the Conwy crossing at Caerhun. This was the Roman ford near the top of tidewater where I had crossed several times before, mostly recently on our way to Arfon. We were all still on the west bank of the river, for the rain had made the higher fords impassable. Even here the Conwy was still running high, but the tide was well out, and the breaking clouds above us shone tawny-red with low sunset light, reflecting in the fast-flowing water and giving an oddly autumnal tinge to the summer-green meadows. Rhun's party, Taliesin and I with them, was heading for the fort where we meant to spend the night, but I could see ahead of us the Northerners bunching up near the ford, as if uncertain whether to cross now or wait until morning. A group of the leaders were conferring on horseback, and among them I recognized Neirin on his gray pony, his hair shining foxy-red in the strange light. I turned toward Taliesin to make some comment, and saw him looking over his shoulder. At the same time I became aware of a drumming of hooves behind us. The black-speared men of Arfon had pulled themselves out of the line of march and were heading for their hated enemies at a gallop, their lances leveled as they charged.

Rhun must have heard them at the same instant I did. With a curse he kicked his big red horse from a walk to a gallop, setting off at an angle to intercept his unruly men, his *teulu* streaming after him like the tail of a comet. The weary Northerners, most of whom had taken turns riding and walking through the thick mud that day, would be no match for the men of the black spears, but they still held hostages, and would not tamely let them go. Without thinking I kicked my black pony into a gallop after Rhun, and this time Taliesin did not stop me. He himself was already in motion close behind the King, his high-bred mare with her light rider gaining on the big red stallion with every stride she took. I kicked my pony again and settled down to ride, trying my best to keep up with them. What I would do when I reached the fight I did not know, for my sword, like Neirin's and Taliesin's, was safely packed in our baggage and out of reach.

Partially dismounted the Northerners might be, but they were not disarmed. I saw swords and spear-points catch the ruddy light as they formed their battle line for what might be their last stand. In the confusion I had lost track of Neirin, but as I came nearer I caught a glimpse of him again, close beside his brother: they seemed to be arguing. At least I knew that he was still alive.

If the men of the black spears saw Rhun and his retinue, they paid him no heed; indeed they may have thought he was spurring to join them. On they swept at a head-long gallop through the fields beside the river, trampling the ripening corn into the mud as they came. I was close enough now to see faces I knew, men I had drunk with or entertained that summer. Red-headed Dai was there, from Cadwaladr's war-band, and my old friend Ieuan as well, though I looked in vain for their canny lord. I saw seasoned men whom I had overhead plotting revenge the night before, young warriors in their first strength, and boys dressed in their fathers' war-gear. Not yellow-haired Blaidd, of course: he was riding like the wind in the *teulu*, just behind Taliesin and the King, his sword in his fist and his strong teeth showing in a wolfish grin.

We were almost within spear-cast when at last Rhun drew ahead of his men. It was not enough, I thought; there was no way he could stop them, and the mounted Northerners were spurring forward already to meet us, breaking ranks with their spearmen on foot. Then Rhun hauled his red stallion back from a gallop to a sliding, trampling, snorting halt, and flung up one hand, crying "Stop!" in a voice of bronze. And Taliesin beside him echoed his cry at such a pitch that I found my hands acting to rein back my black pony before I had fully understood what my ears had heard.

It did not work for everyone; some of the warriors, particularly on the river side farther away from us, charged on regardless; some of the Northerners had already begun to cast their spears. But now Rhun's *teulu* were putting themselves between the forces as well, and other men were taking up the call, including Clydno Eidyn. A few spears found their targets; a few sword-stokes were exchanged; here and there a man rocked in his saddle from a blow, or fell, blood spurting from his wounds; but slowly, like savage hounds hauled apart by their masters, the armies drew back, and a sullen silence fell on the field, broken only by the cries of the wounded.

Slowly Rhun paced forward on his sweating horse, deliberately turning his unarmored back on the enemy and facing his own men. His face was like a thundercloud; the lightening was in his eyes. "Stop there!" he said. "Stop there and let me see you, you who make war without my permission here in my land. I thought you were men of Gwynedd, riding under my banner, but it seems I was wrong. You are no better than raiding Irishmen, or Saxon scum come from across the sea. Who among you planned this attack against my command? If you want fighting, come and fight me now—here I am, ready to take you all on! For if you ride in my despite, you are no men of mine!"

There was uneasy silence for a moment, broken only by the stamping of the restless horses, the jink of bit or spur. Then someone back in the ranks spoke up. "Na, Lord, we ride to defend your honor—to defend your land! It is not right that these thieves should pillage our Arfon and ride away with their spoil. Lead us now, and let us make an end of them!"

"Yes!" cried another. "Lead us now, Lord, and let us cut them down! It is no right thing you do, to tamely let them go!"

"They have shed blood, let their blood pay!" cried a third voice. "*Galanas* is due to us all—let us have it in blood!" Others took up the cry: "*Galanas! Galanas!* Let us have blood!"

"Na!" said Rhun strongly, and they fell silent to hear him.

"And if you die taking it, who will repay you your lives? Who will till your farms and feed your wives and children? Who will lift the black spears to protect them when next the Irish come raiding, if you lie buried here? And what of the hostages, who put their necks in the noose for your sake and mine? Who will repay their deaths, if you betray them and me?"

"Let them take their chances," cried someone back in the ranks. "If they die, you can kill the Northerners' men in exchange."

"*Sa, sa,*" said another, "we hazard our lives as well!"

"Brave dealing!" said Rhun. "Brave dealing to leave men helpless, who risked their lives for you—you who go into battle with bright swords in your hands! Who will stand hostage for you in the future, if you betray these? Not I, I tell you, not I nor any of mine! If that is the reputation you want, you can have it—how the bards will laugh! Your word-fame will run the length and breadth of Britain, and your children will disown your names!"

There was a muttering in the ranks, and I thought Rhun might have gone too far. These were proud men, free tribesmen and not bought soldiers, and their blood was up. But he did not give them time to make up their minds. Reining his horse in a half-circle, he raked them with his glance. "Go back now to your places!" he said. "Set up your encampments on the north side of the fort. I will finish here what you have started—I do not need your spears to aid me tonight! Take up your wounded and go!" And wheeling his horse, he started at a slow trot toward the Northerners' lines where Clydno Eidyn and Rhydderch Hael were waiting, while behind him the Black Spears, baffled and ashamed, did as they were told.

I was about to follow the King when I heard a voice calling my name. Turning, I saw red-headed Dai riding toward me. "Gwernin!" he said as he came nearer. "I am glad I saw you. Come now, please come—come at once!"

"What is it?" I asked, but from his expression and the tone of his voice I knew it was bad news.

"Ieuan," he said. "He took one of the spears. He wants you. Come now, lad, do!"

I looked back over my shoulder for Taliesin, but he was following the King. "Where is he?" I asked.

"Over here," said Dai, starting back the way he had come. I followed him; it was not far.

Ieuan lay on the ground with two men kneeling beside him. They had stretched him out and were cutting away his blood-soaked tunic to come at the wound in his belly. The spear that struck him must have been at extreme range, for it had not gone through him—but it had gone quite far enough. Ieuan's ruddy face was white and twisted with pain, and he was gasping for breath. I knelt beside him and took his hands, which were clenched into fists, and he turned them and took hold of mine, gripping so hard it hurt. "Ieuan," I said, "Ieuan! O Gods!"

"Gwernin," he said through clenched teeth. "Still—not a Christian—boy?"

"Na," I said, "na, I am not." The man who had been slitting Ieuan's tunic was shaking his head; the bandage-linen he laid over the wound was soaked at once, but he went on trying to bind it into place. Ieuan gave a cry when they lifted him a little to get the cloth under him. His face was wet with sweat and his eyes were closed.

"O Jesus!" he said. "O sweet Jesus! Gwernin—!"

"I am here," I said steadily. I had seen men die of their wounds before, but not many, and not friends I had known from my childhood. My tears were blinding me, but Ieuan still held my hands, and I could not wipe them away. "Hold on, Ieuan, they are bandaging you now. Soon you will be better." I knew it was a lie as I said it, and so did Ieuan.

"Tell Anwen…" he said, gasping, "tell her…"

"What shall I tell her?" I asked, giving up the pretence.

"Tell her…best years…of my life. God bless…"

"Who?" I asked. "Who should he bless, Ieuan?" But I got no answer from him. He was choking and coughing; blood was running out of his mouth; his lips were turning blue. Then his eyes rolled up and he spasmed; his body went on trying to live for a little while longer, but Ieuan was gone. My hands were bruised for days afterwards from the clutch he kept on me to the end.

I went on kneeling beside him for a long time after he was still, until his friends brought over his pony. Then I got stiffly to my feet and watched while they threw his body over the saddle of the uneasy beast. Someone handed me Du's reins, and I mounted without thinking. I was about to follow them to the camp, when I remembered Taliesin and Neirin, and turned back instead toward the ford. Ieuan was dead: my duty was to the living: but it was not easy to ride away.

In the short time it had taken Ieuan to die, things had changed: the Northerners were crossing the river. They were going slowly, for the current was too swift for men alone on foot, and they crossed in small groups, one or two dismounted men clinging to each horseman. The water was deep but fairly clear, and the long summer twilight gave them light enough to see their way. On the far side I could see shadowy figures setting up camp; several cook fires were already springing to life, and one of their small herd of bullocks was bawling in protest as he was led to the slaughter. On this side of the river the three Kings sat their horses close together, talking quietly, Taliesin and Neirin beside them. From a little distance Rhun's *teulu* and a matching group of Northerners watched each other suspiciously, like rival packs of hounds. No one paid me much attention as I rode up and joined the Kings, and I was glad to have it so.

"Na, the Romans' road runs straight from here to Deva," Rhun was saying, "and if you march briskly, you may be there in two days. There you can find the ships you need, or make your own bargain with Cyndeyrn. But I want you out of my lands so soon as may be. After two days I will not hold my men back; and if my hostages die, then so shall yours also: be warned!"

"*Sa, sa*, you have said that already," said Rhydderch Hael. "But if we took ship at Deganwy, we would be the sooner gone."

"Na," said Rhun with hard-held patience, "I have told you once, there are no ships such as you need at Deganwy now, and I will not have you camped outside my walls for who knows how long. As well house the fox in the hen-coop! There would be bloodshed within three days—maybe two!"

"Then give us more horses, enough to mount all our men, and we will be at Deva before the sun sets tomorrow," said Rhydderch.

"I am not a fool," said Rhun. "Why do you take me for one? If I remounted you, you would let loose fire and slaughter in Rhos and Tegeingl to match what you did in Arfon and the Lleyn. I would rather take what horses you have, but that would make you too tempting a target. I want no more bloodshed in this matter."

"With that, if nothing else, I am agreed," said Clydno Eidyn smoothly. "You have the whip hand, Gwynedd: we will go to Deva. Are you content?"

"So far as I may be, when good men's lives have been lost," said Rhun. "Go, then, and join your troops: I will be watching you tomorrow." And turning his horse, he rejoined his *teulu*, and they rode off toward the *llys*. Rhydderch Hael, muttering under his breath, set off toward the ford, but Clydno lingered for a moment, Neirin beside him.

"Taliesin," said Clydno abruptly, "I give my brother his freedom for tonight: he has things to tell you. He may rejoin me in the morning." And as quickly as he had spoken, he was gone, leaving the three of us to stare at each other in surprise.

"Well, well," said Taliesin after a moment, shrugging his shoulders, "we had better follow the King now, or we will find no lodging in the fort tonight. Neirin, you can tell us what this means as we ride."

"Na, I am not knowing," said Neirin as we set our horses in motion. His clothes were dirty and rumpled, unlike his usual careful dressing, and his face in the twilight looked weary and bruised. "I did not expect it. But it is true I have things to tell you, and things to ask."

"Tell them now," said Taliesin. "We will not be more private at the fort." And it was true we were almost alone on the road now; everyone else was already about the evening's business. Smoke rose from many cook-fires in the fort and in the fields; war-bands were setting up their camps; horses and cattle were being put to graze in the meadows under the watchful eyes of their herders. In the west the broken clouds were fading to a pale ashy gray as the sun's fires were quenched; the day was done. From somewhere high above us came the bubbling song of a single skylark, tumbling down in a cascade of notes; then it ceased. The beauty of that song pierced my heart; my tears overflowed.

"Gwernin," said Neirin urgently beside me, "why are you weeping? Are you wounded, brother? There is blood on your clothes. Were you in the fight?"

"Na," I said, "na." I could go no farther. Sobs heaved in my breast; my tears flowed down like rain. I tried to wipe them away, tried to regain control of myself. "A friend was killed today," I said.

"Ah," said Taliesin. "That was why you stayed behind—I wondered. Tell us when you are ready; in the meantime Neirin will talk—he is good at it."

"*Sa, sa*," said Neirin ruefully. "True that is. Well, as my brother said, I have things to tell you, and chiefly that we have made peace between us—for the moment! And when he takes ship for the North I am going with him, to sing at his court for a little while and take part in the Contention." This was a great competition of bards held at Dun Eidyn every summer; the year before Neirin had won it, and with it his silver circlet. "I am thinking he feels the need of a good song-smith to bolster his prestige after this failure," said Neirin, and chuckled. "I doubt me I will stay long at his court, though—we are too different, and too alike; we will always strike sparks off each other."

"Where will you settle for the winter, then?" asked Taliesin to keep him talking—for I think he knew.

"With my mother's brother, Gwallawg Elmet, if he will have me," said Neirin. "I would like to spend some time in those hills, and in that grove."

"Bro Arnemetia," said Taliesin thoughtfully. "Yes, there are deep roots there. I shall be visiting it again myself, one of these days—perhaps before summer's end. You were there last year with

Neirin, were you not, Gwernin?"

"*Sa*," I said huskily. I remembered the young grove of oaks on their hilltop, and the things I had seen and heard there: a shadow out of all proportion to the trees; the echo of a brazen horn, faint and far-off, like the horn of Gwyn mab Nudd; and the sound of voices chanting: that, and the touch of hands where hands had rested long ago. "Will we go there soon, Master?"

"Perhaps," said Taliesin, and smiled.

That night while Taliesin and Neirin sang for the King in his hall, I watched the Lord Cadwaladr and his men bury Ieuan. With only one death in their war-band that day, they could take time to do the thing properly. They put him into the earth in the little Christian burial ground outside the fort, with a priest from the nearby *clas* to say the words. I remember the solemn faces in the torchlight, and the thud of the earth going into the grave, striking the well-wrapped body. I remember my own tears—not many, for the well of my grief had almost run dry. I had not loved Ieuan, but I had known him for a very long time, more than half of my life; he was part of my childhood. It was time, I thought, to put childhood away, and be a man.

But that, O my children, is a story for another day.

A Long Summer's Day

Rhun began the next morning by sending half his army home. The men of Arfon, Môn, and the Lleyn had done enough, he proclaimed: it was time they went back to rebuild their ravaged farmsteads and gather such of their harvest as had survived. He would be reinforced that very day by men from Rhos and Tegeingl, Rhufoniog and Dyffryn Clwyd; these, who had suffered no losses, would take up the burden where the first war-bands laid it down, and harry the Northerners out of Gwynedd. Not mentioned, but implied, was the fact that the new levies would have no personal blood-debts to avenge, and might be more controllable in consequence. The men of Arfon, Môn and the Lleyn understood this, but they were weary with fighting and longing for their homes, and they took their dismissal in good part. Most of them set off westward along the Roman road which ran through the Ddeufaen Pass, an easier route than the torturous track we had ridden through Eryri. Meanwhile, the rest of us followed the Northerners along the same Roman road to the east.

Neirin had gone back to his half-brother's camp that morning, according to the terms of his parole. The night before, when the feasting was over, he had bedded down with me in the stables, the two of us sharing my blankets in the dusty straw-scented darkness, full of the snores and rustlings of the other men sleeping there. Lying beside me with his hands clasped behind his head, he told me a little more of what had passed between him and Clydno during the last few days.

"The first night, Rhydderch and the others bade me sing for them," he said, "and when they did not like my singing—for I was not after praising them, I can tell you!—they made for to pay me in kicks and blows. But Clydno stepped between, telling them to be content with what they had got, and not make bad worse by angering a bard; for praise which could only be got by threats was not worth the having, and might change to its mirror-image when the bard moved on. That sort of word-fame, he said, he did not want, and more fools they if they did!" Neirin chuckled softly. "He is good at persuasion, I will grant him that: I watched him drive them as a master charioteer drives a half-broken team. But I will be making sure in the future that he does not drive me so." And with that he turned on his side, his shoulder warm against mine, and so fell asleep, leaving me to lie awake for some time, a prey to my misgivings. I did not trust Clydno Eidyn: it seemed to me that having failed with Neirin one way, he was now trying another; but there was no point in saying that to Neirin, for he would not believe me.

I am told that the Romans used to take two days to march from Caerhun to Deva, though it can be done much faster on a good horse. Half of the Northerners were marching, however, so two days is what it took us as well. It was not hard traveling, such as we had just had amidst the crags and streams of Eryri, for once the road climbs out of the Conwy valley, it runs straight and true along the ridges and over the crests of the gentle green hills of Rhos, until it reaches Dyffryn Clwyd and Llanelwy. There, on the river-meadows near the monks' wooden-walled *clas*—founded not so many years before by Kentigern—we camped for the night, the King's party on the west bank and the Northerners on the east. Rhun had kept them moving at a good pace all day, chivvying at their heels like a sheepdog, and now he set mounted pickets to surround them, lest some of them be tempted to break out and cause trouble in the dark. However, we had a quiet night of it, in a warm and peaceful land—for on our leaving Eryri the weather had reverted to high summer. One more long summer's day would see our enemies pushed over the border, and an end to Gwynedd's grief—though whether the Princes of Powys would be so happy with the results was another question.

"Where shall we go next, Master?" I asked Taliesin the following morning, as our party toiled slowly up the steep eastern side of the valley through the ancient oak forest which clothed its slopes, heading toward the bald sheep-cropped hilltops above. The patches of sunlight dropping through the dark leaves were warm on my face, the trees were full of birdsong, and I was feeling cheerful once again. "You spoke of Elmet the other night."

"I did," said Taliesin, giving me a sideways look. "Are you so eager to go there?"

"I would like to go, yes," I said, and slapped at a deerfly which had lit on my bridle hand. "But I will be happy to go wherever you choose."

"Well, we shall see," said Taliesin. "I think we will be a day or two at Deva before we move on. If we entertain there tonight, what song will you sing? Remember, the Northern Kings will probably be in the hall, as well Rhun."

"Mmm," I said, biting my lip. "I will have to think on that... I had better praise our host Cyndeyrn, then, but I do not know much about him."

"That is why bards must know genealogies and histories—the descent of kings and their deeds," said Taliesin with a smile, and proceeded to give me a lesson. "Do you make a song with that," he said at the end, "and have it ready for me to hear when we take horse again after our nooning." And shaking his reins to get his mare's attention, he rode on up the line of the *teulu* toward the King, leaving me to my work.

The long straight road across the lonely hilltops, silent except for the sighing of the wind in the heather and the distant bleating of sheep, lay behind us, and likewise our noontime halt near Treffynnon—a holy well once sacred to the Druids, and now taken over by the Christians for one of their many saints—before I had completed my song to my satisfaction. Taliesin when he heard it was less pleased, however, and pointed out several areas for my improvement, so with a sigh I set to work again. By then we were riding beside the wide flat estuary of the Afon Dyfrdwy, the river which gives Deva its harbor. The tide was half out, and the mudflats were busy with shore birds, and loud with the crying of gulls. I got a phrase or two from them to add to my lines, and slapped at the biting black flies which had come up from the strand to feast on this moving banquet. Du shook his head in annoyance, but they paid him no heed, settling on his eyelids and around his nose and mouth, so that he snorted again and again. In a while the road led away from the water, and the flies diminished; but the sun which had been pleasantly warm in the morning was now baking down upon us, and the sea breeze had died.

Riding half-asleep in the heat, I began day-dreaming about Deva, a city I had visited once before with Taliesin and Neirin. I remembered with pleasure the comfortable room we had shared in the Prince's guesthouse, and the hot plunge in his still-functioning Roman baths; but chiefly I remembered the beautiful slender girls I had seen on the city streets and in the court. Maybe, I thought, if I sang well tonight, one of them might fancy me... But with this many visiting soldiers and captains and kings in the town, my chances of getting a girl to myself were not good. In a day or two, however, when we moved on, they should improve. I was still thinking of girls when I saw Taliesin waiting for me up ahead. Hurriedly I ran through my refurbished song in my mind. Perhaps it was good enough now, I thought. Taliesin listened to it and agreed, but as if half his thoughts were elsewhere. Across the wide river on the eastern bank, Deva was coming into sight.

Like all the Roman towns, this fortress city had lost much of its past grandeur and population, but it had been a great seaport in its day. Its red sandstone walls with their well-built gates and watchtowers loomed over the shipping anchored at its docks, which ranged from sea-going traders to small fishing boats, and I saw with mixed emotions that there were plenty of ships large enough to take the Northerners home. I would be glad to see the back of them, no question, but Neirin would go with them, and the Gods alone knew when I would see him again.

I said as much to him that evening in Cyndrwyn's guesthouse, where the three of us were sharing a room. We had managed a quick visit to the bathhouse before dinner, and Taliesin had already dressed and gone to the hall; but Neirin, clad only in his trews, was still searching through his pack for some of his better clothes, while

I sat cross-legged on my bed-place polishing my boots and watching him. There was little of the boy left in him now. His dark red hair, combed out to dry, hung thickly curling on his strong shoulders; and looking at his fine beard, I rubbed my thumb and finger absently over my own chin, which still only sprouted untidy clumps of fuzz. "Do you remember," I said, "when we were here last summer, and went looking for girls?"

Neirin glanced up at me from his search and laughed, his amber eyes sparkling with amusement. "Do I not! *Hai mai*, I think your thoughts are running on the same lines as mine, brother! But I doubt me we will be having the time this trip, for I will not be here long. Clydno is impatient to get home before his neighbors come visiting in his absence, and I cannot blame him."

"Na, or I either…though it would be only justice," I said, remembering ravaged Arfon.

"Not to those who would suffer the most, and who never did Gwynedd harm," said Neirin seriously, and then laughed again. "Ah, well, there will be girls enough for me in Dun Eidyn!" And finding the tunic he sought, he began to worm his way into it, emerging after a moment or two somewhat tousled and red in the face. "*Hai mai!*" he said again, smoothing the bright cloth carefully across his chest and flexing his shoulders. "This fit me well enough two moons ago, and now it is tight. Have you been wearing it, brother, perhaps in the rain, to shrink it in my absence?"

"Not I," I said laughing. "You have been growing again."

Neirin made a face. "Perhaps a little." He buckled his bronze-mounted belt across his flat stomach and grinned. "That must be why I am so hungry! Make haste to finish your dressing, and let us go to the hall: I am thinking I could eat half a cow, bones and all!"

In the torch-lit feast-hall we found an unexpected sight. Half a dozen tall richly-dressed men stood by the central hearth, drinking from silver cups and talking amiably, their bright-colored robes agleam with jewels in the smoky firelight. Such a sight was not unusual in Cyndeyrn's hall; it was only the identity of the drinkers which surprised me. Two of them—not unnaturally—were gray-haired Cyndeyrn himself and his warrior son, whom I remembered from my previous visit, but the other four were Rhun, Rhydderch Hael, Clydno Eidyn, and Nudd Hael. A few days ago, I thought, they had been trying to kill each other; now they met peaceably on neutral ground to share a measure of good wine. Such are the ways of kings and of princes.

That night Neirin sat beside Taliesin at the high table, and sang praise by turns to Cyndeyrn, Rhun, and Clydno Eidyn. Praising the last two in the same hall was a tricky business, but he managed it dexterously, speaking as little as he might of war. Taliesin sang as well, and even I came in for a turn late in the evening. The black-browed bard of that hall, Bluchbardd, I did not see, but the Lady Denw, the young unmarried daughter of Cyndeyrn, was much in evidence. Her fair hair, uncovered as befitted a maiden, seemed to gather all the light of the torches to itself; she glowed like a fine beeswax candle, pale and slender and bright. As always she seemed drawn to Taliesin, though he gave her only such notice as was civil; but once or twice I saw her turn her green eyes thoughtfully on Neirin, and once or twice I saw his amber ones watching her in return. Always he had a liking for a golden lass: but this one was far out of idle reach, even for such as he. For myself, I ate good braised cow-meat and drank clear sweet mead and talked with my table-companions, and enjoyed the pleasures of clean clothes and a full belly, and the prospect of a comfortable—if solitary!—bed that night. It was a good end to a long summer's day.

The next morning was less peaceful. Rhun was determined to reclaim the remaining horses stolen by the Northerners, neither letting them be carried off to the North nor sold here in Deva for the reavers' profit, while Rhydderch and Clydno were equally determined not to lose more face than they had lost already. We came to breakfast to find a hot discussion taking place in the hall, with threats and raised voices and hands on knife-hilts, and there might have been bright blood spilled on the flagstones had not Taliesin and Cyndeyrn stepped between the would-be combatants. In the end, words won where steel had failed, and the Kings and their captains went forth to oversee the exchange of horses—and incidentally of the remaining human hostages!—between the opposing armies camped outside the town. This achieved, Rhun did not linger: by afternoon he and his war-bands were a cloud of dust on the western road, and Deva subsided into an uneasy peace.

That evening in the guesthouse as we were making ourselves fine for the feast, Taliesin asked Neirin, "When do you sail, Little Hawk?"

"I am thinking it will be tomorrow," said Neirin. He had been combing his hair, but now he laid aside his many-toothed bone comb and began to gather the dark red mass together and divide it into three parts, before starting to braid it. "Clydno and Rhydderch have made their bargain with the ship captains, and Cyndeyrn has gone surety for them, so there is nothing more to stay for… Will you be setting out, then, for Elmet, or do you bide here yet awhile?"

"Neither the one nor the other," said Taliesin, looking up from the carved wooden box which held his finest jewels, his great enameled brooch in his hand. "We will be leaving tomorrow also, but for Powys Cyndrwyn, not Elmet."

"For Powys—!" said Neirin. "But—I thought Gwernin was going with you to Elmet?"

"What?" I said, breaking in. "Master, are you sending me home? Have I displeased you?"

"Well," said Taliesin, and paused for a moment, looking amused. "No, not exactly, Gwernin—and no, you have not displeased me. It is only that I thought I might see how Talhaearn is bearing up with young Rhys, and relieve him of that affliction if it seems necessary. I thought, too, that you might like to spend the rest of the summer with your girl Rhiannedd, all things considered."

"All things considered?" repeated Neirin, puzzled. "Is there a problem with her, Gwernin? You did not tell me so."

"I—na, I suppose I did not," I said, and felt myself blushing. "It is only—it is only that she is…" I stopped, embarrassed for some reason I could not name.

"She is what?" asked Neirin, frowning in bewilderment. And

then, as I did not answer, he started to grin. "Aha!" he said, his amber eyes sparkling. "My *awen* whispers to me, and I foretell—a birth! Am I not right, Gwion?"

"You are," said Taliesin, grinning back at him. "So, Gwernin—do you stay with me, or not? We will go to Llys-tyn-wynnan regardless."

"I will stay with you, Master, if you please," I said earnestly, "at least until the end of summer."

"Then you may," said Taliesin, and smiled. But Neirin only grinned.

The next morning saw the Northerners go aboard ship. Such horses as they had brought with them—mostly the high-bred stallions belonging to the Kings and captains—were loaded into the holds of the two biggest ships, and Neirin's gray pony went with them. "I can be getting another pack-pony in the North easily enough," he said to me, "but Brith I insisted on taking. He will not enjoy the voyage, poor fellow—and neither shall I if the wind blows as it did last time!—but I could not be leaving him behind." And he went himself, when it was his turn, to soothe the dapple-gray and lead him aboard. From the deck of the ship he waved to us, and we waved back. Then in a little while the sailors cast off the ropes and raised the big mainsail, and the ship, answering to her helm, took her course along the smooth-flowing river and so to the sea. One after another, the other vessels of the expedition followed. But Taliesin and I did not stay to watch them all out of sight; we had a long ride that day to the southwest, toward Llys-tyn-wynnan, and the choices that lay before me there.

But that, O my children, is a story for another day.

Choices

Have you ever been long away from your home, and missed it; yet no sooner were you there, than you were eager to take the road again? So it was with me this time. All the way from Deva—or at least, such of it as I was not kept busy at my duties!—I had been thinking of Rhiannedd: her soft red lips; her dark blue eyes; her hair like black silk between my fingers; her firm white breasts... I had lain wakeful at night with thoughts of her, and during the day my mind had wandered when I should have been listening or composing. Taliesin reproved me for my inattention more than once, and I tried to amend, but always my thoughts went astray, racing ahead of me to Llys-tyn-wynnan and my dear delight.

She was standing in the gateway of the court when we rode up the hill from the river, as if she had seen us coming and stopped to wait. Her arms were full of a willow basket with some green stuff spilling over its edge, and her shape had subtlety altered as the child she carried began to show, but I knew her from afar off, and I think it was the same with her. Even after all these years, I can still remember the joy in her face at the sight of me, come back sooner than she expected; indeed there was but once or twice in my life I saw her gladder. For myself, it was only the fact that I was mounted—and leading three pack-ponies!—which stopped me running to her and scooping her up in my arms. All I could do was call, "Rhiannedd! We are back!" while grinning like a fool.

"Give me the lead rope," said Taliesin as we entered the courtyard. Without more ado I handed it to him, and swung down from Du to go to my girl. She came into my arms gladly, and there in front of everyone we kissed. Indeed, we kissed for a long time, and it was Rhiannedd who drew back first. Then I heard the laughter, and turned around to look. What seemed like half the court was watching us with broad grins, but the person laughing was Rhys.

His short time with Talhaearn had not improved him. Brown eyes, curly brown hair—uncombed—and a wide mouth just now stretched wider with laughter, he was still a thin, coltish figure in an oversized tunic. "Look at the big lover!" he snickered. "I hope he is a better lover than he is a poet—though that would not be hard!"

I felt my face flush hotly with anger, and turned toward him, my hands balling themselves into fists. Rhys continued to grin insolently, though I think he was also preparing to run. Then his eyes slid past me, and the laughter went from his face, leaving it suddenly rather pale.

"A good evening to you, Rhys," said Taliesin coolly from behind me. "Where is your master?"

"I—in the hall, I think," said Rhys uncertainly. He looked sideways at me, then back at Taliesin. "Shall I go and get him?"

"Tell him we have arrived, yes," said Taliesin. "Then you can come back and help with the ponies."

"Yes, Master," said Rhys, and turning on his heel, wove his way rapidly through the crowd and disappeared. Two stable-boys stepped forward to take our reins, and with a few friendly greetings, the rest of the on-lookers went about their interrupted business. Taliesin followed Rhys into the hall, and I started as a matter of habit to carry my gear toward Talhaearn's quarters, then paused. "Where is Rhys sleeping?" I asked Rhiannedd, who still stood watching me.

"With Talhaearn, in your place," she said, frowning. "You can take your gear to the guesthouse along with Taliesin's for tonight—there is plenty of room; no one is using it—and we can sort things out tomorrow. Is Taliesin staying long? Maybe he will take Rhys away with him when he goes, and then we can be comfortable here again."

"Mmm," I said, and paused, my arms full of harps. "I do not think he is staying long, but... Help me with some of this, then we can talk." In private, I thought silently, and without Rhys around.

"Of course," said Rhiannedd, and picked up two of the bundles the stable-boys were unloading from the pack-saddles. "I am so glad," she added as she followed me across the courtyard, "that you are back already. We heard of the fighting in Arfon, and I was afraid... I was afraid. But you were not in the battles, were you? You were only there to help Taliesin, as you told me? Not to fight?"

"Mmm," I said again, shouldering my way into the guesthouse and setting down the harps on one of the bare beds. "I did fight a little—only a little. A bard must know the face of battle, if he is to sing of it and praise the warrior. And as you can see, I am come back whole and well. But of course when I come to be *bardd teulu* to the Prince and his retinue, I must ride to war with them—it will be expected." I had gradually come to count on getting this post in the future, although no one—least of all the Prince—had as yet offered it to me.

"That is different," said Rhiannedd as we headed back for another load. "You will be older, and—and probably not in the front line of battle. Does Taliesin charge the enemy with the King?"

"Not usually," I said, thinking of the field at Caerhun. The image of Ieuan, dead there so short a time ago, came into my mind, and my face set in an unaccustomed bleakness. Rhiannedd looked sideways at me and saw it, and was silent. With an effort, I asked, "Has Talhaearn been well?"

"Well enough for his age," said Rhiannedd, picking up another armload of our gear. Then she giggled. "When Rhys is not driving him mad! Whatever possessed Taliesin to send that boy here? He is horrible."

"I think," I said, draping a saddlebag over either shoulder and picking up my pack, "it was part of the bargain for letting me go with him. Also, they are both friends with his father Ugnach. Also, Rhys has had a good poetic training, and may make a bard someday—if he ever gets any sense in his head! But on the whole, I agree with you. What has he been doing to upset Talhaearn?"

"What has he not done?" Rhiannedd giggled again. "He is dirty—he does not wash unless Talhaearn makes him. He is lazy—Talhaearn must shake him at least three times in the morning to wake him. He is rude to almost everyone except the Prince—even to Talhaearn sometimes! And when Talhaearn beats him for it, he sulks for days on end. He may have a clever tongue—too clever for his own good sometimes!—but no sense of when or how to use it."

"Mmm," I said, setting down the last of our gear in the guest-house. "Maybe Taliesin can manage him."

"Maybe," said Rhiannedd doubtfully. I looked at her, then smiled and opened my arms, and she walked into them.

"Let us not talk of Rhys," I said hoarsely. "We have a little time before anyone will come seeking us—and, oh! I have missed you, Rhiannedd!"

Some time later, while we were lying still close-entwined upon one narrow bed, I felt her stir in my arms. "Gwernin," she said softly, "we had better get up now. It must be almost time to go to the hall; Taliesin may come back at any moment to change his clothes."

"Mmm," I said, and drawing her closer, kissed her. She kissed me back, but after a moment pulled away.

"Na, not now," she said. "We do not have the time." And rising, she began to set her clothes to rights. I lay watching her in the dim light which filtered in around the shutters. She was very beautiful, was Rhiannedd. Her belly was as yet only a little swollen from the child she carried, and her breasts were still high and full. They strained against the blue linen of the sleeveless summer gown she wore, a deep midnight blue like her eyes. She pushed back the dark cascade of her hair, which I had disarranged, and smiled at me. "Get up now, *cariad*. We will have time and to spare on another day, after Taliesin has gone."

"Mmm," I said, sitting up reluctantly and adjusting my own clothes. "I had better tell you, I suppose."

Rhiannedd paused in her arranging of her hair. "Better tell me what?" And then, when I did not speak at once, "Gwernin, you are not going away again? Not again?"

"*Sa*," I said, "I am. But it will not be for long—I will be back before Samhain."

"But why?" asked Rhiannedd. "If he takes Rhys, he cannot need you as well. And Talhaearn does need you—and so do I!"

"Do not press me, *cariad*," I said earnestly. "It is something I have to do. I have learned so much—so much!—from Taliesin already this summer, and to have the chance to travel with him and learn from him for a little longer, is—is a chance that I must seize, even if it means that I must put up with Rhys. It is important—I do not know why, but it is. And if once Taliesin takes Rhys as his new prentice, I may not get another chance."

Rhiannedd looked at me for a long moment. "Well," she said at last, "if you must go, then you must. Only come back to me, Gwernin—promise me that you will!"

"I will," I said. "Though I pass through the Gates of Annwn itself, I will come back. I swear it by my ash spear—by my holy *awen*." And standing up, I opened my arms to her, and she walked into them again. I held her close in silence, her head on my shoulder and my cheek against her dark hair, and her arms tight around me, as though she would never let me go. We were still standing so some moments later when Taliesin scratched at the door and came in.

"Ah!" he said as we fell apart, blushing "Here you are, Gwernin. Talhaearn has been asking for you. Go and see him now—he is in his quarters. Then you can come back and dress for hall."

"Yes, Master," I said, and followed Rhiannedd out the door.

My first thought on seeing Talhaearn was that he had aged a year or more in my absence. His face seemed thinner, and the lines in it more deeply carved; his hands were gnarled and wrinkled, with veins like thick blue worms twisting on their backs. Yet perhaps it was only that having been away, I saw him with fresh eyes, and noticed what had been all the time before me. At any rate, his disposition had not mellowed with age. "So here you are at last, boy," he said as soon as I came into his room. "Where have you been hiding yourself this past hour? I wanted to hear your latest piece before we go to the hall, to judge if it is good enough for you to perform tonight, and now there is scarcely time. What I have done to be cursed with such bone-lazy, absent-minded, ill-advised, incorrigible, unteachable, never-here-when-I-need-them, pie-eyed, pig-ignorant, pestilential puffed-up poetasters as students, I do not know—and each of them worse than the last! It is all very well for Gwion, who as the world knows is never short of young men begging for his attention—ready to lick his boots clean if that is what it takes for him to notice them!—to borrow you whenever I have you halfway trained, and drop some pathetic fool in my lap in return; but I have told him—and I mean it!—that this must stop. Not again, I told him, not even once more, will I lend you to him. Take Rhys away, yes, and welcome! I said, but beyond that he must find his own disciples, and keep them—a plague on all of them!"

At this point he paused for breath. Looking around, I saw a cup and a flask of wine on a tray by the brazier, and pouring out a measure, I took it to him. "And what did he say, Master, in response to all your talking?" I asked. Talhaearn glared at me, but drank a mouthful of wine before he answered.

"As you may imagine, he begged my pardon." The old man sighed. "But being Gwion, he also begged again for your loan—only until Samhain! So of course I told him that you must make your own decision." He paused, and drank more wine. "When will you be leaving?" he asked quite mildly.

"Oh, Master," I said, going on one knee beside his chair. "You know that I do not wish to leave you. It was you, remember, who persuaded me to go with Taliesin the last time. If he needed me then, how much more will he need me when he has Rhys in tow?"

"Very clever," said Talhaearn, and chuckled harshly. "I see that you are learning his ways. Well, I have been without students before, and survived; no doubt I shall do so again. But mind you come back before winter—it is not only I who will be missing you."

"I know," I said. "I have promised her already I will come back—whatever stands in my way. And by my *awen*, I promise you the same."

"Well, well," said Talhaearn, "pretty talking. Let me hear this new song now, which Gwion says I will enjoy, and then make haste and change your clothes for hall. And if you see Rhys on your way"—and here he grimaced—"send him to me. I suppose I can put up with him for one or two more nights."

In fact it was three days that we stayed at Llys-tyn-wynnan, during which time I sang more than once in the hall, and spent my mornings with Talhaearn, and my afternoons with Rhiannedd. Once resigned to my impending absence—as she had not wholly been earlier in the summer—she set to work to send me off in good style, as a wife should. She washed all my clothes in the river and hung them on broom bushes in the sun—we spent some pleasant hours among those bushes while the clothes were drying. She mended my torn trews, and to my delight produced another pair for me as well, which she had been preparing for my return. By this it will be seen that she had got the measure of me and my luck with clothes. Ieuan's spare tunic she also washed and mended for me. After his burying I had tried to send it back to his woman on Ynys Môn, but red-headed Dai had urged me to keep it. "The Lord Cadwaladr will see to it that Anwen does not want," he said, "and there are two or three of us lads there who would, any one of us, be happy to take her to wife, once she is ready to marry again. Do you keep the tunic in memory of Ieuan—that would have pleased him; he was very fond of you." I told Rhiannedd all this story when she asked me where I got it, and I could see it made her thoughtful.

"If I were to get my killing," I said that afternoon as we lay in the deep, green grass beside the gurgling river, "would you be after marrying again, or would you stay unmarried as your mother did?"

"You are not going to get your killing," said Rhiannedd firmly. "You have promised to come back, and you will. Your son and I will be needing you." And she moved my wandering hand to her round belly, and held it there.

"Of course I am coming back," I said. "I was only thinking." I am not sure what answer I wanted, but I did not get one. Instead she stopped my talking with a kiss, and I kissed her back, and after a little while there was no need for words. In the golden sunlight we conversed without them; that was a good day, our last before my leaving.

While all this was going on, Rhys had kept out of my way so

far as he could. I suspected Taliesin had spoken to him again, but I did not ask. It was noticeable, however, that the boy's cleanliness began to improve: a desirable change, since I was likely to be sleeping near him soon. Other than that he was quiet and sullen. Only later did I find out the reasons for this, which were not what I had supposed. At the time I was simply thankful for his silence. One of these days there would have to be a confrontation between us, but I was in no hurry for it: I would win little praise for beating a lad not yet come to manhood, however unpopular he might have made himself locally.

And he *was* unpopular. I heard bits and snatches of it here and there around the court. "At least," said Rhiannedd's mother Gwawr judiciously, as we stood talking outside her hut one afternoon while her daughter finished a decoction, "Taliesin will be taking that little devil away with him. Proud as sin he was when he arrived, or so the priests would say. He sang a boasting song in the hall that first night after his father left, and got more laughter for it than applause. Thirteen, and carrying on as if he were a graybeard, and famous! Talhaearn soon took him down a peg or two."

"A lazy pup," said big red-bearded Goronwy, one of the Prince's *teulu*, as we exchanged a few words in the stable-yard. "Cack-handed with the horses, and the one time he joined the other boys at weapon-drill his spear-casts all went wide of the mark. No discipline—I cannot think how he was raised! As well for him he has a clever tongue—he would never make a soldier."

"His stories are no good," said a little girl in the feast-hall who brought me a cup of ale while Rhiannedd was busy elsewhere. "He uses too many strange words, and I cannot understand him—he talks through his nose *tlike thith*. I like your stories better, Gwernin," she added consolingly. "They make sense!"

"It is Talhaearn's business, of course, what pupils he takes," said the Prince's wife Angharad, while I was putting my harp in its case after harping her baby to sleep. "And the boy's father is of great renown—I remember him singing often at my own father's court in Deganwy, before my marriage. But I admit I will not be sorry to see his son leave. He tries too hard to impress, and fails every way. He has not yet understood that a bard must be more than a good poet."

"*Sa*, I beat him," said Talhaearn that last evening, as we sat in the hall talking before meat. "Three times I beat him, though not nearly so hard as I beat you—but then, you were older. He is letter-perfect on the *how* of poetry—I really cannot fault him. There, his father has done a good job. But he does not understand the *why* at all, never mind the *when*. He does not respect his *awen*; he thinks it is a toy to use for his own prestige, for winning himself fame—or scoring points against his enemies. Were he an Irishman, he might make a good satirist; but he might also meet the fate of Redg, who threatened Cuchulainn." He drank from his cup, and shook his head, scowling. "Na, I might prevail in the end, but I have no more patience with him. Let Gwion take him away, and try whether he can do better: I am done."

The next morning, as we made our farewells in the courtyard, he said to me, "Remember to come back, boy—I still know a few things Gwion cannot teach you."

"I will, Master," I said smiling. "I promised—and I should like to learn those few things. Do you keep yourself well, and I will see you before Samhain."

To Rhiannedd I said, "Take care of yourself, *cariad*—and the babe."

"I will," she said, and kissed me. Her eyes were bright with unshed tears, but she had herself well in hand. Rhys sat watching us sullenly from horseback, holding the pack-ponies' lead-ropes—for this was now his job, to my delight. And Taliesin, as always, watched us all: but what he was thinking, he did not say.

So we rode off into a warm bright morning, the country around us green and rich with high summer, and the wind-rippled corn in the fields turning a pale gold as it ripened toward harvest. Before I came back, those fields would lie stripped and brown from the reaping, and the trees would stand bare in a bitter wind; and I myself would know what it was like for the sheaves, to be cut down in their pride, and broken under the flail on the threshing floor, to yield the grain that would make their masters' bread.

But that, O my children, is a story for another day.

Ghosts

Taliesin's house in Pengwern had a red door, and two glazed windows through which the morning sunlight fell, somewhat cloudy and diffused, to light the polished wooden table where his harp lay. Cynan Garwyn had built the house for him two years ago when Taliesin first took up residence at his court, and had the precious glass brought all the way from Gaul. It was worth, if not a king's ransom, at least a high-born warrior's honor price, and showed most clearly the value which the Prince placed on his bard, on whom he had showered many other gifts as well. And yet Taliesin, or so Talhaearn had said, was planning to leave Pengwern before long, and move on to some other royal *llys*. Even a golden cage could not hold this singing bird forever.

So I was thinking that first morning, as I sat on a padded stool in that comfortable room, eating fresh wheaten bread and new butter—brought to us by a servant without the trouble of going to hall—and watching Taliesin as he studied a manuscript spread out on the table beside his harp. From time to time he took a bite from his own piece of bread, but without lifting his eyes from the page. His right forefinger moved steadily down the column, keeping his place, at a much more respectable pace than I could have achieved. Once he frowned, and taking up a pair of wax tablets and a stylus which lay ready to hand, made a note in tiny, indecipherable characters, then resumed his reading. Reaching the bottom of the page, he advanced the scroll, rolling it up on one side and letting it out on the other, to come at the next section. Then he looked up and caught my fascinated eye. "Do you read, Gwernin?" he asked.

"A little," I said. "I had my letters from the priest at my aunt's urging. It was her hope that I might make a priest myself someday." I grinned. "But she was wrong."

"Clearly," said Taliesin and smiled, his blue eyes bright in the sunlight. "Did you learn much Latin from him?"

"Only a little," I said. "I doubt I could remember it now."

"Then you could not read this book," said Taliesin. "When you go back to Llys-tyn-wynnan—before Samhain!—ask Talhaearn to teach you. He knows more than a little of it, and though he distains it, you will find it useful every now and then. Do you ride out to your uncle's farm today?"

"I do," I said, "providing you give me leave."

"Go as soon as you are ready, then," said Taliesin, still smiling. "But shake Rhys awake before you go. His snoring disturbs my study: his talking cannot be worse."

The evening before, our first in Pengwern, Taliesin had not sung in hall, though he had remained closeted with the Prince for a long time beforehand, and emerged looking tired. Instead it was I who had performed that night, first with a praise-song for Cynan and later with a story. The song was nothing much—I had by then under Taliesin's direction made my first of many such, praising the prince or king for the appropriate virtues, with only his name and a few details changed here or there—but the story was one I had picked up on my travels, and had since polished. It is a tale of a man who travels looking for riches and fame, and comes home disconsolate, only to find that everything he wanted was there already. I told it partly because Pengwern was the place where I got my raising, and there were those there who still knew me: and yet for me the story was not true. All the things I wanted in my life lay elsewhere—some of them behind me in Llys-tyn-wynnan, and some of them yet to be won upon the road ahead. The truth was that Pengwern was no longer my home.

Rhys did not perform that night. Taliesin had put a ban on his doing so until he gave him leave, and loaded that ban, I think, with some threat I did not hear. He did not scold Rhys before me, but only apart and quietly; and yet whatever he said made its mark. Since he had known he was coming with us, the boy had grown more and more silent: and at the time I thought that this was good. Nothing, however, could quieten his snores, which seemed sometimes to shake the very roof-tree of whatever house he was in, and I smiled to myself as I went to do Taliesin's bidding.

I spent a good part of that day on my uncle's farm. He had a free-holding on the north bank of the Severn not far from Pengwern, and it was there I had spent most of my childhood. I had visited my family briefly the previous autumn, on my way back from the North with Neirin, and found things not much changed. The rhythm of the seasons runs much the same on the land—good harvests and bad, cold winters and mild, flood or drought, feast or famine. It is only now and then that events come which break the pattern, and imprint themselves upon the memory of a generation. Such an event had been the Black Year, when I was five years old. Not many who survived it are still alive, and those of us who remember it at all remember only scattered horrors; but its story echoes down the years.

The Year Without A Summer, I heard it called later, when snow fell at Lughnasadh, and what corn had sprouted rotted in the fields. Starvation followed ruined harvests, and plague followed starvation; some of the Roman towns which still survived were abandoned then, left to their forgotten dead, and Viroconium, not far east of Pengwern where Watling Street crosses the Severn, was one of these. I have seen the ruins of that town where I got my birthing—the bones of the buildings, roofless and untenanted; the weeds and young trees growing rank in the streets. I have seen the ghosts walking there in the twilight, and heard their voices on the wind. I did not fear them, for they were my blood kin, my parents and my small brothers. There they died, and there they are buried; only I of all my family came out of that place alive.

It was an old horror which did not disturb my sleep; I was not even thinking of them, that day on my uncle's farm. My mother's-sister and her husband and children were all the family I truly remembered; I had grown up amongst them as well-treated and well-loved as any child could be. It was only now and then that something stirred a memory, only now and then that something raised a ghost from the past, as my gray-haired aunt's words did that day. "So you are traveling now with the great bard Taliesin," she had said suddenly as I was taking my leave of her.

"I am," I had said, a little surprised that she should mention it, for I knew she did not value bards: they were too sinful, too taken up with worldly praise and pride.

Narrowing her faded blue eyes, she peered up into my face for a long moment, as if seeking something there and not finding it. "Your mother," she said at last, "would have been proud of you. She valued his singing highly; more highly, it may be, than her immortal soul. Ah, well, safe journeys to you, *bachgen*. I will say a prayer that I may see you safe again some day, if the good Lord wills it."

"So I would hope," I said smiling. "I will likely see you before Samhain, *boba*, on my way home—on my way *back*—to Llys-tyn-wynnan. And if I do not, I will send you word—when you are a grandmother!"

"Do not name the unborn child," she said reprovingly, but she smiled as well. "I am a grandmother twice already, as you well know—but do you send me news all the same!" After a little more such scolding, she hugged me and let me go, and my uncle, a less talkative man, embraced me in his turn.

"Do not you be minding her clack," he said with a grin. "But you know that, lad, as well as I do. A mystery it is to me, why you must wander the earth rather than settling down to till it, as any sane man would do, but whenever you pass by, stop in and see us. Be off with you now, and mind your master." And saying so, he turned and walked away toward the cow-shed, where someone was calling his name. I mounted my black pony and rode slowly back to Pengwern, thinking of the past. It was a long time since I had heard mention of my parents; I found I could remember little of them aside from their names. Even their faces were faint and blurred in my memory. It was a strange feeling, a sort of hollowness at my core, where I had thought to find firm ground.

Taliesin sang in the hall that night, a graceful praise song to Cynan thanking him for gifts recently received, and afterwards I told another tale. I noticed Rhys once or twice scowling at me from the lowest table, but before I had finished he was gone. When I got back to Taliesin's house, he was asleep—or at least feigning sleep—on his pallet beside my bed in the sleeping-alcove which had once been Neirin's. My own sleep was restless that night after my thoughts of the day. Sometime in the dark hours I woke from a troubled dream of blood and death and storm, to hear real storm-winds moaning around the house, and raindrops rattling briskly against the wooden wall beside me. As I lay half-awake listening to these sounds, I heard another sound beneath them: the sound of human sobs, coming from the pallet beside my bed.

If I had been a few years older, or Rhys a few years younger, I would have got up and tried to comfort him; but the gap in our ages was wrong, and there was no liking between us to bridge it. Instead I lay and listened to him weep, until the sound blended with the weeping of the wind, and I slept again. In the morning when I awoke he was snoring peacefully, and I wondered if I had dreamt the whole. But something in his heavy-eyed appearance when he arose at last told me that I had not.

After breakfast I went to the stables to make sure he was taking proper care of our ponies. Du took his head out of his manger long enough to whicker a greeting at me, then went back to steadily munching hay. I had groomed him myself the day before, and Taliesin's red mare in the stall beside him looked well tended, but I thought the stocky brown pony Rhys himself had been riding seemed somewhat neglected. Catching sight of a stable-lad pushing a barrow full of dung and straw, I asked him if the boy had been around. "Na," he said with a gap-toothed grin, "I have not seen him today. I fed and watered these three with the rest of my string this morning, and will be after grooming the brown cob by and by—I did the red lass earlier, did I not, Rhosyn *fach*?"—this as the mare turned her head at the sound of his voice, her ears flicking forward. "She is an old friend of mine."

"Do not you be worrying about the cob," I said. "I will send Rhys along when I find him—he should at least be tending his own mount. But I thank you for your trouble."

"Na, it was no trouble," said the lad, still grinning. "They are good beasts, all of them." And he went whistling away to empty his barrow at the dung-heap, and come back for another load, the while I went to look for Rhys.

I found him at last down by the river, throwing stones into the smooth green water that surged with such deceptive power along the bank. He heard my steps on the gravely path, but made no move to see who came. Only when I spoke his name did he turn. "What do you want?" he said, showing me an unwelcoming face.

"Why did you not tend to the ponies this morning?" I asked angrily. I had been looking for him for some time, and my temper was short in proportion. "It is your job to feed and water and groom them, not the stable-boy's."

"They were fed and watered already when I got there," said Rhys. "And as for grooming, it will not hurt them to miss a day. Or tell the stable-boy to do it, if you are so concerned. I am not a servant."

"That was not the tack you took when we came to your father's house," I said, remembering. "You moved quick enough then when he gave the orders."

"Let Taliesin order me, then," said Rhys shortly. "I take no orders from you."

"If you did your work properly, you lazy little pig, I would have no need to give them," I said. Rhys' face turned red, but with anger, not shame.

"Be careful, Storyteller," he said, his eyes narrowing. "I have threatened you once before with satire, and I can do it. Beware the kind of word-fame I could give you."

At this I laughed. "You? Give me word-fame? Even if Taliesin had not gagged you, no one would care what songs you make. I heard about your success in Llys-tyn-wynnan—so much for your windy threats!"

Rhys was still holding one of the flat stones he had been throwing into the water; now he suddenly flung it at my head. I ducked, but it clipped my ear as it went by, and I finally lost my temper. I grabbed Rhys by his over-large tunic before he could escape, and slapped him across the face. He yelped and tried to hit me, and I slapped him again. Then he began to kick my legs, which stung. I slapped him harder, then gave him a box on the ear which made his eyes water. All the time he was twisting in my grip, trying to hit or scratch or bite me; it was like fighting a wildcat. I tried to hold him off, but my arms were not long enough; he was the tall son of a tall father, shooting up like corn at Beltane, and even with four years between us he could already look me in the eye.

Changing tactics suddenly, I grabbed him with both hands and shook him, then hooked his feet out from under him and bore him to the ground, landing astride him. Before he could get his breath, I caught his wrists and pinned his arms down. He glared up at me and began to curse me, and I let go one wrist long enough to slap his face again.

"Shut up, you little turd," I said, grabbing the free wrist again before he could strike at me. "Hold your tongue if you value it. I threatened once to throw you in a river, and by all the Gods, I would do it now if I could be sure you could swim. You are not worth doing murder for; you are a plague and a nuisance, a bone-lazy, ill-favored, incorrigible, pig-ignorant, pie-eyed poetaster. The lowest scrapings of the oldest dung-heap in the whole of Wales are sweet and fragrant compared to your stink. You are as shiftless as the day is long; you are not worthy to lick Taliesin's boots clean, or demand a heart-beat of his time; you are only here because Talhaearn was sick of you, yet likes your father too well to simply fling you back in his lap for the useless wretch you are. You know the *how* of poetry but not the *why*; you do not understand that a bard must be more than a good poet; you travel with giants and babble of *your* greatness. You are a fool, Rhys, and if you go on as you are now, it is you who will never be a bard, not I!"

Rhys glared up at me in silence, his mouth half-open in shocked surprise. No one, I thought, in his whole short life had ever spoken to him so. His nose was bleeding profusely, his lower lip was cut; and the red marks of my fingers were plain to see on his face; but he was not much hurt. Only his pride was wounded, and not before time.

"Get up," I said after a moment, releasing him and standing up myself. "Go to the stables and tend to our ponies; and if the stable-boy has done your work for you already, stay and help him with his. After that you can come back and bathe in the river. I do not want to see your face again until it is clean."

Rhys got slowly to his feet. Still silent, he turned and marched stiffly away toward the town, the set of his shoulders prophesying more trouble to come. I followed him, wondering what he would do—or not do—next. Little did I guess the payment I would presently make for that morning's work.

One more day we spent at Pengwern, while Taliesin read in his books and talked with his Lord, and Rhys did his tasks and kept himself out of my sight. I filled the time myself by dallying with the fine, trim, black-haired girl who had poured my wine in hall the night before—it had, after all, been at least three days since I was last with Rhiannedd—and by working on my song for that evening. Here is a snatch of it:

> "A brand in the hand,
> A burning fire;
> He reaps to keep,
> Risk not his ire;
> Your gore will pour
> Ere Cynan tires;
> And his foes will go
> To a funeral pyre!"

Not particularly clever, but a new meter for me. It went over very well in hall; Cynan's war-band was beating time on the tables before the end, and I got a good gift of silver afterwards from the generous dark-haired Prince himself. I told a tale next, and Taliesin finished with a song:

> "The sun climbs up the eastern sky
> to light this land below;
> so bright its beams, yet brighter still
> a sovereign Prince I know:

> in Cynan Garwyn's court no fire
> outshines his matchless glow.
>
> The sun sinks down the western sky
> toward the waiting sea;
> all lands it crosses feel the weight
> of Cynan's mastery:
> all kings and princes fear their fate
> when Cynan's host they see.
>
> The white moon shining overhead
> has not so fair a face:
> the swift stars wheeling at her side
> match not his headlong pace:
> since earth was made no equal his
> in prowess or in grace.
>
> In joy I stand, in joy I sing,
> to praise him is my pride:
> his generosity abounds;
> with him I will abide
> until sad need lay hold on me
> and steal me from his side."

"Why," I asked Taliesin afterwards, "did you sing that you would stay with Cynan as his bard, when I know—or at least, so Talhaearn told me—you are planning to leave him before long?"

We were sitting in Taliesin's house again, sharing a final cup of wine and a few words about my performance before bed. The full moon shone through the glazed windows, adding her ghostly light to the mellow glow of the oil lamp upon its high iron stand. Rhys was already in his blankets, his snores through the curtain drowning out the small noises of the night outside. In the mingled light Taliesin's face looked weary again, and his blue eyes dark as shadows. He sat for a moment silent as if he had not heard my question, looking down at the silver cup which he was turning in his narrow, long-fingered hands; then the corners of his lips quirked up in a smile. "Na," he said, "those were not my only words. I said I would stay until I need to leave. And when that need comes"—he shrugged—"I will go. Cynan was not deceived: he knows it as well as I do. No reason not to offer him sweet praise in the meantime."

"*Sa*," I said slowly, "I see. But that was not how it felt."

"That," said Taliesin, still smiling, "is part of the art of the bard. How it feels is often more important than what it says. Cynan knows that I will leave, sooner or later; he also knows he does not really outshine the sun, or the moon, or the stars. But he took pleasure in hearing me say so, and he will try—at least for a little while—to live as if my words were true. I hold up for him, not so much a mirror, as an ideal; and as he is generally a well-intended man—as are most men—he would like to make himself more closely match that image. Insofar as he does, he will become a better man, and a better prince, for hearing my praise. This is what the Christian priests such as Gildas will not see." He shrugged again. "Or maybe they see it, but do not approve, because it is done through the power of the *awen*, and not through their prayers to their God." Slowly he drank off his wine, and set the cup down on the table in a pool of moonlight. "I am for bed now, and you should be also; we have a long ride tomorrow."

"Go on, Master," I said. "I will take a breath of fresh air outside first; the smoke from the hall is still in my head and in my throat. Blow the lamp out; I can find my way without it."

Outside the night was cool and still, and the moon cast crisp black shadows. I stood for a while breathing deeply, and watching a brindled cat slip in and out of their darkness, silent as a ghost, as it hunted mice. Faint and far-off I heard the hoot of an owl. When at last I went back indoors, all was dark and quiet; even Rhys' snores had stopped for the moment. Only in its pool of moonlight Taliesin's silver cup stood shining like an offering—an offering placed on a stone altar raised to the half-forgotten Gods of the past, like the one I had seen the previous summer in Gwallawg's town of Aquae Arnemetiae where we were going next.

But that, O my children, is a story for another day.

Memory

Cupped in a hollow of the high hills where iron-rich hot springs rise to the surface, Arnemetia has been a holy place time out of mind. The Druids knew it well, and planted their sacred oaks on the round hill which overlooks the steaming waters; the Romans found it, as they found all such places within their domains, and built their own temples there on older foundations. Now grove and temples were alike abandoned, and the Christians celebrated their rites in other places and ways; but the memories of past worship, like the ruins they left behind, still lived on in the stones.

We had been several days at Aquae Arnemetiae, and the moon was halfway through her waning, before I asked Taliesin about the altar. It happened on a sleepy summer afternoon not long before Lughnasadh—the usual time of first harvest, although here in the hills where the spring comes so late the corn would not be ripe yet for some while. Taliesin was just finishing a lesson he had been giving us—he now taught me together with Rhys for some subjects—and as the day was fine and warm, he had chosen to hold our class outdoors rather than in the stuffy dimness of the hall or the guesthouse. Sitting cross-legged in the shade of an ancient oak tree not far from the springs themselves, we had answered all the questions he threw at us about the kings and princes of Britain in Arthur's day, and I was pleased to find that in this field at least, Rhys was not ahead of me. At last Taliesin smiled and rose from the stone where he had been sitting.

"Enough," he said. "You two may do what you will now until time for meat. I am for the hall; my throat is dry after all this talking."

"One question, Master," I said, "before you go."

"And what is that?" asked Taliesin. Rhys, who had been on the point of leaving, turned back again to listen.

"When I was here last summer with Neirin," I said, "he showed me some things which he said you had once shown him.

Things to do with the Druids. I have not gone to look at them again by myself, not yet, but I wonder if you…"

"If I would tell you more about them?" asked Taliesin. The wind, which had been still, fluttered the oak leaves above us, and painted his face with dappled flecks of moving light. "I might, but that answer would not be short, and I am thirsty. Let us go to the mead-hall first; then I will give you the story."

When we were seated in the hall, each with his cup of ale—half-strength for Rhys, as befitted his age—Taliesin sat silent for a while. I waited patiently, but Rhys began to fidget. At last Taliesin sighed and spoke.

"As both of you know—or could guess if you looked about and thought—the Romans were here in Aquae for several generations. They built in the stone which they quarried from the hillside below the town, and much of what they built has endured—it is still around us now." And he gestured at the lime-washed stone walls which supported the timber roof above us. "But they were not the first to build here, not the first to worship at the springs. Some of their temples sites have deep roots. The earth remembers…

"Both of you were at Aberffraw when Talhaearn told his tale of the Black Lake. You heard what devastation the Romans wrought on our land—and upon its people. Because the Druids would not submit to them, they destroyed all the sanctuaries that they could find, and slaughtered all the priests. But though they burned the wooden buildings, some sites of power they afterwards made their own. And I think, Gwernin, that you have seen one of those here."

"A stone altar," I said, "in a ruined temple."

"Yes." Taliesin frowned. "This is not a thing which I can teach easily in words. Drink up your ale, and then, Gwernin, you can show us—what we are speaking of." And suiting his actions to his words, he drained his own cup, and we did likewise.

As I led the way up the hill in the hot afternoon sunlight, I began to have misgivings. In the dimness of the hall it was easy to speak of spirits, but under the bright summer sky it was different.

Maybe my memory of what I thought I had felt last summer had grown over time. Maybe I was about to make a fool of myself in front of Rhys.

The stone-built ruins of the circular building seemed to have crumbled even farther under their clinging ivy, but when I had pushed my way through the elm saplings and the purple flower spikes of willow-herb, I found the place was much as I remembered it. Within the ruined walls lay an open space, floored with summer-green grasses and roofed only with sky, and at its center stood a carved block of stone half the height of a tall man, and an arm's-length across. The figures on its sides were too worn to be recognizable—too worn, perhaps, to have been carved by the Romans, though of that I could not be sure. I stopped a few feet away from it and pointed. "That is it," I said.

"Hmm," said Taliesin softly. He walked up to the altar, but did not touch it. Instead he stretched out his hands and moved them slowly over the surface, a finger's length above the stone.

"What is it?" asked Rhys from beside me. I glanced at him; he looked more excited than respectful. I frowned, and was about to admonish him when Taliesin spoke.

"What did you do last time, Gwernin?" he asked.

"Neirin put his hands on the stone, and so did I," I said.

"Then do so now," said Taliesin.

Stepping forward, I did as he bade me. Most of the altar's top was smooth gray limestone, but there were cracks in the surface where tiny green mosses grew, veins of verdant life in the unchanging rock. At first I felt only the chill of the stone—for despite the warmth of the day, it was winter-cold. Then, as I half-closed my eyes to concentrate, I began to feel something more. The world around me grew paler, out of focus, in a way I was coming to know. I heard a sound which was not a sound, and felt the faint echo of a presence once familiar to me. I took a deep steadying breath, and looked up to meet Taliesin's eyes. They were dark as the midnight sky, dark as the eyes of a man I had met only once before, in a place which was not a place, in a dream which was not a dream, in a time outside time—a man who had died five hundred years ago, not many hours after he had poured out his last offering onto this stone. The name he first bore as a boy I did not know; his second name, got on Ynys Môn when he became a Druid, was Lovernos; but his third and final name was Claddedig—the King in the Ground.

"Yes," said Taliesin, and his voice, which was not his voice, seemed to echo in my head. "Yes, he was here—I was here. You have heard my story—now speak my true name."

How could I speak a name I did not know? I stood and pondered for what seemed a long time, while the chill of the stone crept up my arms toward my heart, and my feet sank twisted roots into the stony ground, and the light of the sun faded from my eyes, and above me the stars came out. "Lord," I said at last, my tongue as heavy as the stone, "I cannot speak it. The knowledge is not in me."

"Then find it," said the voice which was not Taliesin's. "You will find it..."

There was a shock, and for a moment the world spun around me. I blinked to clear my vision, and it was daylight again, a warm summer's day. Taliesin was himself, and the stone altar was only a stone.

"Why cannot Gwernin say your name, Master?" asked Rhys beside me. Looking down, I saw that his skinny brown hands with their bitten nails were resting on the altar next to my own. Then I knew where the magic had gone, but not why.

Taliesin knew. "Rhys," he said very quietly, "why did you do that?"

Rhys looked puzzled. "I wanted to know what Gwernin was doing. He does not seem to be doing anything."

"And what did you find out?" asked Taliesin, still quietly.

"Nothing," said Rhys. "There is nothing here but a stone."

"Not quite," said Taliesin, and placed his own hands onto the stone opposite ours.

Around me was the sound of chanting, of many men's voices raised and blending as one. It was nighttime, but the leaping red light of the torches mixed with the light of the full moon. Some of the men led the sacrifice, a white bull-calf wreathed with green branches. They brought him to the altar stone and held him there for the priest. I was the priest; my knife was sharp and knowing. He died with barely a struggle, and his blood ran into the bowl, steaming in the frosty air as the hot springs had steamed. I lifted it and poured, and the stone drank it in. Next time, the knife would be for me. I knew it, and I rejoiced...

Again the world spun around me, and it was daylight. Beside me someone was screaming. It was Rhys, and he was yelling, "Na, na, na!" His hands still rested on the stone as if stuck there; his eyes were wide, and his face a sickly white. "Na, na, na!" he cried. "Not me, not me, I will not go—I will not!"

"Hush!" said Taliesin, not loudly. Rhys' voice stopped, and his mouth closed, and he stood wild-eyed and trembling, his hands still pressed to the stone. Taliesin spoke a long phrase in a language I did not know, but which rang with music, and lifted his own hands from the stone. And beside me Rhys crumpled down in a dead faint, and lay still in the grass.

I dropped to my knees beside him, feeling for his pulse, but before I found it I could see that he was breathing. Gently I turned him onto his back, wrinkling my nose in distaste as I did so. There was a spreading stain on the skirts of his tunic: he had wet himself with fear. Otherwise he seemed unhurt. "What happened to him?" I asked Taliesin.

"I let him see—what there was to see," said Taliesin dryly. He came around the altar stone and went down on one knee beside Rhys, lifting the boy's wrist to feel his pulse. He touched Rhys on the forehead, and the boy's eyelids trembled. Taliesin stood up again. "He will be all right."

" 'What there was to see,' " I repeated. "I saw things, too, but—why was he so frightened?"

"Maybe," said Taliesin with a slight smile, "he saw things—differently."

We carried Rhys, still unconscious, down to the *llys* and laid him on his bed in the guesthouse. Between us we stripped off his soiled clothes and rolled him in his blankets. "He will sleep the night through," said Taliesin. "It is the best thing for him now."

"I still do not understand what happened to him," I said, beginning to make myself tidy for the hall.

"He was not ready for what he saw," said Taliesin, combing back his shoulder-length black hair. "His experience of the Otherworld is small, and his belief in himself great. So it is with many who have only heard the stories—who have only seen the glow of the fire, and not felt its heat. A little pain, early on, can be a good teacher." He put on his silver circlet and adjusted it until it sat just so. "If you are ready, get your harp," he said smiling, "and let us go to the hall. You still owe Gwallawg a song."

Gwallawg mab Lleenawg, King of Elmet, was a big burly redheaded man with only a little grey in his abundant beard. Neirin and I had spent a few days at his *llys* the summer before, and been richly rewarded for our tales and songs; indeed it was Gwallawg who had given me the sword I had used in the fighting in Arfon. At his court I also rated a place at the high table, beside Taliesin, and only Rhys had been relegated to a lower seat in the hall. Gwallawg was in a good humor that night, talking of a raid he was planning in a few days against the Saxons of Deira, to the east of his mountainous kingdom. "They will be at their harvesting already," he said with a grin, "and we can sweep down upon them and take them unprepared, and be back home in time for our own reaping. It does not do to let them get too sure of themselves, there along the border. Besides, they stole six-score head of my best cattle last spring; it is time for me to go and take them back, plus a few more to cover the increase. Do you ride with me, Taliesin?"

"Not I," said Taliesin, smiling. "I saw enough bloodshed in Gwynedd earlier this summer to satisfy me for some time. I will pass the days teaching my two students and making more praise-songs for you and your war-band, ready for your return."

"Ah, yes, Gwynedd," said Gwallawg, frowning briefly. "Rhun got rid of his enemies there in the end, so I hear, though he would have done better to have killed them all outright. Pretty dealing, to let them sail away again to plot revenge. Dead men bear no grudges."

"So many of Rhun's captains thought," said Taliesin dryly. "But if dead men bear no grudges, that is not true of their living relatives. Better to make peace and have done with it, if the thing can be accomplished."

"Ah, but that does not work with Saxons," said Gwallawg, grinning again. "They believe treaties are only to be kept until it is to their advantage to break them. I prefer to get my strokes in first. What about you, Gwernin—will you ride with me, or is your bloodthirst also slaked for now?"

"I would ride with you gladly, Lord," I said, "supposing my master gives me leave." I was feeling restless with too much study, and had not yet found myself a girl there whom I liked. Besides, I thought, it would get me away from Rhys for a while.

"Well, Taliesin," said Gwallawg, lifting a bushy red eyebrow, "what do you say? Will you let the boy ride with me?"

Taliesin frowned, and drank from his mead-cup. "I—would rather not," he said slowly. "But I have no good reason to refuse. Yes, Gwernin, if that is what you wish, you may go. When do you ride, Gwallawg?"

"Not for two or three days yet," said Gwallawg. "Will that content you?"

"I think that it must," said Taliesin, but he still looked troubled. "And now, Lord, Gwernin has prepared for you—a song."

"That will be good enough for a beginning," said Gwallawg, grinning again, "as long as he has a story to come after." For he dearly loved a good, bloody tale, as I well knew.

"It shall be as you wish, Lord," I said grinning back at him. And so it was.

When Rhys awoke the next day he was quiet, and I think confused. Taliesin spoke with him for some time, helping him to understand what he had seen, and it seemed at first that this lesson might have improved his behavior. As soon as he heard of the proposed cattle-raid, however, all was undone. Why could he not go, if I was going? The difference in our ages and experience he brushed aside: he was as well-born as me, and had as much right to go. A cattle-raid was not warfare, but only the training for it. As to his age, why, he was nearly a man: he would be fourteen before Samhain. And if Taliesin could spare me, then why not him as well? There were plenty of servants in Gwallawg's court who could take his place until he returned. On and on it went: he could think of nothing else. At last matters came to a head on the eve of my departure. The feasting was over, and we were all in the guesthouse, where I was checking my gear once more. I would not be taking much with me, only my weapons and a change of clothes in my saddlebags. In the mild summer nights my cloak would be covering enough. Rhys lay on his bed sulkily watching me while Taliesin sat tuning his harp. "Master," he said at last, for perhaps the hundredth time, "please let me go with Gwernin! It is not fair that I should have to stay behind!"

"No!" said Taliesin forcefully, so that the harp-strings rang in sympathy; even his patience had its limits. "I have said you are not going, and that is final. If you do not like my commands, Rhys, you can always go home."

"Why—as to that, it is a long way," said Rhys uncertainly.

"Not so far as all that," said Taliesin. "Go back to Condate, where we stopped on our way from Pengwern, and there turn west toward Deva. With your good pony on that good Roman road, you can be home in three days. Then, of course, you can tell your father why you left me—I am sure he will be interested to hear the tale."

"I—I will tell him how you and Talhaearn have misused me," said Rhys with a little more confidence. "He will not like that!"

Taliesin laughed, a long peal of laughter such as I had never heard from him before. "Be sure and do so," he said, when he had command of his voice again. "I wish I might see it! Child, you do not know what you are saying. But leave, by all means, if you wish it—I am sure Gwernin will help you pack!"

"Gladly," I said with a grin, fastening the buckles on my saddlebags and laying them down beside my bed.

Rhys said nothing. His lower lip was trembling, and he closed his mouth hard to stop it; his eyes were suspiciously bright, as with unshed tears. I felt a little remorse, but only a little.

"Rhys," said Taliesin quietly, "when you are a man you may do as you wish. But man or boy, if you would remain my student, you must stop arguing with me. Now go and wash your face, and make ready for bed: we will speak of this more tomorrow, after Gwernin has gone."

Without a word Rhys rose and left the room. I watched him go with a slight frown, then shrugged; he would have to sort out his problems for himself. Meanwhile, I had plans of my own. The plump little red-headed girl who worked in the kitchen had promised to meet me that evening after her duties were over, and I reckoned that she should be done by now. It would not do to keep her waiting. Taking my cloak, I stood up. "I will be going out for a while and a while, Master," I said.

Taliesin looked up from his harp-strings. When he saw my cloak he smiled. "Well, well," he said, "I will not sit up waiting. The red-haired lass?"

"Yes," I said, and grinned.

"At least," said Taliesin wryly, "that is one problem I do not yet have with Rhys—thank the Gods! I will see you in the morning, then—a good evening to you." As I went out the door I heard him pluck the first notes from his harp.

My red-headed girl was waiting, and I did indeed have a good evening. And if I was somewhat sleepy in the morning, when the time came for the war-band to depart—why, it was worth that price, and more, for the memory…

But that, O my children, is a story for another day.

Gratitude

Now in my old age, I am grateful for many things: for food and fire and bed, and friends around me; for the sight of my eyes, and the clarity of my mind; for fine weather and the fruits of the season; for the days I have had, and the days that may yet be to come. I am grateful to my masters for their teaching; grateful to my patrons for their support; grateful to the Gods for all the good gifts they have given me in my long life. But gratitude, as I have observed, does not always come where it might be expected, and deeds done with good intent can often lead to ill results. So did it happen to me.

Our first night out, we camped at Mamucium in the grass-grown remains of the old brown Roman fort. We could have crowded into the small court which Gwallawg maintained in one corner of its crumbling walls, but in the pleasant summer weather most of us saw no need, and even the King, who slept in his room there, spent most of the evening with his war-band around the campfires. I sang and told tales, and generally acted as their *bardd teulu*, and everyone seemed pleased to have me along.

It was at the end of one of these tales, looking around the circle of my audience, that I saw what seemed a familiar ghost standing in the half-light behind them. Dark curly hair, dark eyes in a pale oval face, a thin, coltish body in an oversized tunic—yes, it was Rhys. Keeping an eye on him, I finished my tale, and presently made my way out of the circle to join him. He had not come closer while I spoke, but neither had he gone away. "Rhys," I said, "what are you doing here? You should be back in Aquae, and in your bed."

"I am going home," said Rhys defiantly, "unless the King will let me ride with him. Do you know where he is?"

"Somewhere around the fires," I said, "unless he has gone back to his hall. Come and ask him, then—but I know what answer you will get." And I turned away, looking for Gwallawg. Taller than most of his men, and with a big booming laugh, he was not hard to spot; he stood, like many of his soldiers, with a horn of mead in one hand and a dripping chunk of roast cow-meat in the other, talking to a group of his friends. Grinning, I watched as Rhys went up to him and begged his boon.

"Na, na," said Gwallawg, chuckling. "You are too young, boy. Does Taliesin know that you are here?"

"Na, I have left him," said Rhys curtly. Gwallawg's eyebrows went up. "If you will not have me, I will ride on tomorrow—I am going back to Gwynedd."

"That is a long way," said Gwallawg, frowning. "You had better go back to Aquae, at least for now."

"Na, I will not," said Rhys. "Taliesin is—is not the master for me."

"So be it, then," said Gwallawg, shrugging. "Find yourself some food, and camp with us tonight—you are welcome to that."

"Lord," I heard myself saying, for no good reason, "let the boy come with us—I will keep an eye on him, and see that he comes safe back to our master. He is too young to journey so far on his own." I cursed myself silently once the words were out of my mouth, but it was true. Besides, I was still in a good mood from the night before.

Gwallawg opened his eyes wide at my words, then laughed. "*Sa, sa,* I see you are still looking out for others, Gwernin. I remember it was you, last year in Olenacum, who talked me out of killing that Saxon boy we took prisoner; and now here you are, saddling yourself with another hapless fool who should not be on the war-trail. Well, on your head be it. Yes, he can come along—ask my *penteulu* to find him a spear. But keep him out of the fighting if you can—he can help drive the cattle when we get them!"

"There you are," I said a little sourly to Rhys as we walked away from the fire through the shifting crowd of laughing, drinking men. "Picket your pony in the horse-lines, if you have not done so already, and find yourself something to eat—and try not to make me regret this more than I do already!" And turning away from him, I went back to my former audience, where someone was—I hoped!—keeping a horn of beer for me against my return.

The next two days, as we rode through the Pennine hills toward Verbeia, Rhys mostly stayed out of my way, and I began to feel more cheerful. At Verbeia, near the northern border of Elmet, we camped for two nights while Gwallawg sent out scouts toward Deira to the east. Then, on a bright warm morning, we set off toward the Saxon settlements. Out of the hills we came, one hundred men on horseback, our ponies' hooves drumming on the old Roman road as we moved from a walk to a trot, from a trot to a canter. Ahead of us the cornfields of Deira stretched flat and ripe and golden in the hot sunlight, their reapers already hard at work for many hours. In their green outlying pastures the herds of fat cattle were grazing, lightly guarded by boys too young to help with the harvest, and ready to our hands. Black cattle and red in their short summer coats, their winter shagginess forgotten; sharp-horned, sturdy cows with their half-grown calves at heel; young bullocks and massive herd-bulls, all of them grazing, tail-switching against the flies in the noonday heat. Lowing, bellowing, their contentment changed to unease as we came, their unease to panic. We broke down the gates—the herd-boys could not stop us—and drove them out of their pastures and away down the lanes, the loyal herd-dogs barking vainly behind us. In a cloud of summer dust we moved across the landscape, gathering more cows as we went.

Now we found the Romans' Dere Street and followed it southward; and now we began at last to meet resistance. Scattered groups of mounted Saxons came after us, but we beat them off without trouble; a little blood was flowing, but no one had yet died, so it was all good fun. I checked now and then that Rhys was still with us, helping to drive the cattle, but most of my interest was with the running combats on our flanks. The fighting in Gwynedd that summer had not slaked my thirst for glory, but instead had increased it; I lusted to distinguish myself in war—even such small warfare as this. Seeing another party of Saxons approaching, I slowed my pony and worked my way to that side of the drive. Taking one of the light throwing-spears the King's *penteulu* had given me out of its crude holster on my saddle, I hefted its balance as I rode, making ready to throw. But some of the *teulu* riding ahead of me were quicker, being more used to this sport. Their spears arched through the dusty air, and two of the Saxon youths tumbled from their horses. The rest threw their own spears after us, but the distance was too great; they vanished behind us in our dust-cloud, and I sighed and re-holstered my weapon.

Thrice more in that hot afternoon we swept up new herds of cattle; thrice more, bands of angry Saxons came galloping in pursuit and were beaten back. I hit at least one flaxen-haired youth with a lucky throw, and saw him sway in his saddle; and I got a bloody arm myself from a glancing spear, and tied a rag from my pouch around it as I rode. We were heading southwest now, following the declining sun toward the sheltering hills. The cattle were thirsty and tired, moving more slowly, the calves lagging behind their mothers so that they were hard to drive. I was thirsty myself; my belly was empty; and my eyes and throat were full of the pale summer dust which painted us all chalk-white as phantoms, only our faces brown-striped with the lines of our sweat. I looked yet again for Rhys, and saw him some way behind me, swaying in his saddle but grimly keeping up. I eased my pony a little to keep him in my eye; to lose him now would be bad, with more revengeful Saxons bound to be following us before long.

The sun had gone, and the twilight hills were closing in around us, before we halted in a wild glen some way inside our borders and allowed the weary cattle to drink and graze. Stolen meat, so they say, is the sweetest; and sweet indeed were the half-raw, half-burnt chunks of cow-meat we shared around our cook-fires that night. Rhys had tumbled down in the dirt with his share only half-eaten, asleep before ever his head touched the ground, and I wrapped him in his cloak, grumbling as I did so. Then I found someone to bind up my grazed arm for me—you cannot do the thing properly one-handed—and remounted my tired pony to take my turn at guard-duty under the summer stars. After a quiet night, we were up and away with the dawn, following a winding trail deeper and deeper into the forested hills. It was only at midday, when we stopped to rest and water the cattle, that I found Rhys was missing.

At first I could not believe it. I had shaken him awake that morning, and seen him saddling his pony. Asking around, I found one man who remembered seeing him mounted when we were just starting out. But no one had seen him since. Cursing, I realized I would have to go back and look for him: not an appealing prospect. I explained myself to the grizzled *penteulu*, who shook his head.

"Not a good idea," he said frowning. "There may be Saxons on our back-trail, looking for revenge. I understand, though, if you are responsible for the boy."

"I made myself so," I said in annoyance, "when I asked the King to let him come. There is nothing for it; I will have to go back. I cannot return to my master and say I lost the brat somewhere on the road."

"True that is," said the *penteulu*, nodding. "Good luck to you, then. We should camp tonight at Rigodunum—God send we see you there, Storyteller."

It was another warm day, and I was glad that much of my road lay through wooded country. The cattle had trampled down the undergrowth in a wide swath—they had been devils to drive through this area—but after we passed the forest quiet had come back, and the small woodland creatures were once more about their business. Birds sang loudly in the branches, somewhere a green woodpecker hammered on his chosen tree, and red squirrels darted chittering from limb to limb like streaks of living flame. In the churned dirt and leaves of the forest floor, my pony's unshod hooves made little sound. I rode alert at first, tensed for trouble, and expecting to meet it at every bend in the road; but nothing happened, and gradually I relaxed.

I was more than halfway back to our camping place when a difference in the forest sounds ahead of me made me rein in my pony and sit listening. I heard the alarm call of a jay, mixed with a squirrel's scolding bark, and saw a flicker of movement through the trees. Frowning, I reined Du off the trail and into cover, and waited.

The flickering came closer, and resolved itself into a weary Rhys leading a very lame brown pony. With a sigh of mingled relief and exasperation, I broke cover and rode toward him. "So there you are," I said. "What happened?"

Rhys had been startled at first when I burst out of the bushes, but he now looked relieved to see me. "I had to go aside for a while," he said sheepishly. "A long while... My bowels griped, I could not help it. And then, when I tried to catch up, Coch-ddu stumbled and threw me." His dirty and grazed condition testified to the truth of this. "And now he is lame. I have been coming as fast as I could," he ended defensively. "It was not my fault!"

"Well, let us see what we can do," I said, sliding down from Du. The brown pony stood stolidly, but when I tried to lead him forward he limped badly, favoring one foreleg and ducking his head at every tender step. "We will have to go at his pace," I said. "Get up on Du, and I will take him."

"Very well," said Rhys, and vaulted clumsily up onto Du's back. My black pony snorted and danced a little at first, and pulled against the reins. I frowned at this, but after a few minutes Rhys got my old friend under control, and we set out. It was going to be a long way back to Aquae, I thought—but I did not then know how long.

Partway through the sleepy afternoon, when Rhys was drowsing in the saddle, and the forest was quiet, and I was trying to persuade the lame pony to go yet a little farther before stopping again to rest, I heard a faint but regular noise from somewhere on our back-trail, and recognized the sound of many hooves on the forest path. Glancing around hurriedly, I saw some alder scrub off to one side of the trail which might be thick enough to hide us. "Rhys!" I said quietly but urgently. "Into the bushes over there, as quick as you can. Someone is coming!" And turning the brown pony, I led him as fast as I could toward the cover.

"What is it?" asked Rhys, not following at first.

"Saxons," I said tersely. "Hurry—they are almost on us! And be quiet!"

"But—where?" asked Rhys, at last reining Du aside to follow me. "They'll see us!"

"Maybe not," I said at half-voice. "Come on! Dismount! And for the Gods' sake, shut your mouth!" The hoof-beats were louder, and coming fast. Rhys reined Du into the bushes after me, but did not get down.

"Maybe we could both get away on your pony!" he said.

I shook my head. "Too much of a load for him. They would catch us before we went half a mile. Get down, will you not?" And dropping the brown pony's reins, I tried to catch his arm to pull him off Du.

"Na!" gasped Rhys, fending me off. "I will not get down! If you want to be killed, I do not!"

"You fool!" I said, and reached for my sword where it hung from the saddle-horn in its sheath. Thinking I was again trying to pull him off the pony, Rhys kicked out hard at me, catching me in the ribs, and I stumbled back against Coch-ddu, who snorted in alarm. From the path I heard a shout, in words I did not understand but recognized all too well. Turning, I saw two Saxons, with more behind them, spurring their mounts toward us, their spears in their hands.

Rhys saw them too. In blind panic he kicked Du hard, and the black pony, startled, took off at a gallop along the forest path to the west. At the same moment the leading Saxon hit me in the chest with his spear-butt, and I yelled in pain. Then his horse's shoulder knocked me hard to the rocky ground. As I rolled, trying to avoid being trampled, a glancing hoof struck my temple; my head exploded with agony, and I lost consciousness.

I got it back abruptly when someone kicked me in the ribs. I groaned, then cried out and tried to twist away as they did it again. The kicker laughed, and two or three other voices echoed the laughter. Another kick, another round of laughter. I forced open my eyes against the pain in my head. Somewhere above me was a face: yellow hair, yellow beard: Saxon. I was going to die—if I was lucky. O Gods, I thought between kicks, what have I got myself into?

I heard the sound of two horses coming back, and some shouted conversation; I could understand none of it, but clearly the people shouting were not happy. Maybe Rhys had got away, the ungrateful little coward. The Saxons would not know how far ahead our war-band was—too far to help me!—and must have stopped their pursuit for fear of running into our rear-guard. I was distracted from these thoughts by yet another kick from the rawhide shoe of the man on my left, this time hitting me in the shoulder. I covered my face with my arms, and he kicked me in the ribs again.

Then one of the Saxons thought of a new game, and poked me in the chest with his spear-point. When I tried to grab the shaft he laughed and tore it out of my hands, then jabbed me again harder, this time in the thigh. I yelped, and grabbed, and got another kick in the ribs for my trouble. The ensuing laughter was interrupted by one of the men who had failed to catch Rhys. He seemed to be asking questions, and those around me answered him gleefully. Then he came shouldering his way into the circle—another big blond blue-eyed man very like the rest in a faded red tunic and dirty trews. While I was looking at him someone kicked me from the other side, and I twisted away with a yell.

The new man let out an exclamation, followed by an order, and the kicking stopped. Then he went down on one knee beside me, and grabbing my hair, pulled my head around so he could see my face. There was a laughing suggestion from above, and a knife landed point-down in the dirt a finger's-breadth from my ear, but the hair-puller ignored it. Pale Saxon eyes stared into mine from a lean, bearded face not much older than my own—a face with a white scar crossing its tanned forehead, as from an old wound. For a long minute he looked at me; then his thin lips moved in a grim smile. "*Hwaet is ðin nama?*" he said. "*Hwa aert ðu? Saga hwaet ðu hattst!*" And when I stared back at him uncomprehendingly, he repeated himself in heavily accented British: "What is your name? Who are you? Say what you are called!"

"Gwernin," I said in bewilderment. "I am called Gwernin, Gwernin Storyteller." The Saxon gave a bark of laughter.

"Gu-wer-nin," he said, and laughed again. "Know you me? Wulfstan am I called, Wulfstan son of Aethelstan. You remember?"

"Wulfstan," I said, trying to think clearly despite the pain in my head. "Wulfstan... Last summer, at Olenacum. You were the captive, the one the King was going to kill."

Wulfstan laughed again without humor. "Yes, Olenacum. You ask King, not kill me, make me slave. Yes?"

"Yes," I said. "I remember... Did you escape?"

"Na," said Wulfstan, and his face suddenly twisted in anger. "Na, I am slave there one year, then ransom paid. I come back to my people, my name in dirt. I am glad, glad, to see you again, Gu-wer-nin. I remember your face, remember your name. I want, give you thanks for my life. Show you my—my great—grat—"

"Gratitude?" I said.

"Yes," said Wulfstan, and smiled that same bitter smile. "Gratitude. So I not kill you." Letting go of my hair, he stood up and issued a string of orders to his fellows, which were met with the sort of laughter a good joke gets. One of them dropped down beside me and began binding my wrists together in front of me with a leather strap, while another slipped a length of rough rope around my neck and tied it in a slipknot, then drew it tight. With shouts and jests they pulled me to my feet and held me there while I swayed uncertainly, blood running into my eyes from the gash on my temple. Wulfstan remounted his horse and took the other end of the rope. He grinned fiercely down at me.

"Yes, Gu-wer-nin," he said. "I give you what you give me—your life. Now *you* can be slave—in Deira!" He laughed again. "Gratitude," he said, savoring the word, and kicked his horse into motion. I grabbed the rope with my bound hands before it could choke me and stumbled after him. It was indeed going to be long way back to Aquae.

But that, O my children, is a story for another day.

An Iron Chain

The level corn-lands of Deira are not so different from those of eastern Powys, and the reaper's task is much the same in both. As a boy on my uncle's farm, I grew up helping with the harvest: at first, as a child, bringing drink to the reapers as they toiled under the hot sun; then, when I grew older, working with the women and boys who gathered the cut sheaves and loaded them into the ox-drawn carts which would carry them back to the byre; and at last as a reaper myself, before I left to go wandering the roads of Britain as storyteller and would-be bard. Now I found myself cutting the corn on a Saxon farm, one more thrall among the other laborers. My muscles remembered the rhythm of it, but my hands had grown soft on harp-string and ale-horn, and were blistered and bloody-raw before that harvest was done. I made no complaint, but did the work that was given me; indeed I had little choice in the matter. In the wide, busy fields during the day, there was no chance of escape, and I spent each night chained to a post in the out-building where the other thralls slept—chained by the iron slave-ring which the smith had hammered into place around my neck on the first morning after Wulfstan brought me home from his raiding as his prize.

That chain was on me now as I lay in the straw, listening to the snores of the men around me and watching the light which crept though a hole in the gable-end of the thatched roof strengthen with the approach of dawn. Waking out of a half-remembered dream, I had not slid back into the warm cavern of sleep that morning, but instead had lain rubbing my night-chilled arms and thinking. There had not been much time for thought during the corn harvest, when absentmindedness with scythe or sickle could end in a gashed arm or leg, if nothing worse, and I had tumbled down every night exhausted, to sleep until I was kicked awake in the dawn. There was still plenty of harvest work left to do—we were picking the early apples now, and starting to thresh the grain—but I was getting hardened to it, and anyway apples could not turn in your hand and cripple you if your thoughts wandered. Besides, our Saxon masters did not grudge us a few windfalls to sweeten our midday barley bannock and cheese, and I gladly took all that came my way. Many of them were wormy, but there were always good bits if you looked: so far had I come down, from feasting with princes and kings.

Most of the thralls on the farm were native Britons, although not all—the Saxons had nothing against enslaving their own kind as well—and the greater part of them had grown up here, on land which their fathers and grandfathers had worked under Roman and Romano-British masters before the Saxons came. Among themselves they spoke a debased sort of British, thick with borrowed Saxon words and their own argot, and I could hardly understand them at first, though I was getting in the way of it by now. This slaves' language gave me a bridge in turn to the Saxon tongue itself, which I was slowly learning.

The trained memory of a bard is tool as well as resource; words and sounds make patterns in my head, like links in an iron chain. It might be that someone would come from Elmet by and by to ransom me—assuming they did not think me dead there—but I had no mind to wait, or to serve out my youth laboring on a Saxon farm—I who was almost a bard! But until I could understand the speech of my captors—my owners!—my chances of escape were small. So, just as I had memorized Talhaearn's and Taliesin's lessons, I now set myself to harvest the words around me, storing them away for future need. The work-songs and children's songs were the best, whether or not I understood all of them; their rhythm had its own patterns, and a meaning which was more than that of the words alone.

It was not of words I thinking, though, on that early morning as I lay in the straw, but of people. What story had Rhys told, when he caught up with the war-band? Did the King and Taliesin think me dead? And if so, would they send a message to Talhaearn—to Talhaearn and to Rhiannedd, now in her sixth month—I had paused here to count on my fingers—with my child? I could see her face so clearly if I closed my eyes—her feathery brows and thick curling lashes, dark against her honey-pale skin; her soft red lips which I loved to kiss, and her small white teeth; her dark blue eyes, like the summer sky at midnight, and the silken cascade of her hair. I ached for her, and not only in the way of a man for a maid; my arms were empty without her. But she was as far beyond my reach as the Western Isles. I would come back, I had said, before Samhain—before our child was born. I had sworn it on my ash spear, on my *awen*...

The door to our out-building opened, and Wulfstan came in, his face still puffy from sleep, to kick the thralls awake and to unlock my chain. Rolling to my knees to avoid his customary blow, I set aside thoughts of love, and thought instead of breakfast. It was usually oatmeal porridge, gray and gritty as it came from the millstone, ladled out of the huge black cauldron which an old woman stirred over the fire. Sometimes there would be a lump of stale cheese to give it flavor. Eating open-mouthed and quickly, and blowing on my horn spoon between bites, I could often empty two wooden bowlfuls of the scalding stuff before it was time for me to go to the day's work; and even then my belly would not be overfull. I quickened my steps toward the kitchen-court in anticipation, combing my fingers through my tangled hair as I went. My face and hands felt dusty from the straw, and I would have liked to wash, but bathing was not a luxury often afforded to thralls.

After our food, we went to the orchard, carrying the first of our big willow-woven baskets; Wulfstan would follow with more in the cart as soon as the oxen were harnessed. The sun was not yet up, and the air was still cool; in the east the narrow silver rind of the waning moon showed palely through a drift of thin cloud. So had I seen it above Elmet on my last morning as a free man: so would it wax and wane twice more before Samhain night. We reached the orchard and picked up our ladders, setting them carefully against the trees so as to break no branches; we men began to climb, filling our baskets one-handed or dropping the little russet apples to the boys and girls who waited below to catch them. From my perch in the top of the tallest tree, I could see a long reddish-gold line low on the western horizon, like a bar of cloud, but not a cloud: the tops of the Pennine hills of Elmet, just touched by the first sunlight. A long way off, those hills were: too far to reach on foot before the pursuit rode me down. I gazed at them by snatches that morning through the gray-green leaves of the apple trees, until the midday heat-haze rose from the fields to hide them. Even then, I knew that they were there, and gazed on them in my heart.

We finished picking the apples that day, and followed the last cart-load back to the farmyard to carry them into the byre. Some went into the loft, where laid on racks beneath the thatch they would keep the longest; others went into barrels in the cool earth-floored cellar against the north wall. Bruised or damaged ones were set aside to be pressed soon for cider, an activity which the other men assured me I would enjoy. By the time we had done all this, and sluiced the sweat and sweet apple-juice from our faces and hands with a few buckets of well water, the sun was setting and it was time for food.

The hall of Aethelstan Thane, though not so large as many a lord's hall I have known, was good of its kind and not small, as befitted a well-off man who held his lands directly from his king. In the upper part, near the hearth, sat gray-bearded Aethelstan himself and his sons and male cousins, those of them who were not serving in the King's war-band. Wulfstan was not among them; he sat, as I had noticed before, at the next table down, with the free craftsmen and overseers of the farm. Lowest down, near the door, was the place for the thralls, and there we ate our barley bannocks and bowls of stew, sitting cross-legged in the rushes or on the wooden benches along the walls, and served from the same black caldron which had cooked our breakfast porridge. Even here there was status and precedence: as a young man newly come to the farm, I merited only a spot on the bench nearest the door, pleasant enough on an early autumn evening but likely to be exposed to icy drafts come winter.

"Why," I asked the skinny dark-haired lad seated near me that evening, "does Wulfstan not sit at the high table? He is Aethelstan's son, is he not?"

"He be," agreed the lad—Pedr was his name—"but since he done come back disgraced, his dad not be owning him." He paused to swallow another mouthful of stew, then added, "It be not to wonder at, God wot. He be lucky to have home here still—some men will be turning him out."

"Why," I asked, sorting my way through this, "is Wulfstan disgraced? What did he do?"

Pedr chuckled. "It be more what he not do: he not die. For member of King's war-band, as he was, to be taken prisoner is shame. To be made thrall by Cymry, worse shame, like he be coward: can nothing wash that out. Wherever he go, whatever he do, that name be following him." He spooned the last of his stew into his mouth and swallowed noisily; then, looking at Wulfstan's brooding face, he added, "He be better dead."

"I see," I said slowly, and there was a sinking sensation in my belly which owed nothing to my own supper. "Thanks, Pedr. I—think I see."

Pedr grinned, showing broken teeth. "I hear how he catch you, when your pony go lame. Was bad luck to you."

"Yes," I said absently, "it was." I had not told anyone about Rhys' desertion, at first because of the language difficulties, and later because it had not seemed important. "So Wulfstan cannot go back to the war-band, even though he did nothing wrong? I remember he was knocked down and stunned in the fighting when we overran them; he was found among the slain. He did not surrender."

"Makes no matter," said Pedr, wiping his bowl with his last piece of bread and popping it into his mouth. "No one believe him or trust him now. King's war-band must be bravest of brave; he cannot go back, cannot win lands or gold from King. No lands or gold, no bride-price; no bride-price, no wife; no wife, no sons to come after him. He be finished. No life for him here: he will go wolf's head—outlaw—by and by. He be better dead."

That night before I fell asleep in the straw, I thought about it again. I understood now more clearly the reasons for Wulfstan's hatred of me: he blamed me for his ill-fortune, for his broken life. Thank the Gods, I thought drowsily, that the Cymry were not so foolish: I at least, if I escaped—when I escaped!—would carry no shame from my time as a thrall. But until that day arrived, I would have to do my best to keep out of Wulfstan's reach, for my would-be benevolence in the past had given him much to avenge.

This, I found, was easier to plan than to do. As the rhythm of work slackened after the first frantic rush of the corn-harvest, Wulfstan found many small ways to make my life a misery. All farm work is hard, but some jobs are dirtier and more unpleasant than others, and all of these now fell to my lot. If there was a privy to be emptied, a muck-heap to be moved, a load of offal to be carried to the pigs or a dog-kennel to be raked, mine was the hand on the tool. My sleeveless woolen tunic, my only garment—my own good clothes and boots had gone as spoil to the raiders who helped take me—grew stiff with filth, and my long hair greasy and matted; but I was given no chance to wash, until at last even the other thralls began to avoid me. Not only was I unpleasant to be near, but my company might be unlucky: people who seemed too friendly with me attracted Wulfstan's notice as well. And then there was the matter of the dogs.

In addition to the usual herd-dogs who helped with the cattle and sheep, Wulfstan's father kept several hunting dogs: big shaggy gray-brown brutes, hip-high to a tall man and strong enough to bring down a stag. Wulfstan fed them himself, and from time to time would ride out hunting with them to keep them fit and eager. I began to look forward to his absences on these expeditions: not only was my work lighter on days when he was gone, but I often managed to steal time for a midday bath in whatever pond or stream was closest. This usually meant going without my noon meal, but it was worth the price. Our overseer on those days—a stocky, grizzled veteran called Edgar—kept a wary eye on me at first, but made no comment; and if Wulfstan noticed that I was cleaner when he returned, he merely found me another filthy job to do. His latest idea was to make me a dog-boy: I should clean the kennels for his hounds—while the dogs were in them.

This first happened on a cool gray morning late in the harvest month, at about the time when day and night are equal. On such a day, eighteen years before, I had come yelling into this world, the first-born child of the young, dark-haired mother whom I could hardly remember. Looking into the wooden enclosure where the hounds lay waiting, I thought to myself that she had not borne me to be dog-food. But Wulfstan stood behind me, grinning like his hounds, and pulling the lash of the whip he used on them over and over through his lean brown fingers, so I had no choice. Slowly and reluctantly, I opened the kennel door and went in.

Savage and unpredictable even with Wulfstan, the dogs had no mind to be friends with me. Their growling rose to a crescendo punctuated with ear-splitting barks as they advanced, hackles raised, toward me. Hastily I retreated, but the door was closed and would not open for all my pushing: Wulfstan must have latched it behind me. With my back against the claw-scored wood, I said urgently, "Wulfstan! At least give me the whip!"

Wulfstan laughed, a fierce barking laughter that blended with the noise of the dogs. "Na, na, *wealisc*," he said. "You maybe hurt my little dogs—and they worth more than you! Go on, you coward—start work! You not come out until done."

I ignored him and stood still, holding my rake handle crosswise before me with white-knuckled hands, ready to use it as a defensive weapon if one of the hounds leapt at me. Staring at the biggest male, I began to make what I hoped were soothing noises. It was not a success: he redoubled his growling: but I kept trying, though the sweat of fear was running down my face and my mouth was tinder-dry. At last, with a final snarl and a snort, the big dog turned away and padded over to the far side of the pen, where he lay down; but his yellow eyes remained fixed on me suspiciously. With a few more barks and whines the others followed his lead, and something resembling silence fell. Gradually my racing heartbeat slowed to a canter, and I breathed again.

With aching care, I unclenched my hands from the rake handle, and started to sweep the droppings which lay thick on the ground into a pile near the gate. The hounds watched me unblinkingly, with an occasional low growl or bark if I moved too fast, but otherwise suffered my presence. Maybe, I thought, they were not hungry that morning. From time to time I looked over my shoulder, but Wulfstan was still there, leaning on a post and watching me with the same unchanging hostility as his hounds. When all the trash and droppings in the pen were swept into one pile, he opened the gate and shoved in a basket, and when I had filled it, he let me out. Then he latched the gate, and turning, let fly with his whip from behind me.

It curled around my neck and stung like a gadfly, and with a yelp I dropped my basket, spreading dog-shit and gnawed bones everywhere. Without speaking Wulfstan swung again with the full force of his arm, cutting me this time across the face. Throwing up my hands to protect myself, I yelled, "What are you doing?" and got another blow for my pains, this time across my raised arms. Blow after blow hit me; he drove me back across the yard until my shoulders struck a wall, and still he swung with a single-minded determination which was more frightening than the blows. At last in desperation I launched myself at him, ignoring the whip, trying to come to grips and stop the pain. But Wulfstan was expecting this; bigger and stronger than I was, he grabbed my by the arms as I leapt and tripped me, then kneed me hard in the groin. The pain was agonizing, and I collapsed into a whimpering ball, wrapped around myself; I hardly felt the last few strokes of the whip. Faintly through the red mists that surrounded me, I heard him say, "Every dog get one bite, *wealisc*—that yours. Next time you try to fight me, I kill you." And giving me a final kick for good measure, he walked away, leaving me moaning in the dirt.

When I could move again, I dragged myself to the thralls' shed like a whipped dog to his kennel, and lay there in the straw while my blood and my tears dried together on my torn face. Nobody followed me; nobody came looking for me. Only at evening, when the other thralls had came quietly to bed, did Wulfstan follow them to chain me to my post. By the flickering light of his tallow lantern, I watched him with a sullen hatred nearly the equal of his own, while he threaded the cold links through my thrall-ring and snapped the lock closed. But he saw it and grinned. "Good dog, *wealisc*," he said tauntingly, and touched my bloody cheek. "One bite, remember." And then, half to himself, "Gratitude."

That night I slept badly, troubled by pain and by dreams, and every time I turned in the straw my chain rattled like that of a restless hound. Sometimes my dreams were of Rhiannedd, sometimes of Talhaearn; sometimes I thought I heard Taliesin's voice speaking my name, or heard Neirin's laughter. An iron chain wrapped me round, pulled me down; I was drowning in the depths of Annwn, in the sea of Neirin's Dark Path. For once I was glad when morning came, whatever kicks and blows it brought with it. I did not know then that my luck was about to change.

But that, O my children, is a story for another day.

The Singer of Tales

All nations have their poets and storytellers, or so I believe. We British call them *beirdd*; in Irish their name is *filid*; and among the Saxons, *scopes*. Always they are men of art and status in their lands, honored and welcome wherever they go, as I myself have proved. So when, at the end of a long, aching day of labor, I heard that a *scop* had come to Aethelstan's farm, my leaden heart rose up, if only a little way, and I quickened my steps toward the mead-hall. Meat one can have on any evening, but poetry is the food of the Gods.

This happened on a night of wind and rain, a night more appropriate to winter than to autumn. It was a few days after Wulfstan beat me, and by then most of my bruises were starting to fade, although the whip-cuts on my face were still sore. One of them had split the flesh over my left cheekbone and needed salving, but no one cared whether a thrall was scarred or not, so long as he could work. Remembering my herb-lore, I treated it myself as best I could with crushed yarrow and comfrey-root from the field borders, and it slowly began to heal. My worst wound, though, was to my self-esteem. I had been proud of my growing skill in my craft and the respect it had won me; but here, as Wulfstan had made plain, I was of less worth than a good dog. That is a hard blow to endure at any time of life, but especially in one's youth. So it was in half-conscious hopes of some inner salving that I went to the hall that night.

The well-born ones at the upper tables were already seated by the time I arrived, and the serving-maids were hastening back and forth with great platters of tender boiled ox-flesh, and heavy pitchers of foaming brown ale and clear mead. I was cold and tired from working in the rain, and the good smells of food and drink brought the warm water into my mouth, and made my empty belly growl like one of Wulfstan's hounds. Even the thin stew and tough barley-bread we thralls would be served was a thing to look forward to on such a night. I got my share as quickly as I could and found a spot against one wall where I would be sure of seeing the *scop* perform, then began to cram my mouth with food.

I had already spotted him at the high table: a small man of maybe middle years with a bald brown pate surrounded by thinning sandy hair, and a clever wrinkled bearded face which had seen much sun and wind. His clothes were rich and colorful, deep-dyed in the strong reds and blues that the Saxons love, and he wore several necklaces of polished amber pebbles which Talhaearn himself would not have disdained. He sat very much at his ease beside the master of the house, laughing and talking with his hosts on either side. Presently, when the eating was finished and the cups were refilled, he would sing.

It had been in my mind since I heard of his coming that bards and *scopes* travel, and that this man, if he would, might do me a great favor: he could carry news of me to the Cymry, and maybe procure my ransom. Somehow, I thought, I must have speech with him; but how to do it I did not know, for my only free time was at meals, and I could not approach him then. I would have to trust in my Gods to provide: but my Gods had not been kind to me lately, and the Saxon Gods were strange to me. Silently saying a prayer to anyone who might be listening, I carefully tipped my wooden cup and poured a good half of the thin beer it contained onto the packed earth floor by my dirty bare feet. It was not much of an offering, but it was all I had: maybe, I thought, it would be enough.

In the meantime, the *scop* had finished his meal and was standing up to sing. My knowledge of the Saxon tongue was far from complete, but I hoped at least to follow the outlines of his song or story. In the event, I got that and much more.

"*Hwaet!*" he began, striking his small harp – the Saxon word for "Listen!" I heard the words for *kings, good* and *great* go by. There was a long passage of which I understood little, and my mind began to wander. Then, suddenly, I heard:

> "bright blood bursting fountained fiercely
> reddened Hrothgar's high-built hall
> midnight monster broke men's bodies
> ate their man-meat gorged on gore..."

More words passed me by, only now and then a phrase standing out:

> "wood-wrought war-kist, worm-knots writhing...
>
> mail-sark shining fish-scale steel...
>
> mead-hall merry loud with laughter...
>
> moonless midnight cold and clear..."

The leaping rhythm of his little harp kept pace with the words like a heartbeat, now slow and calming, now pounding with excitement or fear. I lost the thread of the story again, and turned my eyes from the singer to his audience. All of them were watching him transfixed except for Wulfstan, who was beckoning a serving girl to pour him more ale. His face was already flushed as red as his faded tunic, and his pale eyes glittered strangely in the torchlight; they reminded me of something seen long ago, something animal. The girl poured for him and would have turned away, but he grabbed her wrist and held her, ignoring her startled protests, while he emptied his cup and held it out to be filled again. As a counterpoint to his actions, the *scop's* voice continued:

> "Fearless fighters strong in shield-wall,
> battle-blooded, dauntless, dear:
> foul false foe-man slew them sleeping;
> word-wrights wergild wrought in praise..."

Again the serving-maid filled the cup, and again Wulfstan drained it. Had his face not been so grim, I could almost have believed he was weeping.

> "One man mighty stayed still sleepless;
> watching, waited goblin grim:
> hide too hard for steel-snake's slashing
> would prove weak to hand-grip's hold..."

Again she tried to pour, but the pitcher was empty. With a curse Wulfstan dropped his useless cup on the table, and pulling her down onto his knee, began to fondle her breasts. She mouthed a protest, but I could see she was afraid to do more. Such scenes were not unknown in this hall on evenings when the drinking was heavy, and besides, everyone else was still listening to the *scop*.

> "stern the struggle, bloody, bestial,
> man and monster strained and strove;
> fiend's frame finally burst with bone-crack,
> shoulder shattered, sinews snapped…"

She was a thin girl, not pretty, and past her first youth, older than Wulfstan by some years. I wondered what her man—she must have one among the thralls—was thinking. Maybe, like me, he was thinking with shame that there was nothing he could do. Wulfstan had threatened to kill me if I fought him again, and I believed him.

> "Screams earth-shaking brought down boulders,
> crashed from crags as mountains moved.
> Troll's-bane triumphed, blood-gush bathed him:
> hero's hands—death-dealer's doom…"

At last, with a convulsive movement, the girl tore herself free from Wulfstan's grasp and scrambled away. Caught by surprise, he made a grab for her, overbalanced, and tumbled from his bench to the floor. In the conclusion of the song few people noticed: drunks are common, *scopes* rare. Under cover of the cup-pounding applause that followed, Wulfstan climbed back onto his bench, his face scarlet with drink and frustrated anger. I looked at him briefly and then looked away, back at the *scop*, but not before he caught my eyes on him. I felt a shiver go down my spine, and my belly clenched with fear. Man-eating night-walkers in a tale were one thing, but Wulfstan was here and real, and he hated me. I did not look forward to tomorrow.

The weather being bad for traveling, the *scop* stayed with us for three days. Each night he sang in the hall, and each night I listened eagerly despite my fresh bruises. Wulfstan, on the other hand, tended to disappear after he had eaten, and sometimes Edger came instead to lock my chain when we all retired. Then, on the fourth morning, it was he who came to waken us as well.

"Where is Wulfstan?" I asked him as he was fumbling with the clumsy padlock. Edgar snorted in disgust.

"Still abed," he said, "and like to be all day. Fell in the yard last night on his way to the privies and broke his head, the stupid sot. Get up now, you are loose."

"Edgar," I said urgently, "is the *scop* leaving today?"

"Well, and what if he is?" said Edgar.

"Let me be the one to saddle his horse. I must speak to him."

"And what will you give me for it?" asked Edgar bluntly. I bit my lip; I had nothing to give, and he knew it. "Well, you can have it, lad—likely I will find something extra you can do for me one of these days. Now go on, get your breakfast. Go to the threshing floor when you are done, they need help there. I will send to tell you when to saddle the horses."

The day was cool and sunny after the rain, and the leaves of the trees around the steading bright with the first autumn colors. I went gladly to the threshing floor, where three men were spreading sheaves of corn on the smooth stones, before beating them with flails to loosen the grain from the husks. It was hard, steady work, and I had raised a good sweat before a small boy came to call me to the stables. The other men were sorry to see me go so soon, but I promised to return when I had done my errand. In truth, I would be glad to do so; it was some of the cleanest work I had done lately, and no one had hit me that morning—though I admit I felt a certain sympathy for the sheaves.

The *scop* owned a little brown mare and a small shaggy pack-pony who reminded me of Talhaearn's Llwyd. I had them both saddled and his baggage strapped on before he appeared in the stable-yard. For a Saxon he was not tall—perhaps a hand's-breadth taller than I—and his wrinkled brown face looked good-humored. He was dressed today in plain russet wool for riding, his hall robes packed away, and he could have passed easily for a groom or an old soldier. "Well, lad," he said with a twinkle, "you do fast work. I see I have nothing to wait for."

"L-lord," I said, stammering a little in my haste, "can I talk you a little? I want ask your help."

"Why, what is this?" the *scop* asked, looking at me keenly. Then, switching to the British tongue, "Are you Welsh, boy?"

"Yes, Lord," I said gratefully. "I was taken prisoner this summer, while I rode as *bardd teulu* to King Gwallawg of Elmet. I am student to Taliesin Ben Beirdd, who may think me dead. If you could send word of me to Elmet, either he or the King would gladly pay my ransom."

"Hmm, hmm," said the *scop*, scratching his grizzled beard. "A bardic student, are you?" He smiled. "Could you give me some proof of this?"

"Gladly, Lord," I said. "What is your name?"

"I am called Aelfwine," said the *scop*, still smiling. "And you are?"

"Gwernin," I said, and closed my eyes for a moment to think. The linked words were there waiting; I opened my eyes and smiled, and softly sang:

> "Aelfwine, answer I ask now of you:
> carry my message, oh, carry it true.
> Gwallawg fine gold and silver will send,
> And Gwernin will stand as forever your friend
> If you take my pleading: ah, pray give me hope:
> Answer me kindly, O Aelfwine the *Scop*."

Aelfwine laughed in delight. "Not bad, boy, not bad for no warning. Yes, I will find a way to send your message to your King, but it may take some time. I am going south and east myself, into East Anglia and the Kentish lands." He looked at me searchingly, taking in my battered face and other bruises. "You have been having a hard time of it here, I think."

I grimaced. "True word that is. Wulfstan has a grudge against me, from things that happened a year ago—it would take too long to tell."

"Then be careful, lad," said Aelfwine seriously. "That young man is a bad case—I have seen them go that way before; the sagas are full of them. He will kill someone before long—do not let it be you."

I swallowed. "I will try to avoid it, Master."

Aelfwine nodded. "If I come back this way before winter, I will stop in and look for you. I wish—" He broke off, shaking his head, then moved his right hand in a curious gesture. "Woden's blessing be on you, lad—he is the patron of *scopes* and storytellers. I will ask him to keep you safe. Now I must go."

"May the Gods protect you on the road, Master," I said, handing him the mare's bridle. "I hope our paths will cross again someday in happier circumstances."

Aelfwine smiled, and for a moment there was a twinkle in his faded blue eyes which seemed familiar. "I am sure they will," he said, and mounting his brown mare and taking the lead-rope of his pack-pony from me, he rode out of the stable-yard. I sighed and went back to my threshing, hoping that Wulfstan's broken head would keep him abed for at least another day. I was getting very tired of bruises.

In the event it was two days before Wulfstan reappeared in my life, and he was somewhat less generous with his kicks and blows. I put this down at first to his fragile state of health—he had broken his nose as well as his head when he fell, and had two beautiful black eyes to go with it—but I think the *scop* may have said a word or two to his hosts on my behalf before he left. Woden's protection is not a thing to be lightly ignored: he is the chief of the Saxon Gods, and a powerful patron. Habit, however, is also strong, and I soon found myself doing all the dirtiest jobs around the farm again. I was not pleased, but I did as I was told and kept my tongue between my teeth. Aelfwine had given me hope, and I planned to follow his advice. It was not his fault that my plans went awry.

Meanwhile the days went by, and the moon waned again toward her darkness, and I had been two months in the Saxon lands. My old life, which had come back to me for a few moments while I spoke to Aelfwine, once again seemed very far away. Also very far away—so far that I could hardly count it—was the last time I had lain with a woman. Dirty as I often was now, my chances were not good, but still I began to look about me. Most of the servant-girls were taken, of course, and those who were left were not appealing, or were too young for it. Still, there were one or two…

One day not long after the new moon, we woke to a pounding rain with a hint of ice in it. Even Wulfstan had no stomach for driving the thralls to work in this—always supposing there was anything useful we could have done—so once the cows were milked and put out to graze again, the chickens and geese fed, the sheep moved into their next pasture, and the pigs given their daily swill, we gathered in the lower end of the hall away from the masters to sit and gossip and work on winter-tasks. I was squatting in a corner, trying with a borrowed knife and a piece of stiff old cowhide Edgar had given me to make myself some rawhide shoes. So far I had been getting by with bare feet and rags, but the cold mud that morning had reminded me of how fast the season was changing. Less than a month now until Samhain… I shut that thought away and went on with my clumsy shoemaking. I needed Gwydion's touch with dulse and seaweed, and I did not have it.

"Gwernin," said someone. "Ho, Gwernin! Be you asleep?" I looked up to see one of the least ugly of the kitchen girls regarding me inquiringly. Godgifu, that was her name, a pale little thing with Saxon hair and dark eyes.

"What is it?" I asked shortly. I had just cut my thumb with the knife, and was in no very good mood.

"We did hear," said Godgifu, "that you be *talu-wer*—story-man. Be that true?"

"It is," I said, wondering where she had heard it.

"Can you tell tale for us now? Pass time good?"

"Well…" I said, my hands full of crudely cut leather.

"Ah, go on, do," said skinny dark-haired Pedr beside her, putting down the wooden ladle he was carving. "I finish shoen for you—I be good shoe-man. Tell us tale."

"Well—why not?" I said and suddenly grinned. "Do you all know of King Arthur?"

"Heard a little," said Godgifu, biting off her linen thread and starting another seam, and one or two of the others nodded in agreement. "You have story of him?"

"Indeed I do," I said, smiling to myself. "This is a tale of Arthur before he became King, when he was only Arthur the Soldier, War-Leader of Britain..."

It was a story I had told often before over the years, one of the first I learned before I went on the road with Ieuan. It tells how Arthur, finding himself benighted and alone on the slopes of Yr Wyddfa, takes shelter in a cave. Smelling smoke, and seeing the light of a fire deep inside, he decides to venture farther in. He finds a great room full of many marvelous things, including an immense cauldron, large enough to take a whole sheep or even a man; a great harp with golden strings; and a huge pile of treasure. Tempted, he decides to steal some of the gold. He fills his pouch; then his boots; then his tunic; and finally his cloak...

"At last, when he had all he could carry," I said, "and that was a lot, for Arthur was a strong warrior—he turned to leave, for it seemed to him now that a night spent on the hillside in the rain might be a better choice than waiting in the cave for its owner to come home. And as he turned, what do you think he heard?"

"Footsteps," breathed Godgifu, her forgotten needle suspended before her halfway through a stitch. In the silence of the hall I could hear the rain dripping from the thatch outside; not only the thralls were listening.

"That is right," I said, and grinned at her. "He heard the sound of footsteps, coming down the passage toward him..."

The footsteps, it turns out, belong to an ugly giant and his even uglier mother. They decide to tie Arthur up, and perhaps have him for breakfast. He spends an uncomfortable night, but does manage to fall asleep because of the beautiful music the giant plays on his harp. And in the morning...

"The giant picked him up and set him, still bound, on his feet," I said. "Arthur saw that the fire had been built up and the great cauldron set in place above it, with a little steam rising from its maw. The giant drew a knife from his belt and set to sharpening it, *wheet, wheet, wheet,* on a whetstone. 'Well, Mum,' he said to the hag, 'what do you think?'

"The hag looked Arthur over from his head down to his heels and back again, her eyes very bright and knowing under the rook's-nest of her gray hair. 'Ah,' she said after a bit, 'it is a bonny lad he is, though there is not over-much honesty in him. Pity it seems to waste him, when a sheep would serve as well.' And she laughed. 'I will tell you this, my lad,' she said to Arthur, 'if you can speak me three undoubted truths before the pot boils, I will let you go.'

"Arthur looked at the cauldron, and saw the steam was thickening above it. After the night he had spent, his head felt solid as a block of wood, and his tongue like a strip of old boot-leather in his mouth. Gazing around desperately for inspiration, he saw the harp sitting silent to one side, and remembered last night's wonderful music. Looking at the giant, he said without thinking, 'You are the best harper I have ever heard!'

" 'Aye,' said the hag, holding up a bony finger. 'That is one!' And Arthur realized he had spoken his first truth.

"From the corner of his eye, he could see the steam over the cauldron was thickening fast. Nevertheless, he could not help staring at the hag. To say that she was not attractive is like saying that the weather outside today is a little damp." There were grins from my audience at this; the wind was moaning at the door, and the rain was increasing again. "The longer Arthur looked at her, the more she amazed him, and without thinking, he said, 'You are the ugliest woman I have ever seen!' "

There was a collective gasp from my audience, mixed with nervous giggles, but I ignored them and went on.

" 'Aye,' said the hag," I said, " 'and that is two!' And she held up another finger." And I held up a second finger as well.

"Arthur cudgeled his brains in search of inspiration, but his wits seemed to have gone right out of him. He looked around the room again, but nothing came to him. The cauldron was starting to make the sort of muttering noise that comes just before it boils, and the giant had begun sharpening his knife again, *wheet, wheet, wheet,* in time with the sound. Arthur looked at the knife, and he looked at the heap of golden treasure which had seemed so valuable to him the night before, and he looked along the passage to where the first sweet gray light of morning was just beginning to show. And without thinking, he said, 'If I once get out of here, I will never come back again!'

" 'Aye,' said the hag, 'and that is three!' And the cauldron boiled.

"Quick as a wink, the giant grabbed Arthur by the hair, and with his knife cut the ropes that bound him. 'Go on, then, man,' he said, turning him loose, 'and keep your word while you can!'

"Arthur took to his heels without a backward glance, and what he had said, he made good. As long as he lived, he remembered that some things are more valuable than gold, and he never came near that part of Yr Wyddfa again. And neither, I can tell you, have I!"

The applause I got was loud and lasted long, and Godgifu's sweet smile was even better. But I could not savor it as I might have. If only, I thought, if only I could get out of *this* place. I did not guess then how soon I would do it, or what the price of my escape would be.

But that, O my children, is a story for another day.

The Kitchen Girl

I have always been a man for the girls. Now that I am old, my need is less strong; but in my youth my ash spear was always ready for the chase, even if my pursuit was not so urgent as Neirin's. Rhiannedd understood me, as much as a woman can, and we never quarreled about what I did when I was out of her sight—nor indeed about what I did when I was in it, for what I did then was done for our mutual delight. So now, though my thoughts went often to her, my body had needs of its own. And looking around me for what satisfaction I might find, my eyes had gone now and again to Godgifu.

Not altogether to my taste, she was, for I have always preferred dark girls, though I have made do often enough with what I could get. She had pale Saxon hair and dark eyes—mixed blood—in a thin, pale face, but her smile was sweet, and her figure not unappealing. Her age was hard to guess—two or three years younger than I was, perhaps—and if she had yet borne a child, I had seen no signs of it, though she could not be a maiden. She seemed to be friends with Pedr, to put it no stronger, and that gave me pause; yet I doubted that thralls could marry, and outside the church-set bounds, a woman may well be shared between comrades—provided the woman is willing.

I had got no farther than thinking, however, when the next thing happened. It came about on an afternoon not many days after I told my tale of Arthur in the fire-hall. That had been well received, and not only by my fellow thralls; some of the overseers such as Edgar, who understood and spoke the British tongue, had been listening as well—there being no better entertainment that evening—and had seemed to enjoy it, though it told of their ancient enemy. One of those who had not, however, was Wulfstan.

Since Aelfwine's departure, he had continued with his heavy drinking, and there were few evenings now when he went sober to bed, as I knew well—for his beery breath when he came to lock my chain each night was hard to ignore. I had seen some of the other Saxons regarding him with disfavor from time to time, and wondered what the outcome might be. To be flushed with drink in the ale-hall is considered no ill thing among those people, but even a thane's disgraced son must work for his keep, not lie drunkenly abed half the day—and this Wulfstan was beginning to do.

It did not keep him from riding out with his father's hunting dogs whenever the weather served. If I had looked forward to these expeditions before, when I merely wanted a bath and some relief from his attentions, I did so even more eagerly now: a man who spends his nights chained to a post must needs do his wooing by daylight. So when I overhead Wulfstan speaking to Edgar one evening in the hall about his plans for the morrow, I pricked up my ears. "Be sure," he was saying, "that the Welshman cleans the kennels well tomorrow while the dogs are out of them. If I find a single bone or turd in them when I return, I will have the skin off his back: tell him that."

"Aye, I will," said Edgar, and took a deep pull on his ale-horn. "But you should use him less hardly, boy. He is a *scop* among his own people, and by the All-Father, it is ill luck to mistreat such a one."

"Are you, too, making a hero of him because he can spin a simple tale?" asked Wulfstan, and spat angrily on the floor. "That for his stories. He is my own personal thrall, taken by me in battle, and if I decide to have his hide off, to make me a pair of shoes, I will do so, *scop* or no *scop*."

"Be careful," said Edgar grimly. "You may do what you will among men and bear the consequences yourself; but if you offend the High Gods, you put us all in peril. Be warned, lad, be warned!"

Wulfstan gave him a venomous look, but closed his mouth on his reply. A few minutes later I heard him shouting at one of the kitchen girls to bring him more beer. It was Godgifu: she came and poured for him—a foaming stream like dark amber into his red-glazed cup—and then moved quickly out of reach when he would have grabbed her. Wulfstan sat watching her go for a long moment before turning back to his drink, and I felt a touch of unease at the sight. Then I forgot it in thinking about the next day.

As soon as Wulfstan had ridden out with the hounds—not very early in the morning—Edgar set me to clean the kennels. "Be sure you do a good job, lad," he said gruffly. "We want no trouble with Wulfstan, and you know how he is."

"I do," I agreed with a faint smile. "I will be careful." I did not tell him I had overheard Wulfstan's threats; there was no need; but never before in the history of the world was dog-kennel and yard raked and swept and polished so clean. I even scoured out the great wooden water-butt—a sort of iron-bound half-barrel where the brutes drank—with a stiff brush, and carefully refilled it with brimming bucketfuls of icy well-water. Then I stripped off my filthy tunic and turned the same scrub-brush and water on myself and my clothes. Wet and shivering though I was when I had finished, it was worth it to feel clean again. By then it was past midday, but Edgar, when he came to check on my work, whistled in amazement. "That was well done," he said with a smile.

"Thank you, Lord," I said, pushing back my damp hair from my forehead and grinning. "May I go to the hall now and get some bread and cheese? I did not want to stop earlier for food."

"Yes, go, lad," said Edgar still smiling. "Then, when you have eaten, you can join Gwrgi and Pedr, who are rough-digging the kale beds in the kitchen-garth—they will be glad of the help." I nodded understandingly and went. The kitchen-garth was well away from the kennels, and working there would keep me out of Wulfstan's sight until evening. Before then, though, I had other plans.

In the smoky kitchen quarters I found several of the women hard at work on preparations for the evening meal, and was pleased to see that Godgifu was among them. She was cutting up turnips and adding them to the big cauldron which boiled all the food for the thralls. As I arrived she looked up, saying to the older woman in charge, "Hilda, I be needing to go out to cold-cellar for more turnips: there not be enough here."

"Go on, then," said the gray-haired woman; then, seeing me,

"Hello, Gwernin. What be you doing here?"

"Come to beg a little bread and cheese, mistress, because I missed my midday meal," I said cheerfully. "Godgifu, lass, if you get me some first, I will come with you and help you carry your turnips back."

Some of the women giggled at this, but Hilda nodded. "Well enough," she said. "Give him what he asks for, Godgifu, and then the two of you can fetch the turnips. Only do not be too long about it, or the stew will not be ready for dinner." At this there were more giggles, and Godgifu flushed as pink as her faded woolen kirtle, but she put down her paring-knife and got me some fresh bread and cheese. I took it and stuffed half of it in my mouth, then followed her out of the kitchen and across the courtyard to the barn.

"You are looking very pretty today," I said to her as we entered it. "That blush becomes you." I had already finished the cheese and was eating the last of the bread, so my compliments came out somewhat muffled and full of crumbs.

Godgifu gave me a sideways assessing look, then she smiled. "You be speaking pretty, story-man. I think you have much practice. Have you girl at home?"

"Yes," I said, and felt the smile leave my face at the thought of Rhiannedd. "Yes, I do." Going to the trapdoor into the cold-cellar, I lifted it up. "How many turnips do you need?"

"Small basketful," said Godgifu, indicating a stack of two-peck willow baskets near the wall. "Wait—you need light." Going to a shelf beside the baskets, she opened the side of the horn lantern which sat there, then began to strike sparks onto a wad of tinder. Once she had a flame, she lit the lantern and brought it over to where I was already descending the ladder into the cellar.

"Give me the basket," I said, "and I will fill it."

"In moment," said Godgifu. "Take lantern first." She knelt and stretched down with it, and I reached up and took it, then stood looking around me while she fetched the basket. I had helped bring the apple harvest here, but had not been down the ladder myself before. The cellar was bigger than I had thought, twice a tall man's height in either direction, and roofed with heavy oak timbers supported on posts sunk into the hard-packed earth of the floor. The turnips, freshly dug, were stored in wicker tubs filled with straw along one wall. I hung the lantern from a nail on the side of one of the posts, then caught the basket Godgifu dropped down to me.

"Come down," I said smiling, "and help me choose the turnips. I would not want to select the wrong ones." Godgifu looked down at me for a long moment, and I saw that she was smiling too.

"That be bad," she agreed. "But cellar cold."

"I think," I said slowly, "that I could keep you warm."

Still smiling, Godgifu kilted up her skirts and began to descend the ladder. At the bottom she turned to me and said, "Can not stay long."

Putting my hands on her shoulders, I leaned down and kissed her, at first gently, and then more urgently. Her arms came up and clasped me in return. In the lantern light her hair was like spun silver, and her mouth was soft and red; her woman-scent was strong. Under her small breasts I could feel her heart beating in time with my own. I stroked my hand down her back and felt her shiver, but not from cold. I kissed her again lingeringly, and she returned the kiss, her body pressing against mine. "I think, Godgifu," I said hoarsely, "that we will have time enough." And we did.

Two nights later I told another story in the hall. It was raining again, and we had gathered early. This time, when I began to speak, I did not lack for listeners; even gray-bearded Aethelstan and his sons and cousins at the high table, most of whom did not speak British, showed some interest. I strove to keep my words simple and my gestures broad—easily done, since I was telling the tale of Cuchulainn's weapon-taking—so that most of the people in the hall could understand me. When I came to the end, and told how the boy-warrior returned from his first raid with three men's heads hanging from his chariot-rail, many of my listeners burst into applause. It was only then, looking up and meeting Wulfstan's baleful gaze, that I realized my choice of story could have been better. Clearly, his face said, I had chosen it to taunt him, the failed warrior, with his shame. There was no way I could explain that I had not meant it so.

That night when he came to lock my chain, I expected to be beaten, but it did not happen. Instead he said nothing; only when he had closed the padlock, he spat suddenly full in my face. As I lay there blinking, my muscles tensed and my hands clenched into fists, he said, "Be careful, *wealisc*. Even *scop* can die like other men." Then he turned and left. Cursing softly, I wiped my face as best I could; but I could not wipe off the shame of my helplessness, and it was long before I slept. Wulfstan, I thought, had taken me prisoner for revenge as a bitter jest, not knowing what I was. Now it seemed that the joke was on him, for whatever he did—keep me, kill me, or let me go—he must lose face. But it was a joke I might well die of.

Three days later he went out again with his dogs. I had been ready, and had arranged with Godgifu to meet again in the barn that afternoon. After a long morning, during which I practically polished every grain of dirt in the kennels and washed myself thoroughly as well, I went to the kitchen to get my delayed meal. "Oh, Gwernin," she said when she saw me, her pale face lighting up, "I be hoping you come. I be needing to fetch apples from cold cellar today, and it be hard to climb ladder with basket. You come and help?"

"Gladly," I said, accepting my bread and cheese from one of the other women who smiled understandingly. "Go on, I will meet you there in a moment." And taking my food with me, I went quickly to the thralls' sleeping-place for the coarse woolen blanket I had just been given for winter use. The floor of the cold cellar was dry and fairly smooth, but it was not soft.

We had not been there long—or so it seemed to me—when we first heard the sound of barking. Distant and distorted by its passage through the barn and into the dark space where we lay, it could only mean one thing: Wulfstan was back early from his hunting. Intertwined as we were, we froze, listening. Then Godgifu began to push me off of her. "Must go!" she said in a frantic half-whisper. "He find us, he kill you. Must go now!"

"Why would he look for us here?" I asked, still listening to the barking, but I began also to get up. "I will go out first, then he will not see you. You can wait until it is clear."

"Can you be carrying apples up ladder?" asked Godgifu practically, straightening her clothes. "Must have them when I go back. Hurry, hurry!" She began quickly to take apples from the nearest barrel and fill her basket, but fear made her clumsy and she dropped several of them. "He be wanting me for long time," she said, picking them up. "I be running away when I can. He find me with you now, he kill you. Oh, hurry!"

It does not take long to fill a willow basket with apples, even a big basket. It is harder to climb a ladder one-handed with the basket clutched to your chest, but I managed it, then turned to give Godgifu a hand as she swarmed up after me. "Take them to kitchen," she said breathlessly. "I wait here, then follow. Hurry, hurry!"

"Do not worry," I said smiling, and turned to go. Behind me Godgifu gave a sudden scream, cut off abruptly. Wulfstan was standing in the open doorway of the barn, staring at the two of us as if turned to stone. In one glance I saw that he knew everything we would have wished to conceal.

What brought him there at that time I never knew. I do not think he was seeking either of us, for in that first moment he looked as shocked as we were. Then, before either of us could move, he started forward, pulling out his dog-whip which he carried thrust through his belt next to his hunting knife—the foot-long single-edged *seax* from which the Saxons take their name. "Bitch!" he yelled at Godgifu. "Slut!" And he brought the whip-thong around in a whistling arc, cutting her across the face. She cried out and stumbled back, putting up her hands to protect herself, but he swung again and hit her other cheek. "Run, Gwernin!" she cried to me. "Leave me, go!" Blood was running down her face, but she was not weeping. Wulfstan swung his whip again and this time hit her arm, and she cried out again.

"Stop!" I yelled, and hefting the basket I still held, I flung it at him, apples and all. The hard red fruits hit him in the chest and shoulders, and he flinched, then turned his attention to me. The anger in his face was frightening to see; I think in that moment he was truly mad, with the berserker rage of his people. "Run!" I yelled at Godgifu. "Get help!" And with one wild-eyed glance at Wulfstan, she did so. Then the dog whip sang again and cut me across the mouth, and I yelped in my turn. Twice more he swung it at me, his blows becoming wilder and wilder, and I caught them on my arms; then, throwing the whip aside, he reached for his knife. Before he could draw it from its sheath, I took two running steps toward him and leapt. I knew quite clearly as I did so that I was already a dead man; there was nowhere I could run to escape. I might as well die fighting.

My attack only worked because I took him by surprise. He was bigger and stronger than I would ever be, a golden-bearded young giant of a man, and he was armed with a razor-edged blade while I had only my bare hands; but I was desperate. I hit him with all my weight, and he went down under me with a crash. I grabbed his right wrist and hung on, and butted him in the face with my head as he tried to get up, hearing him scream as his newly-healed nose broke again. Over and over we rolled on the packed earth floor, scattering apples everywhere, while he tried to draw his knife to stab me and I did my best to prevent him; but I knew there could be only one end to this. His strength was too great for me; slowly I was losing the struggle.

Then there were men shouting, and cold water flung over both of us, and hard hands grabbing me and dragging me off Wulfstan, breaking my death-grip on his wrist. Still struggling, I was wrestled back onto my knees with my arms twisted painfully behind me. Blinking the blood out of my eyes—Wulfstan's blood this time!—I saw that men were clinging to him as well. "Let me go, you cowards!" he was yelling, thrashing about like a madman. "I am going to kill him! I am going to kill him now!"

"No," said a deep voice behind him, and I saw his father Aethelstan standing in the doorway. "No, there will be no *scopes* killed on my land today, not-my-son. Or do you want to leave this place, now and forever?"

From where he knelt, Wulfstan looked around at his father, and some sort of sense seemed to come back into his eyes; then slowly he stood up, and the men who had been holding him let him go. Blood was streaming down his face from his broken nose, and I wondered crazily what the Saxon penalty was for that: in Welsh law blood shed from the nose has no value…and neither had my life just then. Slowly and carefully Wulfstan pushed his *seax* all the way back in its sheath, so that it seated into the snug leather with a little snap. "Make him stand up," he said to the men holding me, and they pulled me to my feet. He took three long steps toward me, until we were almost close enough to touch. "*Wealisc*," he said to me softly in his broken British, "I tell you once, dog gets one bite. Second time, I kill you. But my not-father says, not kill, because you *scop*. So I not kill you—not today." Then more loudly to the others, in the Saxon tongue: "But if I own a stallion who fights the bridle and throws me repeatedly, there is a remedy, is there not, my once-father? I will not kill him—but he will be no more a man. Is that acceptable?"

"It is acceptable," said Aethelstan reluctantly, and there was a muttering of protest from the men around me, swiftly stilled. I opened my mouth to speak, and Wulfstan hit me hard in the face with his fist. Once, twice, three times he hit me with his full strength while the men behind me held me, until red lights spun before my eyes and my face was as bloody as his. Then I saw his knee come up, and twisted sideways to take most of the blow on my thigh; but the pain of it still made me gasp. Wulfstan laughed, spraying flecks of blood into my face from his streaming nose.

"Yes, *wealisc*," he said to me softly, "I not kill you this time—but you will wish I had." And to the others, in a voice of triumph: "He likes the cold-cellar—throw him in there for now. Tomorrow will be soon enough to deal with him: it will give him time to think about what is coming to him, and to bid his stones farewell!" And he laughed again.

Despite my struggles—and now, when it was too late to make any difference, I was fighting like a mad thing—they wrestled me to the edge of the cellar opening and pushed me in. I landed hard on the cold floor, and lay there for a moment catching my breath while my head spun dizzily. Above me the trapdoor fell shut with a crash, and I heard dragging noises as heavy things were placed on top of it, weighting it down. Then they all went away and left me, alone in the dark with my fear.

But that, O my children, is a story for another day.

The Gray Hounds

I am no hero like Cuchulainn. I have been afraid many times in my long life, and I do not blush to admit it. But seldom have I felt such terror as in those first few moments when I lay gasping on the floor in the darkness of the cold-cellar with Wulfstan's last words to me ringing in my ears. Death I could face; I had expected it; but to live without my manhood... The thought of it was unbearable. I would have to get out of this prison, or die in the attempt.

Dragging myself up off the floor, I scrambled up the ladder as far as I could go, and setting my shoulders against the trapdoor, I pushed with all my strength. The ladder rungs creaked ominously under my feet, but the trapdoor barely moved. Again and again I tried it, pushing in jerks, slamming my back against the wood until the sweat was pouring down my body and my breath was coming in gasps, but I could not get more than a finger's breadth of movement from the trap. At last, bruised and exhausted, I dropped back off the ladder and collapsed onto the floor again. With a great effort of will, I pushed my gibbering terror into the back of my mind, and tried to think.

Despite Wulfstan's attentions, I was not badly hurt. My face was the worst of it: my left eye was swollen almost shut, and I thought my nose might be broken; but my jaw still worked, even if it was painful, and inside my bloody lips I still had all my teeth. If I could once get free, I could run—run until I dropped! But how to get free? And when?

Setting this problem aside for the moment, I took stock of my surroundings. Except for the bread and cheese earlier that afternoon, I had eaten nothing since morning, and I felt a growing desire for food. There were still plenty of apples in the cold cellar, and possibly other things as well. The darkness, however, was almost total: only a faint line of light came in along one side of the trapdoor. It was not enough to show me my surrounding, but it would tell me by its going when night had arrived: a better time for escape, if I could manage it.

Meanwhile I found the apples, and settled down with my back against a barrel. With my broken mouth, it hurt to eat, but hunger won out over pain. When I had munched my way through enough of the hard sweet fruit to quieten my belly, I got up and continued my explorations. The line of light by the trap was growing fainter; I could barely see it now. I shuffled along like a blind man, groping with my hands, and almost tripped over the blanket on which Godgifu and I had lain that afternoon, half a lifetime ago. Picking it up, I slung it around my shoulders like a cloak, and was glad of the warmth.

What was happening to her now, I wondered? She must have run for help when she fled, to bring the men who stopped the fight before Wulfstan killed me. Would he punish her? I hoped not, but I was all too aware of my helplessness. I could not even save myself...

It was then that I remembered the lantern. Groping in the darkness, I found it on the post where Godgifu had hung it. The flint and steel took longer to find, but fortunately she had brought them down with her, to light the flame when we had finished our play and needed to see. Carefully I struck sparks onto the wad of tinder and blew them to life; carefully I lit the wick of the thick tallow candle inside its horn door. Then, holding it high to light all the corners, I looked around the cellar for anything that might aid me in my escape.

There were barrels of apples along one wattled wall, and baskets of turnips and other roots along another. There were sacks of grain and bags of nuts along a third wall, and jars of pickled cabbage and jugs of cider here and there wherever they would fit. There was nothing—nothing—that could help me raise the trapdoor, or tunnel my way out through the walls around me. There were no shovels, no augers, no hammers or chisels, not even a knife to help me fight for my freedom when they came for me in the morning. I might set fire to the trapdoor, but the wood was thick and strong, and I had no desire to burn to death, or cough my life out in the smoke—though maybe that latter fate would be better than what Wulfstan had in store for me... My candle was burning low before I gave up. Then, because there was nothing else to do, I drank some of the cider, wrapped myself in my blanket, and lay down to try to rest. Unfortunately, there was no giant harper in this cave to play me to sleep.

Sometime in the night, tossing restlessly on my improvised bed, I had a thought. The cellar was roofed with oak, true, but the wood did not extend far on either side, and the walls were wattle and daub—slender billets of wood woven in and out through vertical posts and caulked with mud. If I could find something to dig with—anything, even a piece of wood—I might force my way through at the point where wall and ceiling met, and tunnel my way out. It was a desperate chance, but it was better than lying here in the dark, awaiting my fate. I lit the lantern and looked around again.

Not all of the apple barrels, I found, were full: there were two or three empty ones at one end of the row. Picking up one of these, I flung it down as hard as I could against its cousins. It took me several tries, but at last the strakes began to work lose, and with one more hard blow I managed to cave in that side of the barrel. Pulling out one of the strakes, I examined the walls for a weak spot, and soon found one, on a side where I hoped nothing was stored in the barn above. The cold-cellar had been designed for short Britons, not tall Saxons, and I could touch the ceiling without stretching, so by dumping the apples out of a couple of barrels and standing on them, I could easily come at my target.

Thrusting my barrel-stave between two of the rows of woven wood, I began to break my way out. The billets were old and hard, but they were only meant to give the wall stability, not to keep in a desperate man. It was not easy work; more than once I lost my balance and tumbled off my perch; more than once I broke my stave and had to return to my barrel for a new one. Before I was finished my hands were torn and bleeding; but I persisted, and slowly the gap in the wall grew. Behind it was only packed earth: easy to move in comparison. Once the hole in the wattle-work was big enough to let me pass, I began to dig. And behind me as I did so, my candle slowly flickered out.

I did not let it stop me. Working now by touch in the darkness, with loosened soil cascading down around me, I dug on. Once or twice as my hole grew deeper I had to get down and add more apple barrels to my pile. The absence of light became no hindrance; I worked with my eyes closed against the sliding earth which powdered my face and body and made me sneeze. It was only when my thrusting barrel-stave met no resistance that I opened my eyes again and saw, faintly limed by pale light, a gap above me where the earth had fallen in. Was it dawn already? I did not wait to see. Instead, dropping my tool and gathering my blanket-cloak around me, I swarmed up through the hole in the wicker-work, and struggling, wriggling, scrambling and scraping, burst my way through into freedom at last.

The glow I had feared was dawn proved to be only moonlight. Standing at the doorway of the barn, still hidden in its shadows, I looked out into a silent silver stillness of thin drifting fog. No sound, no movement stirred in that white light, nor in the dark buildings of the steading. It was well past midnight, for the almost-full moon was westering. I did not stand long to admire it, but made my way quietly toward the stables: I needed a horse urgently to put as many miles between Wulfstan and myself as I could before morning. I had not forgotten his hounds, who would follow a man as gladly as any other game.

Easing the stable door carefully closed behind me, I stood for a moment listening while my eyes adjusted to the straw-scented dimness. Two or three horses were drowsing in their stalls, Wulfstan's tall bay gelding among them. I paused beside him, tempted, but the bay's temper was as uncertain as his master's, and I did not want to be thrown tonight. In the end I chose a sweet-natured brown mare who was more my height. Her saddle and bridle hung ready to hand on the door to her stall, almost as if placed there for me, and I took this as an omen. I was doing up the buckles with clumsy fingers, desperate to be away, when I heard the stable door squeak on its hinges and saw the momentary brightness from outside as it opened and closed. Someone else was in the stables with me.

My heart pounding, I froze. The stable floor was silent packed earth, but I heard the rustle of straw beneath a stealthy foot. Crouching beside the mare, I waited, trying to breathe quietly. My hands had formed themselves into fists: I would not be tamely caged again. The weight of the thrall ring around my neck, to which I had long grown accustomed, pressed heavy on my skin.

The rustling footsteps paused beside the mare's stall, and I saw the looming bulk of a figure, and heard the faint brushing of a hand along the bar where the saddle had hung. Then there was a moment's stillness. "Gwernin?" said a familiar voice softly. "Be you there, lad?"

"Edgar?" I could hardly believe my ears. "What are you doing here?"

"Looking for you, lad," said Edgar. "Or rather, not looking. I could not set you free myself, but I hoped you would break out. The All-Father knows I would have done so in your place, if there was any way at all to do it!" I heard another brushing noise, and the soft sound of something bumping against the stall door. "I am hanging a saddlebag here," said Edgar. "Not for you, of course: I would no doubt have been riding out, come morning, to check something or other in the fields. I expect whoever steals the mare tonight will take it, but that is not my fault. May the High Gods bless your pathway, lad, and guide you safely home." And I heard his feet rustle again in the straw as he turned away.

"Edgar, wait!" I said. "Godgifu—will Wulfstan punish her?"

"Not if I can help it," said Edgar, pausing. "I think he will not be here much longer in any case. Go now, lad, and do not question: follow your own fate, and leave us to find ours." A moment later the door creaked open and shut again: Edgar was gone.

As quickly as I could, I finished my saddling and followed him, taking his gift with me. Across the moonlit yard I led the mare, trying to make no sound, and took the track which led to the west.

The night was still and quiet around me—no barking dogs, no cries of alarm, though I heard a muffled *wuff* from the kennels. Only when I was well away from the farm buildings did I mount and urge the mare into a trot. Ahead of me the road was a ghost track in the drifting silver fog, but the sinking moon showed me my direction clearly enough. I took a deep breath of the cold, free air and settled down to ride.

Dawn found me wandering in a marshy wilderness, surrounded by grey mist and the calls of waking waterfowl. My pony's hooves made sucking noises in the mud of the track I followed—it could hardly be called a road—and the smell of stagnant water and rotting vegetation was strong in the icy air. My hands and feet were numb with cold, and all my bruises had stiffened, but my lust for freedom kept me moving—that and my fear of the great gray hounds which might be even now upon my track. Pulling up by a little stream to let the mare drink, I groped behind me in Edgar's saddlebags, and was delighted to find a soft, cloth-wrapped package in one which proved to contain bread and cheese. I ate a little of it as I rode, and put the rest back for later; presently I would have to see what else he had given me.

It was well past noon before I came, after many reversals and dead ends, to the long straight line of the Roman road which leads from Londinium to Eboricum. Here I paused, torn between two choices. The sun had burned away the fog by now, and I could see the hills to the west again, clearer than ever, across the low flat land which still lay between us. The Roman road was safe and high; it would lead me into no bog-holes, and on it I could make good time. But it led north and south, within the Saxon lands, and would not take me home. With regret I left it and struck off to the west, following another muddy, winding track: but I was worried. In the marshes I had seen few people, and those incurious peasants, but in the drier lands to the west there would be farms—and farmers who would notice a stranger in rough clothing riding a good mare. I was tempted to lie up somewhere until dark—Gods knew I could use the rest!—but always behind me was the fear of Wulfstan and his gray hounds: and so I rode on.

The hills were closing in around me at last, and I was riding half-asleep in the saddle, when my weary mare stumbled and almost threw me. Pulling myself back up with an effort from somewhere around her right shoulder, I reined her to a halt and sat looking around me. No farmers had pursued me, though here and there people had stared at me from their fields or farmyards as I trotted past; and Wulfstan, I thought, was unlikely to catch up with me now. The sun was already behind the hills, and it was time to find a camping place for the night while the light still served.

I found one not far up a little valley where the game trail I was now following took me. There was a small meadow with good green grazing for the mare, and for me a rock shelter—almost a cave—at the base of a steep, oak-forested hill. Indeed, on looking closer, I found that it *was* a cave, with a low, narrow passage at the back leading farther into the hill, out of which came a breath of cold air and a faint sound of falling water. I regarded this somewhat warily, but the remains of old fires in the rock shelter showed that others had camped here before me, and presumably had come to no harm. I still had the flint and steel from the cold-cellar with me—I had dropped them down the breast of my tunic above my rope belt, so as not to lose them in the dark—and with this and an armload of downed branches from the oak-wood I soon had a fire. Edgar's saddlebags proved to contain—in addition to the bread and cheese—a smoked sausage and a rusty belt knife, and a long leather rope to tether the mare. Leaving her grazing contentedly at the end of it, I ate a little more of my food, rolled myself in my cloak, and settled down beside the flickering flames with my head on my saddle. Freedom felt very good indeed.

I cannot have been asleep for long when I heard the hounds. At first their baying was faint and distant, like something heard in a dream; but when I had at last struggled up from the black depths of sleep and lay blinking at the embers of my fire, I could still hear them. Deep-voiced hounds, howling as they ran, like the horn of the wind blowing through a mountain valley, or the gray spectral pack of Gwyn mab Nudd who rides the storm, or the white-bodied, red-eared dogs that Pwyll saw on his hunting of Glyn Cuch—the hounds of Arawn King of Annwn himself. But stumbling to my feet, I knew with dread that what I heard was none of these. This pack, coming rapidly closer even as I listened, was only too mortal and familiar: Wulfstan and his dogs had found me after all.

Grabbing up my saddle and bridle, I ran for the mare, but she had heard the hounds as well. Snorting and plunging at the end of her tether, she did not want to be caught, let alone saddled. Again and again I tried, while the baying grew louder, but each time I got the pad on her back she bucked it off. At last in desperation I loosed the tether from the headstall she still wore, and tried to mount her bare-back. It was a mistake: a few heartbeats later I lay cursing on the stony ground, while the frightened mare galloped off into the night. With the dogs almost upon me, I did the only thing left to me: I ran back to the rock shelter, scooping up my cloak and saddlebags in passing, and plunged headlong into the cave. Maybe I could hold them off in the narrow passage, and maybe I could not, but on one thing I was clear: I was not going back with Wulfstan to be gelded. Death was better, even at the jaws of his hounds.

The passage was low and damp, and soon grew lower, so that I went on hands and knees, groping blindly ahead of me in the dark. As I went in, the cold breath of the hill grew stronger in my face, and the sound of falling water louder. There was something familiar about it, something I had heard before, but I had no time to search my memory. Soon the passage opened out again, so that I could straighten up. Carefully in the pitch blackness I turned around on my knees, looking back the way I had come. The baying of the hounds had changed to barking and snarling; they must have reached the rock shelter. Then I saw a distant flash of fire, like a torch. Wrapping my cloak protectively around my left forearm, and clutching the knife I had found in Edgar's saddlebag in my right hand, I waited. Then I heard Wulfstan's voice, echoing strangely in the cave.

"You in there, *wealisc*?" he yelled. I kept silent. "*Wealisc*, I know you there. Come out, or I let loose dogs!" Still I said nothing. "*Wealisc*, I can wait longer than you!"

"Na!" I yelled back at that. "You cannot! I will die here first!"

"Ha! Maybe you will, *wealisc*!" Wulfstan laughed. The barking and snarling redoubled, and I heard him cursing his dogs and cracking his whip, but nothing else happened: it seemed the hounds would not enter the cave. After a long time he yelled, "Come out now, *wealisc*, or you stay there to rot!"

"I will stay, then," I cried. "Go home to your farm, you drunken coward, and take your dogs with you: I will never come out, though you wait for a year and a day!"

"Stay, then," yelled Wulfstan, and laughed again, a great wild laughter that went on and on. There was a long pause, filled at first with barking and scuffling noises, then with a crunching and grinding and thudding of pebbles, and at last with a great crashing thunder of falling rocks. When it finished there was no more torchlight from the mouth of the cave, no light of any kind. "Goodbye, *wealisc*," I heard Wulfstan yell, faint and muffled and distant. "We quits now. Enjoy freedom—while you can!"

I waited for a long time, but heard nothing more, only the rattle of an occasional pebble from the cave mouth, and the sound of falling water behind me. At last I went groping back along the passage on hands and knees, but I knew already what I would find. Where the rock shelter had been there was only a jumble of boulders blocking the mouth of the cave. Somehow Wulfstan had pulled down the rock-face to seal me into the hill—into the gateway to the Halls of Annwn, the Land beneath the land.

Clearly, then, in my memory, I heard my own voice speaking to Rhiannedd before I left her. *Though I pass through the Gates of Annwn itself*, I had said, *I will come back. I swear it by my ash spear—by my holy awen.* I would have to make good on that promise now, I thought with a shiver, or die in the attempt.

But that, O my children, is a story for another day.

The Halls of Annwn

Even in the blackest night, there is always hope of a dawn. Sealed into a cavern with no chance of escape, in a passage too narrow for me to turn around, and with only unknown darkness at my back, I did what any wise man would do: I put my head down on my folded arms and fell asleep. Either I would find a way out in the morning, or I would not, but there was no longer any urgency in my situation. In truth, I was too exhausted by then to care: I only wanted to rest, to be still.

Morning, however, brought no better counsel. I awoke, cold and stiff and hungry, to almost total darkness. Only a few grains of light sifted through the massive pile of rocks before my face, but it was enough to show me that there was no way out here. Even if I could shift one of these boulders—no light task—it would only be to make room for another, and I might well end like corn under a millstone, ground to a bloody powder for my pains. In this direction there was no escape—no way back.

No way back—the words echoed strangely in my mind. Taliesin had said it, or something like it, during our vigil for Neirin, back in Ynys Môn in the spring, a thousand, thousand lifetimes ago. I could hear his voice now as if he were beside me, as if he placed a hand on my shoulder, warm and strong and kind. Something else important he had said that evening, something about Talhaearn... *Eye-blind is not always head-blind, Gwernin—remember that when the day comes that you need it...* That day had arrived indeed. If I were not to lie before this blocked cave mouth until I starved, I must to learn to see in the dark.

It was one of the hardest things I ever did, to leave those little scraps of light, and push myself, foot by foot, backwards into the immense cold darkness that lay behind me. Only when I reached my discarded cloak and saddlebags did I turn to face that darkness—the Dark Path which lay before me, through the Halls of Annwn itself. Why, I wondered, had Wulfstan's hounds refused to enter the cave? I knew that they did not fear me—of what, then, had they been afraid?

In the flat lands of Powys where I grew up, caves were not common, and I had little idea of what to expect in this one. Bats and spiders, perhaps—I had brushed through a score of clinging webs on my way in the night before, but had barely noticed them in the face of a greater threat. Were there other creatures which lived underground? And what of spirits? Ghosts I had met before, and survived, but in Annwn's Halls there might be many worse dangers. I shivered at the thought, yet I had no choice but to face them.

Before going on, I did three things, three necessary things. I ate a little of my food, just enough to stay my shrunken belly. Working by touch, I used Edgar's knife to cut and tear strips from my cloak which I wound around my arms and legs, both for warmth and for protection against the stones over which I might have to crawl. And I called upon all the friends and protectors I had ever known to help me through this ordeal, and bring me, one way or another, to a good ending. Then with open eyes and a steady heart I set out to walk my path—my Dark Path—which I hoped would lead me home at last.

There was one thing which fed my hope, and that was the breeze: the moving breath of cold air which had flowed out of the cave to meet me on my way in. Somewhere above me, I thought, that air must enter, and if I kept my face toward its flow, I might find my way out again at last. I tried not to listen to the part of me which suggested that air could move through openings too small for me to pass. All I could do was to go and see.

Seeing, however, was something I could not do at the moment. Instead I sat still and listened. Somewhere ahead of me I could hear the sound of falling water. It was not a great roaring cascade like that in Neirin's cave, nor yet an occasional drip such as falls from the eves when the sun strikes the thatch after a night of frost: this was the noise a small stream makes, rushing over a drop in its bed. The moving air came from that direction, too, though it was less noticeable here than it had been in the narrow entrance passage.

Toward the water, then, I must go.

Feeling above me for the roof of the cave, I cautiously stood up and started toward the sound. This was not a good idea: after two steps I bumped my head, stumbled, and fell forward onto chunks of rough stone. Rubbing my head and my bruised shins, I decided to stay on all fours, and started forward again on hands and knees. While my body labored slowly over the muddy floor, where scuttling things ran now and then across my fingers and strands of cobweb tangled in my hair, my mind went looping back to Neirin's ordeal on Ynys Môn, looking for clues that might help me now. Three elements he had met there: air and earth and water. In the sky he had found light to guide him, but here the moving air must be my guide. Through earth and water he had traveled, and there found and retained a prize. I would be lucky, I thought, to get through earth; I would forgo enlightenment if it meant getting out again... Feeling cautiously ahead of me, my groping hand ran into water, and I stopped: I had reached the stream.

The water was cold and fast-flowing, and I scooped up handfuls of it to slake my thirst, for I had drunk nothing since entering the cave the night before. It came from my right, and so did the air: to my right, then, I must go. Crawling along the banks of the stream, I had gone some way before I found the cave wall closing in on me from my right. Then the gravelly bank narrowed until the stream filled the whole opening, and I had to take to the water. Overhead I sensed rather than saw the ceiling coming lower. The stream course climbed slowly at first, then began to rise in steps; sometimes as I labored up one I bumped my head and shoulders on the low rock above me. In the icy water I was soon soaked and shivering, but the faint touch of the breeze on my face had strengthened as the opening narrowed, and gave me hope.

The rocks of the stream bed were slick with a film of limy mud; my rawhide shoes slipped in it, and several times I slid backwards some painfully-gained feet, and had to begin again. Once a many-legged creature dropped from the stone above me and ran across my neck, its venomous feet leaving tiny tracks of pain. The only sounds were my gasping breath and the splashing and gurgling of the water. My hands and feet were growing numb with cold, and I could no longer tell if my eyes were open or closed: in the blackness around me it made no difference. Faint spots of light blossomed and dissolved before me, bodiless and formless as dancing spirits. Odd currents of air brushed my face like ghostly hands. My mind began to play tricks on me: I thought I heard voices. Somewhere Neirin was calling my name; somewhere Rhiannedd was weeping. I tried to call out to them in return, but my words came thick and muffled as if in a dream, and they did not hear me. Their voices died away, and there was only the sound of the water, singing its eternal song, leaping and running in the dark.

Gradually I realized that the cave had opened out again, and I was able to climb out of the stream and rest. Everything here was slimy wet and cold; the rocks on which I sat were slippery with mud, and drops fell continually from the unseen ceiling to strike my head and shoulders or splash in the pools around me. My belly was knotted with hunger, and I scraped the remains of the bread—now reduced to a clammy mush—from the saddlebags and ate it, turning them inside out to lick the last gritty crumbs from the wet leather. I was tempted to eat the remaining pieces of cheese and sausage as well—their scent alone brought the warm water into my mouth—but with an effort of will I put them aside for later, and lay down on as smooth a patch of floor as I could find to rest for a little while. Soon, despite the cold and my hunger, I slept; and in that sleep I dreamed...

I stood on a mountaintop, and it was night. Above me the stars were huge and bright, hanging so low it seemed I could reach up and touch them. Remembering Neirin's efforts, I tried to catch one to give me a light in my darkness, but no matter how I stretched they evaded my grasp. Then they disappeared, blotted out by great wings. I heard the hiss of air through strong pinions as the eagle braked in his descent. Just beside me he landed, and his feathers brushed my face; then they blurred, changing into a cloak, and Gwydion was there. The starlight sparkled in his green eyes and showed me his white teeth as he smiled: so does the wolf smile at his dinner. "Well met, Gwernin," he said; his voice was soft as the fur on the back of a bee, but it sent a shiver down my spine. "Did you call me to ask for my aid?"

"I did not call you at all, Lord," I said, but my voice sounded faint and hollow, like the wind piping through a reed. "I know your help has a price. But it is true that I could use some."

"Ah, but you did call," said Gwydion, and I heard laughter in his words. "Na, na, do not argue with me: I will give you now what you need, and someday you will do me a favor in return. Is that not a fair bargain?"

"Yes, Lord," I said after a moment's thought. "Let it be as you will."

" 'As I will,' " said Gwydion musingly, as though the phrase stirred a memory in him. "Yes, I will have my will." Holding up his hands, he spat deliberately into each palm. "Stand still," he said, and coming closer, pressed his moist palms firmly over my closed eyes. He held them there for as long as it takes to breathe twice, then took them away. Blinking, I resisted the urge to wipe my face, and Gwydion smiled. "Na, do not worry," he said chuckling. "It will not rub off. But look!"

I stared at him, uncertain of his meaning. The night was as dark as ever, but now I could see every line on his face, every thread and stitch in his clothing. Every stone and spring of grass on the mountaintop was as clear as at midday. "What have you done?" I asked.

"Given you clearer sight," said Gwydion. "You will not always have it, but you can summon it when your need is great. Otherwise you should not use it, because it comes at a cost." And he stretched out his arms to become an eagle again.

"What cost is that?" I asked, but the eagle was already in flight. I leapt and tried to stop him, and fell, and falling tumbled down the mountain in the dark…

It was dark, and I was in the cave again. Groaning, I unfolded myself from the ball into which I had curled for warmth. A drop from the ceiling fell on my face, and I blinked and reached up to wipe it away—and saw my hand. Only briefly, there and gone again—but real. I froze for a moment, startled, then sat and thought. Then slowly I looked around.

It was not exactly sight. There was no color to it, or texture. It came as much through my skin, or my ears, as through my eyes. But I knew now where the walls of the cavern were, and where the boulders lay on the floor waiting to trip me, or the gleaming sheets of water which covered deep pools. I saw the faint breeze, like a ripple in the air, which flowed through that place, and the opening in the cave wall where the stream came rushing out. All of these things were part of the darkness that surrounded me, like a carved picture seen with the hands rather than the eyes. I touched and read the blackness with my mind.

Opening the saddlebags, I took out the last crumbly piece of cheese and slowly ate it, and re-tied the woolen wrappings around my legs with cold-clumsy fingers. Then I stood up and started across the cavern following the stream-bank, guided through the darkness by Gwydion's gift.

The stream cleft when I reached it was tall and narrow, almost too narrow in places for me to pass. Sometimes I waded chest-deep in the icy water, while invisible creatures brushed laughing between my legs and tugged at my ragged tunic; sometimes I squeezed myself through wider gaps some way above the stream, bracing my bleeding palms against the water-worn walls. More than once I thought that I was stuck, but always I found a way through at some cost in effort and pain, and always the slight, cold breeze blew steadily in my face. Now and again at the edge of my vision I saw orbs of light, like the eyes of silent beasts stalking me, but whenever I turned my head they disappeared. The air was loud with the echoes of falling water, and again I heard voices: Neirin's voice calling my name, Taliesin's voice chanting in Gwallawg's hall—chanting, maybe, a *marwnad*, a death-song—but for whom? Was it, I wondered, for me? Then the voices faded, and there was only the sound of the water again, ringing and chiming like harp-song heard far off in the hollow hills, crystalline and silver...

At last the cleft opened into a wider place—not a large room such as I had seen before, but a bench big enough to let me climb out of the stream for a while. I sat on it huddled and shivering, my head on my knees, and my arms and the tattered remnants of my cloak wrapped around me for what feeble warmth they could give. I did not know how long I had been in the cave, whether hours or days or years, but I knew that I was coming to the end of my strength. Cold and hunger were wearing me down; one of these times when I lay down to rest, I would drift from sleep into that sleep from which there is no waking. Then all I had learned and done and suffered would be in vain: I had made no great songs, and soon men would forget me. Rhiannedd might bear my child, and remember me while she raised him, but my son would never know his father: he would be like the Druid's son in Talhaearn's story, left with only a name and a tale, and whatever of me he carried in his blood... After a while, still crouched as I was, I slept again, and in my sleep I dreamed...

I was walking through a grove of wind-twisted pines; the sea-smell was strong in the air, and I heard the sound of waves. I came out of the trees to find myself on a cliff-edge above the water. Beyond the cliff, not far away, was a rocky island, with the green sea washing around it; and between the cliff and the island there was a bridge—a sort of bridge. No wider than a sword-blade it was, though it stretched many times a man's length, and shone bright as silver in the sun. On the island, I knew, was the treasure I had come to find, but its cliffs were sheer, and the great waves rushed between us like a storm-tide, or the whirlpool that lurks between Arfon and Ynys Môn to suck ships down. One slip on the slender bridge, and I would be in their waters. More than once I placed my foot on that bridge, and more than once I drew back, frowning. I did not have the courage or the strength.

"Ah, man, do you not have the stones for it, then?" asked a rough voice behind me. Turning, I saw a slight, dark man—beardless as a boy, but not a boy—crouching by a fire over which he was roasting a hare. He poked the meat with one finger to test its doneness, indifferent to the heat of the flames, and then squinted at me through the smoke. "D'ya not have the courage for it, then?" he asked me again.

I looked at the bridge, and then back at my questioner. "I do not think I do," I said seriously. "I am too weary to make the leap, and I fear to fail."

"Then 'tis a fool you are," said the dark man. "If you do not try, you will not fail; but also you will never succeed. You must gather up all that is in you, and make your will as hard as your ash spear was when first you lay with a girl. Then thrust with all your strength, and you will succeed or die: but either way, there will be no shame to you. Here!" And pulling the stick with the hare on it off the fire, he tossed it to me. I caught it without thinking, then stood juggling it while the heat of it burned my hands, and caution warred with my hunger. At last hunger won, and sinking my teeth into the sputtering meat, I tore off a mouthful and swallowed it whole. The dark man laughed. "Aye," he said, "that is the way of it. Now watch." And turning, he ran headlong at the cliff edge and leapt. Landing exactly in the middle of the bridge with both feet, he rebounded as it flexed under him and leapt again like a salmon, shining in the air as he flew… The smoke from the fire blew into my eyes, and when I blinked them clear, he was gone…

Again I awoke shivering in the darkness with the sound of running water in my ears, but this time I was not alone. All around me now I could see them, the creatures of the Underworld, crowding closer and closer to my feeble warmth, impatient to dine on my death. The dark walkers-by-night; the pale riders-on-the-storm; the red-eared and white-shining hounds, gold and green eyes gleaming; the unavenged dead come out of their graves, trailing their blood-stained shrouds behind them; the dragons who gnaw their way through the roots of the earth, and shake it when they meet and fight; the gray hag who by the ford washes the shirts of those about to die; and the restless Gods, once worshiped but now forgotten, yet still alive and hungry—all of them were there, all my fears and nightmares. Their claws were sharp to tear my body, their mouths eager for my blood. The sight of them almost stopped my heart. The short hairs stood up on my neck, my breath came fast and thick, and my bowels cramped with terror; yet with courage I knew I could still defeat them. Sitting there in the midst of that hungry host, I took the last piece of sausage from my saddlebags and slowly ate every bite, then licked the lingering traces of grease from my cold fingers. It was not so good as a roast hare, but it seemed to give me strength. Then standing up and forcing myself back into the icy water, I set out to succeed or die; for me now there was no middle way. The watchers gave ground reluctantly before me, to gather again behind my back and wait. I did my best to ignore them: if only I could reach daylight again, I knew that they would fade away like the ghosts they were.

Gradually the ceiling of the cleft came lower and lower, until I found myself first bent double in the stream, then crawling on hands and knees with my face barely above the surface. My chin was in the water, then my lips; turning my head sideways, I had only a hand's-breadth of space left in which to breathe. The breeze was stronger now, and once or twice I thought I smelled wood-smoke in it, but unless I could swim on my back with my nose in the crevices through which it blew, it would do me no good. At last, groping ahead, I found I had no clearance left at all. How long, I wondered, could I hold my breath? Behind me the watchers were waiting. The dark man's words came again into my mind: *make your will as hard as your ash spear...*

I breathed in and out two or three times; then, taking a final deep breath, put my head down and drove forward with all my strength, half-swimming and half-crawling through the icy current. Farther—farther—farther, and still my groping hands found only stone above me. There was a roaring in my ears which was not the water's, and a pain like a spear-blade in my chest, but still I kicked and scrabbled forward until I felt my consciousness going, and then beyond. Still no air—still no air—the taste of blood in my mouth—blood and flesh and hot fat—teeth and claws tearing me—death—

my ash spear—my ash spear...

I shot up into clear air, and clung gasping to the stony bank while the world revolved around me. Only slowly did I realize that there was light around me as well—dim light, but bright as a blazing beacon after all my time in the dark. It came from somewhere above me—somewhere high above me. My eyes followed its dusty shafts up and up, to the jagged rim of the sinkhole far overhead. Fresh air flowed down through it, fresh air with a hint of woodsmoke, and the scent of trampled grass. I could even see a scrap of blue sky, and hear a faint trilling of birdsong. Up above me on the mountain it was a beautiful late autumn day—and I was as likely to reach it as I was to fly.

With a great effort I dragged myself out of the stream, and finding a good, smooth slab of stone, crawled to it and lay down with my eyes still on that scrap of blue. I had escaped the hosts of Annwn, who could not face the sunlight, and yet it was to no avail. I felt weak and dizzy, and light as a wind-blown leaf new-fallen in the first frost. After a while I found words running through my head, the words of a song—my deathbed-song. And a long while after that, when the light from above was growing fainter with evening, I began to sing it.

> "I was Gwernin Storyteller—
> Tales I told before High Kings—
> Blows I struck in bloody battle—
> Songs I sang to give fame wings.
>
> Circuits made I through the Cymry,
> Through Deheubarth, Dyfed too,
> Ceredigion, Meirionnydd,
> Gwynedd, Powys, my tales knew.
>
> Long I followed paths of knowledge,
> Gathered stories, learned their lore,
> Walked with Gods and talked with dead men—
> All I learned I kept in store.
>
> Rode I through the Pictish mountains,
> Followed rivers to the sea,

>   Gathered treasure as song-reaver—
>   Gold and weapons came to me.
>
>   I was Taliesin's student,
>   I learned songs from Talhaearn gray—
>   Now within this lonely mountain
>   I will die with dying day.
>
>   I was Gwernin Storyteller—
>   Tales I told before High Kings—
>   Blows I struck in bloody battle—
>   Songs I sang to give men wings."

With all the strength that was left to me I sang it, and my voice echoed back from the cave walls. Even on the mountain above they will hear that, I thought. When I was through I sighed and closed my eyes. There was nothing left to do, nothing left to fear: now I could rest. I no longer felt the cold; I was barely aware of hunger. But I was sorry not to have kept my word to Rhiannedd. *Though I pass through the Gates of Annwn itself,* I had said, *I will come back. I swear it by my ash spear—by my holy awen.* I would have liked to have made good on that promise; I would have liked to have seen my son...

I thought I could hear Neirin's voice again, calling my name, but I had no strength to answer him. Again and again he was calling: "Gwernin—brother—are you there? Answer me, Gwernin! Is it down there that you are? Wait for me, brother! I am coming—I am coming!" His voice went away, and then came back, louder, closer. "Gwernin—Gwernin! *Hai mai,* brother, what have they done to you? Only hold on, hold on—I will get you out." I thought he was putting a rope around my chest—I must be remembering that time in the North, long ago last summer, when I fell off the tower. His hands were warm, so warm, and I tried to open my eyes, tried to speak to him, but it was too much effort, and I was tired, so tired... "Can you hold the rope?" he was asking.

"Na," I said, and my voice sounded slurred and strange in my own ears. "Neirin..."

"Never mind, brother. I will get you out. Only do not leave me—do not leave me!" I thought he was weeping, and that was strange, for he had not wept before. His voice was growing more distant now, but that was all right; when he was gone I could rest. Then the rope around me was lifting me, hurting me, and I groaned. My spirit slipped away from my body, and went hurtling down a long shaft into a great darkness, as it had on Ynys Môn. This must be death, I thought, but it is not so bad. After all, I have died once before… No Taliesin here this time, to bring me back to life… Though maybe…Neirin…can…

I was tired of being cold. Being warm was so much better. Maybe I would decide to live after all… And so I did.

But that, O my children, is a story for another day.

The Ash Spear

I sat on a low stool in the steamy bathhouse, dressed only in my trews, my eyes clenched shut and tears of pain welling out from under their lids. "Are you not—done yet?" I asked through gritted teeth. "How much more—is there—to do?"

"Na, na, brother," said Neirin cheerfully. "I am almost finished. Only I do not want to be cutting out any more if I can help it—you are ragged enough already."

"Why not—cut it all short, then?" I gasped. "Neirin—!"

"Na, na, you would not be wanting to come before my uncle tonight looking like a crop-haired slave," said Neirin, working busily with his comb.

"I have been one," I said, touching the marks which the thrall ring had left on my neck. "My hair will grow again before the scars fade."

Neirin paused for a moment. "That is true," he said seriously. "But you carry no shame for it. Besides, if I cut your hair short, I cannot braid it, and I am wanting you to look your best." And with that he returned, if somewhat more gently, to his jerking at the matted tangles on the back of my head, while I set my teeth again to endure in silence.

It was only that afternoon we had ridden into Aquae Arnemetiae, after a three-days' journey—which I could usually have done in two—from the camp on the hillside where Neirin had warmed me back to life. Since then he had been tending me as anxiously as a cat with one kitten, although a few good meals at the farmsteads where we had stopped had put me well on the way to recovery. Now, after a long soak in Gwallawg's bathhouse, which drew its hot water from Aquae's famous springs, I was feeling very much myself again, and looking forward to the evening's song and feasting which Taliesin had promised us.

He had been seated in the courtyard with Rhys when we rode in, enjoying a little late autumn sunshine, and had greeted me with as much joy as I had ever seen him display. Rhys, on the other hand, had been white-faced and open-mouthed with shock. "I—I thought you were dead!" he had stammered when he could speak at all. "I—I was sure—I was sure of it!"

I had stared at him coldly. "You did not stop to be sure, did you, you little coward?" I said after a moment. "Although since you took my horse and my sword with you when you fled, it was dead that I should have been, indeed—had not one of the Saxons wanted me for a slave." And then, while he still gazed at me in horror, "Never mind. I do not ask *iawndal* of you—I think you have made your own punishment." And turning back to Taliesin, I added, "Let us take our ponies to the stable, and then we can talk."

"Gw—Gwernin!" said Rhys. "Let—let me do it! I—I will take care of them for you—you can trust me!" And then, realizing the infelicity of his words, "O God! I am sorry—I am so sorry!" And with that he burst into tears.

I had looked at him grimly, but in truth there was little anger left in me for him. After a moment I sighed. "Take them, then," I said, and to Taliesin, who had watched this with interest, "Let us go to the guesthouse. I want my own clothes again—and a bath!"

Neirin's voice recalled me to the present. "That is the whole of it," he said, drawing his bone comb once more through my remaining hair. "Now I can be plaiting it—so"—suiting his actions to his words—"and covering the thin spots."

"Thank you, brother," I said when he was done, standing up and picking up my towel. Throwing it over my bare shoulder, I ran my fingers cautiously over my face. "Have the bruises faded?"

"Very nearly," said Neirin, peering at me, then grinned. "You will not now frighten the women, always providing that the light is not too strong. Do you have one in mind?"

"There was a little red-head in the kitchen," I said, grinning back at him, "who was not reluctant to know me, earlier in the summer."

"*Hai mai!* I will be careful to hunt elsewhere, then, for a while," said Neirin, and laughed.

In the guesthouse Taliesin and Rhys were waiting for us with wine and a tray of food—cold meat, bread, cheese, and apples—to sustain us until dinner. Neirin and I stuffed our mouths—I concentrated on the first three items, and left the apples alone—and settled down to talk. Neirin had told me a little of his story already, but now I heard it all in sequence for the first time, together with Taliesin's.

"When Rhys rejoined the war-band alone," said Taliesin, toying with his wine cup, "Gwallawg sent a party back to look for you, Gwernin—and I think he was not short of volunteers. Rhys had told them that you were dead, but they found no body; however, they could not stay long to search. After Gwallawg had brought his cattle and his *teulu* safe home, he sent messengers under a Green Branch to King Iffi in Eboricum, but still could get no news of you. I did not believe you were dead, but I did not know what to do next, so I left it with the Gods, and waited. Also I sent a message to Llys-tyn-wynnan, to tell Talhaearn that you were missing, but not yet despaired of."

"Their King would have not have heard of me," I said, my eyes fixed broodingly on Rhys, who was trying to make himself small in a corner. "Those who captured me were raiding on their own account, and one of them took me home with him for reasons of his own, to work on his father's farm as a thrall." I closed my lips firmly, reluctant to say more.

"I saw the place," said Neirin, nodding, "and heard that tale. When I left my half-brother's court in Dun Eidyn, not long after Lughnasadh, I rode slowly south through Goddeu and Rheged, stopping at those two courts to perform. Then, for no good reason, I turned eastward to visit Dunod mab Pabo Post Prydein, whom Gwernin and I met last summer. I had been having dreams I did not like, and was uneasy. Dunod was for sending an envoy to Iffi's court on some business of their borders, and he invited me to go along, to add my bardic weight and prestige—such as it is!—to the party. And at Iffi's court I met a man who carried a message meant for Taliesin, and who gave it gladly into my keeping. It came from

Aelfwine the *Scop*, who had met Gwernin on his travels and wished him well. Once I had heard it, I asked King Iffi for a escort, and rode to the farm of his thane Aethelstan. I arrived there," said Neirin grimly, "to hear that Gwernin had escaped the night before, and fled westward with Aethelstan's son Wulfstan in pursuit."

"Why did you flee then, Gwernin, and not sooner?" asked Taliesin curiously.

"Because," I said, "Wulfstan was going to—he was going to…" I stopped, unable to bring out the words. Since my escape from the cave, I had been trying to put Wulfstan's threat out of my mind, but more than once in the past two nights I had woken from nightmares sweating with fear.

"Na, tell me later," said Taliesin, perceiving my distress. "What happened next, Little Hawk?"

"Wulfstan came back," said Neirin, looking at me with concern, "and told us—with some urging from his father—where and how he had left Gwernin. My escort and I followed his back trail to the hills, and found the cave where Gwernin had taken refuge, but the mouth was blocked as Wulfstan had said. He had"—this to Taliesin, who was frowning—"pulled down a tree from the hill above a rock shelter, and brought down half the hillside with it. I called as loudly as I could, hoping Gwernin was still alive inside and would hear me—though how we could have got him out, I was not knowing!—but I got no answer. So I sent my Saxon escort back to their King, and finding a quiet place, I made camp alone. And that night as I slept, I dreamed of my brother, and knew that he was still alive inside the hill."

"I heard you calling me," I said to him, smiling faintly. "More than once I heard you. But I thought—well, never mind."

Neirin nodded, understanding. "I began to search the hill then, hoping to find a way in, but it was another night and a day before I heard your singing, and found you at the bottom of that sinkhole."

"I could not measure the passing of time in the cave," I said, "but I dreamed of you and Taliesin, and—and of other things as well." I closed my eyes for a moment, not wanting to say more.

"*Sa, sa,*" said Taliesin after a pause, "you shall tell me more later, if you wish. But now I think it is time that we made ourselves ready for hall, before Gwallawg grows impatient for the company of his bards—of all his bards!"

That night I dressed myself with more than my usual care. It was good to wear fine clothes again, though I had to borrow an old pair of boots from Taliesin—the Saxons having taken mine—and a belt from Neirin. At least my harp was waiting safely for me, though it would be a while before my hands recovered sufficiently from the rough work they had been doing for me to play it. Running my fingers over my chin, I thought wryly that my beard had not suffered; indeed, it was thicker than it had been when I left. All in all, I felt I made a good sight in my red woolen tunic and new trews, though nothing to compare with Neirin's bright plaid, or even Taliesin's deep blue. Rhys alone looked plain and ordinary in his oversized brown tunic, but then he would not be sitting at high table with the King: and for once I think he was glad of it. Very quiet, was Rhys, and would hardly meet my eyes that night, or for many days to come. I found it a welcome change.

The meat and drink in hall that night was as good as any I have ever eaten, for King Gwallawg, hearing of my return, had urged on his cooks to unparalleled efforts. He himself embraced me like a father when I entered the hall, and seated me beside him at table. Indeed, his kindness was such that I was more than once hard-pressed not to weep. Neirin saved me, teasing me repeatedly on the supposed mourning which had overcome all the women of the *llys* on my disappearance, and hoping that I would leave one or two for him—not to mention a few crumbs of the excellent dinner!

When the feasting was over, and all the bards had sung—myself among them, repeating a piece I had composed back in the summer—we went to our beds; and very glad I was to go there, for I was weary. I laid myself down on that soft straw mattress, covered by warm blankets, and went sliding down a long smooth slope into darkness. And at first I slept well. Then the dreams came...

I was back in the cold cellar again, but this time I had not managed to escape. I knew it was morning; any moment now they would come for me. My lantern had burnt out; it was totally dark, and I went blindly groping around for anything I could use as a weapon; but there was nothing, nothing at all. Then the trapdoor opened, and dozens of tall yellow-haired Saxons came pouring into my prison. They beat me and kicked me until I could barely move, then they dragged me up the ladder and out of the barn, and stripped me and tied me to the gate of the dog-run. Behind me the hounds were barking and snarling, snuffling at me through the bars of the gate, ready for my blood. Then Wulfstan came toward me with his *seax* in his hand, the blue blade naked and shining. "Now, *wealisc*," he said, "I show you what it really like, to be thrall." The knife came closer and closer, and I screamed…

I awoke in the darkness sweating, with Taliesin's hand shaking my shoulder. "*Sa, sa, sa,* Gwernin," he was saying softly. "Wake up now, *bachgen*, you are safe—it is over. No one will hurt you here."

"O—Gods," I said slowly, forcing myself up from the depths of the nightmare. "I am sorry. Did I wake the others?"

"Na, they are still sleeping—listen, you can hear the snores," Taliesin said, and chuckled. And that was true; Rhys' snoring as usual seemed to shake the walls, and Neirin always slept soundly.

"I am sorry I woke you," I said, looking up at what I could see of him in the dimness. "It—it was only a dream. I—I am all right now."

"Of course you are," said Taliesin, nodding. "But I think you will be better still for talking about it. Let us go outside and sit for a while in the courtyard—the moonlight is bright there, and the night is not very cold. Then you can tell me all the things you have not yet told me, which are *not* bothering you, and after that"—I heard the smile in his voice—"perhaps we can both get some sleep."

It was never any use to argue with Taliesin; I had learned that long ago, and so did not try. Instead I got up and found my cloak, and followed him barefoot out into the courtyard, to the place where he had been sitting when we arrived that afternoon. The moon was waning, but she was still bright, and in her light his dark-bearded face seemed all black and white, a mask of a face in which only the gleaming eyes were alive. And there, sitting beside him on the bench against the guesthouse wall, I finally began to talk.

He was a good listener, was Taliesin; he hardly asked questions at all—only a few times when I was stuck, and then very gently. In the end I told him everything, or almost everything: how I was captured; the beatings and humiliations; the pain and cold and hunger; and the fear. I told him how Wulfstan had found me with the girl he had wanted, and what he had threatened to do to me, and how I escaped and ran and was trapped in the end. And I told him about walking my Dark Path through the cave, and the dreams—if they were dreams—that I had there. The waning moon was high overhead before I finished, and the night was growing old, but I was glad to have the telling over and done with: it was like a fever breaking, leaving me weak and cold and empty, but ready for sleep. I even yawned.

"Yes," said Taliesin softly—he was sitting so close beside me that I could feel his warmth—"I think you will sleep now. And you are right: you truly did walk your Dark Path, or most of it, in that cave. I wonder, now... I will have to think..." He paused, and I heard him yawn in his turn. "But for now, I think we should both go back to bed."

"Will we be returning to Pengwern soon, Master?" I asked him. "I promised them at Llys-tyn-wynnan that I would be back by Samhain. I swore it to Rhiannedd, on my *awen*."

"Then you had better make that promise good," said Taliesin, and I could hear the smile again in his voice. "But we have a few days yet in hand before we must leave. And I think...I am almost certain...there is something we need to do here first. But now it is time for rest." And standing up, he put his hand on my shoulder and urged me back to my bed, where I slept without dreaming for what remained of the night.

I woke late that morning, and found myself alone in the guesthouse. Pulling on my boots—Taliesin's old boots—and setting myself to rights, I went to the feast-hall, where I found him and

Neirin talking quietly over the remains of their breakfast. No sooner had I joined them than the little red-headed kitchen girl brought me food—enough cold meat and fresh bread for three men. I thanked her with a smile, and saw in her answering smile that she remembered our last meeting with pleasure, and was eager to repeat it. This set me up considerably in my own esteem, for girls usually did not look twice at me when Neirin was around, and I fell on my meal with a will.

"I have been talking with Neirin," said Taliesin to me, "about what you told me of your walking the Dark Path in the cave, and we are agreed that there is something still lacking for you to complete it—a sort of magical framing, such as we gave him at the beginning of his. How do you feel about that, Gwernin?"

"Why," I said around a mouthful of pig-meat, "I am willing to do whatever you think is needful. But when, and where?"

"*When* would be starting tonight, I think," said Taliesin, "and running through tomorrow night. And *where* would be on the hill of Arnemetia. At the new moon would have been better, but you need to be home by then, to keep your promises... What do you think?"

I must admit that my first thought was that this meant no meeting with the little red-headed girl that night. However, what I said was, "I like it. What must I do to prepare?"

"Nothing in particular," said Taliesin, smiling. "Sleep all this afternoon if you can, for you will be awake two nights and a day. Neirin and I will do the rest."

I sighed internally, but also I smiled. "That," I said, "I can easily accomplish. Do I get to eat first?"

"Not after sunset," said Neirin, grinning.

"Then I had better wake before sunset," I said, and filled my mouth with sweet roast pig-meat again.

It was long after sunset, and the winter stars were rising high and bright, when the three of us left the *llys* that evening and started up the hill of the Goddess. I had bathed again in the hot springs, and Neirin had combed and plaited my ragged hair. Now I wore the brown woolen tunic which had been Ieuan's—no longer too large across the shoulders—cinched in at the waist with one of Neirin's belts; the new trews Rhiannedd had made for me back in the summer; and my second-hand boots. Also I carried a thick hooded cloak, a present to me from King Gwallawg. His craggy eyebrows had risen in surprise when he heard that his bards would not be feasting with him tonight, but after he heard the reason he only nodded, and sent a servant to fetch one of his own best cloaks. "It will be cold on the hill tonight, lad," he said as he handed it to me, "and I would not have you lose your voice to the chill: I want to hear one or two more of your tales before you leave us for the winter." And he laughed his big, booming laugh, and turned away before I could thank him.

We carried no torches as we went up the hill, but the starlight was bright enough to show us our way. The path seemed steeper than I remembered; steeper than it had been on the summer's day a year and a half ago when I climbed it with Neirin. The young oaks around the hill's crest, which had then been bronze-green with new leaves, now stretched their bare branches imploringly to the night sky, and the dark hollies mixed with them made masses of shapeless shadow. There was no wind, and the air smelled of wood-smoke, leaf mould, and frost. Behind us in the *llys* a dog barked, and in the woods I heard the cry of a hunting owl; otherwise the night was silent except for the crunching of our footsteps in the crisp dead leaves of autumn.

We reached the top and paused. I was remembering again the previous summer, and the large shadow the young oaks had cast, like a memory of things past. Then I heard it again, the sounds that were not sounds, that were more than sounds: the echo of a brazen horn, faint and far-off, like the horn of Gwyn mab Nudd, and the rise and fall of voices chanting. There were torches in the shadows, torches coming up the hill, their leaping red light mixing with the starlight, and in their midst a young bull-calf garlanded for sacrifice, and a man in a white robe leading him… The vision wavered, and faded, and was gone; but in my mind the horn echoed still. I looked at Neirin, and saw his teeth flash white in the starlight as he grinned. Then Taliesin was speaking, and I turned my attention back to him.

"Did you bring the fire-pot?" he was asking Neirin.

"*Sa, sa,* I did, and the place was—just here, I am thinking." Neirin knelt and uncovered the pot of coals he carried; then, blowing on it, raised a tiny flickering flame, which grew swiftly to a blaze when he poured it onto his prepared tinder. Sitting back on his heels, he added a few pieces of firewood from the pile stacked beside him, then stood up, his amber eyes sparkling in the firelight. From under his cloak Taliesin produced a lidded beaker of black stoneware, twin to the one he had used on Ynys Môn.

"This is not the draught Neirin drank last spring," he said to me, "because your need and your path will be different, Gwernin. But it should help you to see clearly…the things that you need to see."

"I understand," I said, nodding. "I think I understand." I felt light and eager and without fear, as a man should feel on the edge of battle. Taliesin smiled.

"Seeker, are you ready now," he asked quietly, "to walk the dark path which lies within the sea?" In my memory I heard the sound of surging waters, and felt their chill.

"I am ready," I said.

"Seeker, are you ready now," asked Neirin, "to walk the dark path which lies between the stars?" In my memory I heard the sound of wings in the darkness, and saw Gwydion's smile.

"I am ready," I said.

"Seeker, are you ready now," asked a third voice—and though it came from Taliesin's mouth, it was not his—"to walk the dark path which lies within the earth?" I knew where I had heard that voice before, and the short hairs rose on my neck.

"I am ready," I said.

"Then take this cup," said the voice which was not Taliesin's, "to aid you on your way, and drain it to the bitter dregs." And he held out the black stoneware beaker, and I took it, and I drank.

At first it seemed only water, with a faint, herbal aftertaste, but it spread a warmth in me like the finest mead. There was bitterness there as well, but I did not heed it; I had drunk that cup already; it had passed me by. I handed the beaker back to Taliesin and met his eyes. They were dark in the firelight, the eyes of the Druid, of Lovernos, the King in the Ground. "The Path awaits you, Alder Tree," he said. "Go you now and walk it, and walk it well."

"I will," I said, and smiled. Turning back to the fire, I circled it once, and sat down cross-legged beside it on my new cloak. The fire leapt and roared; there were pictures in it, and voices… When I looked up again Neirin and Taliesin had gone, and I was alone with the night. I smiled to myself and settled down to watch the flames.

In the east the moon rose, and danced with the turning stars. In the *llys* below the last lights had long since gone out. The white owl hunted through the trees, and I heard her lonesome cry; in the hills to the south two foxes called, each to the other. The night grew colder, and I stretched out my hand to put more wood on the fire, but sparingly, for I had a second night to endure as well. Then, staring into the depth of the flames, I let my mind float free again, seeing and counting and knowing all those things that had made me who I was. I was Gwernin Storyteller… storyteller… storyteller… I was the stories I told. All men were in me, because I told their tales; I gave them life, and they gave life to me…

After a long, long time I saw the east was growing lighter, and I ceased to feed the fire. When it had burned down, I banked the embers with ashes, and stood to watch the growing light. And slowly the sun rose up and touched me with its rays, and all around the hill of Arnemetia, the world woke up again. I was hungry now, but it did not matter; I was safe in the hands of the Goddess. Presently I sat down again cross-legged in the sunshine, and the day went past in one long waking dream. When the sun had set I stirred the banked coals and built up my fire again. Then I drank some of the water Neirin had left me in a stoneware jug. It was sweet and clear, and tasted faintly of the same herbs that had been in the beaker. This time I wrapped the King's cloak around me, and settled down again to watch the flames. There were moving pictures there, and voices… one voice… the Druid's voice…

Some knowledge can only be got by doing; when your time comes, you will know. So Taliesin had said to me on Ynys Môn, while Neirin was walking his Dark Path, and it is true. That night I learned things which I cannot put into words; I can only tell the stories that embody them. In the silence on that hill I listened to the voice of the wind, and the voice of the fire, and the voice of the earth; I tasted water and wood-smoke, and felt the frost that formed on my cloak and my hair. I heard the owl again, and traced the path of the stars, and watched as one single bright one dropped from its place to vanish in the void. The branches of the oaks above me sang in the air; the leaves of the hollies rattled their waxy spines. Under me the earth went down and down, black, hard, solid, and older than time. Somewhere rivers ran through it; somewhere water spoke in the dark, and spirits answered. Above it Gods shouted in the thunder, and whispered in the rain and the snow. Gwydion came to my fire wrapped in his cloak of feathers, and we drank and laughed and talked together in the moonlight, and he told me tales of the very-long-ago. My fire burned to gray ashes, but I did not feel the cold; I was beyond cold; I was the cold itself. And at last the moon sank down toward the west, and the east ran gold and crimson with the dawn, and in the first sunlight Neirin and Taliesin came walking up the hill to embrace me, and to lead me back again to the world of men. And I was glad of their coming, but also sorry to leave the hill. But I knew that always now, somewhere within me, would be the hill of Arnemetia, and the peace I had found there. And I knew also where to begin my search for the tale of the son of the Druid.

But that, O my children, is a story for another day.

Samhain

All journeys, like all stories, come to an end. Riding my black pony under a leaden sky along the road which leads west from Pengwern, I thought back to the partings not long behind me. One of the hardest, as always, had been with Neirin, who was remaining at his uncle's *llys* for the winter.

"Na, I am not sure about next summer," he had said as we sat at table that last morning. "But my Mother's-Brother will make me his *pencerdd* while I stay, and this is a snug place to pass the winter." His eyes as he spoke went past me to the little red-headed kitchen girl—I could never remember her name!—who was watching us both from the far side of the hall. I had managed one meeting with her before I left, but did not deceive myself that she would be breaking her heart over my going—not with Neirin ready to take my place.

"A snug spot for the winter is a good thing to have," I agreed. "But for myself, I think I will give up roving for a while. With a woman, and a child coming soon, I need to be making a name for myself with my Prince, so that maybe he will give me lands."

"*Sa, sa,* give my love to your girl Rhiannedd, then," said Neirin, grinning. "What are you for naming the child?"

"Ieuan, I think, if it is a son," I said seriously. "I owe him that. If it is a girl—well, no doubt Rhiannedd will have a name for her."

"Ieuan mab Gwernin," said Neirin, tasting the name. "*Hai mai!* We must hope he does not take after his namesake, then!"

"We must indeed," I said grinning, and with that we rose and left the hall side by side.

Leaving Pengwern was another story entirely. I stopped there for two nights with Taliesin, and rode out on the second afternoon to say hail and farewell to my aunt and uncle. They were pleased and puzzled as ever with me, regarding me rather as a chicken would who has hatched out a duck egg by mistake, but is still fond of her hatchling. I said as much to Taliesin that evening after our singing was done in hall, sitting with him in his comfortable room over a last cup of wine, while Rhys, already asleep, snored on his pallet in what was once Neirin's place. Taliesin had smiled and nodded at my words.

"*Sa, sa,* that is always the way of it," he said. "Only a bard knows another bard's mind. It is as if I had a son who wanted to be a farmer—I wonder sometimes how I would have dealt with it."

"Have you no sons, then, Master?" I asked, greatly daring. "Sons by blood, I mean—for I think that all of your pupils are in some way sons of your heart."

"Even Rhys?" asked Taliesin, with a fleeting grin. "Na, but I know what you mean... So far as I know, I have no sons of the blood, nor ever thought to have one." He seemed for a moment to be looking into a great distance, and his face was sad. I would have liked to question him more, but did not dare to; there was something final in his tone: a closed door; a locked gate; a sealed tomb.

Instead I asked, "What of Rhys, Master? Does he stay with you now as your prentice?" Taliesin's gaze came back to the present, and he gave me a rueful grin.

"Until spring, at least," he said, "but as student, not prentice; and only because the season is late now for traveling. Then I think I will be returning him to his father. He has had a bad shock with your reappearance, and will be the better for it; but he is young yet for the road, in some ways younger than his years. Ugnach will have to take him in hand again; my patience has its limits, and he has reached them."

"Do you have someone else in mind, then?" I asked curiously. I had not noticed anyone else around Pengwern who seemed likely material.

"I might," said Taliesin, looking at me keenly. "Two years ago when we met at Deganwy, you asked me, Gwernin, if I would teach you the harp. Do you remember?"

"Clearly," I said, "as if it were yesterday. You said you had not the time for it then, and sent me to Talhaearn instead." I smiled. "I cannot remember if I ever thanked you for it, but if not, I do so now."

"It is him you should thank, and yourself," said Taliesin. "You have made good use of his teaching."

"I am glad you think so, Master," I said. "I am not sure if Talhaearn would agree… He assures me, by the way, that he has things yet to teach me which you cannot."

Taliesin laughed. "He may be right at that. Although… Gwernin, would you like to ride with me again, come spring? To be my prentice now? You have earned it. What do you say?"

I felt as if I had been punched in the belly. Two years ago this had been my dearest wish; even this summer I had left my girl, for all her pleading, to go with Taliesin for a while. Now he freely offered me the thing I had wanted—Neirin's place with him, for no asking. And all I could think to say was, "What about Rhiannedd?"

"She could come with you," said Taliesin. "I could find her a place here. Or you could spend the summers with me, and the winters in Llys-tyn-wynnan. That is what you have been doing anyway, these last two years."

This was true, but I was not sure that to continue it would please Rhiannedd. "And what about Talhaearn?" I said. "He is old; he needs my help."

"I could find him another boy to look after him," said Taliesin, still watching me with that searching blue gaze. "It would not be hard; I might even find one with some music in him, who would love to learn the harp." He paused for a moment, but I said nothing. "Well, Gwernin? I am waiting. This time it is for you to decide."

I drew a deep breath, started to speak, and then thought again. To go with Taliesin would get me the best of teaching, and also the chance to stand in many bardic competitions. In a year or two—perhaps three at the most—I might even win one, and become a master bard myself. Then any king would be glad to have me as his *pencerdd*, and give me lands and a home for my family. It was a glittering prize, something any young man in my position would fight for. And I knew, looking at Taliesin's face, that it would only be offered once. If I turned him down, he would find another student—maybe even Rhys, despite all his faults. If I turned him down...

"Na," I heard myself saying. "I am sorry, I cannot do it."

Taliesin sat silent, frowning. "Why not?" he asked after a moment. There was no anger in his voice, only curiosity. "Is there anything else you would need, which I could provide?"

"Na," I said again, shaking my head. "It is only—Talhaearn needs me, and I need him. He has been like a father to me, and—and I love him. And Rhiannedd needs me, and I—also need her. I am not a boy any more, to please only myself. I am sorry." I shrugged my shoulders helplessly. "I would have liked to come with you, Master, only—I cannot. Maybe—maybe Rhys will improve with time."

"I doubt it," said Taliesin, and to my surprise and bewilderment he laughed. "Oh, I doubt it! But I perceive Talhaearn has won our bet after all. Na, do not worry, Gwernin, I am not angry. In truth, I think I would have been disappointed in you if you had accepted; but after all that has happened this summer, I had to ask." He sighed, and drank off his wine, and stood up. "I am for bed now. Do you ride on tomorrow?"

"I do," I said, still shaken and a little confused.

"Then I will see you off in the morning," said Taliesin, and smiled. "Do not let Rhys keep you awake." And with that he turned and left me, and I went slowly to my bed. But I lay a long time thinking before I fell asleep.

Taliesin was as good as his word. As we stood in the main courtyard that next morning under a gray and threatening sky, with all my gear loaded and a silent Rhys holding my ponies, I asked, "Shall we see you again in Llys-tyn-wynnan in the spring, Master?"

"Perhaps," said Taliesin, his blue eyes twinkling. "But I think, not to borrow you from Talhaearn again, Gwernin. You have made your choice, and I will respect it."

Almost I sighed. "Thank you, Master—for your forbearance, and for your teaching this summer. I hope you find a good replacement for Neirin to help you on the road."

"That," said Taliesin almost sternly, "will be hard to do." Then he embraced me. It was only when I was mounted and about to leave that he added, "Oh, and Gwernin…"

"Yes, Master?" I said, checking Du.

"Talhaearn knows many languages. Be sure that you learn them all from him." And with a smile and a wave of his hand, he turned and started back towards his house, leaving me to ponder the meaning of his words as I rode.

Now it was afternoon; the track I was following had begun to climb more steeply, and the mist on the hills above me was turning into rain. I reached behind me for my hooded leather cape and pulled it on. I would be in Llys-tyn-wynnan before dark, and glad I would be to get there. I hoped Rhiannedd was well—there was no telling, with a first child. And Talhaearn was tough as alder roots, but also he was an old man—a very old man. Many things could have happened in three months: my mind played out the possibilities before me. I found myself urging Du unconsciously into a faster pace; I was all at once very eager to get home.

It was twilight and pouring rain when I rode into the familiar courtyard and swung down from Du's back at last. In the smoky light of the torches I could not see the faces of the people peering out of the mead-hall, and I was about to lead my ponies on to the stables myself when a boy came running through the rain to take them. Unstrapping my harp-case from where it rode covered on the pack-pony, I said, "Just get them under cover—I will come for my gear in a while."

"I will, Lord," said the boy, and led the ponies away at a trot while I eagerly climbed the steps to the hall. After the dark evening it seemed bright as day in there, and I paused just inside the door while my eyes adjusted. "Gwernin!" called a familiar voice, and I saw Prince Cyndrwyn beckoning to me from beside the hearth. "What a day to come back, lad! Come to the fire—we were just talking of you."

"Gladly, Lord," I said, obeying his summons. "But with whom

were you speaking?" But I had seen Talhaearn's tall white-haired figure at his elbow, and Rhiannedd standing big-bellied close beside them.

"So you have come back, boy, after all," rumbled Talhaearn as I came up to them. "You cut it very fine."

"Why, Master," I said grinning, "I said I would be back before Samhain, and behold!—that is tomorrow night!"

"True, true," said Talhaearn, while I put my arms around Rhiannedd and kissed her sweet lips. "And how did you leave Gwion?"

"With some difficulty, Master," I said, pausing momentarily in my kissing. "He asked me to travel with him, come the spring."

"And—?" said Talhaearn. "What answer did you give him?" I tore my attention away from my beloved again.

"He said to tell you that you had won the bet," I said, and grinned. And at that Talhaearn threw back his head and laughed, and the Prince joined in the laughter. But I turned back to Rhiannedd, and looking down into her smiling eyes, I said, "I am home—and this time for good."

"Until the next time," said Rhiannedd, and kissed me. For she knew me well, and as usual she was right.

That Samhain night, Elidyr Mwynfawr, who had not been content with one kingdom, lay as cold bones in his lonely grave in Arfon; and if his ghost walked, it did not trouble my rest. For myself, I lay with my beloved, and felt our child stir strongly in her womb, and knew myself richer than kings. But no more than the wild geese of autumn can be stopped in their flighting, can a bard ever truly be anchored in one place. Taliesin's river is always waiting to sweep us away, armed only with our *awen*, on our endless voyaging to the sea.

But that, O my children, is truly a story for another day.

Author's Postscript

The sixth century in Britain is in some ways the darkest part of the European Dark Ages (or the Early Medieval Period, as it is often called nowadays). As direct evidence of people and events in this period, we have a handful of poems, Gildas' *De Excidio Britonum*, a few historical references in accounts written a hundred years or more later, and a set of genealogies of doubtful value. In addition, there is a growing body of archeological material, some of which contradicts (or at least fails to support) the above sources. In attempting to write a series of somewhat historical stories based in this period, the prospective author must leap from rock to rock, occasionally walking on water in between. Inevitably there will be some splashes.

For those who care about such details, then, the following summary is provided. Actual physical locations (i.e., towns, forts, roads, etc.) are based on archeological reports where available, but details (buildings, general appearance) of these places at the time of the story are speculative or wholly invented. Territorial units such as kingdoms fall into this category as well; there are no maps of Wales or of the lands of the Men of the North from the sixth century. Most of the kings or princes are at best names in a poem, history, or genealogy, and their characters (to say nothing of their appearances) are largely inferred from their reported actions. Five of the more important bards are listed (as names only) in Nennius's *Historia Britannica*; from two of them—Taliesin and Neirin (later called Aneirin)—we have poetry as well, although the degree to which these poems may have mutated during oral transmission is debatable. This poetry, incidentally, provides a large amount of the detail for material and social culture in the courts of the time.

The story of Elidyr Mwynfawr, his expedition to Gwynedd, and its results is based on a passage in *The Black Book of Chirk*, as quoted by Rachel Bromwich in her encyclopedic *Trioedd Ynys Prydein: The Welsh Triads*, which also contains *The Descent of the Men of the North*. Another valuable collection of this sort of material is Peter Bartrum's *A Welsh Classical Dictionary*. A full bibliography of my sources would run many pages, but since this is a novel and not a thesis I will only mention—somewhat at random—Nick Aitchison's *The Picts and Scots at War;* Leslie Alcock's *Kings and Warriors, Craftsmen and Priests in Northern Britain, AD 550-850;* C. J. Arnold's *An Archaeology of the Early Anglo-Saxon Kingdoms;* P. J. Casey's *Excavations at Segontium (Caernarfon) Roman Fort, 1975-1979;* Thomas Owen Clancy's *The Triumph Tree: Scotland's Earliest Poetry AD 550-1350;* T. M. Charles-Edwards' *The Welsh King and His Court* and *Early Christian Ireland;* H. E. M. Cool's *Eating and Drinking in Roman Britain;* Wendy Davies' *Wales in the Early Middle Ages;* Karen R. Dixon's *The Roman Cavalry;* Stephen Evans' *The Lords of Battle: Image and Reality of the 'Comitatus' in Dark-Age Britain;* Patrick Ford's *The Celtic Poets: Songs and Tales from Early Ireland and Wales* and *The Mabinogi and Other Medieval Welsh Tales;* Gildas' *The Ruin of Britain;* Ann Hagen's *Anglo-Saxon Food and Drink;* Dorothy Hartley's *Food in England;* Marged Haycock's *Legendary Poems from the Book of Taliesin;* Sonia Chadwick Hawkes' *Weapons and Warfare in Anglo-Saxon England;* N. J. Higham's *Britons in Anglo-Saxon England;* Dafydd Jenkins' *Law of Hywel Dda;* Barri Jones' *An Atlas of Roman Britain;* Catherine E. Karkov's *The Archaeology of Anglo-Saxon England;* Fergus Kelly's *A Guide to Early Irish Law* and *Early Irish Farming;* Thomas Kinsella's *The Tain;* John Koch's *The Gododdin of Aneirin: Text and Context from Dark-Age North Britain* and *An Atlas for Celtic Studies;* Lloyd Laing's *The Archaeology of Celtic Britain and Ireland: c. AD 440-1200;* Kevin Leahy's *Anglo-Saxon Crafts;* Frances Lynch's *Gwynedd: A Guide to Ancient and Historic Wales;* Rowena Mansfield's *Wild Herbs of Anglesey and Gwynedd;* Hywel Wyn Owen's *Dictionary of the Place-names of Wales;* Penelope Walton Rogers' *Cloth and Clothing in Early Anglo-Saxon England;* Anne Ross' *The Life and Death of A Druid Prince: The Story of Lindow Man* and *Pagan Celtic Britain;* Alfred Smyth's *Warlords and Holy Men: Scotland 80-1000 AD;* Iii Sullivan's *The Mabinogi: A Book of Essays;* Gwyn Thomas' *Y Traddodiad Barddol;* Richard Underwood's *Anglo-Saxon Weapons and Warfare;* Sir Ifor Williams' *Canu Taliesin;* and Barbara Yorke's *Kings and Kingdoms of Early Anglo-Saxon England*.

With regard to Gwernin's and Neirin's otherworldly experiences at the beginning and end of this book, there is little evidence for (or against) shamanistic or Druidical practices among the early Welsh bards, and the idea is now somewhat out of favor academically; but when a writer consults her *awen*, she must go where it takes her. The *idea* of the Dark Path is my invention, but many of its components are not, and reflect fragments of practice known historically among the Gaelic poets. Gwydion mab Dôn, of course, may be encountered at his *locus classicus* in the Fourth Branch of the *Mabinogion*, but shares his nature with Tricksters everywhere. The King in the Ground, Lovernos, is based on Lindow Man.

– G. R. Grove, *Beltane 2009*

Appendices

A Note on Welsh Pronunciation

The spelling used for Welsh words and names in these stories is mostly that of Modern Welsh. The most important differences between the English and Welsh alphabets are these:

Welsh	English
c	k
dd	th (as in "breathe")
f	v
th	th (as in "breath")

The Welsh "ll" has no English equivalent; an approximation can be reached by putting the tip of the tongue against the roof of the mouth behind the teeth and hissing—good luck!

Names of Some People and Places

key: **historical** invented *legendary/mythical*

(**accent** usually falls on the next-to-last syllable)

Anwen (**ăn**-wĕn) – Ieuan's wife on Ynys Môn

Blaidd (Gwyn mab Dafydd) (blăīth) – warrior in Rhun's war-band

Brochfael Ysgithrog (**brōch**-văĕl ĭs-**gīth**-rŏg) – Prince of Powys before Cynan Garwyn

Cadwaladr (**kăd-wă**-lă-dŭr) – Lord of Caer Lêb on Ynys Môn

Clydno Eidyn (**klēd**-nō ī-dĭn) – King of Gododdin

Cynan Garwyn (**kĭn**-an **găr**-win) – prince of eastern Powys whose court was at Pengwern

Cyndeyrn (kĭn-**dāē**-rĭn) – (invented) Prince of northern Powys whose court was at Deva (=Chester)

Cyndrwyn (kin-**drū**-in) – Prince of western Powys whose court was at Llys-tyn-wynnan

Denw (**dĕ**-noo) – daughter of Prince Cyndeyrn

Deva (**dē**-wă – Chester

Dun Eidyn (dŭn ī-dĭn) – Edinburgh

Dwywei (**dooē**-wāē) – Neirin's mother

Elidyr Mwynfawr (ĕ-**lī**-dĭr mooĭn-**vă** oor) – King of Aeron

Eryri (e-rŭ-re) – Snowdon and the mountains around it, "land of the eagles"

Gododdin (gō-dō-thĭ) – kingdom centered around Edinburgh

Gwallawg (**gwăll**-ăoog) – King of Elmet

Gwawr (gwăŭr) – herbalist and mother of Rhiannedd

Gwernin Kyuarwyd (**gwĕr**-nin kē-**văr**-wĭd) – Gwernin the Storyteller

Gwion (**gwē**-ĕn) – Taliesin's boyhood personal name

Gwydion mab Dôn (**gwĭd**-yŏn măb dōn) – Gwydion son of Dôn, the magician (Mabinogion)

Gwynedd (**gwĭ**-nĕth) – kingdom in northwest Wales

Ieuan mab Meurig mab Pedr (**Yē**-ăn măb **mīr**-ĭg mab **pĕd**-ŭr) – Gwernin's friend Ieuan

Lleyn (tlēn) – Lleyn peninsula

Llys-tyn-wynnan (llēs tēn **wĭn**-nan) – Cyndrwyn's court, near Caer Einion in mid-Wales

Maelgwn Hir (**măĕl**-gūn hēr) – "Maelgwn the Tall", King of Gwynedd (deceased)

Mordaf Hael (mōr-dăv hāĕl) – cousin of **Rhydderch Hael.**

Mynyddog Eidyn (mĭ-nĭ-thŏg ī-dĭn) – title of the King of Gododdin (my conjecture)

Neirin (nāĕr-in) – Taliesin's bardic apprentice; the poet Aneirin

Nudd Hael (nēth hāĕl) – cousin of **Rhydderch Hael.**

Pengwern (pen-gwĕrn) – Court of Cynan Garwyn, possibly located on the site of modern Shrewsbury

Powys (pō-wĕs) – kingdom in east-central Wales, including part of today's Shropshire

Rheged (hrĕ-gĕd) – kingdom in the north of Britain

Rhiannedd (**hrĕăn**-neth) – Gwernin's girl at Llys-tyn-wynnan

Rhun mab Maelgwn Gwynedd (hrēn măb **măĕl**-goon **gwĭ**-neth) – Rhun the son of Maelgwn Gwynedd

Rhydderch Hael (**hrĭ**-thĕrch hāĕl) – King of Strathclyde

Rhys (hrēs) – Ugnach's son and pupil

Talhaearn Tad Awen (**tăl**-hāĕărn tad ă-wen) – Talhaearn "Father of the Muse", Taliesin's and Gwernin's bardic teacher

Taliesin Ben Beirdd (tă-lē-ā-sin ben bāĕrth) – Taliesin "Chief of Bards", most famous bard in 6th century Britain

Ugnach mab Mydno (ēg-nach mab **mēd**-no) – bard of Caer Sëon who competed against Taliesin at Caer Seint; possibly legendary.

Urien Rheged (ēr-eun **hrĕg**-ed) – King of Rheged in the North of Britain

Viroconium – Wroxeter, Shropshire

Ynys Môn (ĭn-is mōn) – the Island of Môn (Anglesey) off the northwest coast of Wales

Yr Wyddfa (ŭr **wĕth**-va) – Snowdon, the highest peak in Wales

Other Welsh words

afon (**ă**-von) – river

annwyl (**ăn**-wĭl) – beloved, darling

awen (**ă**-wĕn) – poetic inspiration

baban (**bă**-băn) – baby

bach / fach (băch / văch) – little, dear, dear one

bachgen (**băch**-gĕn) – boy

bardd (bărth) pl. beirdd (bēĭrth) – bard

bardd teulu (**bărth tăĕ**-lē) – bard of the war-band

boba (**bō**-bă) – aunt

bonheddig (bōn-**hĕth**-ĭg) – noble

caer (kăĕr) – fortress, castle

calon fach (**kă**-lōn **văch**) – dear heart

cantref (**kăn**-trĕv) – an administrative unit, notionally of one hundred townships

cariad (**kă**-rēăd) – dear, beloved

cerdd tafod (**kĕrth tă**-vod) – poetry; literally, "craft (of) tongue"

clas (klăs) – early Welsh religious foundation, monastery

coch (kōch) – red

Cymry (**Kŭm**-rē) – Welsh (people), singular Cymro (Kĭm-rō)

du (dē) – black

dyffryn (**dĭ**-frĭn) – valley

ferch (vĕrch) – daughter (of)

galanas (gă-**lă**-năs) – blood price; compensation paid for a death

glas (glăs) – blue, gray, green

gwas (gwăs) – lad

iawndal (**yăwn**-dăl) – compensation, damages, atonement

ie (ēā) – yes

kyuarwyd (kĕ-**văr**-wĭd) – storyteller (Middle Welsh)

llwyd (tlōēd) – gray

llys (tlēs) – court, fortified complex

mab (măb) – son (of)

Nos Calan Haf (**nōs kă**-lăn **hăv**) – Beltane Eve, literally the eve of the first day of summer; now called Nos Calan Mai, May Eve

pencerdd (**pĕn**-kĕrth) – chief bard, master bard, bard of the court

Pencerddiaid (pĕn-**kĕrth**-ē-īd) – plural of pencerdd

penteulu (**pĕn-tăē**-lē) – chief of retinue, leader of the body-guard

rhyd (hrĭd) – ford

sarhaed (**săr**-hĕd) – insult price; compensation paid for injury or insult

taeog (**tăē**-ŏg) – bound peasant, slave

teulu (**tăē**-lē) – retinue, war-bard (modern meaning: family)

uchelwr (**ēch**-ul-ur), pl. uchelwyr (**ēch**-ul-ēr) – nobleman, literally "high man"

Old English Words

scop *(pl.* scopes*)* (shōp) – poet, bard

wealisc – Welsh, Welshman

Printed in Great Britain by
Amazon.co.uk, Ltd.,
Marston Gate.